Lewi's Journey

Lewi's

Journey

PER OLOV ENQUIST

Translated from the Swedish by
Tiina Nunnally

OVERLOOK DUCKWORTH
New York • Woodstock • London

First published in 2005 by
Overlook Duckworth, Peter Mayer Publishers, Inc.
New York, Woodstock, and London

NEW YORK:
141 Wooster Street
New York, NY 10012

WOODSTOCK:
One Overlook Drive
Woodstock, NY 12498
www.overlookpress.com
[for individual orders, bulk and special sales, contact our Woodstock office]

LONDON:
90-93 Cowcross Street
London EC1M 6BF
inquiries@duckworth-publishers.co.uk
www.ducknet.co.uk

The translator would like to thank Seven T. Murray for his assistance in
translating the hymns included in the text.

⊖ The paper used in this book meets the requirements for paper
permanence as described in the ANSI Z39.48-1992 standard.

Cataloging-in-Publication Data is available from the Library of Congress

Book design and type formatting by Bernard Schleifer
Manufactured in the United States of America
FIRST EDITION
ISBN 1-58567-341-2
ISBN 0-7156-3367-8 (UK)
9 8 7 6 5 4 3 2 1

For Maja

Contents

Lewi's Journey

God's Acre

1.

EFRAIM MARKSTRÖM WAS BURIED ON SEPTEMBER 16, 1982, IN Christiansfeld, a town in southern Jutland near the Danish border with Germany—a country, by the way, that he had never visited. It took place under the auspices of the Unitas Fratrum congregation, within the Moravian church in Christiansfeld.

That's how I found out that he had become a Moravian. I thought he was a Pentecostal. Perhaps toward the end he had turned to his own kind in a foreign country, and only just before death had sought out his true home; which meant that during his lifetime he had lived in the diaspora, in a spiritual exile, but now he had returned to where he truly belonged, which made me feel strangely upset, almost hurt, because I had always believed that Efraim was in all ways anchored in the Bureå parish, in northern Västerbotten, which was also my true home.

"True"—what did this really mean? It made me wonder.

Perhaps the truth was that the diaspora was the natural home of the Moravians. The periphery was their safe center and, like a network of tiny capillaries, they ran through the entire twentieth century in Europe.

Besides, where were the children of the revival to be found if not in the diaspora?

I received an invitation to attend the burial since the deceased had no relatives. He had once told me that I might "be considered" a relative since at least I was Swedish, "like himself," and lived in Copenhagen, so the travel expenses wouldn't be "burdensome" for me.

I hadn't seen him in many years. I had almost forgotten him.

* * *

The morning after the funeral, on September 17, I went out early.

The sun had just come up and hung low in the sky. It had rained during the burial, and everything was damp. I walked over to God's acre in Christiansfeld. That's what the Moravian cemeteries are called, or so I had learned. The idea was that a human being was sown, grew up, and stood erect like a blade of grass, no, like a stalk of grain. Then he was harvested and put back into the earth, and once again he found himself in God's acre.

The cemetery had a gate on which it did, in fact, say in Danish: God's Acre.

Since the late 1700s it had stood at the end of Kirkegaards Allé. Thousands of horizontal gravestones, with nothing in between but bare earth. The land was uncultivated soil; the human race had come from it and would return to it.

Here the Moravians of northern Europe had been buried since 1773. Here they were gathered in God's acre. Here grass was not allowed to grow. All the stones were exactly the same shape. The human being who was returned to God's acre was no greater or lesser than his peers. In God's acre their existence was marked by stones of precisely the same shape, rectangular, and horizontal. Just as in the meeting house men and women were assigned to separate sides, here the men lay on one side, the women on the other, in neat rows, half a meter apart. Separated by bare earth.

Here no grave affiliation existed. No family graves, no wife at her husband's side. The earthly affiliation had been replaced by an affiliation with Christ. No conflicts about grave affiliations after death were possible.

Alone, in the end. Or, as Lewi expressed it in his last sermon: One by one. Before God.

On each stone an inscription: name, place and date of birth, place and date of death, and an epitaph. Efraim did not yet have a stone, for obvious reasons. But he would have one someday.

The sun was so low in the sky that the chiseled grooves of the text cast shadows; the very old grave inscriptions were suddenly visible, not erased by nature or God's hand. Yesterday I wasn't able to read more than a few of them. Now the almost horizontal morning sun made the letters legible. They would remain that way for several more minutes, then the names would disappear. For a few minutes God had illuminated His acre for me, then these lives would be relegated to the oblivion of daylight and the names would become invisible.

A name, date of birth and death, then an epitaph. The pious sense of trust was everywhere. Although occasionally with a different tone.

"She was humble, but she did her best."

All those names. They were born in Falun and Viby and Herrnhut and Hamburg and Graz and Hirtshals. It was like a choir of voices whispering in the slanting morning sun in God's acre in Christiansfeld, the town that had been named after the little, insignificant, and perhaps insane Danish king, Christian VII. His royal physician was Johann Friedrich Struensee, whose father was a pietist and Moravian. As was the son. The one who strayed from his faith but perhaps returned to it. Or so I believe. Returned before the axe severed his hand and head, and his dismembered body was tossed into the cart. This same Struensee had once, in November 1771, granted a concession for the Moravian colonization of this as yet nonexistent community.

God's slanting sun was now illuminating God's and Struensee's acre, making the names visible for a few minutes. They had come from east and west, from north and south, to gather in God's acre. And now Efraim was united with them. For a few minutes in the slanting morning sun they were distinguishable, these people who had been returned to God's acre. It was like a choir of names and voices, it was the piety of the European radical pietists, without societal or imperial dreams, which was something very unusual and by now nearly annihilated. The great whispering European choir of voices from people who were humble but who did their best.

Why did Efraim want to be buried here? I didn't understand it. And why had he invited me?

He was buried by the Unitas Fratrum church in Christiansfeld. It was the largest Moravian church in the North.

Outwardly it also bore a Moravian shape. It reminded me of something. Efraim must have come here while he was alive. I recalled that in a conversation he had once mentioned Christiansfeld, particularly the church, "that gigantic transverse meeting house." When I went inside I understood what he meant. It was transverse, like a meeting house turned crosswise. The church consisted of one large hall, with the pulpit in the middle against one of the long walls, and the benches in ten rows, along the nave. A free-standing roof. No pillars. No decorations. Everything completely white and made of wood, with a kitchen in a room behind one of the end walls.

Of course there had to be a kitchen. The meeting houses and other premises of the free church differ from the sanctuaries of the state Lutheran church by virtue of their kitchens. Why was there always a kitchen? It meant that food could be prepared there for the faithful.

The revivalist movement had kitchens. The state church did not. That was quite clear.

Behind the pulpit was a long wooden bench where the elders of the congregation sat, facing the congregation. It was the same at Rörstrandsgatan, where the elders of the Pentecostal congregation gazed out at the others. It was something they had copied from the Moravians.

Up there the leading brothers.

Down there the sea of women.

Efraim Markström, born in Gamla Fahlmark, Bureå parish, six foot two and powerfully built with big hands, was buried in Christiansfeld. A long journey. Why had he summoned me after his death?

There wasn't much to go on. I had come here from Copenhagen. Efraim lay in his coffin outside the church door. There was something extraordinary about the whole scene.

A light rain had begun to fall; it was audible on the roof. The congregation and the mourners (who had perhaps never met Efraim, no, undoubtedly they hadn't, but then what did I know for sure?) had positioned themselves as the rules prescribed. The men on one side, the women on the other, separated, just as they were in God's acre.

I sat in the very back; I too was separated. Efraim had sent for me. He wanted to send me a message written in Moravian Braille, and I couldn't yet decipher it.

Everyone sang the introductory hymn, slowly and mournfully.

So far everything was familiar. It was the intonation of the Västerbotten hymns sung in the meeting houses fifty years ago, before the new theological times had broken through. The same tempo! That languor with which the dragging, almost howling grief over sin, death, and the proxy suffering of Jesus on the Cross was supposed to take shape in the plaintive tone itself, that protracted liturgical lament.

"Now have I vanquished, with the blood and wounds of Jesus," we sang. I remember so well the outrage many people back home felt when the new cantors, trained in Stockholm, entered the Västerbotten ecclesiastical circles and stepped up the tempo of the hymns. That new haste! Almost blasphemous! That almost modern interpretation of the mystery of the rites! Inflicted on us! That centralistically correct but despised new interpretation of the tempo of grief and fervor which for many years made the congregation, in protest, stubbornly lag behind the quick march tempo enjoined by the organ.

The new times had broken through, but we resisted.

The music far ahead, followed by the voices, like an echo of lamentation. It was as if the congregation were still reluctantly being dragged along by the demands of the new era, but had not yet entirely given up the fight. Two colliding hymns arose, one the defiant, lagging lament of the true and genuine believers, with a very quick and martial-sounding hymn in the lead. Modernism marched ahead, but it left the people behind.

The theologically correct tugboat in a furious tempo out front, and then the people dragging like a stubborn lifeboat far behind. Modern spirituality in the lead, without any sense of the fervent need for lamentation, especially when they sang "O head, bloody, wounded," while the congregation lagged far behind. With a defiant sorrow that refused to be hauled along. But here, in the Moravian congregation of Christiansfeld, at the funeral of the Swede Efraim Markström, in the presence of his visiting relatives, which meant only me, they sang very slowly, plaintively, in the proper fashion, with the true, languorous sorrow and with the proper words, the ones about the wounds and blood of Jesus.

Then came the ringing of the bells and the reading of one text from the Old Testament and one from the New. The liturgical text of the service was listed on the distributed leaflet.

I followed along with a strange feeling of guilt. It had been a long time since I had actually participated.

As an adult I had taken communion only once: at the old folks' home in Bureå, the year before my mother died. If you weren't saved, you didn't take communion. It was a mortal sin; that's what she had taught me.

She taught me everything. No doubt that was what Lewi meant by a Traveling Companion.

Back then, the year before she died, everyone had gathered in the communal hall of the assisted living building in Bureå. A chaplain walked around among the old people and I sat at her side. She was in a wheelchair. This was between her second and third stroke, and that time I took communion too.

It just happened. I couldn't very well refuse. Perhaps I didn't want to.

We formed a circle, as if around an altar. She was sitting on my right. On my left sat an old woman who might have been ninety, paralyzed and mute, or at least that's what I thought. She couldn't say a word. She was hunched over, drooling a little with her mouth half open, seemingly far beyond all contact, scarcely conscious that the body and blood of Christ would now be given to her. When the pastor presented the chalice, she tilted her head upward with unspeakable effort, stretched out her gaping, slightly drooling lips toward the chalice, and partook of Christ's blood, which had been spilled for her sake.

Out of the corner of my eye I looked at her, feeling a strange mixture of sympathy and aversion. It was as if her hunched, barely conscious form didn't fit with the ritual, and yet it did, as if she were one of those humble ones who was now doing her utmost: one of those who, before death, would partake of the body of Jesus, the blood of Jesus.

She was humble, but she did her best. But how much did she understand?

And at that moment, as the pastor, murmuring, moved on to the next old woman and was just bending down to her, about to raise the chalice to her lips, I saw how my huddled-up and supposedly completely mute communion neighbor, with a tremendous effort, turned her head toward the pastor. And in a surprisingly strong, sharp, piercing, thunderous voice, she broke through the pious and devout silence to bellow:

"Hey, I didn't get enough!!"

I don't think any of us smiled. There was no room for that. Nor did anyone come to the conclusion that the paralyzed old woman's sudden and extremely clear roar was the disappointed cry of an alcoholic wanting more from the chalice, which was the only liquor given to the pious.

No, we all knew that it was something else.

The blood of Christ. We had been raised on it. The Västerbotten revivalist movement in the wake of Rosenius was Moravian to its core. We all knew that—those of us who were long-time, ardent believers, those who had little faith, and those who no longer believed at all. The Evangelical Homeland Mission breathed heavily of the mystery of blood and Moravianism; we had the blood in our blood. We couldn't escape it, would never be able to escape it, no matter how hard we tried.

The blood of Christ, spilled for you.

2.

Three days after the funeral I returned to Copenhagen. I brought copies of a text with me, sections of Efraim's *Lebenslauf*, the account of his life. Back then I didn't know that the message he had sent me was not about his own journey but about Lewi's.

It wasn't actually in Braille, and yet. When I ran my fingertips over the nonexistent symbols, they sometimes felt so familiar. But I didn't understand. It's possible to be born into something, and to grow up with it, and still not understand. Perhaps that was Moravian logic. For nearly a century, from the early 1700s until the mid-1800s, Moravianism was the leavening that influenced the whole revivalist movement in Europe and in America.

And in me?

It seeped in everywhere, very calmly and quietly, since the Moravians had no ambitions to create a society, merely to recreate humanity. And me too? It had a lasting effect on Swedish pietism, and created in Sweden the real basis for all Swedish popular movements, from revivalism to the temperance movement to the labor movement.

The symbols of the Braille seemed to say: It's impossible to understand the development of popular movements in Sweden without Moravianism. Yet after a hundred years it had slipped away as quietly as it had arrived in this country. It was a great idea that was injected. Then Moravianism disappeared, almost with a tiny submissive bow. It simply went away. We don't wish to intrude, we're merely speaking about humanity's relationship to the existential questions. We don't want to create any state religions or societies, we don't want to become powerful.

Merely permeate. A popular movement is a movement in the hearts of the people, an idea and not an organization. If the idea becomes an organization, it dies. We don't want to be visible, we don't want conflict but peace—and fervor. The core of Christianity is not catechism but the fervent union of the heart with the Savior. This is not a state-building religion, this is something private, a thought. We present an idea, and if the idea is accepted by other societies, that's fine. Then we disappear, like the morning mist when the sun comes up.

We no longer exist. But we live on in everyone.

Perhaps this is what Efraim wanted to leave behind with his secret message, which was the mystery that took me so many years after his funeral to decipher.

I was not entirely ignorant.

In fact, all the forefathers of Västerbotten were Moravian. Soldiers from Västerbotten, who had been imprisoned in Siberia, had encountered German Moravians and then returned home. In that sense it was quite typical. Moravianism always crept in. It was Christ-centric; it never created theological superstructures that might cause disputes. In a certain way it was chameleon-like. It could creep into any society and take on its color and intonation, as long as one condition was met: total empathy with Christ's suffering, immersion in Him, in His death and atonement.

It viewed the human being as a religious territory, a territory that received religious impressions. This occurred intuitively and emotionally and had to be separated from all logical thinking.

Religion had to be "something else." Count Zinzendorf did not regard the Bible as something finished and final. The Bible was being written every day. Some sections of the Bible were good, others were not as good, but in all cases they had been created by human beings. That's why the Bible should be regarded as a "work in progress." His Christology had strong ties to the Enlightenment, with an emphasis on Christ's humanity. But Christ was not alone in his humanness; the Holy Scriptures were human too. It was a thoroughly human book, filled with errors and follies, and above all contradictions, since human beings, who were contradictory, had created this text.

Yet the unfinished nature of the Bible was its strength. The sacredness of the Bible should be organically united with the sacredness and folly of the human being; the Bible should be constantly renewed.

New parts should be written. His favorite examples of renewal were the Christ hymns by Bernhard de Clairvaux. The important thing was the road to the religious experience. And we built that road ourselves.

Perhaps that's what interested me.

No one looked askance at me in that church. I didn't need to worry. I was alone among those who were united, like a stone in God's acre, without grave affiliation, but without shame.

How much guilt there was in those wordless dreams about the religious experience! And how can those dreams not be associated with other urges, especially sexuality?

It was the language and the images that became problematic, almost sexual. The congregation literally sprang from the body of Christ: when the soldier stuck his spear into Christ's side and blood and water spurted out, that's when the congregation was born from the wound, from Christ. It was as simple as that. Then something was born that could be called orgiastic theology, the almost sexual union with the bridegroom Jesus Christ.

That's why in the meeting houses on the coast of Västerbotten we always ended our prayers with the words "for the sake of the blood." That's why Christ's wound was a shelter, and a warm, enticing, almost female slit. Almost the most forbidden of all. That's why the blood was warm and protective, like amniotic fluid, and not frightening. The blood was love, not violence. That's why sexuality was something so dangerous—forbidden and frightening, and yet always, night and day, present in our religiosity.

Zinzendorf's hymns still existed, even the strangest ones from his "sifting-out period" of the 1740s: those deranged, comic, peculiar, and strongly sexual poems that would end up obscuring or utterly destroying his reputation for a very long time. Yet they expressed, with greater clarity and truth than any ecclesiastical orthodoxy, the absolutely incomprehensible, sensual, and enticing world of religious mysticism.

A little worm in my wound,
in love with my four dear nails,
a bird of the cruciform sky

sick with the torment of love
for my side reliquary.

Little side wound, little side wound,
little side wound, you are mine.

Dearest little side wound,
I want to hide inside you.
For us, lowly friends of the Cross,
the side reliquary can be
the whole Lamb.

Little side wound, little side wound,
little side wound, you are mine.

What was that all about? Was it nonsense? Faith as insanity driven by sexuality?

Or mysterious images that conveyed to human beings better than theological logic that this is not something rational but instead a moist, pulsating, life-giving dream?

A very strong, uncontrollable dream. I think the Braille wanted to say that Lewi, the rational master builder, had also built in this uncontrollable dream like a brick in his great cathedral.

We sang, we listened to the rain, which fell harder, washing over Efraim's coffin outside the door; soon the ritual inside the church would be over. I didn't understand why I was there. Mumbling, I followed along with the liturgy.

Perhaps that's what I had been doing all my life.

Then the tone of the organ changed; it grew brighter. We were singing for Efraim, the whole time the same ambiguously light, symbol-laden texts about the union of the Congregation with the Bridegroom. "*I am a part of your body, I know that in my heart.*" The Moravians sang different texts, depending on their civil status. One song for a married man, another for a bachelor, another for a widower, another for an unmarried woman. This religious sexuality!

My lot down here
is to seek Him
My striving is clear

to sing His praise
Here I await Him
how my heart longs
Till He meets me there
the goal of my songs.

Tender, enticing, ever warmer sounds. No longer plaintive. No lamentation.

His blood, like amniotic fluid. For the sake of the blood.

Then a new sermon began. But this was a different sort of reading.

I suppose I should have been prepared. But I wasn't.

From his briefcase the pastor took out a folder containing a stack of papers that must have been ten centimeters thick. He placed it on the pulpit, cast a somber look over the congregation, opened the folder, paused, and then began to read.

It was the first time I encountered a *Lebenslauf*. It belonged to Efraim Markström. And, as I understood much later, to Lewi.

It was actually quite simple: Every member of the Unitas Fratrum congregation, every Moravian, was expected to keep a running chronicle of his life. Life was a novel that had to be written down, life was a "work in progress," in which chapter should be added to chapter, as if life were the Bible itself and each person an evangelist. And when a person's life was over, the chronicle of that life would be read before the congregation, a more or less symbolic reading of excerpts, but the entire text would be available.

A *Lebenslauf*. Recorded while life lasted.

And now he was holding Efraim's *Lebenslauf* in his hand, reading from it.

I don't remember much about the sections he had chosen. There was his youth spent in the forests of Västerbotten and his work in Vänersborg and his meeting with Lewi. After that Lewi's name was repeated again and again. The pastor intimated, as he almost apologetically raised his eyes from the sheaf of papers, that Efraim had made a significant contribution to the Pentecostal movement.

And why not? No one seemed bothered by the fact. After all, Moravianism could be found in every society. I was the only one who didn't understand.

Then he closed the folder and we sang another verse of the hymn. People slowly got to their feet and went outside, with the little brass band leading the way. The musicians wore tall, black top hats. They looked quite comical, almost circus-like. Their music was turning more and more cheerful. It was still raining, but not as heavily.

We fell into formation. First the brass band, setting off to a merry melody, not entirely in tune but almost lively: oompah, oompah, oompah. Suddenly everything seemed cheerful and bright. The coffin had been placed on a small cart. No horses. The congregation did the pulling, four men. Then came the pastor. Then me. The pastor had taken my arm and given me a friendly nod since I was the closest relative.

We were observing, the pastor explained in a whisper, a "liturgical moving day." A person moves "from the congregation that is waiting for Him here," to "the congregation that is with Him back home."

We walked along Lindegade, turned onto Museumsgade, and then headed via Kirkegaards Allé to the burial site. The coffin was placed over the grave. The pastor said a prayer. Then the coffin was lowered. The pastor said another prayer. Everyone sang.

I don't remember anything else. I remember that the last songs were happy-sounding and lively and that the pastor explained that now we had sung away our grief and should sing in our joy.

I don't remember. I was thinking only of Efraim's *Lebenslauf.*

We left God's acre together, the pastor and I, and I asked him about Efraim's *Lebenslauf.* And the pastor said, "Of course. Come over to the archives tomorrow; that's where we've preserved all the *Lebenslauf* from the congregation since 1773. That's where Efraim's will be archived. Anyone can read it. You're welcome to come. We have no secrets here."

"Isn't his life a secret?" I asked.

"No," replied the pastor. "He has left it behind now and entered into the greater mystery."

That's how he expressed it. The greater mystery.

3.

I met Efraim for the first time in November 1972. He had known my mother's brother Aron quite well. I was writing a book that would come to be called *The Musicians' Procession.* At that time I didn't know that Efraim was a Pentecostal.

Or rather: I knew but I didn't care. He had opinions about Lewi and about Sven. I listened but didn't understand how it all fit together. Later I learned more, and I did care. He told me a great deal, but I didn't understand everything he said. Perhaps this would be a better book if I had understood. I don't know. It's impossible to understand everything at once.

Later we met many times, although not at all during the last two years of his life. Then a letter arrived with an invitation to his funeral in a Danish community called Christiansfeld.

That's how it happened. That's the whole story.

The archives were located at Lindegade 12. I had gotten up early and taken another stroll through God's acre, in the slanting morning sun. I told the pastor about the suddenly decipherable texts. He was standing outside the archive door, smoking a Cecil cigarette.

He had nothing to say about what I told him. Efraim's folder was lying on a table. A straight-backed chair stood nearby. I sat down to read. That was the first time. Later on I went back to Christiansfeld twice. Folders were not permitted off the premises, but I could make copies.

I don't know how many thousands of *Lebenslauf* there were. Some were not written by the individual but had been briefly summarized by relatives. But most people had written their own.

That was the great European choir. Efraim had written his by hand.

In among the handwritten pages had been inserted photostat copies of texts that he had not written himself: pages from Lewi's and Sven's memoirs, always with comments in the margin; a collection of interviews by Sune Jonsson with members of the revivalist movement (wasn't there an interview with Efraim too? That's not clear to me); and newspaper clippings.

One clipping had a picture from the parliament session when the Christian Democratic Party was founded.

At the very end of Efraim's *Lebenslauf*, which consisted of at least a thousand pages, there was a page torn out of a notebook. It was the last note in his handwriting, definitely written by him but this time in pencil and in a strangely feeble hand.

As if it had been stuffed in there, by someone.

I imagine that this was found on his night stand, on his last night, like a nighttime dream that at all costs had to be recorded.

This note was dated with unusual precision.

"February 12," it said, "at about 9 p.m. on Rörstrg when L attacked on the platform and Lewi thanked me, I realized deep in my heart that it was necessary to defend LP. Go through what I've written so that no injustice will befall the one who at this moment I realized I loved."

That was the last of his life's account. The abbreviations are easy to decode: the Filadelfia church on Rörstrandsgaten, Lidman, Lewi Pethrus. And the date. It was easy to understand what event he meant.

But what about the phrase "at this moment?" Was it the moment in the past or his last moment, just before he died?

It's impossible to know. It has to be reconstructed.

I sat at the table at Lindegade 12 in Christiansfeld, holding the page from the notebook in my hand and staring at it. The pastor had to leave. He said that I could stay there and keep reading. He asked me if the whole thing was difficult to decipher.

"Yes, it is," I said. "Why do you Moravians do this?"

"Yes, hmm, why do we do it?" he said.

"It seems so overwhelming. You're preserving all these lives. A lot of them are probably quite uninteresting," I said.

"That depends on how you look at it."

"But you end up with a bunch of fragments," I said. "How do you know that you've chosen what's important or merely deleted what you wanted to hide?"

"Yes, you do have to reconstruct," he said. "According to your conscience."

I'm not sure whether I heard an undertone of criticism in his voice. If was as if he had taken up position among the dead, like a member of the great European choir, the one that was lying out there in God's acre and whose voices had been pressed in between the pages like flower petals.

"According to your conscience," he repeated.

"Yes," I said. "I suppose that's what I have to do."

"You can never be sure that it's right," he said. "When I read during the service I can only choose brief excerpts. I don't know whether Efraim's excerpts were the right ones."

I didn't answer. There was no need to.

"Efraim's seems to be quite extensive; I mean, it covers long periods," he said a little defensively, as if he were afraid that he had offended me.

"The entire twentieth century," I said.

"Yes, he lived a long life. I suppose it covers everything."

"I don't know," I said.

"You knew him well?"

"No," I said.

"Well, then you can form your own opinion," he said and left.

4.

You might say that I found myself in Doctor Struensee's kingdom.

He was the one who had founded Christiansfeld. That was in November 1771. It was his last decree.

Then came his arrest, imprisonment, trial, execution, and dismemberment on the wheel. The last document he signed granted rights to the Moravians, as if it were a farewell gift to his childhood faith. After that he did nothing more.

He was the one who said: The sacred is what the one who is sacred does.

Back when we met in the 1970s I had mostly asked Efraim about his memories of the childhood of the labor movement in Västerbotten. And you only get answers if you ask a question.

I had no idea that he might be more interested in the sacredness of human beings. Who's interested in that today, anyway? One time I asked a couple of teenagers why they thought you shouldn't kill another person. There was a moment of hesitation, perhaps surprise, and then came their answer.

You weren't supposed to kill because . . . because it was forbidden. Forbidden by law. Was that the reason? Yes, it was forbidden by law, and if you broke the law you'd end up in prison. You shouldn't break the law. Was it right for a person to be executed for it, as punishment? Yes, it was right. Because it was such a serious crime. Did that mean it was right to execute, or kill, another person? Yes, if someone had broken the law in that way. Any other answers? One of them said that it was wrong to kill any kind of living creature, especially dogs. A brief debate then ensued: What was a "living creature?" An earthworm? A cow? Was a birch tree also a living creature? Could a birch tree think or dream?

I tried to steer the discussion back to human beings.

It was wrong to kill a human being. But why? They gave me reasons. Some were legal, others ethical. After a while the discussion came to a halt.

I felt a sense of disappointment. Or emptiness. I hadn't told them what to me was obvious: that killing a human being was a crime against the sacredness of human life.

Human beings are sacred.

I assumed they would have asked me what I meant by sacredness. And back then the only answer I could have given them was: That's what I was brought up to believe. That's how I was raised. I was taught to believe that. It's obvious. It comes so naturally to me that it releases me from the obligation to think for myself.

But for them the obvious was unknown.

That's one thing.

The other thing was more troublesome, but it had to do with something else that was obvious to me, although it didn't become apparent until I had read through Efraim Markström's account.

His *Lebenslauf* was evidently not recorded chronologically. But it does have an internal timeline.

In one place he mentions that he "once approved of" a book that his respected mentor Lewi wrote in 1941, "after returning home from exile." It's called *Today We Play—Tomorrow We Cry*. I ordered it from the library a couple of years later. It was a collection of sermons. It was also a guide to how a person should live his life, and to his morals. It was an entire catalogue of sins: the sinfulness of theater, movies, sexuality, passion, desires, playing sports on Sunday, homosexuality, vanity, dancing, folk dances, everything.

Absolutely everything was included: a guide for the perfect fundamentalist person who was cast all in one piece.

It was frightening. But the most terrible thing of all was that it in no way deviated from the values found, for example, in the town where I grew up in northern Västerbotten. It was all so familiar to me. That was exactly how I had been raised. It was *me*. I had merely forgotten. It was as if time had placed a membrane of ice over my life and then suddenly a breath blew it away and a face emerged that was my own face, although I had forgotten. This was me. The terrible thing was that back then it wasn't terrible, only natural. That's the way it was. I had grown up with these values.

That was the way I had become a human being.

The sacredness of humans was not the only thing that had been imprinted. This was too. It was how I had become a human being.

I locked the door of the archives. It was dark. I walked across God's acre to my hotel.

Reconstruction. According to your conscience. Perhaps in some sense the material was to be found inside myself.

5.

When I was a child, I spoke as a child and thought as a child. In the winter I would go out late at night and lie down in the snow to try to make sense of everything.

Because it all depended on learning the correct answers, the ones we were supposed to memorize to the questions about good and evil and sinfulness and guilt and the meaning of life, and the answers were very simple even though the questions were very hard. That was the whole problem! The fact that these hard questions had such simple answers could almost make a person doubt, even though it was a sin to doubt! Maybe even a mortal sin! This incomprehensible doubt about what didn't make sense!!! And this doubt, like the Beast in the Book of Revelation in the family Bible which had illustrations of this Beast, could tear a person apart, even if that person was very small, only a child—and because everything depended on learning the answers, a feeling of uncertainty arose.

Then you would feel at your wits' end, then it was a matter of making sense of it all.

Then it helped to go out in the snow at night to make sense of things. You had to dress warmly so there would be no need for any scoldings from your mother about remembering your thick mittens or two pairs of socks inside your boots. Then you went down below, down to the ice-covered rosehip hedge which on one side, where the snow had drifted up, looked like one long wall of ice blanketed with snow. As if it were very close to the North Pole. But on the upper side that was sheltered from the wind you could see the sprawling branches and realize what it was. It was a rosehip hedge. Then it was no longer believable. Then you were not at the North Pole. But from farther down the hill near the spring it definitely looked like an ice barrier, like the one that Lieutenant Crozier sat on when he was protecting his dead colleagues from the polar bears. This was confirmed in *From Pole to Pole*. Confirmed! Not recounted, but confirmed! It was important for history to be confirmed!

Just as it was confirmed when reading *From Pole to Pole*.

At that spot you were very close to the North Pole, which was confirmed by the fact that the house was not in sight. It was important to find just the right spot, not near the house but somewhere else, maybe at the North Pole, and someplace where the rosehip hedge was out of sight, because a rosehip hedge like that wouldn't be found at the North Pole.

But below the rosehip hedge, on the gentle slope down toward the spring, that was the right spot. That's where you could make sense of everything. That's where the answers could be confirmed. There you could lie down, cautiously, and sink thirty centimeters, creating that soft, warm snow hollow that made it possible to look up at God, who was up there beyond the constellations.

The constellations themselves were not very interesting. I had learned to sketch them on sandwich paper. It wasn't so hard to memorize them. The Lyre and Cassiopeia, and the others. They were no more difficult to draw than a map of Sweden with the surrounding Nordic kingdoms. It was possible to memorize the constellations.

But beyond them was what could not be drawn.

On cold winter nights the starry sky was so clear and almost lightning-bright that the stars seemed to spread out in multiple layers above the snow hollow. First the familiar stars, the ones you could draw on sandwich paper when you lay on the floor in the kitchen; then the ones that could not be drawn.

The starry carpet beyond, beyond! the visible stars—that was what could not be drawn. That was the explanation for why the questions were so hard and the answers so simple that you almost couldn't believe it.

But if this was clearly confirmed, then you didn't need to be torn apart, as if by the Beast.

There was a difference between what could be drawn: the visible, and what lay beyond: God's dusting of stars. But then how could you understand God? It was so exhausting and hard to make sense of it all. That which was beyond what could not be drawn.

The trick was to understand what could not be drawn.

I would lie very still in the snow and feel it getting clearer and clearer. One (it was important to think of "one" and not "I") was a tiny human being in the snow. And the snow was warm and felt like Mother's sheepskin rug. But high above the ignorant and bewildered human being, who was at his wits' end, stretched the stars like layer upon layer of scores of sheepskin rugs even though it was actually sandwich paper: first came what you could understand and had drawn, and then beyond it the smaller stars that were almost unknown, and then even farther beyond, like scattered flour, came what was almost terrifying, the mystery itself.

The mystery no one could explain.

If you strained as hard as you could, you could transport yourself in among the various layers. Even closer to the dusting of stars. Into the infinite. And if you breathed very slowly, your body would feel weightless. And then you could rise higher and higher, and suddenly you could sense that there, tremendously far away, was what people talked about as God, what people called God.

What was given that name was there. It was entirely possible.

Lewi's last words before he died were: "It cannot be explained."

Perhaps he had also experienced something beyond the sandwich paper.

Yet in the *Lebenslauf* only Lewi's more sensible words were included from his autobiography. It was not much different from my own experience. It's true that he was fifteen, while I was younger. What was similar was that God did not exist as a form but only as movement, a tremendous lightness.

It happened somewhere in Norway, on a steamboat. "On board everything was quiet and still. Everyone was asleep in their cabins and there was nobody on deck. There I stood all alone and watched the sun come up over the sea. The magnificent natural spectacle greatly appealed to me, and God, the Creator and Preserver of this whole wondrous world, became inexpressibly alive and grand for me."

"The magnificent natural spectacle greatly appealed to me." It sounds as if he had read that somewhere. It doesn't ring quite true, but, well, it does come close. Yet that's not how it actually happened. It didn't take place anywhere near the North Pole or behind Crozier's wall of ice where he protected his dead colleagues from the polar bears with a rifle in his hand (the moment of death! and what came afterwards? and what did any of it mean?)—but at any rate: didn't it come close?

A ship, a young boy on deck "where I stood deep in prayer, it was as if my whole inner being melted before His penetrating, warming presence"; no, but it was getting close. And then the tears came. "As I stood there like that, deep in prayer, I spoke the words that I myself did not understand. At that time I had no thought of speaking in tongues."

In the *Lebenslauf* there is a photocopy of this page from Lewi's memoirs. In the margin Efraim has written, in clear, almost defiant block letters:

THE RELIGIOUS EXPERIENCE IS INDEED
VERY HARD TO DESCRIBE

Perhaps Efraim thought the same as I did.

Was what ended up on paper merely a nature experience, not something incomprehensible like the dusting of stars above the snow hollow when everything suddenly made sense? But why was there no fear of the Beast, why no attacking polar bears or wall of ice or terror? Had Lewi truly understood something that was just as immense as the pool of stars?

Just as I, on those nights in the snow, understood what it meant to be a human being enveloped by the universe. But perhaps Lewi believed that what is sacred is what the one who is sacred does.

But how the stars boomed! How they boomed!

In the late 1970s Efraim once asked me, "By the way, what's your own relationship to Jesus?" Only much later did I understand why I felt so uncomfortable.

There was an echo of something cloying.

Well, maybe something cloying can't have an echo. It was more like a faint scent—or feeling!—of something cloying and unpleasant from long ago.

Was it fifty years ago?

"What's your relationship to Jesus?" A cloying question with a faintly unpleasant scent, after fifty years. Revivalism had its cloying side, not showing people respect or leaving them in peace! To be left in peace was important! And there was a pastor in the Swedish Missionary Society—wasn't his name Stjärne?—at a tent meeting. I must have been thirteen. He took me by the arm and pulled me aside. And we went off to the side. Off to the side. I was rigid with fear and discomfort. And then he asked me: "What is your relationship to Jesus?"

What was I supposed to say?

The demand for a personal conversion contained a dream of purity, and also something cloying, a cloying fear. The next time I saw Efraim I asked him about it. No, he didn't understand what was so cloying. He had quite often asked "young people" about their relationship to Jesus.

But later I read in his *Lebenslauf* about a boy who said no. I suppose that was some sort of answer.

No doubt Lewi asked too. No, nothing cloying about that. No, Lewi had undoubtedly pulled "young people" "aside" in order to "ask" them about their relationship to Jesus.

I said, not really knowing why: "I think the cloying part was the reason I never had a truly good relationship with the Savior Jesus Christ, and it was Pastor Stjärne's fault."

6.

For Efraim, in the beginning, there was nothing cloying about it. Otherwise Efraim is strangely anonymous and reticent about himself.

It's the others—Lewi and Sven—who interest him.

Efraim knew what his relationship was to Jesus. Perhaps it was somewhat similar, but no, it was different. He never lay in the snow hollow and realized that God could be found beyond the dusting of stars. Nor had he ever had a nature experience. His tremendous leap into religious conversion did not really look like that.

Occasionally he hides himself in quotes about other people. As if he were someone else. But he's probably modest and doesn't want to seem special. A photocopy in Efraim's *Lebenslauf* apparently stems from the Sune Jonsson interview collection. Efraim has added comments in the margin. Judging by appearances, the interview has been abridged.

But it is definitely Efraim Markström. It's almost the only personal item in the *Lebenslauf*, and it comes very late. He seems to be using it as a commentary on his own expulsion from the movement.

He has hidden behind an anonymous voice that is nevertheless his own.

No doubt he was properly raised, and he knew that a person wasn't supposed to put on airs but should conceal himself.

It was three pages long, written in pencil, with a final comment that was perhaps ironic, considering how he and Sven were expelled: "At this time congregational chastisement not necessary."

The text was as follows:

"This is what happened: A girl had come from Vinliden. She arrived in Norrbyberg, which is just past Avanäs. About ten kilometers.

"One of my uncles from there came to see me one day at about five o'clock and told me about that girl. She was a goat-herd and baptized in the Spirit. In the past those who were baptized in the Holy Spirit would actually fall down and lie there, as if they were quite helpless. They were completely transformed. That's why the first friends were called 'fallers.' They fell, and that became their nickname. It was quite natural. This girl had also fallen into a faint when the Power came upon her, and some people ridiculed her and thought of all kinds of ways to make fun of her. If you looked at her, you might think she was trying to draw attention to herself. That's why the girl decided, along with the other friends who went to the meetings and felt the Power come over them so that they fell headlong to the ground, that they would try to hold onto the big shelf high up on the kitchen wall, because falling was regarded as something bad.

"The first time the Spirit struck in a powerful way, it was this girl from Vinliden who experienced it. She was the first. There were differing opinions about what happened. Most people viewed it as something bad. At that time I had not yet been converted, but on the other hand I couldn't understand why falling should be the work of the Devil or something that came from the world of Darkness. On the contrary. Perhaps they had a stronger belief in God's Word, and suddenly I felt a great longing to experience it myself.

"It's true that I had previously surrendered myself to God, but it was mostly lip service. What was happening now was that many people experienced it in a powerful way. In my home district things were starting to happen as they had on the very first Whitsunday. I truly began to feel in my heart a great longing to be saved. I had been unhappy. We lived in such a remote area back then, after moving from Bureå, that I hadn't landed in sin as deeply as certain other people. I had played cards, but I had gone without hard liquor. I had never tasted a drop, nor had I ever done any dancing. It was by the grace of God that I had escaped. But there was no doubt that in my heart I had loved ungodliness and things associated with it.

"I'm talking now about the early days. This was before I went south to find work, first of all in Jörn. By the time I met the Baptists in Vänersborg I had already been granted grace in Vinliden, although it wasn't as powerful as it was for the fallers.

"It happened at a meeting. Napoleon Bjur was preaching. He was a revivalist, but still part of the Evangelical Homeland Mission; only much later did he become a Pentecostal. Yet it must have shone through in Bjur in some way, through his powerful evangelizing, that he would become a Pentecostal. This was also before his time in the Holiness Church. Bjur started out with the Homeland Mission, then joined the Holiness Church, and finally the Pentecostal movement.

"I had done a great deal of brooding over what it would feel like to be lost and relegated to eternal darkness and filled with remorse. Because there would be plenty of room for remorse. Bjur had preached so powerfully that I felt it come over me, though I didn't fall. But that's the thing about confession. What was characteristic of his evangelizing, what made a person become sanctified, was that there was a before and a now. It was necessary. When the revival came, accounts had to be settled. You had to confess. The same held true for me. The important thing was to purify yourself, it was necessary. I had been a sinner, and it was particularly important to settle accounts with God, but also with your fellow human beings. The part about other human beings, and confessing about it, was hard. The fact was that I had been out marking trees. They were trees that were to be cut down. That was before I went south and met the Baptists there. At that time I was only fifteen, but one of the tree markers. And I was not yet saved. That meant I had no direction. If you have no direction, you can prey on someone else. That's what I did, in the sense that I marked a number of trees as smaller than they really were. And it was to my own uncle's detriment that I did this. That was the worst thing I had to confess; yet I didn't dare the first time that Bjur preached so powerfully, but rather two months later.

"I had been struggling for several months and was in a state of disintegration before I got started and confessed this.

"It so happened that when I then came under the Power, I felt quite small. But I can't recall that anything else in particular occurred. Some people were as calm as could be when they were baptized in the Holy Spirit; others you might think were somehow making a lot of unnecessary fuss. People are different, but God is always the same. The main thing was for you to 'come through,' or be reborn. It's impossible to describe exactly how it felt back then. Words are too paltry."

Was that Efraim himself? It was undoubtedly Efraim because he believed that an outcast, and a Judas, could defend himself only in this way.

Farther along in the interview, he talks about what it felt like.

"I would say, if I remember right, that it felt almost like tiny electric shocks. You almost wished that it would last a little longer. But some people were very afraid that they would end up disgracing themselves. I had friends who prayed to God about this. Asking that they might be spared, or helped, so they wouldn't fall or yell. It was the same as for the people who held onto the kitchen shelf. It's true. They prayed: 'You must not come to me, Jesus, my Savior, in such and such a way.' They didn't want to yell or grow boisterous, but the one who asked for such things from the Savior might very well be the one who shouted the loudest when God came.

"But that was in the beginning, when things were still grand. I still remember with joy in my heart how things were back then. It didn't matter whether it was a big meeting or a small one. Especially in the summertime back home. Then large groups would gather, and people would come from other towns too, even if they had to walk ten or twenty kilometers. We went into the woods in small groups. Prayer groups. We went into the woods and prayed. We fell to our knees next to rocks and stumps and prayed to God the Almighty. And the whole forest was filled with the murmur of prayers, and the Spirit fell upon us. You have to understand that if things are to be right again, we need to come back to this.

"There were even prayers out in the barns. If someone prevented you from going to the prayer corner indoors, you could go out to the barn and pray to God there. That often happened. And then there was another matter. We were only able to meet very seldom; the farms were all so far apart. But we never parted without a prayer and an invocation. No, never. Before we parted there had to be a prayer meeting. It was a given. But somehow the custom was lost. It became something else. Not that the prayer meetings disappeared entirely, but they were somehow lost. It was something that upset me greatly. It became the root of what happened later, the fact that this custom was lost.

"I don't know who should be blamed for this. No one person.

"But it can make you feel very sad that it disappeared."

I gave the key to the archives back to the pastor.

"This Lewi," he asked, "who was he?"

"Well, he founded and built up the third largest religious community in Christendom, though he didn't call it a community," I told him. "Today it has over 250 million members all over the world."

The pastor seemed distracted and merely said, "Is that right? Was he Swedish?"

"Yes," I said. "Very much so."

"That's an odd thing to say," the pastor replied. "Is that what it says in the *Lebenslauf*?"

"I don't know," I said.

Then he lost interest in asking me any more questions, since what I had told him didn't sound plausible. He stood on the stairs and smoked a Cecil, the strongest Danish brand of cigarette, which was later banned.

"Are you going to come back?" he asked.

Once again I took a short walk through God's acre. Efraim had not yet been given his stone. No slanting morning sunlight, and most of the inscriptions were still invisible.

Book I

March 1901–July 1910

CHAPTER 1

The Proletarian Writer

1.

THERE IS A BLACK HOLE IN THE *LEBENSLAUF* THAT EFRAIM FILLS in quite late.

It has to do with Lewi's childhood.

He would return to it, almost at the very end. This was during the events of Lewi's exile in 1941. That was the first time he seemed to discover his childhood.

Perhaps that's the way it is with national monuments cast all in one piece. People forget about the child who has been cast inside; he's screaming and wants to get out.

By the way, Lewi was given his own museum. It's in Kaggeholm Castle, which became the folk high school of the Pentecostal movement.

I visited it for the first time in the spring of 1999, seventeen years after Efraim was buried. The museum was very quiet. Faint sounds came from the soccer field, where the young Pentecostals were playing a game. Lewi's study had been restored. The activities at Kaggeholm were quite lively and productive. The Pentecostal movement now offered students courses in media and IT, as well as film technology including digital editing.

Time passes, after all. Attitudes change. Yet the battle for minds goes on; Lewi and Gramsci agreed about that.

The movement's newspapers reported that the question of an association was once again relevant: Should the movement become an association, contrary to the traditions of Lewi and Herrnhut? Lewi was a vague but active reference point in the debate. Someone brought up what he had said in 1919 at the revivalist meeting in Kölingared. Representing 102 Pentecostal evangelists he had declared that "for purely spiritual reasons we consider it best to distance ourselves from the present association's organizational entity, and to make it our prayer to God that the free congregations in our country may remain untouched by all such organizational entities."

Yet now, eighty years later, they wanted to build an association, an organization like those of all the other churches. But some people objected, speaking of Lewi and the betrayal of his dream. Once there was even a popular movement that was transformed on God's great acre, and some people still dreamed about the tongues of fire of the first Pentecostal era, the tongues of fire that ought not to be organized away and die out.

Lewi was a museum. His glasses were there. His library. A vast selection of American literature from the 1930s. *Grapes of Wrath* in English.

Who was this Lewi, as he had taken shape in this museum? The curator, who was very young, little more than a boy, wasn't quite sure. An apostle, he thought. The creator of the Christian Democratic Party.

I said, "He was different right from the start."

"Did you know him?" asked the boy.

"No, certainly not. But I had a friend who knew him from the beginning."

"What was he like?"

"Well, he said that right from the start Lewi was different."

"Different?"

"Yes, different."

"Lewi purchased Kaggeholm Castle in 1942 and gave it to the Pentecostal movement," he told me.

"Did he have money for that?"

"Yes, he claimed to have bought it cheap; he said it was a good buy."

"The members of the movement were poor and had no money, but the money appeared, and Lewi said it was a miracle, as well as hard work," I said.

"Hard work? But didn't he give it away?"

"Yes, even though it was clearly inexpensive, and he said that it was a good buy. He himself had no money," I said, "so it must have been both a miracle and hard work. Because if a miracle didn't occur, then Lewi usually worked even harder, and then it was a miracle after all."

The curator nodded, but I'm not sure that he understood.

I told him, "Well, for an empire-builder he was quite frugal." I could tell that my words fell flat, even though they were true. "Frugal like God's Per Albin," I added in explanation.

"Who?" said the boy as he placed a stack of scrapbooks filled with clippings on the desk.

Lewi's little museum was now completely silent. The sounds from the student soccer field had ceased.

"From the very beginning he was different," Efraim had written in his *Lebenslauf*.

Now that I think about it, whenever I went to see Efraim to talk about Uncle Aron and Nicanor, we frequently talked about the movement, meaning Lewi.

Efraim would often be lying in bed when I arrived.

He would get up with great effort and an apologetic smile. "God's peace," he would say. He uttered that fine old greeting almost defiantly, with a little embarrassed smile. It had gone out of fashion. The fault of a film in the '30s, as he explained. It had apparently starred Fridolf Rhudin and was very funny, although he had never seen it himself. Films were sinful. Well, he wasn't terribly strict back in the '30s, since he was an adult after all, but it had been deeply ingrained in him. It had been deeply ingrained that films were sinful, and so he had never seen it.

But people had talked about how it happened that the peace greeting ended up being ruined. In any case, it had to do with a film starring Fridolf Rhudin. And he was terribly funny and entertaining, after a fashion. He played a Pentecostal pastor in the film. The audience laughed and laughed, and he kept saying "peace" all the time, both when it was appropriate and mostly when it wasn't. Then people sat in the movie theater and practically roared with laughter every time he said "peace." And when they left the theater after seeing the film, it began to spread. Boys started walking around saying "Peace!" to each other, and then everyone would laugh and make fun of it. So that's how the peace greeting ended up being ruined. But Efraim had grown rather stubborn in his old age, so he said "peace" or "God's peace," even though the greeting had been ruined. In some sense it proved to us that it was true: Films were sinful.

Yes, well, there were plenty of other things that were sinful. Plenty of things. Almost everything in the end.

Were there lots of rules?

More and more of them. Playing marbles and card games and even chess, and definitely theater and what kind of clothes you wore. In the end it was even hard to breathe. It was like a second book of laws, and it contained the strangest rules about sins. It was more like an etiquette book. We called it the sin catalogue. That's what people said. It got thicker and thicker. It seemed as if we had tossed the Bible on the trash heap and taken to our hearts *Manners and Etiquette in the Pentecostal Life*. There were rules for everything, especially for women: how they should dress, how they should wear their hair, and whether they were allowed to wear jewelry. People actually started longing for a Jesus who would drive this out of the temple. In fact, Efraim could grow quite furious when he thought about it.

That was later. But peace. Peace. And later Efraim believed that toward the end Lewi came to share this opinion.

And Lewi? What was he like?

Well, in the beginning he was very different. Back then he was not like anyone else. At first he was quite seriously saved, but then later he was about to abandon his faith. He was going to be something else entirely. I think it was actually the great goal of his life, even though he gave it up.

Gave it up? Do you mean Lewi?

Yes, gave up what he truly dreamed of becoming. And he actually never changed. I think that was his secret. Later he was almost ashamed of it. But that explains things.

Efraim asked me, "What was the first film you ever saw?"

"*Call the Doctor*," I told him.

"And how old were you back then?"

"Fifteen."

"That was young," said Efraim. "To be going to the movies."

2.

In the margin of a text that talks about "how Lewi became a human being" Efraim has added two words, heavily underlined twice.

It says: "Traveling Companion!"

No further explanation. It's apparently not an allusion to himself. Or to Sven.

Simply: "Traveling Companion!"

Efraim writes in his *Lebenslauf* that he met Lewi for the first time during the winter of 1901. That was when both of them were working at the A. F. Carlsson shoe factory in Vänersborg, and three years before Efraim went back to Bureå and the dealings with Nicanor took place.

What he remembers about Lewi and their first encounter was related to a trade union meeting. And it came toward the end of it. There were fourteen people present, and they were all sitting on straight-backed chairs. "I remember that it was a basement room, and I noticed at once that a newcomer was among us; we were all experienced young men and workers." The previous speaker had finished his long presentation with a "harangue," which more or less boiled down to "there damn well better be agreement on this, and thanks for listening, comrades," and then the new person raised his hand and asked to speak.

The youth was very short, with a round face and pale complexion; quite insignificant, not someone you'd even notice. He had dark hair with a lock falling over his forehead, and he seemed quite endearing, although insignificant. He may have come to the union meetings before, but if so Efraim hadn't noticed him. Normally those who were new would be quite shy the first few times. And there were strict rules at the union meetings. The new people didn't know the rules or how to behave when votes were taken or motions were passed. Or about the procedures. And there were plenty of those. Anyway, now he had raised his hand to make his voice heard for the first time.

When Efraim thought about it, this may have been the first time that Lewi ever made his voice heard in a public forum.

"Comrade Jonsson has the floor," the chairman then said.

That was the proper thing to say. Things were run very formally in the trade union, so you had the feeling that you were a small part of a great organization that had strictly established rules, which signified an overwhelming power. And the fact that it was all so precise seemed to elevate the proceedings above the ordinary. In fact, it was almost like a church service.

But then this new person promptly corrected the chairman.

"Johansson."

"All right then: Comrade Johansson."

The young man stood up. His hair had been plastered down with water, although one lock was still sticking up. He was wearing a serge suit and looked quite endearing. He spoke in a voice that sounded tense at first but soon grew confident; it was surprising how quickly his confidence grew even though he was so new.

"Comrades," he said, "I have only one thing to say."

Then he paused, as if he wanted to create some kind of anticipation or reflection with his words, or as if he wanted the others to be curious. Then he repeated what he had said.

"I have only one thing to say. I think that those of us in the workers' union . . ."

"The trade union," the chairman corrected him. And then, for a moment, the youth seemed slightly flustered, but he pulled himself together and continued, in an even more confident voice.

"The trade union. I just wanted to say that I refuse to be a member of the trade union if people are going to swear. Then I don't want to belong. I don't think we should take God's name in vain in the union. I object, and I want it to be entered in the minutes. I'm a socialist, but I'm also saved. Thank you for listening."

For a moment no one said a word.

"I see," said the chairman in astonishment. "I see. So Comrade Johansson is saved?"

"Yes, I am."

There was some murmuring, followed by bewildered silence. People began to fidget.

"Is that a motion?"

"Yes, it's a motion." And the newcomer faltered for a moment as he looked around uncertainly, but then he gathered his courage. "It's a motion, and I want it to be entered in the minutes!"

The chairman cleared his throat but looked as if he didn't for the life of him know what to do. He looked around, but everyone was staring at the floor without saying a word.

"Well . . ." he went on, when the silence began to feel uncomfortable. "I'm certain that . . . that . . . that everyone present will respect Comrade Johansson's feelings regarding this matter. The motion is that we . . . won't swear?"

"Or curse."

"Swear or curse. During the meetings. Shall we put the motion to a vote?"

A faint murmuring.

"Perhaps we don't need a show of hands?"

General murmuring that could be interpreted as agreement.

"Is it hereby resolved that we will not swear?"

Faint assent.

"Anyone opposed?"

No one opposed. Sharp rap of the gavel.

"The motion is passed. Unanimously. Item eight, guidelines for the fight against international capitalism: passed. Item nine, the right to place your lunch box under the workbench, also passed. Item ten, other business: the floor is open."

That was how Efraim met Lewi.

Together they had strolled through Vänersborg to the lodgings where Efraim lived. They walked along, talking, side by side. It was foggy, and they kept each other company all the way to his door.

"No," Efraim told Lewi, "you're not the only one who's saved in the union. But there aren't many of us."

"Two isn't bad," said Lewi. "By the time this century ends, we'll be many in number, no doubt the majority. By the dawn of the next millennium, human beings will have risen up from their sin and oblivion. And we'll be able to look around at a white-clad army of socialist believers."

"We won't be alive then," replied Efraim.

"If God is willing," said Lewi. "His is the Power."

"But we'll be over a hundred years old," countered Efraim.

"His is the Power!"

After this exchange they had wandered through the deserted streets for a long time, silent but thoughtful. Then Lewi may have realized that his new friend and ally might not have a faith strong enough to imagine that they could live to be over a hundred, so he added:

"Two isn't bad. A spark can ignite a prairie fire, as they say in the great land to the west."

Then Efraim asked in astonishment, "Are the two of us going to ignite . . . a prairie fire?"

"The two of us," replied Lewi.

3.

The dates in the *Lebenslauf* are often unreliable.

Early one summer, several years after the day when Lewi had compelled the motion of no swearing to be entered into the minutes, he joined up as a soldier in the standing army at Axevalla Heath.

By then something has happened to Efraim. Yet he seems unwilling to discuss his own life. He leaves gaps. "There were many who went to America, but I stayed behind in Sweden." He writes nothing about why he stayed behind.

This was also several years before the incident with Uncle Aron took place, and Efraim gathered the potatoes Aron left on the ice of Bure Fjord.

They had met regularly, not just at union meetings, and "they were now the best and most loyal of friends."

Lewi was the one who came up with the idea of handing out brochures in the evenings to the soldiers.

Efraim had reluctantly gone along. "Socialists weren't very popular at the time. We were regarded as lice, but Lewi thought it was of utmost importance to widen the organization and awaken the young soldiers to the cause of the labor movement. He was very keen on organizing, and thought it wasn't enough to hold meetings at the shoe factory, because a movement also had to reach those who were not believers."

By the second evening, disaster struck.

The first evening everything had gone well, but on the second evening, a Saturday, there was a party going on in the officers' quarters. Great roars could be heard from inside. It was a dark and hot August night, the windows were open, and inside the barracks they had obviously been boozing. The expression was Efraim's. People boozed or hit the booze or got mixed up in boozing. He himself had never hit the booze, though he had played cards, but only for a short period.

Dancing, the third deadly sin, was never mentioned in the same way. You couldn't say that someone had "gotten mixed up" in dancing. The term mostly applied to liquor and card games.

That evening a loud commotion could be heard from the officers' quarters. They were officers from Stockholm and not under anyone's jurisdiction, so they were boozing without restraint. But shrill women's voices could also be heard. "They were whores."

It was early evening, and fornication was in the air. Efraim and Lewi paused for a moment outside the officers' quarters, then continued on to one of the troops' barracks to distribute brochures.

An hour later they were arrested.

That peculiar word "fornication."

What was it about this puritanical country that made fornication so enticing? Why could fornication be found running like a secret, dark current deep beneath the revivalist movement, when at the same time fornication was the greatest enemy? The child of revivalism and the child of fornication—weren't they twins before the throne of God and the Lamb? Efraim, who was also a child of revivalism, must have known.

We all knew, though we seldom admitted it.

Desire and ecstasy and faith and sexuality. What was the dark, deep-running current if not sexuality? And yet it was the most forbidden. To partake of Holy Communion without faith, to falsely receive His Holy Body and Blood with doubt in your heart, was not the only deadly sin. There was something much worse. It was to show before the Lord! before the Lord and His Holy Scriptures! a particular desire for the female body—that was the linchpin of the deadly sin.

The female body was, of course, the source of all sin.

Naturally everyone knew that the revivalist children, the young adolescents, would take the Åhlén & Holm catalogue out to the privy under the pretense that those old catalogues could be used in place of the much too sharp shithouse sticks. But there they would sit and look at the pages with advertisements for bras, at the photos of the headless torsos in which the almost sheet metal-like, armored brassieres concealed the enticing images of sin—but not entirely, because the pages were used for something, though they were never torn out.

The fantasy was there in the power of fornication.

The adolescents touched themselves before these images of fornication and spilled their seed. But that was in the shithouse, and only before the Åhlén & Holm catalogue. What was worse was when the adolescents sometimes used the Holy Scriptures.

That was the ultimate deadly sin.

The family Bible contained pictures by Doré. And some of the large illustrations showed the naked female body. And this Doré was a talented artist, he was truly a man of skill. Every single body seemed alive. The worst sin of all, the one that no one talked about, was when a young man, someone who had perhaps come through and been baptized in the Spirit, still felt tempted. And so he opened the Holy Scriptures. The family Bible. And perhaps he studied one of Doré's pictures, perhaps the one depicting the Deluge in which the flood waters are washing over the desperate and despairing souls. Including women, who are being flung around naked in the surging waters. And their bodies are depicted exactly as they were. And if the young man then exposed his member and touched it, to give himself pleasure, and if he did this before the Holy Scriptures—was there anything worse? No, there was not.

It was said that a young man in Klutmark had been caught in this act, and afterward he felt such despair that he went out and hanged himself from the rafters in the stable without receiving redemption.

Efraim and Lewi had paused, very briefly, outside the officers' quarters and listened to the laughter. "They were whores."

What is it about that tone of voice?

Some of the soldiers must have slipped away and reported what was going on to their superiors.

Efraim and Lewi were taken to the hall where the party was in progress.

Four reserve officers had come out while two scantily clad women stood in the window watching until they were hauled back inside. Then Lewi and Efraim were taken to a remote, empty barracks to be interrogated.

The four reserve officers were wearing uniforms, yet they appeared to be scantily clad, perhaps because of the women. It was possible that they had just risen from the bed of lust and hadn't quite managed to dress properly. That's how things were in the vipers' nest. Doré had made a drawing of that too, when the vipers, in mortal terror, wrapped themselves around the naked women in the roiling swells of the deluge.

You could just imagine.

But the reserve officers seemed to liven up at the sight of their lucky catch, in spite of the interruption to their carousing. Efraim and Lewi had been stripped of their pamphlets and were now sitting on straight-backed chairs, while one of their merciless tormentors was reading from the text in a loud voice, as if he were a judge.

"Death to capitalism?" he then exclaimed in an agitated voice. "This is inciting to murder! How can you justify this?"

Another one of the reserve officers, who had a neatly trimmed beard and a strikingly well-groomed mustache, started to laugh, not with ill intent but as if he thought his colleague was an idiot. Then he pulled himself together and said he would take over the interrogation.

"What's your name, you devil?" he asked.

"Petrus Lewi Johansson," Lewi replied.

"What kind of devilish God-forsaken name is that?" the reserve officer remarked, laughing. And then Lewi asked him not to misuse the Lord's name in that way.

Several seconds of astonished silence followed. Efraim thought this really wasn't necessary. It was the same as last time, at the trade union, but perhaps not necessary. In a sense Lewi was repeating himself. But the situation was different now, and it wasn't necessary.

"What impudence," said the reserve officer in a menacing tone.

Lewi sat on this chair, round-faced and apparently calm, but sweating. And the man who was the interrogator and had laughed when his colleague said that "Death to capitalism" was inciting to murder, asked in a scornful voice for an explanation.

"I am saved," said Lewi, and you could hear a slight quaver in his voice. This was a confession, after all. It always created a certain tension to confess your faith in Jesus Christ. But this was not like in a Baptist congregation. Here they were among heathens. And they were being persecuted like the first Christians.

"Religious?" the interrogation leader asked with a surprised expression, as if he couldn't make the contents of the brochure mesh with the fact that Lewi was saved. Then he said, slowly but emphatically:

"I think we ought to set up a penal colony in Africa for socialists and strikers. That's where those lice should be deported. And be kept under guard! By our army. To keep the hooligans in check. That's my creed. Besides, I'm a poet, and my gospel is the praise of love."

Everyone was staring at the reserve officer after this rather surprising confession.

"Have you ever fucked?" the reserve officer then asked, turning to look at both Lewi and Efraim.

After a moment's hesitation, both of them shook their heads.

"Do you want to see how it's done so you'll understand the gospel of love and turn away from all this socialist drivel in the future?"

"No," said Lewi. "No."

There was a long silence.

"Pious socialists," the reserve officer finally said, "ought to be baptized in the faith of the body and the power of love. That's what I think. They need to be converted. From socialism and sectarianism to love. Don't you want to be baptized into the faith of desire?"

"No," said Lewi.

"We'll see about that," the reserve officer with the neatly trimmed beard then said.

They led the two men to the water trough at the corner of the barracks. Joking, they shoved their heads way down into the water for a brief moment that seemed very long.

Repeatedly.

"Do you want to see?" the officer said after each dunking. "Do you want to see?"

And at last they said yes.

Afterwards Efraim was so agitated that he couldn't hide the fact that he cried. Lewi, on the other hand, said nothing, but in the dark outside the gate, he threw up.

It was the water, he explained. He had swallowed a lot of cold water.

Later in life neither of them ever said a word about what happened. Only once did Efraim ask Lewi about it. That was in the 1930s when Lidman had been saved but conflicts were starting to appear. That's when Efraim asked Lewi whether the reserve officer who had baptized them wasn't actually Lidman.

But Lewi curtly denied it. And Efraim had never wanted to ask Sven, even though there was something in his memoirs that indicated it might be true. But memories could be wrong. And it had been very dark. And what happened that night was not something that ought to be confessed. It was too inconsequential. You should only confess to what is important, to something that possesses an inner greatness. And

Efraim himself may have remembered wrong; it was a very dark night and he had been terrified, fully believing that he was going to drown. And then there came the part with the women and their reserve officers in the vipers' nest, like in the drawing by that artist Doré. He wanted to forget. No doubt Lewi felt the same way.

But the interrogator was a poet.

Lewi had denied it with a firm voice: No, it wasn't Lidman. That was not their first encounter. Definitely not. Spoken in a voice that clearly stated that the matter was now closed. And Efraim Markström should no longer have any doubt about it.

But the desire! The desire!

4.

In the *Lebenslauf* there is a curious comment about Lewi and sports that require physical strength.

The fact of the matter was that according to a resolution passed by the workers' union in Vänersborg—which was actually a trade union —during the years when Efraim and Lewi worked together and were actively involved, it was determined that one of the purposes of the union was to develop the traditional athletics of the labor movement: sports requiring physical strength. First and foremost this meant wrestling, boxing, weight-lifting, and other sports that might be considered preparation for the revolutionary struggle. But not shooting. Lewi had agreed with this, but at a meeting he voiced an objection to boxing, which he did not think he could reconcile with his Christian beliefs.

In order to comply with the spirit of the bylaws, they had agreed that certain sports of a peaceful nature would meet the definition of both "sports requiring physical strength" and "peaceful competition."

For his part, Efraim had suggested the shot put, and Lewi had agreed. So that's what happened. Later on there weren't many people who associated Lewi Pethrus with the shot put, but Efraim wrote that "in truth" it was a fact.

He and Lewi had found a lump of iron shaped like a ball, and in an open clearing in the woods they practiced the shot put. "It was quite primitive, but we drew a line in the sand and paced it off." It was necessary to take measurements because they wanted to know whether they were getting better results. So how was Lewi Pethrus as a shot put athlete? He was quite good, even though he wasn't particularly big. But he was superbly disciplined, which meant that he got better results than Efraim, who was actually a better athlete. Efraim was much bigger than Lewi, but Lewi got better results. They knew that because they took measurements.

One question that arose was: How did Lewi view this type of athletic practice?

According to the *Lebenslauf*, Lewi grew increasingly skeptical. He didn't believe in engaging in sports that required physical strength, and under no circumstances on Sunday. In his opinion we weren't going to change the world by increasing our throw from 17 to 19½ feet. No matter how good an athlete a worker became, it made no difference.

It was through thinking, and the organization of ideas, that the world would be changed. In this he had seen a parallel to his conviction of faith. Conversion and faith—that was something inside a human being; it was a matter of coming through, of salvation. In that way a person could improve; yes, in a way it was like the shot put, in the sense that it was the responsibility of the individual person.

Personal responsibility.

But no matter how many muscles a person developed, it didn't make the wages for piecework any better. It didn't destroy capitalism. It didn't free the slaves from sin. Or fornication. That was faulty thinking. The shot put was entertaining, but it was an individual effort. He would rather organize the labor movement than achieve better results in the shot put. To organize the working class successfully, you shouldn't start with the muscles.

You should start with the spirit.

You should first conquer the way they think. Improve their morals. Drinking, cravings for pleasure, moral decay—all of these things weakened those who were oppressed. People had to be rehabilitated from within, and then those who were morally rehabilitated had to be organized.

But how could this be done?

Well, Lewi felt that their way of thinking had to be conquered first. He saw many similarities between the revivalist movement and the labor movement, in the sense that the conscience had to be conquered first. That was the way to break through. If the workers' way of thinking was conquered, an organization could be built that capitalism could not touch. Every single worker would then become a member of the resistance, and then thousands of small forts could be built that would organize thousands of small cells all over Sweden which would not be held together by a central leadership. Not an association that capitalism and the oppressors could touch, but a group united by a way of thinking. Like the Moravians.

That was the basic idea. First conversion and morals. Later an organization that was decentralized. And then a combined force.

He never did become a shot put athlete. Or a bodybuilder. Instead he became a builder.

5.

There are plenty of details, but the big picture is blurred. Lewi had also sought something that he later concealed.

It was his secret dream, afterwards denied.

During his time in Vänersborg Lewi happened to "brush up against the fate of the poet Birger Sjöberg." There was something about Sjöberg that fascinated Lewi. He had met Sjöberg, but kept a kind of deferential distance even though they were the same age. Yet one time Lewi had his photo taken in the studio where Birger Sjöberg worked.

He hinted at some sort of identification: "The poet from Vänersborg."

He describes both an inner and an outer similarity. Both were marked by a deep religiosity. They had both worked as manual laborers. Both had known poverty. Their first frustrated romantic encounters occurred at approximately the same time. In the *Lebenslauf*, page references are cited from Lewi's memoirs. In those passages Lewi writes with an odd tone of yearning repudiation that "Birger Sjöberg's fate might also have befallen me." Or, later on, the dissociation is almost complete; now he speaks from a distance, having been spared, yet there is still that vague undertone of sorrow and longing. "Since I've followed the writing and eventual fate of this Vänersborg boy, I can better understand what dangers lay in wait for me."

Lewi dreamed of becoming a writer, and that frightened him.

Efraim met him again several years later when Lewi was studying at Bethel Seminary, the training institute for the Baptist seminary. For Efraim the image of a young Lewi has several obvious gaps. The time that Lewi spent in Norway was something that Efraim had only read about; it doesn't seem to interest him. That itself was a glaring gap in Efraim's recollections. Not a word about Lewi's friendship with Georg, who was Lewi's brother-in-law. He refers to what Lewi wrote ("well, so much was written, and you can accept it if you want"), to the books about Lewi, to Lewi's own meticulous account of history, the road to his great career. Yet at the same time there are puzzling nicks in the early picture of the conscientious, friendly socialist, the man cast in one piece.

God's Per Albin cast in one piece.

Yet there was something about this monumental image that confused Efraim. He had seen something that was out of the ordinary. The story was that Lewi wished to become a preacher and had entered a preacher training school, even though he would later vigorously criticize the idea of training preachers. His distrust was part of his contempt for theological hierarchies. The great exemplars Spurgeon and Moody had never gone to any preacher training school. They had acquired a distrust of theological academicism with the Moravians: training to preach belonged to the cancerous diseases of the centralized church. A person's speech should be untrained and pure and powerful. "Lewi believed strongly in a type of preaching that was untrained; it was impossible to train to be either a preacher or a poet(!)"—yet he had entered the seminary.

That's where Efraim met Lewi once again. And it was a strangely changed Lewi that he encountered "during the few days we spent together in friendly fellowship."

Lewi had discovered the library at the preachers' school. He had read Viktor Rydberg's biblical teachings about Christ many times, and they had clearly shaken him. He talked a great deal about all that was meaningless in the "sin catalogue" of the revivalist movement, about what was permitted and what was a sin, and the fact that he had repudiated the concept. He had adopted a position of "tolerance." He had also—and this was the first shock Efraim experienced—started smoking and had "gotten mixed up in boozing."

The latter may not have been particularly serious. But he had tasted liquor several times. And his world view seemed to have changed. He no longer took it for granted that he would become a preacher.

On the second evening he showed Efraim his novel.

He had actually written a novel. It was his dream of becoming an author that had overwhelmed him. He was going to be a socialist proletarian writer, he declared. He didn't want to be a preacher, that was nothing but a subterfuge. He was going to describe reality for the masses as it really was. Lewi the socialist had returned, but he was no longer so inflexible; he no longer corrected comrades who swore. He left them in peace, and they had to take responsibility for themselves. His own responsibility was to be a writer.

The novel was quite lengthy and "interesting." At Björck & Börjesson's antiquarian bookstore Lewi had found an old report of the proceedings from poor welfare cases in Stockholm, and from this documentary material he had written a novel that now "was in a state of near completion."

Efraim was allowed to read it.

He lay on the floor in Lewi's room with the pages in a big stack, and as he finished reading each page, it was placed in another neat pile. And afterwards Efraim felt greatly moved; he remembers that well.

It was good, Efraim concludes in the *Lebenslauf*. It was quite terrifying, but it was good. And there were no spelling mistakes. "I've never gone to the university, you know," Lewi had said. Anyway, there were no spelling mistakes.

But this praise for his spelling seemed to throw Lewi off balance. He didn't want to be praised for his spelling, Efraim recalls. Later Lewi talked a great deal about the fact that those who went to the university had an advantage, but it was not something insurmountable, because the good thing about someone who was born in a two-room house with nine siblings and enormous poverty was that he had experience.

And this compensated for the fact that he had never gone to the university.

That's why an uneducated writer could be just as good a preacher as someone who had gone to the university but had nothing to say.

He had asked Efraim over and over what he thought about it.

It was a matter of self-confidence.

Lewi said that he actually had no self-confidence. The real writers, those who were educated—did they have something that he could never achieve? Was there a particular gift, or could he become like them?

Deep inside he didn't believe that what he wrote was any good.

Not really. It sounded forced, he said. Didn't it sound forced? Almost stiff? Or what did Efraim think? Did what he was preaching (!) possess the proper power so that those who read it would come through and be practically bowled over and not be able to hold onto the big shelf (it was Efraim's own voice and images that suddenly intervened in this recollection—Lewi had never actually encountered a faller at that time, or a big shelf).

The important thing was not that the novel contained no spelling mistakes. What was important for a proletarian writer was to come through and exert power. That was not something the educated writers could do. That was the difference. Yet deep inside Lewi was still uneasy. It wasn't enough to know how to spell. His grades in school had been excellent, but now he was dreaming of becoming a proletarian writer; that was his calling.

The whole time he emphasized that it was his calling.

In his novel there was a chapter, or rather an episode, that Efraim remembers well because he didn't find it very believable, and he said as much.

"That part wasn't very good," he said. Lewi had merely nodded in silence.

It was about the novel's protagonist, who was named Petrus. The name was later crossed out and changed to Johannes, but it was clear what the intent was from the beginning. And this Petrus was a boy from the slums of Söder, the south side of Stockholm, and he had endured the most terrible suffering. He had poor siblings who were starving. So one day the boy decided to knock on the parish pastor's door to beg for a few scraps of bread for his siblings, but the pastor callously slammed the door in his face. Then Petrus, or rather Johannes, lost his faith and resolved to change the world himself and become a socialist.

To a certain extent this was prompted by the hypocritical and callous state church pastor who had refused to listen to him. At any rate, this boy Petrus, or Johannes, sat in the meeting house and listened to the singing, and then he suddenly had an overwhelming experience. Jesus came to him, as if He had walked right up from behind. And He leaned down over the shoulder of this boy Petrus, and He was surrounded by light. He placed his hand on the boy's arm, but in such a way that the wound and nail holes were visible, and then in a terribly kind and cautious manner he whispered in the boy's ear:

"Petrus, you will be the rock upon which I will build my congregation."

And then Petrus understood that He meant socialism. And Jesus was endearing, and it was a magnificent experience. That's what the chapter was about.

Efraim had told Lewi that this chapter was not as good as the others. It was like mixing up two different topics. Making Jesus a socialist was a great idea but not very plausible.

And Lewi had nodded. No, it probably wasn't very plausible.

But it could still be true.

Birger Sjöberg was a real writer. And he too was uneducated. But he got mixed up in sin, and things had not turned out well for him.

Lewi wondered what real writers were like, deep inside. He wished that just once he might get to know a real writer—personally, that is. And understand what it meant. "It" was something secret, filling a person with a sense of both longing and dread.

This was like a question that he tried to answer his whole life. And there's a note in the margin of the *Lebenslauf*, almost teasing in tone, saying that Lewi would actually meet a real writer one day, but it was not Birger Sjöberg.

That's all.

And that's how things turned out. This writer would change Lewi's life, and he would love this writer more than Birger Sjöberg, and the writer would love him in return.

What kind of love was it? Love cannot be explained, after all. Not even love for Jesus Christ.

Almost nothing about how it all started.

Not a word about Lewi's childhood.

Except what is most commonly known: that Lewi was born on March 11, 1884, in Västra Tunhem in Älvsborg County.

CHAPTER 2

————•—•——

The Poet

1.

SO MUCH IS UNSAID YET STILL IMPLIED IN THE *LEBENSLAUF.*

"The two of us," Lewi said on the evening after the meeting at the trade union.

The two of us. Perhaps it was this "two of us" that chafed like a grain of sand. But it didn't turn out to be those two.

Only in one place in Efraim's *Lebenslauf* is there any hint of a connection between Lidman and Moravianism.

Efraim had read one of Sven's books, *Blood Inheritance* from 1937, and quotes from it, almost reluctantly.

Sometimes I think that he didn't really care for Sven.

Sven writes about one of his ancestors, the paternal grandfather of his maternal grandfather, whom he claims to have detested. "I realized how falsely and wrongly I had judged him when, thirty years later, I found him depicted in Hilding Pleijel's book *Moravianism in Southern Sweden* as the defender of Moravianism in Karlskrona, fighting the righteous and pious persecution of W. P. Henschen, the admiralty's pastor, both within the admiralty's consistory and elsewhere. A peculiar trembling passed over me at the boundless context of fate in which our brief little lives on earth are ensnared, also from a human genealogical point of view. In reality, hadn't my great-great-grandfather, whom I for so long had scorned and reviled as a 'neologist,' stepped forward as the defender and protector of what I used to call the Pentecostal revivalism of the 1700s? Moravianism."

The *Lebenslauf* is filled with references to Sven's autobiographical works, frequently occurring only as code words and page citations. But after this quote a brief remark appears, written in pencil. "True, but how ensnared he seems by human genealogy in this wretched book."

No further explanations for this hostile tone. Was it because of "the two of us"?

2.

At one place in the *Lebenslauf*, Efraim Markström dwells with sorrow and anger on the fate that befalls Faithful in John Bunyan's *The Pilgrim's Progress*.

Christian and Faithful are the best of friends. Along their way to the gates of Heaven they have encountered a number of temptations and threats, and suffered derision. Just before his fate is sealed, Faithful uses sharp words to repudiate Talkative, whose devotion consists merely of words, not deeds or truth: from his pulpit he speaks falsely and bewitches his listeners. Then the friends reach the town of Vanity and wander through Vanity Fair, where they are imprisoned. At the trial that follows, Faithful bravely condemns the godlessness that exists at this market where everything is for sale: houses, official positions, promotions, horses, pleasures, harlots, children, lives, blood, bodies, souls, gold, silver, and precious gems. Then these hypocritical merchants are seized with fury because they want to continue their godless lives in which, at this market, they're also allowed to see jugglers, entertainments, plays, jesters, monkeys, scoundrels, and rogues. Christian and Faithful are mocked and berated, but only Faithful is condemned to death. He is executed in the most gruesome fashion since the members of the jury—Mr. Blindman, Mr. No-good, Mr. Malice, Mr. Love-lust, Mr. Live-loose, Mr. Heady, Mr. High-mind, Mr. Hate-light, and Mr. Implacable—decide that his loyalty and fortitude have made him dangerous. First they whip him, then they beat him with their fists, stab him with a dagger, stone him, run him through with a sword, and burn him at the stake.

That is the end of Faithful. Christian is then allowed to continue on his way.

It's not fair. What's unfair is that he disappears from the story. Efraim was apparently indignant about this.

It's not fair.

* * *

The two planets of Lewi and Sven are still very far from each other.

It was now May 1905, and Sven had found his first congregation of devotees and believers. He had gazed out over the congregation and felt a simple warmth in his breast and realized that they shared the same feeling.

They truly wanted to hear his poems, and they were loyal. The congregation was small, consisting of five prostitutes at Västerlång-gatan 24, one of the smaller and yet well-respected bordellos in Stockholm.

There were over five hundred of them.

It was early afternoon at the beginning of May. The girls happened to be unoccupied, as was almost always the case between two and five in the afternoon, especially on Thursdays. They had had a cup of tea and sampled the Madam's home-baked Rosinante cakes. The dark red curtains were drawn, it was a fine afternoon, and the girls were enjoy-ing listening to Sven read his poetry.

They were quite familiar with the fact that poets were young, poor, and unhappy. Sven had clearly confirmed this notion, and they were very fond of him. He usually came in the afternoon when every-one was well rested and waiting to start work for the evening. Those hours were a time for silence and reflection: precisely the right time for listening to poetry read aloud. And afterwards, after he had read to them, one of the girls who was willing—and strangely enough many of them were willing, none of them needed much urging—one of the girls would take the young Lidman behind the draperies and render him a small service free of charge, in exchange for the reading, for the pleasure they had enjoyed when he read to them.

The whole place had such a nice homey feeling of comfort and warmth. Many of the girls who came from the provinces, especially one from Malung named Ellen who was actually a native of Norway and spoke the Dalecarlian dialect with a Norwegian accent, many of them experienced these hours (which were generally on Thursdays) as reminders of their childhood growing up in pious households. There was an atmosphere, or at least very delicate echoes, of the perhaps more sleepy reading hours spent in the kitchen back home when someone would read aloud from Luther's book of sermons. Quiet hours, perhaps, when Mama and Grandma and the neighbor women would listen while they knitted or crocheted. That's why some of the girls had fallen into the habit of bringing their needlework to the gatherings with Lidman on Thursday afternoons.

Many of the poems were quite difficult, but it was well known that young poets both endured difficult circumstances and wrote difficult verse. Perhaps it wasn't necessary to understand everything, or even any part at all. It was enough to listen to the despairing tone, which said so much. Sometimes just the tone could make them cry. Sometimes Lidman cried too, and then they would pause for a while and take him behind the curtain.

> My soul is sick
> my body is sick
> and diseased is my mind.
> All is consumed, burned up, useless,
> but sickest of all what I left behind.

Sometimes he would arrive at the Thursday gathering quite upset, with red-rimmed eyes; he would be in despair even before he began to read and would want to go behind the curtain. But the Madam told him it would be unseemly unless he read aloud first, and then he would comply.

Yet it was understandable that a young man like him should suffer from such great despair that it could descend on him quite abruptly. Sometimes his audience would become upset too; that was when he read his seditious poems. When that happened, they were actually glad that the curtains were drawn and no one was going to run off and report to the police.

On this particular afternoon he started by explaining that he was going to read a poem about the King. He said that he had written a poem about that cowardly rat who refused to take up arms against Norway, and when he said "cowardly rat" the girls all shivered and glanced at each other. The Madam stood up, her face quite pale, and left the room. But Sven paid no attention. Speaking in a powerful voice, he began to read.

> In Stockholm Palace an old man cries,
> may we curse his memory
> with him our Swedish greatness dies
> and our spirit, so manly . . .

Then the girl from Malung, the one named Ellen who was very short and plump and spoke the Dalecarlian dialect, could no longer contain herself. She interrupted Sven and said, "Just imagine if there's a war, Sven. It would be so awful if he started a war!" But Sven was not angry or despairing. He merely looked at her with a gentle smile, perhaps because she was so short and plump and the one who most often took him behind the curtain whenever he was struck with despair.

"Sweetheart," he said, "my lovely little bird. Don't interrupt the man whom Oscar Levertin has called the greatest poet of the younger generation. I'm the one he means, my dear little friend. And by the way, what I've written about war is what I honestly think about it, and I stand behind what I say. 'War is a decree from God. Like the lightning bolt slicing through the thunder-filled summer heat of a sultry idyll. Bringing with it destruction and the rain of renewal.' Isn't that beautiful?"

But she merely shook her head in silence.

"Did I read it too fast? Should I start over?"

"But if you joined up to fight in the war against Norway," she persisted, not wanting to hear about the lightning of destruction again, "what would your mamma say?"

Slowly he folded up his manuscript, as if the reading were over before it had barely begun. For a long moment he stared at the girl named Ellen from Malung. Then he said in such a low voice that she could hardly make out his words:

"She'd be happy."

"She'd be happy???"

"Her maiden name was Wolff, and in that family they're all wolves. She thinks I'm a damned failure. In my family all the Lidman men on Pappa's side have been heroes and officers. If I were shot in the war, even if I were only a reserve officer, she would be able to grieve for me as a failed hero instead of a failed poet. And a failed son. That would be a wonderfully happy ending to a failed life, and then she wouldn't have to keep supporting me."

"Shame on you!!! You mustn't say such awful things about your mamma!"

He didn't seem to hear her as he stubbornly clung to his own thoughts and almost mechanically rattled off the words:

"If she received a letter from General Uggla saying that I had

fallen at the head of my company, to be mourned by the entire regi-
ment, the king, the nation, and all my sisters and brothers-in-law, then
she would be happy! Happy!"

"Hush! You're being terrible!"

"Shall I read the poem about the king again, from the beginning?"

"Yes, do that! That's better than . . ."

Then he smoothed out his manuscript and continued his reading,
though with an odd lack of conviction, as if he were thinking about
something else the whole time.

"*In Stockholm Palace an old man cries . . .*"

But the girl from Malung named Ellen, the one who so often had
comforted him behind the draperies when he read his poems and was
seized by great despair, she now began shouting again:

"I don't believe your mamma is like that! You're just telling lies
about her to make yourself seem important!!! She's not like that at all!"

He fell silent, staring at her with vacant eyes. Then he said:

"No one has ever explained to me what my mamma is like, so I can't
really know. But I believe that I'm a Lidman, with a wolf inside me."

The next day Sven felt strangely depressed. He sat in the little two-
room apartment that he shared with his mother, holding a book in his
hands and pretending to read. But for the most part he stared without
seeing at the book and forgot to turn the pages.

His mother could tell there was something peculiar about his
mood, and she talked to him as if she didn't care that he was absorbed
in reading one of his difficult books.

"Aunt Gerda called," she said. "Everyone is talking about how
famous you are just because of what it said in *Svenska Dagbladet*, and
Gerda says she's pleased, but you can hear that she thinks it's odd you're
not going to get any money for that poetry collection so you could
support yourself, and she's worried about the fact that you're thinking
of leaving your officer's career for . . ."

"Mamma."

"Just imagine that it was Levertin! She clearly thought that was
extraordinary, but the fact that I have to support you, Sven, that's nag-
ging at her. She says it's shameful for a grown man to be a burden to
his mother, but I told her that . . ."

"Mamma!"

"I've sold my uncle's Empire table, and that made her so indignant. She started harping about you finding a job so I wouldn't have to . . ."

"A poet has to starve."

"Or have a mother who goes out cleaning, like I do," she said with a suddenly sharp tone. But when she noticed that he looked up, as if he had heard, her voice became gentle again and she continued, "Dear Sven, you know that I love you, and of course it's nice that you can pass the time writing verse. I always thought you would be a real Lidman, but I'm actually quite content, let me assure you of that, but Sven, do you think there will be a war?"

"No," he replied.

"But surely a reserve lieutenant wouldn't be on the front lines to face the enemy, it's more likely that . . . Where are you going, Sven?"

He had slowly closed his book, stood up, and moved toward the door, as if he were at his wits' end and had to do something.

"I'm going out, dear Mamma."

"Oh, sweetheart. Could you buy a copy of *Aftonbladet*?"

"I don't have any money," he said after a slight pause.

"Here's five öre," she said.

"Thank you, dear Mamma."

"But don't spend the money on anything else!"

He gave the coin a long stare, and then slowly stuffed it into his pocket.

"No, dear Mamma. I promise not to buy a bottle of champagne for five öre. Thank you, dear Mamma."

She smiled at him nervously.

"Sven?"

He stopped with his hand on the door handle and said in a perfectly calm and friendly voice:

"Yes, dear Mamma?"

"Come back soon, and don't go off with any of those awful friends of yours, Sven."

"I promise, Mamma."

"I'm going to bed now, so if you come home late, don't make a lot of noise."

"Yes, Mamma."

"*Aftonbladet*. Nothing else."

"Yes. Dear Mamma."

Then he left. He closed the door carefully, so it wouldn't slam.

3.

Efraim cited two other references to *Blood Inheritance*, but without comment.

He never dwelled, as Sven did, on the significance of biological inheritance. I actually have no idea what Efraim's own family meant to him. I know only parts of it. No doubt there wasn't much to talk about. Perhaps he thought that Sven talked too much about his ancestors. Tried to make himself seem important. What does the biological blood inheritance mean? Why dwell on it? The blood of Jesus was a different matter.

The only person Efraim dwelled on was his Uncle Aron, but that was probably because I asked about him.

Sven cut across the intersection of Jakobsgatan and Malmtorgsgatan.

As he walked through the twilight, he imagined that it was like making an entrance on stage, from the side. He moved from being completely hidden to being completely visible. Then once again completely hidden in the merciful darkness. What was important was that brief moment in the light, when you established a connection, before being hidden again. There ought to be a spotlight or a street lamp; he should come out of the darkness from the side and suddenly emerge into bright light and pause.

All around, in breathless silence, were the others, waiting. The others were the ones who decided and confirmed whether you existed. And whether you were a human being. Then you should quickly and calmly step back into the dark, but forever connected. The important thing was to be connected. But not have to unmask yourself.

A very brief moment.

Afterwards people would know that he had stood there, as if in a photograph, immortalized, a photograph that would be studied later on, in a thousand years, with his face turned toward the ones who are studying it, almost with a smile. They would try to interpret that brief moment when he was visible, what he was like and why, and in which direction he was moving, and why he had left behind this startling and lucid document of his life. But he would have chosen darkness and loneliness afterwards.

The image, the photograph, would remain, like a piece of a life, a photographic document that never left them in peace. They would interpret and search, but he would have passed into the twilight.

He would be left behind, like an itch in their dreams, but without needing to unmask himself.

For those who were not connected with anything, there was only eternal death.

He cut across the intersection of Jakobsgatan and Malmtorgsgatan, and from the darkness he saw a group of five people, four men and a woman. For a moment they paused in the light of the street lamp; the five were visible to him, but he could not be seen by them.

He noticed at once that the woman was very beautiful.

She was wearing a dark red coat. She had dark, faintly copper-colored hair. She seemed to be the natural focal point of the group, and she was perhaps thirty-five years old. He judged her to be older than he was, but very beautiful. He recognized one of the men in the group. He knew he was the editor-in-chief of *Aftonbladet*, although they had never met.

They were all talking very loudly. He judged them to be slightly intoxicated. The woman was very beautiful. She seemed somehow familiar, but he didn't know why. He had always been attracted to women who were older than he was, perhaps in the belief that they possessed a secret sexual experience that he might share without having to take responsibility for it. The group was still standing in the light of the street lamp. To acquire their experience without responsibility would give him freedom. They seemed to be speaking English. At the same time their experience was frightening, and thus enticing. He was convinced that he had never loved anyone, and never would. This filled him with a strange feeling of elation, because it meant that he would be invulnerable. He had his hand in his pocket, wrapped around the coin. To be invulnerable was important. It was only in his poems that he could be invulnerable. He was convinced that he had never loved anyone, except that time during his military service when he had loved a comrade so intensely, almost the way the Greeks had, a fierce love, but he had been rebuffed. His comrade had fiercely rebuffed him after a month. They agreed that he had misunderstood. It was only in his poems that he was invulnerable. The woman looked right at him, even though he was invisible in the dark. If I walk past them, through the spotlight, he thought, she will see me; then I can speed up my step.

He stepped into the light, and she looked at him.

"Oh . . . aren't you that great young Swedish poet . . . Stockholm's Bellman . . . Sven Lidman?"

The four men didn't seem to hear her. He stopped. The light was intense. She placed her hand on his arm.

"Oh . . . aren't you Sven Lidman?" she went on softly, switching to Swedish. "The author of *Primavera*? Let me shake your hand. I thought it was so . . . fine. I think I can . . . 'On this night of stormy and orchestral intoxication . . . the velvet-dark weave of dusk takes on a border of purple light . . .' You see, I know it by heart."

"How nice," he said, hearing instantly how odd that sounded.

"So, may I shake your hand?"

She held out her hand to him. Instinctively he held out his own, realizing too late that it was the hand clasping the five-öre coin. Closed to make a fist. She stared for a moment in bewilderment at the fist he held out, then gently took it in her hand and tried to open his fingers.

"My, my . . . what have we here? Do you have a secret that you don't want me to . . . reveal?"

He opened his hand. There lay the five-öre coin.

"Oh . . . how lovely," she said in a low voice. "A five-öre coin. Is that all a poet has to live on? Is that really enough to live on?"

"Well, it's not enough to die on, at least," he said softly.

She peered up at him. What a strange thing to say. The others were continuing their conversation behind her, not paying any attention. They were all standing in the spotlight; now he too was there. Now the brief moment should be over, now he ought to continue on, into the merciful protective darkness. That would be the right thing to do. He had been seen in the light, but without responsibility. Now she was connected to him, and he to her; now it was absolutely necessary to keep going.

Yet he stayed.

"Well," she said after a very long pause, "my husband and I would be honored to invite you to Rydberg's Bar."

He closed his hand around the five-öre coin again. He nodded stiffly. He had not continued on into the dark.

* * *

Her name was Margot Brenner. Or rather, that's what he called her in his autobiography *Desire and Retribution*. But no one would ever learn her real name.

It would remain the best-kept secret.

He didn't understand the situation. They walked together to Rydberg's Bar, and the editor-in-chief of *Aftonbladet* was completely occupied with his American guest.

The woman's husband didn't say a word.

When they went into the restaurant, she sat down next to Sven, leaning toward him, blatantly uninterested in the others, who were speaking English; her husband, in particular, seemed completely non-existent. Was she jealous and trying to take revenge on her husband? Her name was Margot. She didn't speak to her husband. What kind of game was this taking place right in front of him? Was he in the spot-light, or was he outside of it?

Once when he uneasily cast a glance at her husband, as if to draw him into the spotlight, she took Sven's hand, like a hasty signal, as if to say: "No. Don't look over there. Forget him."

We are the only ones here.

What did she want? This, he knew, was both pleasure and terror. He had no control. What was it? This was nothing like the usual girls for whom he was accustomed to read his poems, not the safe little Ellen from Malung who took him behind the curtain, not Rosinante cakes. This was not the usual, it was something else, perhaps it had to do with power, or control.

Yes, perhaps it was control. He thought he had an idea what it might be: the enormous temptation of being conquered, and the ter-ror of being owned.

She was drinking. He didn't know what he should do. She was talking, in a low, intense voice. "Herr Lidman," she said, "we should meet sometime, to talk about the conditions of creation, do you know what I mean? I've tried to imagine the conditions required to write poetry, how it slowly emerges, or breaks through. I've always wondered about how art is created. Does it come from inside or is it something that is given to the artist, like a gift, a storm of fire, something from God that suddenly—"

"Not from God," he said. "I don't believe in all that religious non-sense."

"No, I don't either," she said. "How interesting that you don't believe either; I thought as much. Not from God. From inside."

"I don't know."

"But how does it . . . a poem . . . actually come to you? Is it like being intoxicated . . . or like . . . being in love?"

"It's not something you know, after the fact."

"Do you think I'm a fool?" she suddenly asked, looking him in the eye.

"No."

"But just once," she said after a long pause, "just once I'd like to create something myself. That's all."

"I can understand that."

"Just once in my life I'd like to be able to write a poem. And know how it feels. Like a storm of fire. Or like falling in love."

"Afterwards you know," he replied.

Rydberg's Bar was almost full; they were enveloped in noise, yet he felt as if the spotlight had shrunk around them, as if the din and laughter had become a protective grotto into which they had crept. She was drinking but seemed incapable of getting drunk. He suddenly remembered the five-öre coin in his pocket. It was so humiliating. Why did he always have be humiliated? What did she want? She asked more and more questions. She did not seem importunate. Afterwards he thought that what she had asked him was actually quite importunate, but at the time it didn't feel that way; it just seemed natural. "Are you married, Herr Lidman? Oh, what a silly personal question. You're not living with a woman? I merely ask because your unusual insights into the mysteries of love seem to belong more to a very old man, someone experienced, almost at the end of his life, but you're not at the end of your life, are you?"

"Occasionally I think I am."

He could hear how false that sounded. And then her silence and the way she looked at him.

"That would be such a shame," she said at last, putting her hand on his arm. Just at that moment her husband abruptly cast a quick glance at them, much too quick. It was unbearable. She turned to her husband and said very matter-of-factly:

"Don't worry. I'm just curious about how a young poet works. And lives."

"And how do you live, sir?" asked her husband in a harsh tone of voice that made the situation very clear.

"All alone."

Then the others resumed their conversation in English. She drank some more. Suddenly he noticed that she was crying, uncontrollably crying, without moving a muscle in her beautiful face, as if she had lost control on the inside but had preserved it intact on the outside. He sat there motionless. After a while she took out a handkerchief and hastily wiped her face. The moment had passed; it vanished quickly. Now it was over, and she looked at him again. Everything was normal. With a little smile she shook her head, everything's fine, you saw and you understood, don't say anything, don't say anything.

She drank some more, very cautiously.

"All alone," she said, quite dryly, as if she were commenting on or simply repeating his reply to her husband, which he had uttered quite a long time ago.

"Yes," he said.

"Where were you headed when we met you? What were you going to do with the five öre?"

No answer. What should he say?

"Buy a talisman, perhaps? Something very simple, for a beautiful girl?"

"I was going to buy *Aftonbladet* for Mamma," he merely replied.

At first she started laughing; softly, as if he were joking and the joke was rather perplexing. Suddenly he saw that she had very beautiful teeth. That's what he saw. He didn't like the fact that she was laughing. He looked at her, for the first time in all earnestness and without feeling afraid deep inside, and she understood suddenly that he wasn't afraid, and then she stopped laughing.

"*Aftonbladet* for your Mamma. I don't believe it. But it was a nice thing to say. It sounded so nice. But it was . . . poetry, wasn't it?"

"Yes. It was poetry."

"A little poem?"

"Yes," he said. "It was a little poem, and I made it up right now, and afterwards you can't explain how it happened."

He came home and walked very cautiously, noticing that he was quite drunk, but he managed to shut the door almost without a sound.

He tried to be quiet.

"Did you remember the *Aftonbladet*?" he heard his mother say in the dark.

He didn't answer. He lay down in his alcove and stared up at the ceiling. "I'm a seething cauldron," he thought. It didn't help. "The heat of this existence was generated by friction between absolute opposites, and the fiercely conflicting hereditary elements inside me," he thought. At that moment he thought it sounded fine, almost brilliant, and he grew calmer, but later it seemed merely false. His mother had started to snore.

"I'm no good," he thought. "I'm no good."

CHAPTER 3

Azusa Street

1.

A QUESTION HAS BEEN INSERTED INTO THE *LEBENSLAUF* IN PASSING.

It was Lewi who built the movement, but it was William Seymour, the one-eyed lame black man, who had ignited the spark. Yet, why was the spark ignited on Azusa Street in Los Angeles in 1906 by the black man Seymour, and not in Texas where he was baptized in the Spirit back in 1901?

Not until the very last pages does Efraim answer this question. The answer is quite simple. Yet he seems to have brooded over it.

How did the spark occur? That was the question. And how did the fire reach Lewi?

There was an event in Lewi's life that Efraim returns to, an event that seemed to be a turning point. It was like coming through.

That's when Lewi suddenly acquired power.

Afterwards he held onto that power for a very long time. He lost his power over the course of a year at the very beginning of the 1940s, then regained the power during the summer of 1941, on July 22. After that he kept his power until he was called home to his Savior. But the first time he journeyed through the Slough of Despond and found his way out of the Forest of Despair, it was in connection with the incident concerning a boy named Enar who received grace.

This is what happened.

* * *

It rose up like a wave, didn't it? Yes, in truth, it rose up like a wave.

The wave rolled through almost an entire millennium, from Hus in Bohemia in the 1300s to Herrnhut in the 1700s, and then westward to the Methodists and the New World, to the Baptists, and to the Pentecostal movement. That's the truth! Efraim was suddenly filled with joy; this was bigger than Ocean Lake! Yes, bigger! And bigger than Lake Hornavan! This was the sea of God! And the mightiest a person could imagine.

There was something majestic about the very image of a wave. Efraim returns to it. Lewi had once used the phrase: "the spark that ignites a prairie fire," but that was the most beloved metaphor of rationalism and the Enlightenment. What did the revivalist movement have in common with the Enlightenment?

But they were metaphors, like in the Bible.

A wave, a spark, and tongues of fire.

Those who came through and acquired the power often didn't have a real gift for words. It was more a feeling. Those who were Spirit baptized wanted to speak like the Lord Himself, in metaphors. But if they were lacking in words, they would speak in tongues. There was an arrogance about those who had words. They looked down on those who lacked words. And then they were told that it was sheer babble. Those who spoke in tongues were babbling. Efraim himself had viewed it as a wordless song, like a harp melody from the far reaches of space. And he didn't presume to judge, even though he himself had never spoken in tongues.

Perhaps they were trying to sing forth something that could not be expressed in words. It was impossible to know. A wordless song, as if from the far reaches of space, from the sea of stars.

It might as well be described quite simply: "It rose up like a wave."

But why?

Why this revival of those who were mute in spirit, God's poke in the side of those who were asleep? Not the regular churchgoers; they slept on. Those bloated regular churchgoers! Those spiritual toads of the state church! No, those who were revived were the socially fallen and demeaned, those without hope, those who had come to hate life. But why were these shouting voices suddenly raised? Why this reckless ecstasy, why this power, why the fallers, why the big shelf, why the speaking in tongues, why the tongues of fire that, like a mark of favor from the Holy Spirit, descended on all those impoverished and deprived heads, like a diadem in the midst of life's filth? Why?

Why did it begin to blaze?

Was it like the peasants' uprising in Hunan, a great wave that would wash away everything in its wake, into the Long March? No, it was not. No march, no war, no killing. Was it the torch of reason that would bring light to the darkness? No, not the wave of rationalism. No, Lord Jesus our Savior, no, that's not how it was.

Not clarity, light, or rationalism. It was the black torch of mysticism that had once again been lit; but it was certainly an uprising.

Then there was the part about the blood.

The blood of Jesus and the wounds of Jesus. Especially the blood, so thick and red and warm. Like suckling-warm mother's milk. Was the bridegroom even a man? How could a person be sure? This figure with his long hair and kindly outspread hands had an opening, after all, like a woman. Didn't women have just such a forbidden and desire-filled opening? Wasn't this figure a fabulous cosmic mother, a female Sovereign of the Universe, enticing with that warm opening, enticing them to abide among the forbidden mucous membranes in the pulsating interior, the most forbidden, the wholly mysterious? And there find a benefactor, like Nemo deep inside his volcanic crater?

What was it that enticed Lewi and Sven? The life-giving blood, the Sovereign of the Universe, or the dream of purity?

It didn't make sense. And that was precisely the reason.

And at the site where the Pentecostal movement was founded, in the little chapel on Azusa Street in Los Angeles, with its sawdust-covered floor, there it was also the blood of Jesus that was supposed to purify, the blood in which a person would submerge himself, hide himself. Through God's work on Azusa Street, "the meaning of the blood of Christ had been rediscovered for the congregation"—it was not merely baptism in the Spirit but baptism in the blood of Jesus.

But "rediscovered"?

The wave, that great wave that rose up like the peasants' uprising in Hunan though it was not at all the same thing, not at all, that wave spoke not only of purity and the importance of re-establishing the original Christian congregation. It also spoke a sensual language, light-years beyond what the state church preached, and that language had a secret, enticing undercurrent, a deep-water current that no one talked about, though many people would be helplessly sucked down by it.

2.

Efraim attached particular importance to the testimony about the Welsh mine horses.

Several witnesses claimed that it all started with the revival in Wales. And that it spread from there to Los Angeles, then to Kristiania in Norway, and then the wave reached Lewi. That was the simple explanation.

Although it had existed deep inside of us the whole time, as he writes.

Efraim recalled a report from the revival in Wales, about what happened with the mine horses that became confused by God's spirit and power. In Wales, in the mid-1890s, there was great misery. People out in the country moved to the cities because famine was spreading through the countryside. People were crowded helter-skelter into tiny rooms, and immorality was rampant. Children had no idea who their father was, almost everyone got mixed up with boozing, and there was nothing but lice and hopelessness. But then the time of the visitation came to Wales. And it spread like wildfire; yes, in truth it did. It was like the prophet Joel says, the sun shall be turned to darkness, and the moon to blood, though in the reverse; the darkness turned into light. And in a matter of months. The newspapers wrote more about the revival than about sports or politics or entertainments. On the streets people sang revivalist songs, crime disappeared, and all the liquor bottles were smashed. And the children had food. The taverns stood empty. Old debts were repaid, and stolen goods were returned. And the workers in the coal mines became spiritually transformed, it was like a spiritual revolution in their lives. The conversations they had previously carried on inside the mines were filled with curses and quarrels. But now they spoke the new tongue of Canaan.

That was when they caught sight of the dumb beasts. The mine horses, which had previously been whipped and abused down there in the mine passageways—yes, let me tell you, those poor miserable nags never saw the light of day, they endured blows and lashes and oaths and were subjected to abuse—those mine horses started acting confused when their former persecutors gave voice to prayers and practically snuggled up to the poor horses. They were used to curses and the whip! When all that stopped they couldn't recognize their masters. Now the men started each shift with communal prayers and Bible reading, and the horses were transformed. They grew very nervous, began to neigh and whinny, as if they were giving voice to prayers and asking that their tormentors be whisked away to eternal punishment. God's spirit had reached even those poor horses. They would stand there whinnying with amazement and inexpressible joy, as if they were praising the Savior; that was the animals speaking in tongues. There was speaking in tongues and songs of praise, and the poor horses were perhaps the first to speak in tongues. And no one called it babble.

And that was just the beginning. But if baptism in the Spirit could reach even the tormented mine horses underground, yes, in truth it did, then this spirit of Pentecostalism could reach everyone.

And that's what happened.

But the origin?

The answer was found in the Holy Scriptures. There alone. You might also talk about "what came before but was later than the beginning." You might begin with the Methodist revival in America, Efraim thought, the one that took place in the 1770s. It grew out of lawlessness, drunkenness, gambling of various kinds, wild fights, and immorality. It began with the Circuit Riders, lay preachers who rode around and gave fiery revivalist sermons, and they had no salary—no, they didn't!—only a travel allowance of $64 to pay for ferry tolls, for shoeing their horses and feeding them, and to some degree for feeding the preachers themselves.

That was before arrogance entered the movement, and the preacher began calling himself "pastor," something that Lewi never liked; oh yes, Efraim would return to this.

Yet how he could remember it now!

And then came the Holiness movement, yes, in truth, and the Methodists. Efraim felt that the preaching of the Methodists contained the birth of democracy in religious life. Just look at someone like Wesley! talking about the importance of equality! And individual responsibility, and the equality of human beings before God. Everyone equal.

But most important of all: the Baptist preacher William Seymour, who became the leader of the revival in Los Angeles.

This Seymour experienced a magnificent baptism in the Holy Spirit and became, in truth, a great leader of the white people in spite of the fact that he was black, blind in one eye, and lame. Many of the first Pentecostal preachers were black. J. A. Warren and Lucy Farrow were black. And yet half of the first Pentecostal congregation in Los Angeles was white. Or, as they said, "The color line was washed away in the blood." As Seymour used to say.

In the blood. In the blood!!!

Black, half-blind, and lame. And chosen by God. For the sake of the blood. Amen.

It was the Methodists, in particular, who took a democratic view. Individuals had a personal responsibility, and all people were of equal worth.

It came from America.

Of all the differences between the Old World and the New, the idea of a state church system was the most conspicuous. Half of Europe's wars, from the Monophysitic struggles in the Roman Empire that Efraim had read about—he seems to have read a great deal in the old days—to the German Empire's cultural battles in the nineteenth century, had arisen from some sort of theological strife, and since the church was a state institution, it led to war! And enmity among the state churches over the true faith. And this eternal intermingling of worldly power and religion became a misery that people escaped in America, and we Europeans should have escaped it as well.

If religious freedom had existed, that is, and not merely conflict and the intermingling of state and faith.

That was his point of view.

This whole chapter, which was in truth so terrible, about blood-baths between state churches, this chapter in the great book of life was unopened in America. Because in that country there was no state church.

There all religious affiliations were equal before the law, and were not questioned. Weren't there more than two hundred religious denominations and congregations in America? And peace reigned among them. Only theological conflicts, not a war of weapons. Yes, in truth. And he thought that when revivalism came to Sweden, in particular the Pentecostal movement, there was such opposition, such hatred, because everyone had grown accustomed to the idea of a state church. Everyone loved the state in the name of God and the church. Even the atheists and intellectuals who never opened a Bible went crazy when they thought about the Free Churches like the Pentecostal movement, because this sense of a religious embrace by the state was embedded in the very marrow of their bones.

That was the reason for the hatred toward the Pentecostal movement.

It became apparent when the conflict with Lidman occurred in 1948. By then Lidman was a believer and one of the movement's leaders, so there was only a little mud-throwing against him. The intellectuals viewed him as a sort of traitor to his class. It was because they hated the Free Church and didn't understand the idea of freedom of belief; they had taken in the notion of a state church with their mother's milk. And singing and rejoicing were foreign to them. It was a relief to them when Sven left the Pentecostal movement, a great joy for the citizens of Stockholm and the intellectuals, the ones who wrote for the newspapers and had never opened a Bible, but in whom the notion of a state church was embedded in the marrow of their bones, even though they were not believers.

That was when Lidman became a hero, when he left the movement.

Yes, it's a common occurrence. Whenever a socialist joins the bourgeoisie and testifies, it's always the same tune. They become instant heroes, credible witnesses. Yet they're nothing but hypocrites.

The handwriting here is slightly trembling, perhaps indignant.

Yes. "In truth," as he writes over and over. There's no doubt he was indignant.

But the foundation of the Pentecostal movement, of course, lay in the Bible. It was the second chapter of The Acts of the Apostles:

> *When the day of Pentecost had come, they were all together in one place.*
> *And suddenly a sound came from heaven like the rush of a mighty wind,*
> *and it filled all the house where they were sitting.*
> *And there appeared to them tongues as of fire, distributed and resting on*
> *each one of them.*

And they were all filled with the Holy Spirit and began to speak in other tongues, as the Spirit gave them utterance.

Now there were dwelling in Jerusalem Jews, devout men from every nation under heaven.

And at this sound the multitude came together, and they were bewildered, because each one heard them speaking in his own language.

And they were amazed and wondered, saying, "Are not all these who are speaking Galileans?

And how is it that we hear, each of us in his own native language?

Parthians and Medes and Elamites and residents of Mesopotamia, Judea and Cappadocia, Pontus and Asia,

Phrygia and Pamphylia, Egypt and the parts of Libya belonging to Cyrene, and visitors from Rome, both Jews and proselytes,

Cretans and Arabians, we hear them telling in our own tongues the mighty works of God."

And all were amazed and perplexed, saying to one another, "What does this mean?"

But others mocking said, "They are filled with new wine."

But Peter, standing with the eleven, lifted up his voice and addressed them, "Men of Judea and all who dwell in Jerusalem, let this be known to you, and give ear to my words.

For these men are not drunk, as you suppose, since it is only the third hour of the day;

but this is what was spoken by the prophet Joel:

'And in the last days it shall be, God declares, that I will pour out my Spirit upon all flesh, and your sons and your daughters shall prophesy, and your young men shall see visions, and your old men shall dream dreams;

yea, and on my menservants and my maidservants in those days I will pour out my Spirit; and they shall prophesy.

And I will show wonders in the heaven above and signs on the earth beneath, blood, and fire, and vapor of smoke;

the sun shall be turned into darkness and the moon into blood, before the day of the Lord comes, the great and manifest day.

And it shall be that whoever calls on the name of the Lord shall be saved.'"

Efraim had copied it out from the recent Swedish translation, the one from 1917.

There was a certain beauty to the text he had copied from The Acts of the Apostles. I thought I could hear his Västerbotten accent as an undercurrent in the account of the first Pentecost. This story about how the tongues of fire descended upon the congregation, on each and every one of them, so that all of them received grace. And then the fact that everyone understood!!! without exception.

The great ecumenicalism, but also the great equality between one human being and another.

The great story had come to all of them, the great story that knew no boundaries of language but existed above language, like a wordless song from the Sovereign of the Universe, "And how is it that we hear, each of us in his own native language?"

You have to try to imagine how they lived an existence that was like a desert.

And then the great story arrived.

It was this speaking in tongues that rankled, and attracted, and aroused suspicion.

Efraim could certainly tell about that. They had learned to live with suspicion. And what about the first time that Barratt arrived in Kristiania at Christmastime in 1906? He had come from Los Angeles, bearing the message of Spirit baptism and speaking in tongues. And then he was to speak. But he was so overcome that he merely stood there and wept. He just sobbed. The whole time. No message, no speaking in tongues, he just cried. The congregation was completely bewildered, and the newspapers wrote about the weeping preacher.

What was the meaning of this?

There were various interpretations. And scorn. The intellectuals in the papers saw it at once. There was something pathological about the phenomenon. Something sick.

"Acquainted as I am with the laws of the hidden forces of the human soul, through my studies and later through experience, I venture to claim that all the aspects that have thus far been associated with this movement can be found under the following labels: hypnotism, mesmerism, somnambulant forces, telepathy, suggestion, auto-suggestion, trance, clairvoyance, monomania (insanity that results when a person directs all powers of his soul toward a single objective), mental derangement, and possession by spirits."

The intent was malicious. They had not understood. But could it actually be the same night sides of the soul that manifested themselves in Mesmer, Charcot, and the one-eyed Pastor Seymour?

The one-eyed lame black man named William Seymour keeps showing up more and more often.

"The first person to start speaking in tongues in Los Angeles was a young lad. Then one person after another acquired the gift. The preacher was a rather insignificant, lame, one-eyed black man by the name of Seymour, but his words had such power that the strongest opponents would fall to the sawdust on the floor and shout for mercy and salvation."

The Pentecostal movement was born in the sawdust of the Methodist church on Azusa Street, which was a little, dilapidated warehouse for old lumber and other junk. "It was filthy and miserable. They cleaned it up, spread sawdust over the floor, and set the place in order as best they could. The space was not large. People had to sit on boards resting across old barrels of nails. The boards were covered with newspaper. There was seating room for forty people. Two empty packing crates were used for the pulpit. The boards were arranged in a rectangle with the primitive pulpit in the middle."

The reports of what took place on the sawdust floor reached the Swedish press surprisingly fast, within a few months. There seemed to be something very special about the spiritual earthquake in Los Angeles, something that distinguished it from the countless other revivals, spiritual storm surges, revelations, and apoplectic fits that history could present, especially during the latter decades of the nineteenth century.

Spirit baptism and speaking in tongues. They had occurred before. But something was new. If the beginning of the Pentecostal movement can be precisely dated to June 1906 on Azusa Street in Los Angeles, then the effects of this earthquake of the spirit made an unbelievably swift appearance in Sweden.

Perhaps there was an entirely different reason why particular attention was focused on California in the year of Our Lord 1906. The earthquake of the spirit was preceded, as if by divine coincidence, by the San Francisco earthquake on April 18, 1906. That settling of the earth's crust! That fist of God that killed the godless! That reminder of human insignificance that unleashed so many prayers and such great

despair and a newly awakened insight into the wrathful power of
God!! That divine giant's hand that razed San Francisco and unleashed
so many prophecies about the end of the world if human beings did
not reform!

As early as September 18, 1906, the Swedish newspaper *Närkes-bladet* ran a lengthy account of what was taking place in Los Angeles:
"About three months ago a Negro preacher by the name of Seymour
arrived in Los Angeles. He began holding meetings in a Negro church
in the darkest section of town. The sign in front of the church read:
'The Apostolic Faith.' They baptize themselves like the Baptists and
others. Since Pastor Seymour's arrival, they have held meetings every
day except for the week when they held a baptism ceremony at the
ocean one day and then rested for the remainder of the week. The
meetings start at 10 in the morning and last until almost midnight. In
spite of the heat and the bothersome flies, an intense interest has continued the whole time. Many people have gathered, including
strangers from various states in America. The goal is for God's people
to be filled with God's Spirit so that signs and miracles as mentioned
in Acts of the Apostles 2 will occur, since the people of the earth will
soon be struck by judgments. Many have been filled with the Spirit
and have spoken in many different tongues, since the Spirit prompted them to speak. Others have been present and interpreted the
words. A young Jew heard Hebrew. Languages from India and Africa
were spoken."

The altar a plank between two chairs. Almost all the windows broken.

But evangelists are created quickly.

"The first ones to present themselves for the Lord's service were
several Negroes. They began with a ten-day fast and prayers, and they
wound up seeing the holy fire come down. The premises on Azusa
Street were well concealed behind a lumber yard and some old stables.
The ceiling of the first floor was barely three meters high. It was an
easy matter to climb up onto the chairs and place your hat on the
rafters beneath the roof. This simplicity was perhaps one of the reasons
why a number of preachers who came there refused to step inside but
turned around to leave, saying that it was the work of the Devil."

Whether it was the work of the Devil or not, quite different political interpretations would quickly follow.

The wave refused to subside. That's what was alarming.

"Toward the end of the nineteenth century, as socialism, material-ism, and modern science broke through all layers of society, many pious people viewed the wave of revivalism approaching from the west as divine intervention to rescue the nation and its people. The Anglo-American holiness movement was the answer to many people's prayers."

But if baptism in the Spirit was salvation from trade unions, social-ism, and social democracy, if speaking in tongues was a ritual invoca-tion that would persuade the wrathful hand of God not to jolt other cities like San Francisco, and if revivalism was the answer to the threat from the labor movement, this was hardly something that the one-eyed, insignificant, lame little black man from Texas realized when he became the spark that would ignite a prairie fire.

3.

There was the matter of speaking in tongues.

According to Efraim, it was a tremendous worry. That's why he devotes so much time to it. Adult baptism was one thing. Baptism in the Spirit was another matter, a step beyond. A step farther. But speak-ing in tongues? There was always the question: How would a person know for sure that he had been baptized in the Spirit? Some said it was only by speaking in tongues that certainty was assured.

That was the sign.

And that might very well be true. It could also be unpleasant. And to some extent, that's where the problems started.

Particular attention was aroused by a young man named A. G. Jansson, who had recently returned home to Sweden from America. In Los Angeles he had visited the Baptist church on Azusa Street, and there he had listened to a preacher named Seymour.

This young man ended up causing a great stir in the Swedish press.

At a meeting in Skövde, one of the participants had started speak-ing words that no one could understand. A tremendous commotion arose at the meeting. Young Jansson, who had recently arrived from America (something that was constantly repeated), stepped forward to interpret. He claimed to be an expert in this area, and calmed the agi-tated souls. What they were witnessing was completely normal, some-thing he himself had experienced. He assured everyone that the revival had now appeared, and then he too spoke in tongues.

At subsequent meetings God's Holy Spirit had fallen upon several more youths, and the news quickly spread over all of Skövde. In the newspapers this Jansson talked about the preacher Seymour in America, putting special emphasis on the fact that he was one-eyed, lame, and black, and yet he had been chosen by the Holy Spirit. But many people mistrusted this Jansson, who was said to have led an ungodly life before his Spirit baptism; this Jansson might be spreading the contagion of sin, he might be a criminal, and according to the correspondent from *Dagens Nyheter*, which influenced the views of many people, "he lived a not entirely impeccable life." It might be a contagion of the Devil that this young Jansson had brought.

And that's why he had to be mistrusted. The fact that he "screamed, stamped, and gesticulated" was a sign of the Devil. It was a contagion that he had brought back from America.

They then decided to call in a Pastor Ongman from the Filadelfia congregation in Örebro. After this Ongman had seen with his own eyes and heard with his own ears the young Jansson, he declared that he could vouch for this Jansson. What was happening at the meetings was a true spiritual revival; there was no need to doubt it any longer. The words of the Prophet Joel, that an outpouring of spirit would come during the last days, applied here.

Pastor Ongman, who was well-versed in both the Holy Scriptures and in church history, now became a guarantor for Jansson, whom he also invited to make a personal appearance in Örebro.

Later, in *Närkesbladet*, young Jansson gave a detailed report of his experiences at the revival in Los Angeles, testimony expressed in a positive spirit. But on January 9, 1907, *Dagens Nyheter* countered with a more critical eyewitness account from the Elim Chapel in Skövde.

"After several testimonies had been presented, the young man Jansson, who had been in America, stood up and quietly began to testify. But gradually the ecstasy took him over. With clenched fists he gesticulated wildly, and his voice was unnaturally loud as he invoked God and Jesus. His eyes rolled and his mouth opened up enormously wide. One had the impression that an epileptic fit might occur at any moment. But he did not speak 'in tongues.' At last he regained his composure and sat down, exhausted. Later during the meeting Jansson appeared for a second time and then began speaking in tongues. The words were soft and rich in vowels, and in the opinion of this reporter, it was a real language and not just a haphazard sequence of sounds.

Occasionally he would mix Swedish into his speech, and one had the impression that this was supposed to be a translation from some other language he was speaking. During this second speech, he reached an even greater state of ecstasy than the first time. He shouted so loudly that it hurt the ears, and he gesticulated wildly with his face horribly contorted. All over the room cries could be heard of 'Thank you, thank you, dear God! Oh, Jesus, come to us! Save me from the grip of Satan!' And on and on. A gentleman who had traveled in India claimed that the young man's speech reminded him of an Indian dialect he had heard. It seemed to this correspondent as if the sound of the words was occasionally reminiscent of Finnish, and he had the impression that a majority of those present were of honest and sincere intentions."

That was the extent of the first report in the leading newspaper of the day in Stockholm.

Disturbed by the incident and perhaps even more by the flood of reports that were now streaming in about the spread of speaking in tongues throughout Sweden and Norway, *Dagens Nyheter* quickly responded with a strictly scientific analysis of the phenomenon. Speaking in tongues, asserted *Dagens Nyheter* in its analysis, is something that is natural and can be explained in scientific terms.

"It is a state of ecstasy when the human brain finds itself undergoing activity that is extraordinarily strenuous and powerful. Impressions that were once made on the brain and were stored away, so to speak, now step forward. A preacher, for example, has a linguistic and speech organ that is especially well-developed and loaded with power, as it were. If this individual has worked with people who speak different languages, and his brain has consequently absorbed and stored various impressions of these foreign languages, without even understanding them, and if this individual is then plunged into ecstasy, it is possible for those overheard phrases that have been stored in his brain to be brought forth, and that is when speaking in tongues occurs. Regarding the matter of the fire that is sometimes reported, the so-called tongues of fire, this is undoubtedly a completely normal phenomenon of nature. An example from Livy's history of Rome can be cited in which the head of a sleeping boy, who later would become emperor of Rome under the name Servius Tullius, seemed to catch fire in the presence of many witnesses. Presumably this is an electrical phenomenon, in that the body's electricity (which, as everyone knows, can occasionally be seen crackling in people's hair, and on certain animals, such as cats, can look like tiny flames in their fur) increases in a state of ecstasy. In some senses it is reminiscent of such natural phenomena as will-o'-the-wisps and St. Elmo's fire, although they have nothing to do with the human body. In the same way the miracle of faith-healing can be explained in a scientific manner. When someone seeks a cure, he enters into an ecstatic state in which the brain starts working under high pressure, and consequently the electrical discharges that occur in the brain greatly increase. At the same time sores, boils, severe pains, and the like become healed. Everything has a scientific and natural explanation if one takes into consideration the posture that the supplicant manifests under these circumstances, namely kneeling with clasped hands. The fact is that this specific posture has the peculiar ability to promote the aforementioned discharge from the brain."

The science writer for *Dagens Nyheter* states, in conclusion, that he finds it difficult to explain in words precisely what he means, but he advises the reader to "try to assume, at a convenient time, the described posture (without praying), and afterwards he will notice an increased vigor, increased physical strength."

That was the explanation.

4.

And what about Lewi?

In January 1907 he was still at the Bethel Seminary. Efraim had visited him for two days, and conversed with him about doubt, and about Lewi's novel. Lewi's wish at the time was to become a proletarian writer.

Nothing else was discussed. What is his opinion on speaking in tongues? No comment in the *Lebenslauf*. He is still reading the teachings about Christ in Rydberg's Bible.

The prairie is burning, but the prairie has often burned with the fire of revivalism, only to be extinguished. The sporadic ecstasy in Kristiania is now very strong—soon it will fade, but it is still strong. There a preacher named Seland is arousing attention by "first shaking and then entering into a certain unconscious state, during which he speaks a language that no one understands, but that is presumed to be Armenian." And his wife, "uncommonly strong and by no means a nervous woman, suddenly was overcome by ecstasy and began speaking a foreign language, which, after she awoke, had no adverse effect on her physical well-being."

By no means nervous?

Do we hear an echo from Charcot's experiments with female hysteria in these descriptions? They had taken place quite recently. In 1891 Charcot concluded his experiments with hysterical women at Salpêtrière Hospital in Paris. Two years later he died, but his most esteemed actress, Blanche Whitman, was still alive and working as an assistant with Madame Curie. Soon this very beautiful and esteemed Blanche, this erotic medium whose spastic fits had enchanted an entire intellectual world, or at least the many intellectuals and authors who had been drawn to her convincing fits of spasms, evoked by applying pressure to scientifically determined points on her body—who, by the way, was considered to be very beautiful, and who during the séances became partly uncovered so that they could see her naked bosom and often other parts of her body, which writhed in enticing convulsions—soon her subsequent and not nearly as public work with nuclear radiation would cause her arms and legs to be amputated.

By the time the wave rises on Azusa Street, she is no more than a torso. Her limbs can no longer make those attractive, convulsive and strangely enticing erotic movements that would be interpreted in such an interesting manner by the assembled intellectuals who, and here Efraim was right, had never opened their Bibles.

Blanche Whitman a motionless torso, Charcot dead, but perhaps her spirit lived on in Kristiania?

"By no means nervous."

What is the human spirit?

What is a human being? A machine? What is sacred about a human being? A kind of cloud or babbling or the dream of rationality and civilized development? A wave? A prairie on fire, a rebellion against the inner silence, against the inner death? But perhaps the fire will soon be extinguished, leaving a scorched plain behind, as so many revivals have done, so much speaking in tongues, so many outbursts of faith and despair, surrounded by so many rational analyses about what is scientifically natural and what is a miracle.

Warning cries and Hallelujah.

In spite of the warning cries in the press, the revival spread.

During the winter of 1906–07, only six months after the constantly cited miracle when the spirit came to Azusa Street through Pastor Seymour, the revival had made great progress in Mellösa, Asker, Lännäs, Pålsboda, Närkes-Kil, Kumla, Åsbro, Svennevad, Norrbyås, Fellingsbro, Vinön, Zinkgruvan, and many other places in Sweden; in fact "it was almost impossible to count how many," in Efraim's opinion. It was reported everywhere. In the Kinnekulle region, in Dalsland and Bohuslän, Arvika in Värmland, Småland, Östergötland, Gotland. In Norrland the revival spread to Gästrikland, Hälsingland, Medelpad, Härjedalen, Jämtland, Lappland, and Västerbotten.

Västerbotten? Yes, but there only within the Salvation Army. As well as within the Baptist congregations and the Swedish Missionary Society.

No Pentecostal movement yet?

No, not yet.

And Lewi? What did Lewi think about speaking in tongues?

Regarding this matter, Efraim writes, he was never quite clear.

In his memoirs, Lewi is evasive. "I wasn't actually expecting to speak in tongues, because at that time I didn't believe that speaking in tongues was a necessary consequence of Spirit baptism. At that time I had not yet discussed the matter of speaking in tongues as a sign of baptism in the Spirit."

He wrote this much, much later. The truth is that he never really cared for it. It was somehow a bit too uncontrollable. Yet he realized that he was dealing with a power he truly did not understand, though it had to be used in the movement.

Perhaps this was a way of avoiding a painful subject. Later on it was not as sensitive, but in the beginning it was. It seemed to carry weight. And it seemed to indicate those who had been chosen.

Those who had come through.

In the beginning no one really understood what it was. Lewi didn't either. He had traveled to Kristiania to study Barratt. He had listened and watched. But Lewi had his own dreams. At least during those days in January when Efraim visited him. And soon he would come to a crossroads.

And then Lewi would seize hold of organizing the irrational, so that it wouldn't fade away and end up lying there like an armless and legless torso.

5.

Lewi had returned from Kristiania and the Bethel Seminary in Stockholm to the very small congregation in Lidköping, and everything was still unclear.

In the photos Lewi looks surprisingly young and childish. He has wavy hair and full lips; his glance seems almost innocent. He has dressed up for the photographer (could it be Birger Sjöberg?), and he is wearing a little checked bow tie on his white, starched collar. He looks charming. Quite slender, not at all like a shot-putter, but charming. He bears a remarkable resemblance to the portrait of my own father as a young man. There is something innocent and pure about him. Actually quite a handsome young boy; later he would hardly be called handsome, absolutely not handsome. But here he is endearing and handsome, having carefully combed his hair into a sweet wave and squeezed it tight, but so it would seem casual, almost windblown.

Such an endearing preacher. Actually much sweeter than Sven. Is it all right to say "sweet?" Yes, he looks sweet. Far more captivating. But Sven, at the time this photo was taken, was still allowing his life to be centered on Margot Brenner; he is not yet present in Lewi's consciousness. The two young, quite captivating twins of God—of which Lewi is the more charming, even the more handsome, or at least the more captivating and the one who radiates innocent purity—they are both still running along parallel paths.

Lewi is a Baptist preacher in Lidköping, and it's February of 1907.

"I wasn't actually expecting to speak in tongues."

Not entirely true. Lewi, too, is writing his own story, not always as it happened, but as it ought to have been. He knew, after all, that the revival was roaring all around in Sweden, though perhaps not as much around him.

It was very quiet. Was that his fault? Was that why he constantly repeated: "I'm no good, I'm no good?"

In his preaching he had started using the word "Hallelujah," which at first aroused surprise but later won general approval. He preached about baptism in the Spirit, and people constantly asked him whether he himself had been Spirit baptized. And he had always answered yes.

But with a certain anguish. Was it true?

There was something frightening about all the people he saw around him and had also seen in Norway. These people who were seemingly without volition and without shame and confessed without doubt and spoke in tongues. In some way they took over the stage, which was the congregation, and without any shame. He himself was quite shy. The first sermon he gave had lasted five minutes; that was as long as his shyness could master. Yet speaking in public, from a dais, was a different matter. He could prepare for it. He had the Bible. He was meticulous.

But speaking in tongues was something else.

Those outbursts! That state of being outside yourself. Of suddenly becoming someone else, and without inhibitions, outside yourself! And in front of the others. If a person was shy, this was something unprecedented. But plenty of shy people did it. How could they? And were they the only ones who, in all seriousness, came through, who received grace? Wasn't he, deep inside, a hypocrite, a false confessor? Why hadn't the Spirit possessed him so that he could avoid this internal distrust of himself? He was supposed to be a shepherd. And such a person could not lie.

He paged through Bunyan. Who was he in reality? Perhaps Little-Faith? Was that his failing?

"As true as God's word is trustworthy," he used to say, "I have been baptized in the Holy Spirit." But each time he could hear that tiny quaver in his voice, as if from a hesitation that he realized with horror might reveal him to the sheep, who had this untruthful shepherd.

He tried to push it aside. Perhaps it wasn't necessary. Perhaps speaking in tongues was not a necessary consequence of Spirit baptism; but this yearning! This unbearable sense of waiting in his soul! This dream of the complete breakthrough that was supposed to happen, praise the Lord, oh, merciful Lord, give me this breakthrough. Let me come through to relieve the anguish of my soul.

The turning point came at an afternoon meeting in February 1907.

He had spoken, and things went as usual. It was quiet, and no one had received grace to speak in tongues. Lewi sat on his chair up front and sang along with the hymn, and suddenly he noticed in the congregation a young man, or rather a boy, someone he recognized. He was perhaps seventeen, with a pale face, and he kept his gaze lowered, focused on his clasped hands. Lewi knew that this young man had been saved during the winter and was now seeking baptism in the Spirit. Which he had not received.

The boy looked nice but unhappy.

That same day in the evening there was another meeting. Before the meeting the boy's mother came to Lewi, and she had a request. She asked Lewi to place his hands on her son, because he longed so fervently for baptism in the Spirit. If Lewi was Spirit baptized, and she knew that he was, and Lewi himself had confirmed it, then the Spirit would fall upon her son when Lewi placed his hands on him, as it had during the time of the Apostles. And it would be confirmed.

He would speak in tongues as of fire.

Then she went back to sit down at her son's side, clasped her hands, and looked at Lewi with a bright and grateful smile.

What should he do?

Lewi led the small congregation in prayer and started in on a song and felt completely paralyzed with fear.

This was the moment of judgment. He had experienced nothing of a baptism in the Spirit. He had never spoken in tongues. He had not trembled beneath God's power. He had not fallen to the ground. He had not spoken Hebrew or Chinese or rattled off words that no one could decipher; no, none of these things. But he had confessed and testified that he had done all of them. Wasn't it a mortal sin for him to say he was something that he was not? And now he stood before the moment of truth.

The song came to an end, there was an embarrassing moment of silence, then he started on a new song. The congregation looked up at him in surprise, but obediently joined in. God was the one with the power. He could do anything, even forgive. The song sounded faint, and not at all like a roaring flood, and he moved his lips to sing and knew that he was a poor, miserable, lost creature, and that he would now be revealed. No, he would not go over to the boy. His hands would not touch the boy's head. The moment of degradation would not happen, nor the judgment day, not that.

They reached the last verse. It was now.

And he thought, "This too I must place on Your shoulders, dear Jesus. This too You must do for me, my dear Savior. You will actually have to stand behind the truth of Your words. Perhaps I've spoken falsely and lied, but perhaps You have merely hidden Your face from me. Perhaps it was right, what I promised them, but You are the one who decides. Because I may have believed rightly: that I possess the power that You gave to Your apostles in the past. And now I simply wait for You to fulfill Your promise. And it is Your responsibility, dear Jesus, the Savior of the world, because I myself am at my wits' end."

The song came to an end.

Silence followed, as when the archangel has blown his horn for the fifth and last time; and everyone looked up at Lewi and wondered what he was going to do, whether he would pray or preach, as usual. And then Lewi stood up and went over to the young man and said: "Let us pray for Enar, so that he might come through." And the boy understood that he should kneel down on the floor. And then Lewi placed his hands on the boy's head and said: "Let us all pray together for Enar, that he might receive the grace of the Holy Spirit."

He heard the congregation begin to murmur a prayer all around them. And at that moment he had no sense of alarm, he felt only the boy's head under his hands, and his hair, which was soft and fair, and Lewi barely managed to begin his prayer before the Holy Spirit fell upon the boy with tremendous force. And the boy, whose name was Enar, was struck to the floor by God's power, which had streamed into him through Lewi's hands; he abruptly fell over, face down although slightly to one side, where his mother was kneeling, and he praised God in a loud voice.

Then the murmur of the congregation rose up even louder, and it became a blessed choir, and Lewi leaned forward from his knees and touched the boy's hair, and at once the bands on the boy's tongue were loosed, and he became the first in that congregation to speak in the new tongues. It was Sunday, February 22, 1907, at eight o'clock in the evening, and it happened through Lewi's hands. Later the boy, whose name was Enar, left for America, and after that Lewi didn't know how his life turned out. In that sense he had disappeared from the story. But for Lewi, the moment when he placed his hands on the boy's head and God answered him and allowed His power and grace to stream through them, for Lewi—and he later witnessed and wrote many times about what had happened—this was the decisive moment in his life. *Yes, if I hadn't dared act because I had no experience, perhaps I, like so many others, would have waited for the baptism of the Spirit for years.* And afterwards grace would also come to Lewi himself, that very same evening the power would come. *When it became clear to my consciousness what had happened to me, my whole being was filled with inexpressible and glorious joy, and at the same meeting, later that evening, I spoke in tongues and sang in the Spirit.*

And he had come through. And after that all doubt had vanished.

That's what he confirmed later when he wrote down his story, and he didn't want to write any other story, but it was undoubtedly true, in some way: the truth was the tremendous anguish of being a poor, sinful human being who had claimed to be greater than he was, and who thought himself too shy and lowly to become like those who could step out of themselves and speak in tongues, without fear, and somehow stand next to themselves without feeling ashamed; and the truth was that, even so, he had gone over to the boy, whose name was Enar, and placed his hands on his head, and the truth was that it had worked.

God's Spirit had worked through him, through Lewi. He was chosen, an instrument. *He* was the instrument, and at that moment he had felt something that he could not explain, perhaps it was joy, or almost a kind of intoxication, or great and heavenly gratitude. Or power.

That was the beginning. After that he was never afraid, except during the year when he fled, but that was another story.

And the revival took hold all around. He realized that now it was important to organize, to let his hands work, that they were allowed to rely on God's power, but for safety's sake, he needed to strengthen the organization and campaign, also in the press. Later that year, on December 8, he wrote for *Närkesbladet*, which would become the main publication of the revival, a brief account from the opening of the premises in Göttene, an account that in many ways pointed far into the future.

It said, in its entirety:

> The heavens seemed to open for us. Showers fell. Hallelujah! Please send a number of sample copies to Lidköping. We have already collected almost 30 subscriptions for your newspaper for the coming year.
>
> Yours, emancipated in the blood,
> Lewi Petrus

But why did that Seymour first begin to preach in Los Angeles in 1906 and not in Texas in 1901? Why that five-year delay? Why had God's Spirit tarried? Why the wait?

The answer was quite simple, Efraim later writes in the *Lebenslauf*. At a revival meeting in August 1901 in Texas, this Seymour had been Spirit baptized and started to speak in tongues. That's when he felt the call. But since the race laws of Texas forbade blacks from preaching God's word indoors he had been forced to undertake the long journey to California, where no such bans existed regarding blacks preaching indoors.

That's what had happened. That was the simple explanation. That's how the spark was ignited, that's how it was spread, and in this fashion the spark had finally been transmitted, with a five-year delay, from Texas to Azusa Street by the lame, one-eyed black man named William Seymour, and then at last reached Lewi, who was the one chosen by God to build His Kingdom.

CHAPTER 4

The Droplet in the
Sea of Women

1.

EFRAIM HIMSELF HAS PRINTED THE GERMAN WORD *LEBENSLAUF* ON
the file, on the outside of the folder, and signed it.

I don't think he knew German.

It's impossible to know why exactly he wrote it. It's rare that anyone knows why he writes something. In Efraim's *Lebenslauf*, by the
way, there is almost nothing about his life outside of the revival; it's as
if the Pentecostal movement, and Lewi, were everything. When he
reaches the political year of 1909, there is nothing about the constitu-
tional reform that involved universal suffrage, although women were
excluded, and abolition of the 40-grade scale, which allowed the rich
to cast more votes, or about the great strike—only about Lewi.
Whenever we met, on the other hand, he never said a word about the
Baptist faction that had started up at Uppsalagatan 11 during that year
of 1909. Not a word about it, even though the small congregation
would soon call Lewi its leader. But in the *Lebenslauf* he writes that this
was an event equal in importance to the great strike.

Surely he was joking.

It's a matter of deciding what's important. Or: he had changed the
lenses in front of his eyes. It didn't matter that the world was changing. The only important thing was to change the lenses, to see something different.

It was Efraim who recounted the story about how Uncle Aron died:
his long struggle to chop a hole in the ice, and how his knapsack had

gotten stuck, but with the utmost strength of will he finally had set off on the long dizzying passage down to the deepest depths of the sea.

The anguish of sin. How many destroyed lives were there, actually, for every joyously saved soul?

Or: how did it all fit together with the vault of stars, and what existed beyond what could be sketched on sandwich paper? How did it fit together with Doré's drawing of the Deluge and the naked women's bodies, and the beloved little worm in the wound, so secure in the side wound of the Savior in Zinzendorf's hymn? No, that question could not be answered. Nor could the ones about the language of the ritual, or the dream of coherence, or what actually drove us, or what the sacred was, or why it was so sullied by life-giving urges, or what love really was, or how it all fit together.

It was necessary to change lenses once in a while, in order to understand—that must have been the reason.

The brothers up on the platform used to call the congregation down below the sea of old ladies. Or sometimes the sea of women, if anyone was listening. My mother, whose name was Maria although she was called Maja, never attended a Pentecostal meeting, as far as I know. It was the wrong sect, so to speak. She was twenty-nine years old when my father died, and she was still beautiful. She never remarried. But sometimes I think I can see her face, down there in the sea. Actually, I see her all the time, with her face lifted in hope and prayer, like one of them, like a droplet in the sea, with her gaze turned toward Jesus, lovingly waiting for the answer from Him, the answer to the question about love, and how everything fits together, and whether there is a meaning, imploring that there must be an answer, although it was so lonely; it was love for Jesus Christ that was the meaning. And she was like a droplet in that sea that kept asking and asking.

Maybe that was why.

2.

Sven had closed the door to his room and drawn the curtains around his bed.

His mother was asleep on the sofa in the kitchen. He had asked her not to disturb him while he was writing, but sometimes she would come over, open the door a crack, and say:

"Sven? How's it going? Have you written any poems today?"

There was a connection, he was practically convinced of it, between poetry and sexuality. Not that he absolutely had to write about love in all his poems—no, it was that sense of an itch. It was as if the itch, the ever-present images of naked female bodies, the thought of how he was going to penetrate, simply penetrate bodies without faces, female bodies for the most part, but sometimes the female body shared with another man; as if that ever-present itch increased with every second that he wrote.

Or at least when he was truly writing, when it truly came alive and he wasn't merely imitating, and he knew deep inside that he wasn't just moving the pen to win Levertin's favor. He had recovered from the dissolution of the union and was no longer planning to shoot the treacherous king. There was another sort of fame. A person had to choose what to strive for. When he was truly able to write, he felt a steadily growing agitation urging him closer to himself and at the same time shutting him off. It was extraordinary. Shutting him off. The itch and the agitation had to be present for him to write, but if they were too strong, he couldn't write. Sexuality was the prerequisite for a poem, but it also shut the poem out. He had started walking for several hours every day, but it didn't help; the itch kept growing. "It doesn't help to walk," he thought. "I have to assuage the itch." But not even the girls to whom he read his poems on Thursdays could help. Not even the plump girl from Malung and the sweaty sessions behind the curtain when he read with such emotion that he would break down. Nothing helped. Not even liquor. He started borrowing money from his friends and would often come home drunk to lie in bed and stare at the ceiling, knowing that he couldn't write a line. Everything was dead, dry, and crackling; nothing had any life.

Just this extraordinary restlessness, which was gradually taking on a face.

And he knew whose face it was.

After the night at Rydberg's, he had seen her a couple of times. Once she had returned his glance with an almost imperceptible little smile, and nodded.

But she had not stopped.

Finally he had called her.

Her response was seemingly cool, yet she was immediately willing to arrange a time to meet. They had arranged a time. He was the one who had called, she seemed cool, but it was too late to change his mind; they had agreed on a time.

She opened the door, and it struck him at once, like a wave of desire: she was extremely beautiful. She was wearing a green, sleeveless dress. She led him inside.

There she introduced him to her little nine-year-old daughter.

"Oh, Herr Lidman," Margot said, "my little girl is having such trouble with mathematics. I wonder if you could help her with her math today. Is it . . . Would you?"

"Of course," he said.

He sat down at the dining-room table with the loathsome little nine-year-old. With relief he realized that he knew enough math for a nine-year-old. The girl stared at him with lovely, bored brown fish-eyes and didn't seem to understand a word. He controlled himself and tried again. Every once in a while Margot would come in to offer encouragement.

The whole thing was deeply humiliating.

At last the nine-year-old announced that she understood everything and no longer needed any help. Then Margot came in and began manically talking to Sven, but without looking at him.

It was unbearable.

She had loved living in the United States, she told him, but her husband wanted to move back home to Sweden. She hadn't really understood why he wanted to be in Sweden, there was nothing here, nothing, not a single man worthy of respect except for the Social Democratic leader Branting, although why he would want to marry that Anna, but men never could make the right choices, especially talented men, who always seemed to have such poor judgment, while idiots . . .

"Fru Brenner," he said at last, "I must go."

"Oh, what a shame, can't you stay another half hour and have dinner with us? By then my husband will be home from Dalarö. He would be so happy to see you, I'm sure of that."

He declined.

At the door he took her hand to say goodbye but was suddenly seized by a tremendous rage and said in a very low but very clear voice:

"I didn't come here to tutor a child in math. I came because of you. But I haven't seen a trace of you."

An expression of despair or shame or perhaps merely pain flitted across her face, and she began to explain.

"You must understand . . . it wasn't . . ."

"You've been toying with me," he said. "You've been toying with me." And then he left.

The next day she called him.

It was his mother who answered the phone. She called for Sven, gave him a surprised look, and said that there was some woman asking for him.

It was Margot Brenner. He knew that his mother was listening the whole time.

She wanted to apologize.

"I didn't mean to humiliate you. That wasn't my intention. It was just so . . . wrong."

He listened.

"Are you there?" she asked after a moment of silence.

After a pause he said, "Yes."

"Things aren't easy for me," she then said.

And she hung up. He stood for a moment with the receiver in his hand, staring at it. Then he carefully put it down.

"Who was that?" asked his mother.

"Nobody," he said, and went into his room.

She followed him. He could see that she was uneasy, perhaps scared, that she wanted to know.

"You said almost nothing. Why didn't you say anything? Only that single 'yes.'"

After a moment he said, "I have to write for a while now, Mamma. Dear Mamma, don't worry."

"But I am worried," she said. "I am."

An hour later, after his mother had gone out to do the shopping, he made up his mind.

It was Margot who answered.

"Forgive me," he said.

He heard a sudden faint sound on the telephone, as if she had started to cry, or at least was taking a deep breath.

"Can I see you again?" he asked after a brief pause.

"Yes," she replied. "Yes."

* * *

Lewi is still far away.

Perhaps Sven and Lewi could be pictured as two planets that are connected in some way, tremendously far apart but in orbits that are slowly converging on one another. The planets seem to attract each other. But still faintly. Their orbits are slowly converging, extremely slowly.

In the first hundred pages of the *Lebenslauf*, Sven is largely absent. Later a few indignant, occasionally doubtful references to his autobiography. Suddenly a comment that is difficult to interpret: "I knew Lewi so well that I understood why he would allow himself to be ensnared by that snake-charmer."

By Sven?

The orbits of the planets were moving toward each other. Soon these two very different but peculiarly complementary beings would turn their faces toward each other, and from the enormous distance of history, and with expressions of mistrust, loathing, surprise, or perhaps it was actually love, they would discover that they were alike and thus had to become loving enemies.

Who ensnared whom? I understood what he had written, that Lewi had allowed himself to be ensnared.

As if he were a helpless child.

Wasn't it Lewi who ensnared Sven? Efraim must have been mistaken. It was difficult to explain. Even though the great driving force of the story is a beloved little worm in the wound which, sick with the anguish of love, longs for the little side wound of the Savior, which is easy to explain.

3.

Margot Brenner was now wearing a low-cut pink dress; the apartment was empty this time.

No loathsome nine-year-old, no demands for math lessons, no threatening spouse on his way home from Dalarö. This was entirely different. She was beautiful and charming but in some strange way furious, and Sven knew that he was completely bewitched, and it filled him with desire and fear.

Great desire was always tied to the fear of being ensnared. He was very close to that right now. He knew it. He also knew that he had no control whatsoever.

Her fury had to do with her husband, her fortunately or unfortunately absent husband.

"He's truly amazing," she said. "He leaves me a little handwritten note saying he has to go to Dalarö on business. I knew that, there's always some kind of business, but he knows and I know that there's a little Fru Yderberg, and he thinks he can fool me. That's what makes me furious. The greater his infidelity, the more beautiful the little love notes that he leaves on a slip of paper. Let's have dinner. Or would you rather not dine with me?"

"No, I would rather not," he said.

"No? Then what do you want?"

He was sitting at her feet; for a moment he had an unpleasant memory of those Thursdays at Västerlånggatan 24. It all raced through his mind, the girl from Malung, the red curtains, the poetry reading, reading poetry before desire. But no, this was different, completely different, much more dangerous and more amazing.

And he had no idea where it would end.

"I'd like to read to you."

And she replied, "Read."

He had no book, but he knew his poems by heart. He had written them himself, after all. He thought it was his duty to memorize them, and besides, in his solitude he had read them so many times since they were published. He knew every intonation. He had experimented with every intonation and modulation. He recited them from memory.

At last he fell silent. He didn't know what she was thinking, and softly and almost cautiously he asked her:

"Shall I give you more?"

Then she touched his hair with her fingertips, slowly and almost meditatively, pausing before she finally said, "I don't want you to give, but take."

And he was not too young to misinterpret the expression of a woman issuing a command.

And so he obeyed. And then he took.

They made love in the couple's bed.

Yet to make love in the marriage bed that had been besmirched by the spouse was, in the long run, repugnant. It did no good that before Sven arrived and Margot's daughter had been settled in some safe, distant place, and with her husband away, she would always put on clean bed linen.

So he rented a room in Gamla Stan.

It was necessary. He had managed to get it quite cheaply. Money was actually not a problem, since Margot was the one who paid. She had money, or rather her husband did, though neither of them ever mentioned that.

The room contained a bed, two chairs, a table, a wash basin and water pitcher. He called the room a "love nest." In reality they both thought—this was something they agreed on—that the room was awful, but they had agreed to be practical.

They met in the afternoons according to an ingeniously arranged schedule, and after taking the necessary precautions. They never entered the building together. Right now they were lying naked on the bed, and it had been magnificent.

That was exactly the word he was thinking: "magnificent."

He studied her face with curiosity; it was pale in the afternoon light. A moment ago it had been ecstatic, but now it was pale, perhaps despairing, for all he knew. He knew nothing about her, or which of them was in control or which of them was exercising power—if power was what they were exercising, calling it love or desire.

"I'm writing better now," he said. "Yesterday I wrote two long love poems, and it went fast."

She didn't seem to be listening.

"Sweetheart," he went on, "you're the first married woman I've ever won."

"What did you say?"

He didn't repeat what he'd said, since he could hear something in her voice that frightened him.

"The first married woman ... Is that what you said? That you've won?"

"Yes."

"Is that something you've dreamed about? About winning? A married woman?"

"Yes."

"And who have you won me away from?"

"From your husband."

"And that makes it something special. Like the Holy Grail. To win from someone else. You've won a small part of his good name by humiliating him, and that gives you more prestige for yourself."

"That's not what I meant. I've won . . . you."

"I hope you don't think you've won me away from myself."

He didn't know how to respond.

"A married woman. That makes you a little . . . excited? Since it's forbidden?"

"Yes," he replied with a tone that was almost hostile. "Perhaps a little excited. Danger is always exciting. Like killing. Like war."

"And therefore enticing?"

She lay there for a long time, silent and motionless. The expression of satiety or desire or despair or whatever it was that he absolutely could not decipher in her face had disappeared. She slid her hand over her body, as if she wanted to reassure herself that it was still there.

"So I'm a grail. How cold that feels."

He was silent. He knew that he had said something wrong, but he didn't know how he was going to get out of it.

"Something completely forbidden. Do you know what my completely forbidden thing is?"

He didn't say a word.

"No, you don't. But it's you. Though you don't know why it should be precisely you. And you'll never find out. You'll never ever find out."

They lay there in silence for a long time, but then that too passed.

Perhaps they were waiting each other out, and then became practical and strangely enough even more passionate: as if a membrane had been pulled away from reality and they began to see everything more sharply and clearly, with distinct colors, like after a heavy rain; not the passion they had dreamed about but something else, stronger but more painful. And that's why desire and passion became less enveloped in an impossible dream.

They began to caress each other, and then made love again in that love nest with a bed, two chairs, and a table and wash basin and water pitcher, and Sven was a planet in the ice-cold universe of love, and somewhere far far away was the other planet called Lewi, but so far away. What was he doing? Efraim, what was he doing?

Efraim?

Lewi had applied for a pastor position in Lidköping.

And love? And the well-masked dream of writing?

He had applied for a position as preacher and head of the congregation in Lidköping. He was only twenty-three years old, and he was no longer writing novels. When he had to preach for the first time, he was afraid, but it went well. Didn't it go well? Oh yes, it went well, he won praise, his sermon was short, five minutes, his supervisor had praised him and said that God doesn't count the minutes! But that same evening Lewi wrote a letter to a Norwegian girl he had met, Lydia, with whom he was "smitten."

It was a farewell letter.

He wrote that the calling to be a preacher (his calling!!! What had happened to his dream of being a proletarian writer? Had he given it up?)—he wrote that the calling to be a preacher was now his, and that he would never be able to afford to marry, and that's why he would have to live alone, and he didn't want to lead her on, and it was a big responsibility to provide for her, and so on, one excuse after another, and Lydia would have to understand.

His song of praise to God's eternal love had lasted five minutes, but God does not keep time, and his twin, Sven, had rented a love nest; they were not aware of each other. And so Sven and Lewi, those two planets, continued to circle each other for a little longer in the ice-cold space of love. Only slowly, very slowly would they approach each other, with their secrets, with their absolutely forbidden enticements, and their secret reservations, and at the center of this passionate ice-space of love there was a midpoint which they would later mutually, in a duet of faith, call the Savior Jesus Christ, the gravitational midpoint of ecstasy and ritual, the vast power.

It actually existed inside themselves, though they didn't see it.

No, they didn't see it.

Not yet a sea. Merely two drops.

Lydia in Norway must have read the letter, which so nobly renounced love, but no one knew what she thought of it.

And Margot Brenner was so right, and she had understood so much when she told Sven that her secret, her most forbidden, was something she would never tell him. She would keep the shameful secret of love to herself, embracing it with her arms, like a fetus in the belly of love; no, like a newborn child that has to be protected, while the great planets circled around her in that ice-cold space of love.

4.

Five years had passed after Efraim Markström's funeral before I returned to Christiansfeld. Everything was the same; the number of members in the congregation had decreased by twenty-two. That had no significance. God's acre had acquired new stones.

Efraim's stone, as well as those of the others.

A section towards the end of the *Lebenslauf* seemed to have been written as a direct answer to me, to a question I must have asked. I had forgotten about it. It had to do with which passages in the Bible he thought should be rewritten, or excluded, if the Bible was a "work in progress," as Zinzendorf claimed.

Efraim thought, for example, that the parable about the prodigal son should be rewritten and made clearer. My question must have concerned Uncle Aron; I can't think of anything else. The Pentecostal movement was not something that interested me.

Perhaps the question was whether Uncle Aron, who had raped Eva-Liisa and made her pregnant, should also share in the grace.

I may have asked this because Aron was actually the son who stayed home. Not the sinner who went off carousing into the world and was received with rejoicing. But neither was he the faithful son who had never sinned.

Was there also grace for him?

Now, like a voice from God's acre many years later, he replied. Efraim thought that the parable was unfair, and that consideration should be given to the matter of sin.

There was, he said, both a good and a harmful idea behind our sin catalogue in the movement (and by this he apparently didn't mean the labor movement but the Pentecostal movement, although sometimes they seem to merge for him in a completely natural manner). It was this catalogue that was supposed to indicate what was totally forbidden for a Pentecostal, or what might tempt someone to do what was totally forbidden.

The idea was to shut out all experience of sin, or the risk of such experience. This was partially direct sinning, fornication and liquor and the like, but also what might be enticing. The latter was what might entice vanity (a woman's hairstyle or the wearing of jewelry), or those situations that almost inevitably led to sin (dancing on dance floors when bodies could easily be pressed against each other and entice the sin of desire), or sinful ideas (movies with erroneous ideas) or theater performances, which could of course be both good and bad. Or women in general.

As an example of what the movement could accept, he mentioned Carl Dreyer's film version of the Kaj Munk play *The Word*, which as late as the 1950s was presented at private showings for members of the congregation, and which made manifest the possibility of miracles, and the idea that resurrection was possible.

That was fine. But as a reply to the question about Aron, the Dreyer example was difficult to interpret.

Nowhere the word "compassion," except with regard to the compassion the movement exercised in connection with the soup kitchens.

He asked me when I saw my first film. "When I was fifteen," I told him.

"That was young to go to the movies," he said.

When I said fifteen, it wasn't quite true. Sometimes they showed 8mm silent movies at the annual meetings of the Army of Hope. It was always a film about the harmful effects of alcohol and what it would lead to. There was a young athlete who was good at cross-country running, and he had a blonde fiancée, and then he won the district championship. But the next evening he fell in with a bad crowd that wanted to win his favor, and they went out boozing. They drank hard liquor and beer. And he got caught up in sin. And then there was a crime, and the police arrived. But in prison he came to believe in the Savior Jesus Christ, and he came to understand how it had all happened, and his fiancée wept, but everything ended up fine: he was saved and gave up sports and alcohol and was saved and thanked God.

It was like *The Boy in the Choir*, except shorter.

But that wasn't a real movie. It was in the meeting house, and for the Army of Hope, where I was the secretary.

My mother and I had made a strict and unshakable decision that I would not attend any showings of movies. Nevertheless, when I was only fifteen, in all secrecy and without telling my mother, I was enticed by a cousin who was a couple of years older and not saved—that was Doris—and I sneaked off to see a movie being shown at the House of the People in Bureå. It was the film version of Einar Wallquist's novel set in Lappland and titled *Call the Doctor*.

It was about a doctor and some moose poachers. The poachers got their just punishment. Since I had never before seen a movie, it was a tremendous experience, but I kept it from my mother and did not confess.

Several days later, as I was drying the dishes with my mother, I used an entirely different technique that was new to both of us. I picked up a stack of plates, dried off the top and bottom of the stack, and then placed the top plate underneath and continued in this manner. My mother watched and asked me in a sharp tone of voice why I was doing that and where I had learned it. I then felt a strong urge to confess and told her that I had seen a woman drying dishes that way in the kitchen in the film *Call the Doctor* by the Lappland doctor Einar Wallquist. So I ended up telling her about going to the movies. At first my mother had tears in her eyes, but then she pulled herself together and said: "There, you see what bad things you can learn at the movies?"

I thought this was unfair but did not protest, merely asked for forgiveness, and that evening we knelt down together and received forgiveness through the grace of the Savior. But this whole thing about drying dishes, which I had learned in the sinful darkness at the movie theater, has ever since remained irrevocably etched into my memory.

I don't know why. But the sin seemed to me much too small, and the method of drying dishes in that way seemed sensible.

The analysis contained in the *Lebenslauf* could be a sort of posthumous response.

There was a problem with the sin catalogue. The intent of the rules was to preclude sin and the possibility of sin, but all it did was to create such an extraordinary interest in sin that certain people almost went crazy. They were like alcoholics who were no longer drinking. They thought about the bottle all the time. It was as if the bottle were a god; yes, he didn't hesitate to say that.

That's how it was with sin in the movement.

There was so much talk about sin in the Pentecostal movement that a huge interest in sin arose. At the same time, there were few real sinners. Not that they didn't exist. The real sinners, out in the villages! Especially those who were saved, and there were plenty of them, the truly heartless: he could have talked on and on about them. Hard, hard-hearted! and strict law-abiders! No, those people never confessed to their heartless and damning deeds. They would simply point their middle finger at the sin catalogue and say that the good Lord on Judgment Day would submerge all the unsaved sinners who had not received grace into boiling oil, pull them up again, and then lower them back in, up and down, up and down, year after year; yes, sometimes it was hard to understand what use there was in describing all the suffering that would befall them.

And it was worse for the children who had to listen to this. Afterwards the poor children couldn't sleep at night. No, there were plenty of sinners among the truly pious who were saved. Although this was never talked about.

It was the same with sin as with the forbidden bottle. Those who were saved were all too conscious of sin, in spite of their ignorance.

And that's what created this temptation.

Sometimes, Efraim writes in his *Lebenslauf*, when I think back on what happened later, with Lewi and Sven, who were so different and yet like Siamese twins, who seemed almost turned away from each other but in some sense were grown together, yes, with the same backbone, at any rate . . . What Efraim sometimes thought about was that there was a great need for a real sinner, who had somehow been pulled from the black sea of sin. Who could tell them how terrible it was. Who had the experience that the movement denied those who had come through. And who could talk about it.

There was a need. It sounds shocking, but later, when Sven was saved, there seemed to be some merit in the fact that they could sense how deep he had sunk. Before he came through. It seemed as if a tiny shiver always passed through the congregation when he stood there, as if bathed in radiance, because there was a true radiance about him, but with a border of black around the radiance.

And that explained things a little. Yes, how it fit together with this—well, almost love!—that people in the movement could feel. The fact that there was a need.

But Lewi did not have that type of background. No, he certainly did not, in truth.

Was that a fact?

Yes, as far as anyone could tell. Only Our Lord knows, of course.

All anyone could understand was that there almost seemed to be a need for the other in Lewi. That was what Efraim meant by the front side of sin. It was as if those who were saved secretly thought that sin, if it was so deep, had somehow ennobled the one who had come through. It was an experience, and a cleansing bath, and only those people could become true preachers who had come through, who had been down in the mire.

It was almost like envy. Yes, in truth.

Although this could not be said aloud. Because in that case it would be like exhorting those who were saved to dive down into the slough of sin and come back up, somehow wiser. And that these people would then have an advantage over the ones who had kept themselves pure the whole time.

This was precisely what was wrong with the parable about the prodigal son. Efraim had always thought it was the most difficult parable to understand. Not the fact that the person who had landed in sin received forgiveness. That was in keeping with the very spirit of the commandment of love. But the fact that this rogue who came strolling home should be somehow superior to the one who had kept himself pure.

That was hard to digest. But later they saw how it would all turn out.

5.

The relationship with Margot could have been perfect. Yet there was this insidious fear.

Sven had always had a secret wish that someone, anyone, would be able to see him, to see! And then from the outside, and with complete honesty, tell him who he was.

What his qualities were. What other people thought of him. A sort of total, objective evaluation. No, not an evaluation.

A testimony, quite simply.

Someone would testify to him about himself. It would be established fact. And afterwards he would be calm, no matter which way the testimony went.

What scared him most about Margot was that she might be this witness, and she might be capable of saying something extremely unpleasant. Not that he had demonic qualities. That was something he could live and die with. In fact, to be truly evil or demonic was something that was associated with great artistry. But he worried that she was about to expose him as a person who lacked qualities, lacked a center.

That's what she was about to do, he could sense it. Very soon she would utter the decisive words.

He had two choices. One was to flee right now. But then he would never find out what she said. The other was to stay and await her testimony. But then she would have power over him forever after. Then it would be like Phaedra and Hippolytos, and he had always found that work by Racine most unpleasant. She would see something in the younger man, he would arouse an incomprehensible passion in her, he would become branded into her, like a branding iron on an animal, unable to love in return, and become hated. And then, suddenly, Phaedra would utter the decisive words: *You cannot love, and you are nothing beneath your shell.*

He could flee, and learn nothing. Or stay, and become helplessly ensnared.

While waiting to make up his mind, they manically made love. He was scared. Very soon she might utter the decisive words. That must be what love is, he thought. Exhausting yourself while waiting to be exposed. But what if there was nothing to expose?

Once, after only a few months, she was about to say something. She was very close. He had turned ice-cold with fear. "You're like an onion," she said.

It could have been a joke. She was familiar with *Peer Gynt*, after all. Maybe it didn't mean anything special. And so he waited. That must be what love is.

On the practical, meaning the purely organizational, level it had become a somewhat calmer and less agitated sin.

Stockholm, too, had grown calmer. When fall arrived, Sven noticed, as if in passing, how wonderful it was that the great strike was now over. It should have been crushed with the help of the military. But worse was the sense of filth.

Stockholm was filthy during that summer of the great strike. He couldn't think a pure thought; not that it meant anything for the two lovers. They had their love nest, after all, but it was this feeling in the air of hatred, or envy: it was like coal soot around their love. It became slightly soiled, no matter what they did or didn't do or thought. When the strike was over, everything seemed cleaner.

They were in the habit of going to the outskirts of Stockholm. Margot seemed to have unlimited funds and could access them without difficulty. He would receive a phone call, directions to a specific intersection, and there find a horse-drawn cab. The driver knew where he was supposed to go. Sven became accustomed to these brief words on the phone, and his mother no longer asked any questions, merely kept silent and seemed to be crying to herself.

He no longer took the trouble to say, "Little Mamma, don't worry."

They had found a very secluded bay on the archipelago outside of Vaxholm, and a practical little grotto in which they made love. There was an overturned wooden boat, with its keel in the air, forming a tent or a hut. "Rousseau's hut," he thought and tried to write a poem about it, but he never got further than the title.

He found the place beautiful, in an almost poetic way; but the poetry of the site hadn't worked, it produced no poems. That's the way it often was with the poetry of a site, it turned out to be too inconsequential. When fall arrived, it brought colors and fog; the fog could be quite thick, and that's when it was best. And she would bring along a blanket, and he would spread it out on the ground beneath the overturned boat, and they would make love, quickly, wordlessly, without taking off their clothes.

Sometimes she seemed hostile. He didn't understand what that was about. He asked her if she was displeased. She found his question idiotic, refused to answer.

"I've read all your poems," she said. "They're erotic, and that's wonderful, don't deny it, that's amazingly wonderful, but something is missing. That's what I'm displeased about."

He didn't know what she was getting at.

"But what is it that's missing?"

"They're cold. It's nothing but eroticism. There's nothing more, just beautiful images. It frightens me."

"What do you want me to write about?"

"Surely you must know."

"I don't know what's missing," he said, feeling absurdly submissive or defensive, knowing that he should have kept silent.

"Well, what do you think? You must know. How are you going to continue after this?"

He could have said: "What do you mean by 'this'?"

It always excited him to make love outdoors, in the cold, with only parts of their bodies uncovered.

A covered body, wrapped in the cold. There was something about "warm skin against yellow leaves" and "cold fog" that attracted him, like a potential poem; but afterwards he sometimes felt slightly annoyed at her chatter about what was missing, and he didn't know what to say.

"Tor Bonnier wants me to write a novel instead of poetry. But I don't know if I can right now. I might not be able to do anything anymore. Do you think it's over? What will I do? Have I gone dry? Am I all used up? I'm scared."

"Scared?"

"I could always write about you, about our love, but later, after I've written about that . . ."

"Yes?"

"When that's over, that too, then I suppose I'll have to shoot myself."

No, that was bad; he could hear it himself.

He thought that otherwise he had really made an effort, up until the bad part about having to "shoot himself." He had spoken to her tenderly about how important she was to him for his poetry, that he was sure that great and amazing poems would come out of their love, but she didn't seem to understand.

What was magnificent evaded her. She seemed simply to freeze up, and it was not the autumn fog, it was something else.

"Is that why . . . you're with me? To have something to write about? Is that why you're with me?"

A long silence followed. She had not understood. He didn't speak. She didn't deserve an answer; besides, what could he say?

"So you're studying me? And maybe I'll turn into a poetry collection? One that Fredrik Böök will like? And then you'll drop me? Like a snake skin?"

He simply kept still. It was true, and unfair, but she shouldn't have said it.

"You're using me. Is that right?"

Then she suddenly relented and kissed him, and after a while it was almost gone, and they had almost forgotten, and she said:

"We should find a bigger apartment. So you have a little stability and won't have to live with your little mamma your whole life."

And when he was offended by her tone of voice and abruptly got to his feet, she regretted her words and said, very softly:

"You mustn't think of me as a holy grail. Or just something to write about. You have to realize that I'm obsessed with you. I don't know why, or maybe I do, though I'm not thinking of telling you, but you've become burned into me."

"Like a branding iron on an animal," he added, almost without understanding why, but later he remembered, it was Phaedra, yes, precisely.

"But I'm not an animal," she said.

When winter came, they carried out their trysts in his somewhat bigger apartment, which he had procured all on his own and which had been arranged without difficulty, and besides they never talked about money or where it came from.

It came partly from a book advance, partly from her husband.

She seemed desperately anxious to get inside him.

"And what do you dream about?" she used to ask. "What do you actually dream about? Aside from getting rich? Or just famous? Do you dream of sailing trips out to Vaxholm, and admiring glances, or becoming part of literary history, or what?"

He always refused to answer. One time he said:

"That someone, just once, could tell me who I am."

Then she started to laugh.

"My own Peer Gynt," she said. "I keep peeling and peeling and I never get to the core."

On the afternoon of February 21, 1910, just as she put on her coat and was about to leave, she made up her mind.

There was something she needed to clarify. She turned around at the door, came back into the apartment, sat down on a chair, and did not take off her coat.

"Sven, my dear Peer Gynt," she said in a perfectly neutral tone of voice. "What do you think your mother would say about Margot Brenner as her son's wife?"

He turned completely rigid. She noticed.

"As your wife. Haven't you ever thought of me as your wife?"

No reply.

"Not just as your lover. Or a holy grail."

He merely stared at her. And with that she had her answer.

Slowly she took off her coat, giving him a kind of smile that he had never seen before. It was a smile, but completely rigid. As if he had struck her in the face and she had decided to look happy, even though she knew that she was going to kill him.

"It was just a joke," she said. "Come on. After a joke like that, we should make love again. Don't you want to try again? And afterwards you can write a poem about everything, how we made love, how I put on my coat to leave, how I asked you that silly question, how you didn't realize that it was a joke, how I took off my coat again, how the embarrassing moment passed, and how we made love again. Love comes and goes. It will be our finest poem about our love."

He didn't move. He didn't say a word. They didn't make love. She left.

No, it wasn't always like that.

They reconciled the next time, they made love, and then everything was fine once again, her face very beautiful.

Afterwards she said:

"Sven? Do you know what I wish?"

"No."

"That you weren't so young."

"Is that right?"

"You're so young."

"Yes."

"I wish you weren't so . . . young. I wish you weren't so innocent. So young and so cynical. Or so conceited. Or so cold. Or so charming. Or so talented. Or so terrifyingly guileless and yet finished and cast all in one piece."

He didn't reply.

"I wish that your soul would start to burn. And that you would too. That you would be wrenched along and smashed to pieces and not be so perfect. That a great fire would seize hold of you and that you would start to burn. Swept along. Burn. As if from some great rapture."

And to that he merely said:

"I don't know what would make me burn."

6.

How quickly rumors spread!

Perhaps the hansom-cab drivers weren't very discreet, perhaps there was something odd about that apartment, perhaps she had been observed in the doorway. She was a beautiful woman, one of those conspicuously beautiful women with a solemn face and lowered head whom everyone turns around to look at, a woman who carried her strangely shy ability to attract like an invisible veil, making people wonder and arousing gossip.

An invitation arrived for Sven.

Perhaps Brenner, the husband, had been spurred by her to quell the rumors, to neutralize them. Perhaps he had good reasons for making a contribution to neutralizing them. And that's why Sven was invited to a neutralizing, very official dinner with the Brenners, with excellent food, and the loathsome little child just happened to be away, and cognac with coffee, and conversation.

Sven, who found the situation thoroughly odious, grew more and more intoxicated, laughing loudly. Herr Brenner seemed to be enjoying the situation. He liked to see Sven drunk. He grew more and more cordial toward Sven. It was obvious that he hated the young poet. Afterwards he drew Sven into the library to have a talk, man to man.

"Herr Lidman," he said as he smiled and looked at his hated young friend. "Please believe me. I have never been jealous of you. I know there's been talk. Talk! But I have never doubted my wife's virtue. Never! And when I look at you!!! How could I even for an instant believe . . . when I look at you! No, never!!! How could she!!!"

He noted that for a moment Sven seemed about to get up and leave, as if, in spite of everything, he was sober enough to understand the little insult that wasn't really so little, but then he stopped himself. No, it was too soon, he didn't want Sven to leave yet, there was much more to say.

"Forgive me! I didn't mean it that way. Not like that! I meant, when I now see your character! Your young, pure character!!! I've never had any doubts. And for so many reasons. One is that . . ."

He checked himself for a moment, as if to listen for sounds from the other room, as if to assure himself that his wife wasn't listening, though he knew that she was, that was the whole point; and then he went on.

" . . . one is that I know my wife. I know my wife! She is virtue personified. Beautiful . . . and virtuous. But . . ."

He leaned forward, as if to confide the utmost intimacy. It was unpleasant, extremely unpleasant, but he continued implacably in that low, friendly, purring tone of voice that was still loud and clear enough that anyone who was listening in the next room would be able to hear him.

"But she's cold. Cold. Confidentially, and just between us men. I know that you'll keep this confidential. You're my friend. We can confide in each other. I trust you. I tried . . . before our marriage . . . one evening in Chicago to take her to bed. Got her drunk. It didn't help. She was as virtuous as a prudish nun. Clamped her legs together. Had her on the bed! She clamped shut! Do you understand! Not a chance. I was forced to marry her virginity."

Sven sat there, completely rigid. What was he supposed to do?

"I had to marry it! Do you understand?"

"I understand."

"Marry her virginity! Virtue personified. What I didn't know was that she would clamp shut! Regularly! That this virtue was so excessive! Excessive! Do you understand?"

It was terrible. He sat there as if paralyzed, unable to stand up. What was he supposed to do? And that low, purring voice that he knew was bent on hurting them, wounding them, permanently, trying to cut them apart.

"She has given me a child, in spite of it all! And we're both happy about that. But now something is finished . . . finished! Inside of her. She can't have any more children. Unfortunately. She's completely finished as a woman."

"I understand."

"Virtuous. Beautiful. Marvelous body! If you only knew! If you only knew! But she can no longer have children. Her tremendous virtue has . . . in some way . . . petrified her . . . vitality! Do you understand?"

"I understand."

"This is just between us . . . between us . . ."

"Of course."

"Can't have children. A deeper inner virtue that has made her barren, sterile, cold!! That's why, Herr Lidman, that's why I trust her."

At that moment Margot appeared in the doorway. Her face was perfectly calm.

"How nice," he said. "Do come in, Margot. I'm talking about my days in Chicago."

7.

Which of the three was the most humiliated? He didn't know. But they made each other ugly.

Afterwards events seemed to happen very swiftly.

He had the feeling of being swept along by a river, one that was initially very calm and wide, the wide but exciting river of sin, but then suddenly a precipice, a waterfall, whirlpools, desperate breaths, then yet another fall: and then absolute calm, a great dead body of water, tree branches resting on an oily surface that was covered with dead algae; and encompassing everything a peculiar smell that he couldn't identify. Like the smell of death, or guilt, or a life that had ceased but was floating around in shiny, oily water.

Four weeks later they were sitting in a café at Drottninggatan 74, sitting very properly, across from each other. It was the proper afternoon hour for tea, for a conversation that no doubt included literary questions. The passersby couldn't misinterpret; everything was precisely as it ought to be: two literary acquaintances engaged in a perfectly normal conversation. And then suddenly Margot leaned toward him and in a low but calm voice, very calm, said it quite bluntly.

"I'm with child, Sven."

His face was like stone. He was impossible to read, but she saw that he had turned pale.

"I'm with child, our child, Sven. And I want to keep this child."

"That's impossible," he whispered after a moment.

"No, it's not. I file for divorce, we get married, I give birth to our child."

"I thought . . ."

Then he fell silent.

"What did you think?"

No reply.

"That I couldn't have any more children?"

He seemed paralyzed, perhaps he didn't know what to say, or not to say.

"Ohhhh ...Was it him? His days in Chicago? Oh, how I hate him. But I'm with child."

"Are you absolutely sure?"

"You thought I couldn't have children? I didn't think so either. But I can. I've longed so terribly for . . . I've longed so terribly for . . ."

He didn't say a word. Why didn't he speak?

". . . for this child."

And then she practically whispered:

"Sweetheart. I want to have this child."

Of course he was scared.

He tried to think about it in poetic terms. Fear was much too simple. To fall through the rapids, then a flat, foul-smelling body of water, another fall, a gasping breath: he seemed to have lost all sense of time.

Merely to be carried powerlessly by a river, and then a fall. And that peculiar smell.

He strolled through Östermalm with Margot. He was very matter-of-fact and not at all poetic, but the whole time that stubborn smell. He couldn't explain what it was. Perhaps he was coming down with a cold.

The important thing was to be very matter-of-fact.

The next day they were walking up Slottsbacken. He tried to remember what she had once said to him. What was it she said? She had dreamed that he would burn. Burn? But how could he burn, how could anyone ever burn in this ice-cold city, where so few alternatives existed, and no solutions. Sweden was not the sort of country that burned; and then that persistent smell which he was sure, quite sure, did not come from himself.

Was that how fear smelled?

"We have to get rid of it," he said in the voice that did not burn but was merely practical. "I've made arrangements."

"Arrangements!!!"

". . . and it costs . . . it only costs two hundred kronor. I've got an address, and it's completely . . . it's all right . . ."

"Two hundred!" she said with a sneer. "Two hundred!"

"Two hundred. I've gotten an advance from Bonniers, so money isn't a problem, and I insist, as a man!!! on paying for it; I'm not taking money from . . ."

"Two hundred."

"Two hundred. Is there something odd about that?"

"Two hundred!!!"

She seemed completely off balance. She was obsessed with that number. She mechanically repeated it. It was very unpleasant, but he was convinced that she was off balance, which was understandable, but in any case unpleasant since they were in such a public place.

"Well, it's expensive, but . . . Forget about the two hundred; what's so strange about it?"

She walked very quietly at his side, muttering her monotone "Two hundred! Two hundred!" over and over, and it was making him nervous. He didn't understand what she wanted. And she said:

"Oh, dear God. Two hundred. You say 'two hundred' as if it were the price for a side of beef. But I want to have this child, and . . ."

"That's impossible."

Then she stopped. He stopped too. And she struck him across the face with her bare hand and screamed:

"Two hundred!!!"

Everyone around them stopped. What was going on? Was this completely normal, or had something happened?

He turned around and started walking, then stopped again and stood silently staring at her.

No, there was no way out. No river falling freely. Just a calm body of water, dead driftwood, and that smell. They stood motionless in the snow at Skeppsbron and looked at each other, and then everything returned to normal and they could continue on. No waterfall, no time that had disappeared, just everything completely normal.

And that smell.

In spite of this they made love often.

And Margot said:

"You're never going to change your mind. I know that."

And she was right. She went to have the operation, alone.

She hadn't known what the word "modality" meant. So she asked. That was stupid. She shouldn't have let on that she didn't understand. The abortionist, who called himself a doctor, was very kind but used the word "modality," and during the whole procedure that word had run through her mind, almost as if offering some kind of protection or safety. And afterwards she thought: "This is something I'm going to hold onto, this knowledge of the word 'modality,' for all eternity."

"There are several modalities I have to clear up first," the doctor had said, pulling on a pair of gloves.

"I know," she said. "Two hundred."

"No, no. That's been . . . the gentleman has . . . paid. In advance, so there's no problem."

"Oh," she said. "Of course."

"That's been taken care of. The gentleman was anxious for all the modalities to be clear."

"What does 'modality' mean?" she asked. "Does that mean the two hundred kronor?"

He gave her a long look.

"It means two hundred kronor, that's clear. But the modalities also mean that you sign a statement that I am undertaking a simple corrective operation of the cervix. Just in case."

"In case?"

"In case."

And then she understood that "modality" meant two hundred kronor, and this written statement, and an "in case."

He walked restlessly back and forth along Västerlånggatan in the snowstorm, thinking that nothing lasts forever and that this was an experience, no doubt minor in a historical perspective. And that he shouldn't magnify things, that art was greater and more important than life, in a philosophical sense, no doubt that was true, but that life created tragedies and difficulties, and that the definition of tragedy, as Aristotle had defined it and which was true, was the conflict between two just and good principles; that's where tragedy arose, that which was greater than life itself.

Just before he reached Lejonbacken, a prostitute called to him, and he stopped and stared at her, obediently, as if he were a dog.

"Five kronor," the girl said, "but preferably not in a doorway, because this horrible snowstorm makes it . . ."

"Can't do it," he replied, thinking that he was standing there like an obedient dog.

"And if the gentleman has a little place we could go, we can discuss the price."

"Yes," he said.

"Yes what?"

"I do have a little . . . place."

"Well, then we won't have to freeze, and the gentleman certainly does look miserable. Are we agreed?"

"Don't know," he said, and thought that a tragedy is the collision between two just principles, but wasn't there a third, slightly dirtier and smaller, which is the tremendous human desire to sully the great tragedy, to be dragged down into the whirlpool, not to create the great tragedy that is the collision between two good principles, which is the third principle, that of the utmost degradation, what happens then, what happens to me, what is a human being in reality, and do I have a heart of glass, and how is that glass going to be shattered, and I'm standing here like a dog, and what good is that?

"Are we agreed?" she repeated.

"Yes," he said.

Later he confessed.

Margot Brenner sat on a chair, looking oddly rigid, in their lovers' lair as he confessed, and she turned white in the face. He explained how necessary it was for him to confess; there was an odd muteness about her, as if she didn't understand how important it was for him to confess, to report this tawdry act. That it was necessary to tell her, that the confession was important to him, that he felt soiled and that the confession would cleanse him.

Though he didn't mention the latter, but it was true.

"You didn't have to tell me," she whispered at last, very quietly. "Not that you went to a whore. Not on that day. You didn't have to."

"I wanted to be honest," he said.

And then, perhaps it was the word "honest" that unleashed it all, then she completely lost control. It began as a resolute stream of words, almost as if they weren't directed at him but just as much at herself, although he was the one she was talking to. "Honest? What crap, honest, honest!!! I don't want your confessions and your honesty, I don't want you to hurt me again, I don't want to see your honesty, honest! just so you can write about it someday, I get rid of my child and you go to a whore and the only thing that's important to you is to confess and be honest . . ." And it was impossible to stop her torrent of words, now she was no longer looking down at her hands but straight at him and it was unbearable and she had, he realized, because of her depression, lost all control. " . . . but it wasn't because you wanted sex, but because you wanted to be able to confess to me afterwards, so you can feel truly worthless, like the great artists! Artists!!! Those damned fakers!!! And then write a poem about it afterwards, but you don't know anything about life, and that's why you hurt me, just to find out what pain is like, but you don't know a thing, you're dishonest, through and through, and you took her into our bed, our bed! Yours and mine!!! Just so you could hurt me . . ." and she couldn't sit still but had begun to pace back and forth in the room, "and then you had to confess, and you killed our child and . . . two hundred kronor . . . and . . . two hundred! And I signed my name to the modalities!!!"

He couldn't say a word. Finally she fell silent.

She sat down and looked at him. Then she started in again. "You're a child," she said in a new, low, terrifying and strained tone of voice that was barely audible. "You're a child, and you have all the wickedness and innocence of a child. You're never going to grow up, Sven. I don't hate you, I may always love you in some way, but at this moment I pray to the God who perhaps exists, who perhaps has to exist in order to punish these evil and innocent children that He has created, I pray to Him that if you ever marry another woman, that He will make you suffer everything that I have suffered for your sake; oh, hear me, God, oh dear God, hear me in this hour of need, and You must make their first child die because You are righteous and cruel and know how to punish Your evil children."

He sat in utter silence.

"Why don't you say anything?" she asked after a moment.

He said, hesitating:

"I was just thinking—that this was true hatred—or passion perhaps—I wish I could write it down—so horrible and at the same time . . ."

She looked at him, her face rigid with loathing.

"Write it down? So that's what you're thinking. You should write it down. Oh, God, why do You make Your evil little children able to write? Why do You give Your evil little children the ability to write?"

Then she left. And he would not see her again for over thirty years.

CHAPTER 5

———•◆•———

Grains of Manna

1.

THE SQUARE IN FRONT OF THE TEMPLE ON RÖRSTRANDSGATAN ON this November morning is utterly quiet. No people, November fog. Raw and cold. As usual, I read the bulletin board, the schedule for the Pentecostal meetings.

It's an anniversary year.

They're remodeling; a glassed-in café will soon be finished at the corner facing Bråvallagatan. The Filadelfia temple is celebrating its seventieth anniversary. Does that means it's ninety years since the Pentecostal movement was founded, or is 1913 considered the founding year? That's when Filadelfia in Stockholm was spit out from the mouth of the Baptist Union and Lewi got his own congregation, his own house.

Lewi was not given any kind of monument. No equestrian statue, no bronze bust. Yet he did receive a monument, a cathedral; it's still standing there. I visit it more and more often, Lewi's monument, which in reality is an equestrian statue, though not in bronze.

And not cast in one piece.

2.

Still nothing in the *Lebenslauf* about Lewi's childhood.

Here and there brief remarks. "Lewi had eight siblings, and their house was 7 meters by 4.25 meters, as measured from the outside." "Lewi's hatred for alcohol stems from his father who got mixed up in boozing." Or, most puzzling of all: "Lewi's mother was the Kristina who did not emigrate."

When I was a child and found myself in a quandary and at a complete loss, I would go to my grandmother, whose name was Johanna but whom I called Josefina in my novel *The Musicians' Procession*, to ask for help.

What happened next was that she would stick her thumb into the Bible at random, open it up, and read the Bible verse on the page. Then she would fold her hands, sit in silence for several minutes, close the Bible, and go back to whatever she was doing. That was how I got help and no longer felt confused.

The custom goes back to Zinzendorf, who, for the first time in 1728, gave the congregation in Herrnhut a Bible text chosen at random, called the Watchword of the Day. Later this was developed into quite an extensive system of haphazardly selected Bible texts, often written on slips of paper, placed in a bowl, and then chosen at random, as in a lottery. For every situation, from a financial crisis to seeking advice or making a decision on the choice of a marriage partner, it became the practice to write Bible verses on slips of paper, place them in a bowl, and then in this way receive an answer to whatever was causing the confusion.

At a prayer meeting just two weeks after the Filadelfia congregation was formed within the Baptist Union in Stockholm, on August 30, 1910, the question arose as to who should be summoned to preach.

The congregation consisted of twenty-nine members.

They read aloud a verse from Isaiah 60:22: *"The least one shall become a clan, and the smallest one a mighty nation,"* and it had given all of them strength. Except for Engzell the wholesaler, everyone in the first diaconate belonged to the working class, with jobs as masons or metal workers. Yet most of the twenty-nine members were women, the majority of them young and single and skilled workers. No woman in any of the lead positions. At this prayer meeting it was decided that for guidance regarding the question of a preacher, they would draw a "grain of manna," one of those Bible verses written on slips of paper and placed in a bowl. It turned out to be from The Acts of the Apostles 10:5: *"And now send men to Joppa, and bring one Simon who is called Peter."*

Someone pointed out that a certain Lewi Petrus—at that time he spelled his name without an "h"—who was young and unmarried but was proving capable in Lidköping, had been asked, but he had said he was going to leave his preacher position and become a manual laborer, or turn all his attention to social concerns and work within the congregation only as a choir director, since he was very interested in music.

They then selected another grain of manna.

It was The Acts of the Apostles 12:7-8, which says: *"and behold, an angel of the Lord appeared, and a light shone in the cell; and he struck Peter on the side and woke him, saying, 'Get up quickly.' And the chains fell off his hands. And the angel said to him, 'Dress yourself and put on your sandals.' And he did so. And he said to him, 'Wrap your mantle around you and follow me.'"*

The summons is dated September 14, 1910.

Lewi Petrus had by this time experienced the event with the young boy named Enar, the event in which Lewi received the power; he was no longer wandering in the Forest of Despair, as it's called in Bunyan's book.

In his heart he had once more decided to leave his preaching position to do social work, and that's why he had again taken up the idea of becoming an author, particularly of proletarian novels. At first Lewi, without hesitation, declined the offer. He happened to be living with a family named Blomgren. At coffee one day, this Blomgren suggested they should choose a grain of manna, to receive guidance. The family's little daughter, six years old, asked if she might choose the slip from the bowl. She put in her hand, and the Bible text she chose was Jeremiah 1:17-19.

It says: *"But you, gird up your loins; arise, and say to them everything that I command you. Do not be dismayed by them, lest I dismay you before them. And I, behold, I make you this day a fortified city, an iron pillar, and bronze walls, against the whole land, against the kings of Judah, its princes, its priests, and the people of the land. They will fight against you; but they shall not prevail against you, for I am with you, says the Lord, to deliver you."*

Lewi asked if he might have the grain of manna. And then he accepted the offer.

In the Baptist congregation in Lidköping they were greatly surprised, because theirs was larger than the new Filadelfia congregation in Stockholm, which consisted of only a few dozen members. And it was unusual for God to summon a preacher from a larger congregation to a smaller one.

Yet, in the end, he did not hesitate to obey the words of the Savior

Jesus Christ, as they were given to him by the six-year-old girl whose name he later forgot. He would go to Stockholm.

He would become, as the Bible text stated, an iron pillar and a bronze wall against the whole country, against its princes, against its priests, and against the common people.

That's what it said. Almost everyone would stand against him. But that only filled him with greater confidence.

That's how it began.

BOOK II

August 1910–June 1921

CHAPTER 6

The Seers

1.

EVERYONE WAS ASKING WHAT IT WAS.

The woman left behind an account of the event at Uppsalagatan 11 when she came through at a prayer meeting. This is one answer.

She was saved but had not previously come through. And she was troubled about that. At the time of the incident she was twenty-nine years old and lived alone with one child.

It was around seven in the evening. Surrounded by sisters and brothers, she had been kneeling in the sight of the Lord for a long time. She felt torn to shreds. To God she said, "If You, Lord, will not do anything right now, then nothing will ever happen, because I have tried everything." Then she began to sense God's power. It started working in her left shoulder, and the force became enormous, taking hold more and more. At last her whole body was overcome.

The sisters and brothers began rejoicing and praising the Lord. God's power was so great that she was raised up from the floor as she convulsively grabbed hold of a chair which stood near where she was kneeling. Then the Spirit filled her heart with words from Psalm 81, verse 10: *"Open your mouth wide, and I will fill it."* Then she thought: It's now or never. Her spirit was filled with an exuberant bliss and joy. It felt as if her pores were opened and her corporeal life was forced out of her body.

She writes: "But it was heaven, that much I can say. God came in love, sweetness, purity, in an irresistible power to my soul. It was such a revelation of blood that I lost all control of myself, as far as life forces are concerned. There was such power in the exhalation of my breath that my throat widened and my vocal cords had to take on a different form than they had ever possessed. Oh, how strange! Now the Spirit spoke through me in a foreign language. Then the Spirit released me, and the power grew fainter, and I thought: Maybe this is something special, something of the soul. But then the power of God's Spirit seized hold of my jaws and vocal cords again, and this time I said: 'No, no, no, no, no' for a long time. Now I was convinced that it was not me who was talking but someone else. And a tremendous power came over me, and I spoke in tongues for two hours. My companion was able to interpret a good deal of what was said. I myself was conscious of everything, but not present. I was not on this earth. I was in heaven. When we got to our feet it was midnight. By then five hours had passed, but for me it felt like only a few minutes. Then the power left me, and I felt calm. Oh, I can never praise God enough for this blissful experience. Now Christ had conquered me."

Otherwise no information about her life, or her living conditions. Not even her name. She is but a drop in this sea, she too. My mother was also twenty-nine years old when she ended up alone. There's a similarity to her, the seeress who came through. But my mother never participated in a Pentecostal meeting, never spoke in tongues, was never Spirit baptized. She was beautiful, she received the commandments, but never the ecstasy.

Perhaps I begrudged her that.

There are a number of testimonies: "My companion was able to interpret a good deal of what was said."

That's the other face of speaking in tongues. The interpreters of the seers.

Comets pass, God's hand shakes San Francisco apart, Norway frees herself from her neighbor, the children of misery call out their distress, and the turning point is near. Then the seers speak to us in tongues. What are those incomprehensible voices saying?

In the first part of the *Lebenslauf,* there is a transcription that is said to be "interpretations of speaking in tongues." Someone has "taken shorthand" and afterwards "interpreted" a speaker of tongues who testified during one of the first years at the meetings of Filadelfia in Stockholm.

This was during Lewi's first period as head of the congregation. It is not known who took down the shorthand notes. Nor who interpreted them. At the very bottom of the last page a single word has been added: "Lewi?"

The interpretation is by no means confused or babble. The text is a statement: this is what the speaking in tongues means, or the babble, or the insane mutterings, or the despairing cry for help, or the secret message of the seer. Interpreted by someone who, in turn, may have had a specific intention.

This then is what it said.

"Be still before my countenance, and I will tell you what will soon come to pass. The earth, the wretched earth, which is a mute witness to all the abominations that have been carried out since Adam, and which has absorbed in its womb all the righteous blood that has flowed since the beginning of existence, will soon be free of the terrible weight resting upon her. The sins of humanity have reached their limit. The boundary that has once and for all been drawn can never be crossed. Alas, wretched earth, you are already faltering, and your foundations are trembling and starting to crack. The prince of the abyss has spewed a good portion of his spawn over you, and the effect is obvious to everyone. Woe to you, all those who scoff! Woe to you, all those who have not given the worker his wage! Woe to you, all those who have drunk of injustice like water! Woe to you, all those who have collected taxes in these final days! Woe to you who have oppressed the poor! Your cries, prayers, and lamentations have reached my ears, and I shall know how to administer a just sentence, says the Lord!"

And then the added word: "Lewi?"

No, this is not his language. But perhaps Efraim had taken note of the peculiar mixture of objectivity and revolutionary apocalypse that existed inside the correct young preacher from Lidköping.

As to what the "babble" meant: the interpreter assumes the role of the seer. And the speaking in tongues has many faces. But perhaps it's possible to imagine that the seer being interpreted was, nevertheless, the twenty-nine-year-old woman who seemed to be raised up off the floor and could feel the power spreading from her shoulder into each ever-widening pore, that her experience was hers, on her own terms, and that next to her sat a companion, perhaps one of those that Efraim later called "the men of 1912," one of the workers who later disappeared from the movement's leadership, an interpreter, perhaps not so much of her yearning as of his own rage, and this brother and sister in faith had somehow become united in an earthly and heavenly song, incomprehensible as the harps of heaven, and yet possible to decipher, like a poem.

2.

Now Lewi and Sven were in the same city.

Sven, too, was dreaming of burning. But since perfect form was the iron corset a person was forced to don in order to attain eternal fame, that's the fashion in which Sven wrote: in perfect form.

Sometimes he wished for a form that was a scream, but that type of form required courage, and that sort of courage he did not possess. Why did poetic ecstasy require this prescribed corset? And yet he submitted.

Why was the world of art so fundamentalist?

In the press he read about the babblers. That was the word that was used. The babblers were growing in number. It was like a menacing rumble of thunder before an imminent catastrophe. The world would shake and war would slay humanity, and blood and fire, that's why the babblers were sprouting like mushrooms and speaking in tongues. The babblers were rumbling within the revivalist movement, and the press was offended. But they're seers, he thought. They were prophesying.

Why couldn't he write a poem that was a babble, like the babble of the seers? He dreamed that a babble of art would shatter the iron corset that was slowly suffocating him.

He was sitting in a café with the celebrated Swedish author Hjalmar Söderberg.

Sven felt honored. He thought that nothing of the episode with Margot was left inside him, since he now seemed to be clothed in an outer armor. He felt that "clothed" was the proper word. He had always felt inferior to certain of the leading intellectuals, because the talents he possessed that were good, or superior, were shared by everyone he admired, yet they also possessed talents that he did not.

In Doctor Glas, the protagonist of Söderberg's novel, he seemed to see himself.

Every month he now received, from Bonniers Publishing Company, one thousand kronor. He suspected that in his heart Hjalmar despised him. Each day Sven groomed his beard and lamented that it was too thin.

His dream of the great devotion remained a dream that was fading; he feared that it was no longer his. That's why he had decided to despise it.

The poems he wrote, without hope, contained great beauty and nothing of value.

Hjalmar had not replied to his sharp-witted remark about an inner death. To sit in a café with Hjalmar Söderberg was a social coup of great significance; that's why he controlled his nervousness and acted witty. He didn't mention his background as a reserve officer, since he sensed that an artist, if he is alive, should not be a reserve officer. At death, in battle or by suicide, perhaps the rank of officer and the role of artist could be united. Poetry was different from prose in that it had shorter sentences and was written by idlers, Hjalmar had said. Sven laughed nervously as if this were a joke. Hjalmar had apparently not meant it as a joke.

Everything Sven wrote was beautiful and possessed of rigor mortis.

He wished he were very rich. Hjalmar Söderberg was not very rich, yet he was in some way enviable. The day before, Sven had seen Margot Brenner, together with her husband, on the other side of the street. She had not said hello. At the café he told Hjalmar about Margot. They were sitting in a place that Hjalmar had chosen. Söderberg gave Sven a long look and interrupted him before he could finish his account of the abortion. Hjalmar said, "You shouldn't have told me this."

It was incomprehensible.

"I just wanted to be honest," Sven replied. "Like in my poetry," he added after a pause that lasted far too long. "A poetry collection about the inner death, for instance, would only have life if it was candid," he added further after another long and troubling silence. Hjalmar then said that candor is nothing more than a speaking in tongues to protect one's own pain.

Hjalmar did not explain. All this talk of speaking in tongues! The newspapers wrote of nothing else. Sven found the comparison with poetry ridiculous, but he said nothing. Hjalmar had hinted that he knew Margot. That was puzzling. He said in a teasing voice that a man shouldn't talk about women and his experiences with them.

"Only in poetic form," Sven then replied. He was afraid that Hjalmar was growing bored and decided not to act witty anymore. The streets were muddy, Stockholm stank.

"This is not a clean city," Hjalmar said after a long silence.

"How can a person retain his inner purity in this outward filth?" Sven elegantly retorted.

"Why are you looking for purity?" asked Hjalmar.

That night Sven couldn't sleep, and finally he broke down and sobbed.

The next morning he made up his mind, and all day long he controlled himself and refrained from thinking about the end of their conversation, which, though carried on in a courteous tone, had still unsettled him.

"What are you looking for in a woman?" asked Hjalmar. "A great prize to conquer?"

"A great rapture," replied Sven.

"Like the preachers?"

"What preachers?" Sven asked uncertainly.

"The ones who speak in tongues," was the reply.

"Madmen," countered Sven. "Those madmen aren't artists; they ought to be put to death."

"Then," said Hjalmar with a slight smile, "then all hope is lost, and you might as well come with me tomorrow night to visit the very heart of the great Thiel fortune."

"What would I find there?" asked Sven with a teasing smile which he hoped would make an impression.

"You'll find the daughter, Carin, and she's beautiful. She's everything you're looking for in a woman, especially wealth; then you won't have to write a bunch of damned poems anymore."

Something in his tone of voice gave Sven the impression that Hjalmar didn't think much of his poetry. He didn't dare ask. Afterwards he thought that he should have established clarity with a provocative question. Only clarity and aggression aroused respect; of that he was convinced. But he hadn't asked, except in a veiled way.

"Does that mean I'm finished as a poet?" he wondered without wanting to hear the answer.

"Can you free yourself from the inner death that you praise so eloquently in the person of Doctor Glas?" Söderberg asked.

"I don't know if I want to," replied Sven, not knowing why his words sounded so strangely stiff, as if they were terrified or contrived. "But," he added, "perhaps I do wish that—if it would enable me to create a great poem, the way you can."

"In that case," his friend told him, "you should come with me, because there's a poetry collection hidden inside her."

"In every woman," Sven had wittily remarked. "That's the very raison d'être for women."

"Then even Margot has a certain *raison d'être*," said Hjalmar after a brief moment of silence.

Söderberg used only her first name.

"Yes, like the poets, the ones with the inner death," said Sven, realizing that this conversation had to come to an end; it was starting to repeat itself. He regretted having started it. It was the beauty of the words that had made him do it, the words "the inner death," the ones about beauty and rigor mortis: but to break it off abruptly seemed much too dangerous. He noticed that his words had acquired an increasingly stiff and literary character.

The whole time Hjalmar gazed at him with an oddly interested smile, as if he were searching for some inner meaning behind the well-formulated sentences of his young friend.

It was quite unpleasant.

Then Hjalmar insisted on paying the bill and said he needed to get back to his work.

It had been an unpleasant meeting.

Maybe Hjalmar was his enemy now. He didn't know why, but perhaps it had something to do with the inner death, or the story about Margot, or the word "rapture," or because he knew that the poems he was trying to write possessed great beauty and an absolutely terrifying inner death, and that something was missing, and Hjalmar had seen it.

He had seen it. Maybe he knew Margot. Sven shouldn't have told him.

Hjalmar had almost certainly seen that Sven was dead and would never experience rapture, and that this inner rigor mortis was manifested in his witty remarks, no matter how much he tried to control himself, or perhaps for that very reason.

That year Lewi and Sven found themselves in the same city.

3.

Lewi gave his debut sermon in Filadelfia, and it aroused a certain attention and discussion. Efraim relates a conversation that he had with Lewi the following week. Filadelfia was still part of the Baptist Union; this was before the split. Efraim would say "such as it was."

The situation was such that the leading brothers asked him to speak to Lewi.

"It was a good sermon," said Efraim. "I agree with you. You know where I stand. You know me better than anyone else. I was born like you were and have seen the filth. We are called by God but want to work for socialism."

"Fine," said Lewi, "but the goal is salvation."

"But there's one thing you should know," said Efraim. "The brothers—well, not all of them—but the leading brothers have heard that you have ties to the trade union. They've discussed this and asked God for guidance. Some of the Baptist brothers consider unions to be the new Leviathan. And someone made a joke about your name, but I admonished him."

"I know," Lewi replied.

Efraim's *Lebenslauf* follows no chronological principles.

Perhaps Efraim is searching for an inner logic. Perhaps he wants to say: "This was before Lewi's expulsion from the Baptist union." Perhaps he wants to hint that the political differences were an explanation for Lewi's extraordinary calm when he was thrown out. Perhaps Lewi regarded the concern that the somewhat older brothers felt about the union's Leviathan as a sack of stones he would gladly be rid of.

"The brothers wanted me to talk to you," Efraim repeated. "They don't want any division. No doubt the brothers think that politics is something that shouldn't concern dedicated believers. They see trade unions going against God's order. God created poor people and rich people. Someone who is saved should put his trust in God and not interfere with His order."

"I see," said Lewi.

"That's what I was supposed to say, in my own words."

Lewi had "pondered" for a moment and then replied "both clearly and pensively":

"I have sought God's advice. And He said that the poor and the oppressed should not merely acquiesce. He said that 'the educated' become ensnared and dissipated under materialism's network of slavery, that the masses are systematically robbed of their life's bread, that the multitudes of youth are led down into irreverence, hedonism, and moral indolence. He told me that the churches stand empty and with abandoned Communion bread, that He has heard about the congregations where faith in Christ is largely dead. He told me that He has heard and seen all this; there is misery among the people, and it's a matter of their very lives."

"True," said Efraim.

"But it's also a matter of fighting for people's spiritual lives. The spiritual degradation. Degradation!"

"I have a feeling that the uneasy brothers would have nothing against it if you talked about the spiritual degradation. Morals, in their opinion, are less political."

Lewi then looked at him with an odd smile and said:

"And that doesn't make them nervous?"

"What do you mean?"

"They're not uneasy about the battle for moral . . . purity?"

His voice had a tone to it that Efraim couldn't properly interpret. But he noted that this was the first time Lewi had used the word "purity" in their conversations. Efraim then, almost in jest, said:

"You really should have been a politician. The labor movement could use someone like you. And the Social Democrats."

Then Lewi said quite wryly:

"I doubt there's any place in Social Democracy for 'someone like me.'"

And Efraim merely replied, evasively:

"Yes, well, that's true. A shame, perhaps. In a way."

But the word he remembers best from their conversation was "purity." He writes that it might have been a fork in the road.

But they didn't see it.

CHAPTER 7

The Lice King

1.

THE TEXT OF EFRAIM'S *LEBENSLAUF* IS NOW MORE DETAILED. THE reason is that Lewi has arrived in Stockholm.

They were reunited.

As for Efraim, after moving to Stockholm he had hired on as a longshoreman at the harbor and taken lodgings on Högbergsgatan and was absolutely miserable. It was a distressing time, he would say. He feels confused, which is unusual. Halley's comet had passed by the earth in May 1910; the prophecies about the end of the world had proven false, yet what anxiety! What uncertainty! The following year the newspapers write about the uprising led by the peasant leader Emiliano Zapata, and Efraim tears out the articles, or rather cuts them out with a scissors, nice neat borders, and pastes them into the *Lebenslauf*. This revolt seemed to be fateful; perhaps, in fact, a portent.

So many portents. That faint rumbling of thunder.

Efraim apparently made regular visits to the Elim congregation. On this point he is quite effusive.

Elim became a sort of storm center. It was in this connection that he met Axel Hammar. He was a well-read fellow from Uppsala who had trained to be a missionary at Livingstone College in London, and he had been out in the field in Rhodesia. That was rather unusual. But the missionaries weren't afraid of foreign countries. That had been part of their work since the time of the Moravians. But Hammar was quite delicate, though not small in stature, and he was struck with all manner of tropical diseases, worst of all malaria. And he was very nearly called home by his Savior. But he pulled through, although he returned home to Sweden after two and a half years.

For Hammar, the experience down there had transformed him.

There had almost been more work with the bodies of the poor than with their souls. The conditions among the blacks were so wretched that the soul was secondary. And when Hammar came back to Stockholm and saw how things were there, it was as if he were seeing Rhodesia in Stockholm. Things were quite miserable. These were the pre-war years, and people were starving and unemployed and, in truth, it's impossible to describe. This Hammar seemed to see a starving heathen people in the middle of Stockholm. And he began working with their bodies and souls, but most of all with their bodies.

Because how could the poor be saved if they were already dead?

Efraim met Hammar at the congregation and became his work colleague.

That was how he once again made contact with Lewi.

Lewi also met Hammar in Stockholm. In many ways they were alike. Neither of them could forget the frail bodies of humanity. Both had seen the starving heathen folk in the middle of the capital, and they cared about them. Although Lewi had never been to Rhodesia.

Hammar and Lewi were actually very similar. At least at that time. Later on things were a little different. Efraim used to think about that group of founders of the Pentecostal movement as "the men from 1912." They burned for social causes; most of them were from the working class, and they were indeed fiery. It's possible to imagine fiery middle-class citizens, of course, but in this case most of them were workers.

Later the leadership changed completely. In the end Lewi was the only one remaining from the working class. That's why it was hard for him, and this difficulty seemed to stay with him. It was somehow both invisible and difficult. But it explains a great deal.

According to Efraim. Though he was only a witness. Merely a witness.

And yet.

The Elim congregation in Stockholm was one of the Baptist congregations; this was before the split, and among the Elim group there was real turbulence. It was not calm in the eye of the hurricane.

That explains what happened when Lewi came up from Lidköping.

People have forgotten how hard it was. And how they struggled.

And prayed. How there was a sort of breaking apart among the Baptists. When Spirit baptism and speaking in tongues arrived, it was a matter of life and death. Those who were in favor of speaking in tongues, who called themselves the reformers, were almost as hateful as those opposed. It's impossible to understand that things could be so hateful back then. John Ongman, who was the preacher in Örebro and Spirit baptized, was the one who had met young Jansson from Los Angeles. He wrote a fierce article in *Vecko-Posten* about those who opposed speaking in tongues and Spirit baptism. He said that "those who are skeptical about this movement or openly oppose it should desist while there is still time, because it is impossible for things to go well for such people in the long run. They will either be struck by some specific chastisement from the Lord, or they will be unfit for God's acre. If a person takes it into his head to vigorously oppose God's work, then the Bible and history as well contain astounding testimony about the ways in which God has gotten rid of such individuals."

Those were harsh words. Then a preacher named Hellström, who was against speaking in tongues and Spirit baptism, wrote a rebuttal to Ongman. That took courage. That clearly took courage. But only six months later Hellström suffered a cerebral hemorrhage and died. And then the *Tribune* published an editorial saying that this was God's punishment for those who opposed the reformers. And this Hellström had been warned, both verbally and in writing.

They wrote that it's difficult to swim against the current. It was understandable that God had gotten rid of such individuals.

Later, however, it wasn't just the revivalist newspapers that spewed hatred. When Elim became the center for the Spirit baptized and reformers, this took place in Stockholm. And Stockholm was different. In that city there were newspapers that hated everything about revivalism. All the newspapers were full of hatred, without exception, and they worked people into a frenzy.

It all started when a young man by the name of Bernhard Olsson attended a speaking in tongues meeting at Elim and began speaking in tongues himself, but later he actually went mad and killed himself with a shotgun barrel in his mouth. And then they wrote about how a neurotic man had become over-excited and taken his own life.

The point was that it was the babblers at Elim who had driven him to his death.

This suicide victim, Olsson, gradually became many, so to speak.

He was multiplied in the press, even though he was the only case. He became the example. And then it seemed as if the suicides were legion. Almost every day there were headlines about gruesome new events at Elim. This Olsson achieved a kind of eternal life in the Stockholm newspapers, even though he was dead. And demands were made for the police to stop the madness.

One paper called it the killer congregation and another the hotbed of the plague.

Things didn't get any better when John Ongman was summoned from Örebro to comfort the brothers and sisters suffering such scorn and explain things to the newspapers. Explain! He couldn't explain. It was like setting the fox to mind the geese because in Örebro things were even worse, and there they were normally considered insane.

It was like pouring gasoline on a fire. Ongman was practically the worst. And as for speaking in tongues and the Stockholm fallers at Elim, Ongman merely told the newspapers that they were "lively," but then "I am too."

This lively Ongman was ridiculed, but he had, in truth, asked for it.

Then Professor Bror Gadelius was summoned. His specialty was criminals and the insane, and that's why he was asked to give his professional opinion about the Elim people. He wrote in *Dagens Nyheter* that the Elim church was "a spiritual hotbed of the plague" and that it was a matter of "hysterical split personalities." And as if that weren't enough, *Svenska Dagbladet* called on its own expert, an associate professor at Långbro Hospital, which was the insane asylum at the time. His name was Olof Kinberg. He later became famous for writing a book about the criminally insane, and he said the same thing as Gadelius.

Since Kinberg was a specialist on the insane, he was allowed to comment on the saved at Elim. "This is an epidemic," he wrote. True, the meetings were stirred up. But he thought the whole thing was of a transitory nature. Time would heal the wounds of these sick people.

Otherwise there was always Långbro to care for them.

It was an utter frenzy. And the Baptist press, for its part, wrote that the journalists were vultures in a holy war. So it was truly a lively debate. And it was in this situation that Lewi was called from Lidköping.

Efraim himself had worked mostly with Hammar and those who were unemployed and starving. It was the Baptists who did such work, up until 1913, that is, when the Pentecostal movement was started and then they did that work too. This was something that people always forgot. The revivalist movement encompassed almost everything: both Spirit baptism and relief work. It was screams and a hotbed of the plague and a madhouse, and specialists on the insane were recruited who wanted to call in the police. But in reality most of the work was with the poor. They took the most time, and the most money. But the revivalist movement was practically everything at once, in truth. It was the tattered proletariat and food coupons and Spirit baptism and fallers all rolled into one.

But for the most part the newspapers wrote only about the fallers. That's what sold papers. People would rather read about those who went mad at the meetings and killed themselves with a shotgun stuck in their mouth. The ones who just lay there and starved to death didn't sell papers.

Yes, it was an acid test, in truth.

2.

Five men met Lewi at the train from Lidköping.

They all wore their best clothes, but still look oddly shabby. Embarrassed and somber, they greeted the twenty-six-year-old man who was now going to lead them through the storms that everyone knew were coming. Only one of the men embraced him, in Christ's name: Efraim.

"It's been a few years," said Lewi.

Then they escorted him to his lodgings, which consisted of two small rooms, a bed, and a wash basin. More pieces of furniture would be brought up later, they assured him. Brother Bengtsson hinted that they were fumigating them for lice.

Someone had put up wallpaper made from old newspapers, but there was none from the evangelist press, so there wasn't much reading material. Or at least nothing edifying.

"We have great hopes for you," Bengtsson said. "And they say you're a good organizer. Well, there are only twenty-nine of us in the circle of brothers and sisters, so I'm sure everything will go just fine."

Lewi looked at the curtainless window and said:

"Well, at least there's a window."

"There's another one in the hallway," Brother Bengtsson said with "a disarming smile."

Efraim then retorted:

"No doubt Brother Petrus will pray to God for curtains for the window; we're no followers of Lestadius, after all. And then I'm sure that God will provide them for him, because Brother Petrus can be quite stubborn."

Then Brother Bengtsson said:

"And a woman. Surely Brother Petrus needs a wife. We can discuss it at the prayer hour tomorrow."

Brother Petrus didn't reply, and he seemed ill at ease, but the brothers laughed, and after a moment Brother Petrus joined in since all the brothers seemed to be in such agreement on this topic.

A wife. In Christ.

The next evening he gave his inaugural speech.

The congregation had turned out in force. They looked at him tensely, but kindly.

There is a record of the sermon, which was apparently written down and not, as was his custom later on, merely improvised. It might be his own manuscript. "Brothers and sisters in Christ," he began. "God looks with sorrow on the world that we have created. Our young congregation is born into a world in which a battle for life and death is being waged between the propertied classes and those who have none, the unemployed, hungry and starving, who have finally awakened to consciousness of their human worth. The bent backs are straightening up. The slaves are shaking off the yoke. The tenant farmers, farm hands, maids, servants, and day laborers are starting to grumble. But children still roam around begging for a scrap of bread, or they steal a turnip from a farmer's field and are sent to the spinning house or sold at auction. Brothers in Christ, I know this world, I was born into it." And then he continued, and at the end, after a fervent prayer, he picked up a piece of paper and read what it said: "Sisters and brothers in Christ, we who have received grace through His blood, we are a small congregation, and we are in need of bylaws, and I have here a bylaw proposal. I suggest that Paragraph 1 should read as follows:

§1

The Filadelfia congregation in Stockholm is an association of confessors in the teachings of the evangelical Lutheran faith, who have come together to share religious services and mutual Christian edification, as well as for the express purpose of caring for and tending to the poor and otherwise needy children, to rehabilitate and help onto the correct path those who have fallen, but also, within our power, to help those in distress or to undertake Christian humanitarian activities.

He then paused, looked out at the congregation, and said:
"We'll take the paragraphs one by one. Shall we adopt this one?"
A brief moment of silence followed.
"Shouldn't the authorities be doing those things?" said a somber voice from the congregation.
"Oh yes! But they're not!" Lewi snapped.
"No, I guess they're not."
"So we must do it! Anyone opposed?"
Utter silence. Then someone asked for an adjournment. And the only thing we know is that these bylaws were not adopted until five years later, on March 27, 1916. On that first day he was unable to get passed that first remarkable paragraph, and they worked without bylaws. And that worked fine. But in March 1916, it was passed: perhaps the most extraordinary preamble that a revivalist movement ever adopted. But there was something in his voice that made them realize that although this small group within the congregation might be inconsequential, it would grow quickly, and soon they would more and more compliantly nod approval to this little preacher, and would continue to nod, for an entire century, until this cathedral-builder of God was one day called home to Jesus Christ, his Savior, benefactor, and ally.

3.

If a person dreamed of the happy, pious, and harmonious nuclear family as the foundation of existence—and this was a dream that Lewi gradually came to seize hold of with all his might, almost out of desperation—then there wasn't much hope to be found in that city.

Stockholm was a rubbish-heap, smelly and freezing and starving. The infant mortality rate was high, and the overcrowding abominable. The working class, which had grown in recent decades, was packed into indescribable hovels, except during the summertime when they could build little wooden huts on the rocks of Södermalm. And promiscuity was widespread. The great debate at the end of the nineteenth century was about sexual morality, chastity for men before marriage, and freedom for women—the "Glove Morality," as it was labeled, after the Norwegian playwright Bjørnstjerne Bjørnson called for male chastity in his play *A Glove*. This debate was carried on in a very thin stratum of air, very high up, among intellectuals in all of Scandinavia, since the great authors traveled back and forth between Kristiania, Copenhagen, and Stockholm and aroused attention with their radicalism. But rarely did the debate penetrate real life, as it existed in Stockholm. Particularly not to people of the working class, who were crammed into tiny ice-cold rooms, who were starving and copulating recklessly, without hope.

Of course families did exist. But one third of all families in Stockholm in 1910 consisted of single women with children. These women were not mentioned in the preamble of the Filadelfia congregation. But it was these single women who were at the center of the misery. And going lower down in the social strata, almost half of the new working-class families consisted of these single women, widowed or deserted, or simply impregnated through some random copulation.

There was no need even to mention rape. It was the misery itself that was the rape that engendered these "defenseless children," who, by the way, were dying like flies, with the highest infant mortality rate in Europe.

Almost half of all families were these families without a provider, nuclear families without a core.

On one of his first days in Stockholm, Lewi went to visit Axel Hammar's rescue mission for homeless men.

Hammar welcomed Lewi, talked about Rhodesia, called himself the Lice King, and led Lewi through the gloomy hell that was Stockholm, if you disregarded the fashionable Strandvägen and Djurgården's lovely little restaurants. And Lewi was not naive; in Lidköping he had started an orphanage for "motherless" children (fatherless was such a common state that it didn't need to be mentioned), and a soup kitchen that swelled almost beyond the financial control of the congregation. But here in Stockholm the need for help seemed almost hopelessly great. Hammar had also started a "home for the unemployed" on Kindstugatan in Gamla Stan. He asked Lewi if he would be the supervisor, and Lewi accepted.

This was in obvious conflict with his work as head of the congregation. But his mission was quite clear: "I was supposed to initiate the work in the capital among the poor, the down-and-out, and those who had sunk very far, and God would be with me and give a special blessing to this work."

Yes, he found himself in the Swedish Rhodesia.

The first year he didn't sleep much. There were so many bodies during the day and souls in the evening, Efraim recalls.

The first summer Lewi lived among the workers, for practical reasons, since Hammar was away and someone had to take care of the soup kitchen. There are hints of conflicts with the leaders of the congregation, noted in Lewi's autobiography. "Leading figures in our congregation rebuked me sharply for this. They regarded the work as much too demanding for me to take on such duties. It was particularly unsuitable for me to live with these men, which included all types, and there wasn't much peace at night."

Soon the activities were expanded. They found a little room at Köpmangatan 15 for the soup kitchen to feed unemployed and destitute men. "The misery that is rampant among these unemployed and homeless men cannot be described in words. They often go without food or shelter for days, and they barely own enough to cover their bodies," he writes in a letter.

Suddenly his dream of becoming a proletarian writer had caught up with Lewi, and reality had raced past him. The court records he had ordered from Björck & Börjesson's antiquarian bookstore, about the relief practices for the poor in Stockholm during the nineteenth century, had become manifest in the reality surrounding him, and this reality was worse than in the records.

It was necessary to be practical, and to organize.

The room at Köpmangatan was too small. The collection of money among the "propertied classes," as he expressed it in his sharp inaugural sermon, had to be more effective. Surely some of these propertied people had good hearts. But it was the congregation that responded to most of the collections, with their own funds. Besides, it was necessary to be practical. Those who were starving would not be fed on sharp words. The efforts at Uppsalagatan 11 were more effective. There they served rice pudding, although they started with songs and prayers, and after the hungry ate their fill, they continued with talks and songs. There was a good atmosphere. Later they served split pea soup with pork, which was cooked in the furnace room of the wash-house, and songs were sung in unison.

Perhaps Lewi dreamed of anchoring the movement among the tattered proletariat. His companions among the leaders of the little Filadelfia congregation would wait and see.

Where would all this lead?

Ever-expanding social work. It was growing.

Lewi found a little room next to Uppsalagatan 11, and there he received visitors every morning at eight o'clock. There were food coupons to distribute, or food, and words of encouragement, with prayers if there was time. The lines kept growing longer, and then the prayers got shorter. The congregation, which sang and prayed in the larger room in the evenings, began complaining about the lice problem. The gatherings for the poor in the morning brought an invasion of fleas and lice that settled on the faithful in the evenings. This was a problem. "During my consulting hours I used to sit at a table and write out chits for overnight shelter, and the line would start pressing forward. Sometimes Fru Engzell would discover lice crawling over my clothing when I went upstairs after the consultations. Finally the shop owners began complaining about the lines of unemployed outside their businesses. People were afraid to go into the stores."

So that was the beginning. And the hundreds of people seeking help soon became thousands. Then they rented premises on Krukmakaregatan, and started a place for "the clothing of poor children" and a small orphanage, and it grew.

Where did he get the money?

From charity, prayers, the consul's wife Maria Ekman, the organization, long lists of contributors' names: faithful brothers and sisters; Fröken Ljunggren, 2 score eggs; H. Nilsson, 50 kg potatoes; Eggetorp's Baptist congregation, clothing; from sisters in Uppsala, 7 large woolen sweaters, 6 large caps, 1 pair mittens, 4 pair stockings; Ida Johansson Jonsered, 50 öre; a collection box, 3 kronor, 55 öre; tailor Larsson, 1 krona, 50 öre; as well as to a certain extent God's supervision and grace as mediated by the general overseer Lewi Pethrus.

But that's not what the newspapers wrote about.

They wrote about speaking in tongues.

One day Lewi received a call from the Konradsberg psychiatric hospital. A nurse asked him to come to the hospital. Someone wanted to talk to him. He went there and was immediately escorted to the person who was waiting; it was Professor Bror Gadelius, the medical superintendent of the hospital, professor of psychiatry at the Karolinska Institute, and fellow of the scientific council of the Medical Board.

At issue was the fact that the newspapers were demanding that the revivalist meetings be stopped, that they were harmful for emotionally unstable people, that speaking in tongues was a danger to society, worse than the threatening social unrest, which it might even be provoking, though that was a matter of contention. Which was the chicken and which was the egg? Yet everyone was agreed that revivalism was a hotbed of the plague. A long list of calls to the police had come in after the articles appeared in the Stockholm press.

Certain interventions had been undertaken.

The authorities could no longer sit by with their arms crossed. The opinions expressed in the newspaper editorials required action.

And they did start to take action.

From Filadelfia, for instance, a man had been admitted to the Långbro insane asylum. He had been saved during a meeting at Filadelfia, and had confided in Lewi. He confided that while unemployed he had been guilty of several criminal acts. Lewi had then exhorted the man to go to the police, and he would accompany him. But the man had gone alone to the police and confessed, but told them that he was saved, and at that point he began sobbing loudly. The chief constable then concluded that the confession was made under duress and the weeping was clearly a sign of mental illness, fruit of the unhealthy zealotry in the revivalist movement, as depicted in the latest newspaper reports. The confession, the tears, and his connections to Filadelfia clearly proved that the man was insane.

He was promptly confined to the Långbro insane asylum.

After several months members of the congregation started to wonder where the man had gone, and they grew uneasy. They had their answer when a newly released Långbro patient secretly contacted Lewi and, "whispering," begged him to go to see this man, who didn't seem crazy and who was worried about his old mother, for whose care he was solely responsible, because he envisioned a forced incarceration that would last for many years.

Lewi went at once to Långbro.

There he met with the saved colleague who, dressed in asylum

garb, was walking around mowing the lawn in despair. Lewi demanded to speak with a doctor. They exchanged sharp words. Lewi main-
tained that a person could not be considered sick because he wanted
to give up his criminal activities, and being saved in the blood of Jesus
Christ was not a sure sign of the outbreak of insanity. If they wanted
to commit everyone in the revivalist movement who was saved, the
facilities of Långbro insane asylum would hardly be sufficient.

After an hour's discussion, the doctor said:

"He'll be released tomorrow."

The conversation with Professor Gadelius lasted three hours.

Gadelius was very friendly and asked interesting questions. He
asked whether evangelism meant influencing people. Lewi said that of
course that was the case. He would be a poor speaker if he didn't influence his listeners. All preaching, religious or political, contained a measure of suggestion. Gadelius then asked whether the accusation was true
that hypnosis was used. Lewi said that he had no knowledge of hypnosis. Then he was asked whether meetings of this nature, with such strong
emotion, could cause insanity. Lewi replied that insanity existed among
all categories of people, also within the revivalist movement, and his
understanding was that many severely tested people avoided insanity
through their faith in the gospels, but he would leave it to Professor
Gadelius, who was the medical expert, to answer that question.

They talked for three hours. Their conversation was very thor-
ough, and agreeable. Professor Gadelius warmly thanked Lewi for the
interesting conversation, said it had been very elucidating, and was
friendliness personified.

During the conversation he had in no manner expressed the idea that
all religiosity was more or less a sign of insanity, as one of his colleagues
had claimed. On the contrary, in a newspaper interview a week later, he
was quite restrained in his discussion of the Pentecostal movement and
declared that "a person can never go insane from too much religion."

But what was that conversation about? What had it actually dealt with?

It took place under great secrecy. Lewi was summoned but not
told who he was going to see. The nation's top expert in psychiatric
problems had interrogated him for three hours.

Were the human rights of the people in the revivalist movement perhaps called into question?

Or what was that conversation about?

Afterwards Lewi began to wonder.

Was it possible that in reality, during those three hours, Lewi had undergone a brief mental examination, but had passed the test?

CHAPTER 8

The Lovers

1.

EVERYTHING WAS ENCHANTING UPON ENTERING THE THIEL PALACE. Sven strolled in at Hjalmar Söderberg's side, and it was all so enchanting.

He was escorted inside. How radiant the intellectual and financial elite were in this beautiful and spotless Swedish capital! How surrounded by beauty! Wasn't it just like a painting, the way the Nordic light filtered down through the foliage of the trees to the figures who had gathered for conversation, reflection, brilliance, debates, and discussions about the latest ground won by the new ideas? The way they were gathered on the steps leading up to the Thiel palace, which now, on this summer afternoon, formed a frame around the leading artistic vanguard; that's how Sven would express it in his mind: vanguard, an unusual word, but apt.

The way the beauty of the place framed everything with its balance and artistic sense.

He was properly dressed, if proper meant a coat that fit correctly; he had made a proper entrance and noted that people looked at his friend Hjalmar with respect. He knew that most of the people there that evening were enormously wealthy; but respect was not always measured in terms of wealth. He knew that among these people who appeared so enormously successful on the outside, there were secret dreams of becoming an artist, and an almost nervous insecurity with regard to people like himself. Since artistic talent could not be bought, it seemed very precious to those who were immeasurably rich, almost unattainable, like a priceless diamond. That was why he could move among the very rich with a sort of humble arrogance, as if he represented a dream that for them was secret but unreachable.

But the important thing was to say the right words.

He was allowed to be intense but only in a very calm fashion, almost whispering; that was the way to spark interest. It deepened the latent interest in artists that merchants already possessed. Sven succeeded in finding the right tone. Maria Thiel, in particular, who was Ernest Thiel's new wife, found him exciting. She always read all the reviews, often gathered artists around her, and she knew that Oscar Levertin regarded the poet Lidman as the young lion. She found his calm nervousness intriguing; it was basically the expression of his alienation among these financiers, something that she found proper and in fact natural for creative artists. Anything else would have surprised her.

"Herr Lidman," she asked, "when you compose a poem, what are the forces that initiate the actual . . . spark . . . the actual . . . do you understand?"

"For me it's a miracle every time," he replied in such a low voice that she almost couldn't hear his words.

"Would you explain . . ."

"How can anyone explain a miracle? Lazarus rises up from his bed, they ask him, 'Why are you alive?' and he doesn't reply. What should I say, Fru Thiel? How does a work of art rise up from the inner death?"

This last comment was the only thing that was in any way true; a truth had suddenly appeared in the midst of his words, did she understand that? He had an uncomfortable feeling that he had revealed himself, even though he was merely intending to sound witty, or at least brilliant.

"I understand," she said, almost breathlessly. "And do other people play any role in this? A woman, for example?"

He was calmer now, and found the proper words.

"She is a sword that pierces my blindness," he replied.

She looked at him with new appreciation.

"You are very lonely, Herr Lidman," she said.

Now he was feeling quite confident, didn't have to formulate his responses, they were there, they poured out, almost without resistance.

"History is an echo chamber within me, and that's why I am never alone, Fru Thiel," he replied. "The Lidmans, my family, are there, although nearly all of them have committed suicide, died on the battlefield, or drowned. I can hear their voices and will never be rid of them; their fates are like invisible voices in the fog. I know their despair and bewilderment, but I let their voices live on in my poetry; that's the curse in our family, that echo chamber! If I ever have children, my voice may echo in everything they do, everything they say; I hope not, but it's a curse. No, I'm never alone, Fru Thiel. I wish I were alone."

"Wish?"

"That's why I swallow my despair until I have written what I have to write."

"I understand."

"Swallow my despair."

He didn't notice that Hjalmar Söderberg had come over and was listening to the latter part of the conversation. When Sven repeated the phrase "swallow my despair," he heard a faint groan behind him, saw his friend turn on his heel and leave. Then Sven was struck by a great nervousness. He was almost certain that he had said something wrong. It was a groan that he heard. Had he said something that was poorly formulated, or formulated much too well?

He turned back. Fru Thiel was moving away. That was perfectly reasonable. He too had turned away. Though very briefly, perhaps only for an instant.

He was almost certain that she had seized it as an excuse to flee.

He saw Hjalmar talking to a very beautiful young woman. He knew that she was Carin, the daughter of their host. Later in the evening he managed to approach her. He asked if he might read some of his poems for her sometime.

She merely said:

"I'm not interested in poems. Only architecture. Are you an architect?"

So she didn't know who he was.

"No," he replied. "Only interested in the architecture of the body."

Later that night he had a brief conversation with Tor Bonnier and complained.

"What does she mean 'only interested in architecture'?" he said. "How enormously trite. Architecture."

"She means architects," said Tor Bonnier. "It's that Ragnar Östberg."

"She's rich, beautiful, unapproachable, and only interested in architects. How the devil can God create such monsters? It's driving me
crazy."

"Calm down," replied Tor. "You're drunk."

"It's driving me crazy."

Later that night he went out on the lawn. The morning light was
starting to appear, that Nordic light! He was standing next to a tree to
take a piss. He no longer cared if anyone saw him. That Nordic light.
He let the stream flow for a long time as he looked up at the balcony.

There he saw Carin and Ragnar Östberg. They were kissing. He
realized that nothing was enchanting anymore. He suddenly felt
tremendously drunk, and determined.

Her. No one else.

2.

Her. No one else.

With surprise Sven noted that it was easy for him to make friends
among these immensely rich people. These friends were pleasant and
didn't try to force their way inside of him, into the space that he didn't
believe existed, the innermost part, because he still remembered
Margot's words that he was an onion. But he had found some friends.

He mobilized one of them.

The friend was Count Oxenstierna, who was held together by an
outer shell, which was his title, but who had not yet decided on his
path in life. This friend, who was called Oxis because he was not brilliant but good-natured and only thirty-two years old, had a great
admiration for people who were mentioned in *Svenska Dagbladet*, especially on the cultural page, and this included Sven. Without hesitation,
Oxis declared himself willing to help with the modalities. He dressed
up as a coachman and got himself a carriage and horse. The equipage
drove up, and the friend got out and knocked.

Carin opened the door and looked with amazement at all the fin-
ery and exclaimed:

"Oxis! What are you up to? Are you just dressed up like a coachman, or have you actually started to work?"

Oxis, young Count Oxenstierna, then explained that a secret admirer
was waiting for her in the carriage. Giggling, she followed him out and
opened the door to the calèche.

There sat Sven Lidman.

"My beauty, my supremely beautiful admirer of Swedish architecture, I would like to invite you on a little drive, for supper!"

Laughing, she climbed in. Oxis clambered up to the coachman's seat. They drove off to what he called "the arrangement."

That's how it started.

It was what he called, while he was making plans, a love feast, though those were not the words he said to her, and afterwards he forgot all about them.

The little gazebo stood in the park.

The "arrangement" consisted of a cold buffet with red wine, and she grew quite tipsy. Sven took care to remain sober, but kept pouring more wine into her glass. He was entertaining and spoke with contempt about expensive wines that acquired bouquet and vitality only when a few drops of Crown aquavit were added, and he talked about his uncle Sam who used to make a blend of one-third Crown and two-thirds expensive French château wine to remove the insipid taste of the scarlet French dishwater.

The words "scarlet dishwater" were enough. They were proletarian and crude, and he sensed that she was interested.

Yes, after a while she found it enchanting. There was something about this mixture of refined abductor and crude proletarian that was irresistible. She understood that he was obviously a man with a genuinely artistic nature: the story about the Crown aquavit in the vintage wine was the door that opened into him, and the realization of his bizarre character.

Oxis had discreetly withdrawn to the main building. It was a beautiful summer evening. Inside the little round dining room there was a tiny room. A sort of sleeping alcove.

She had noticed it but refused to acknowledge it.

He started to sing, and then to dance with her.

"Ohhhh God . . . Herr Lidman . . . you're such a terrible dancer . . . is your poetry equally bad . . . ooohhh . . . help . . . poetry . . ."

He spun her around and into the inner room with a calm, humorous resolve.

"Oh God . . . I'm so drunk . . . oh, please, what was in that last glass . . . it wasn't Crown, was it . . ."

"My beloved Queen," he whispered in her ear. He noticed that she was sweating and that her hair had fallen over her cheek. "My beloved beautiful . . ."

"Oh no . . ."

"You want to . . . I can feel . . . Can't you feel this . . . to just give in . . ."

He was hazily conscious that what he was saying was not from the true world of art; that the images and words he used in his love poems, which were praised in *Svenska Dagbladet*, were now mixed with words and images that seemed to be taken from other texts, as if the afternoons and conversations and teasing with the girls at Västerlånggatan 24 now unbidden, or rather involuntarily, became jumbled up with the language of the exalted love poetry that had made him famous, or almost famous, or perhaps would someday make him extremely and thoroughly famous. But she wasn't listening.

"Let go . . . no, I don't want to . . . oh God, I've gotten so drunk . . . won't you read me a poem, Herr Lidman . . . no, I said . . ."

"My Queen . . . my Queen . . ."

Did he rape her?

No, he thought afterwards. She surrendered to her enormous passion, which broke through the armor of ice; art conquered the icy membrane of architecture, deep inside she wanted to, deep inside she undoubtedly wanted to.

Deep inside she undoubtedly wanted to.

3.

It was almost daylight. She walked across the grass toward the main building and pounded on the windowpane.

She pounded for a long time, furiously, and at last the young Count Oxenstierna appeared.

Yes, it was dawn. Mist hovering over the ground in the park.

He opened the window and looked at her. Her clothes were in disarray, she hadn't bothered to straighten them. Her face was very pale. She had vomited on her clothes.

"Coachman!" she said in an utterly ice-cold voice to Count

Oxenstierna's astonished face, and then he promptly realized that he was the coachman.

And for the rest of his life he would never be anything more than a coachman to her. And he would never be forgiven. And that's why he had to obey.

She turned on her heel and walked toward the carriage. Sven was sitting there, sitting on the ground, leaning his back against a wheel, and smoking.

No one offered an explanation to the coachman.

Who can we talk to? Who can we open our hearts to? Where is the benefactor who in the hour of need will hold his hand over you and save you? Who sees you in your need? Who sees you?

She knew there was only one person. Her father.

On September 26 she went into his study in the Thiel palace and told him that she was with child. She was standing at the window, and her father was sitting at his desk and then she said it, simply that she was with child, and that the father was the poet Sven Lidman.

A very long silence ensued.

"How delightful," he then said in his most neutral tone of voice. "What delightful news."

She didn't reply.

"Do you love him?" he asked. "What I remember is that we had a reception, and you talked to him, and then you said that you thought he was hideous."

"He is hideous."

"On the other hand, I remember that my beloved wife was quite taken with him. But as far as I know, she's not with child."

She said nothing.

"And how did this happen?"

She still said nothing, but could no longer contain herself. She was standing with her back to him, stubbornly staring out the window, and she began to cry but did not put her hand to her face; no, she wasn't going to hide her tears. She wept openly and furiously at the beautiful park, but he couldn't see it.

"Well. I'm sure it will be a delightful child. And the two of you won't want for any material needs. You'll have to get married."

Then she said:

"Pappa, I'm scared."

"Of him?"

She tried to breathe slowly and calmly, making an effort to hold back her tears so that at last she could turn around to face him and rush into his arms. But that was impossible. She had to stay where she was and speak in a tightly controlled voice.

"There's no reason for it," she heard his voice, which sounded perfectly normal though in reality he was furious. "Are you really scared of that . . . poet?"

He said "poet" with such subdued contempt and rage that she was almost frightened. Although in some sense she understood.

"You mean, Pappa, that whoever is your daughter, the child of such an immensely rich man, and who stands in the cool shadow of your money, never has to be afraid?"

And he calmly replied:

"Yes, my child. Something like that."

It was very unpleasant and very proper.

Ernest Thiel was extremely serene, speaking in a low voice, never losing his temper but regarding Sven with eyes that never wavered even for a second. It was as if he never blinked. "As if lizard eyes were looking at me," Sven thought afterwards. Was that the way lizards stared at their victims? No, not lizards. Snakes.

It was enormously unpleasant.

"Herr Lidman, the facts are as follows," said Thiel the banker. "The girl is with child, and we're going to sign a contract. You will get married, a magnificent ceremony that will have a touching and heart-warming undertone of young love. You will marry in the presence of a large number of literati, who will praise your youthful, shimmering happiness, Sven, as well as your improbable and thoroughly undeserved good fortune at marrying into the world of high finance. Yes, I see you notice that I used your first name; so I suggest that we should switch to a first-name basis to mark our newly won kinship, if not love for each other."

"Thank you very much."

"You don't need to thank me. I take your gratitude for granted. You're going to be taunted, but you will be magnanimous in the face of those taunts. Just don't get too drunk, because then you're bound to grow tactless and reveal yourself to be a boor, Herr Lidman. Or rather, Sven. I beg your pardon, I'll have to remember that. Then you'll go on a wedding trip to Berlin and Italy. Berlin is dismal, but that's where an author has to go, that's the proper thing to do, otherwise he loses prestige, and that's not something you can afford to do. I'll arrange for a suitable residence at Djursgården, I recommend the gamekeeper's house on the promontory of the park. You should acquire a library for yourself, Herr Lidman. Otherwise no one will believe that you're an intellectual, Sven! Sven! And you'll receive a monthly allowance from me. A stud fee, you might call it, since you have impregnated my daughter. Allow me to congratulate you on your achievement. We don't need to draw up a written contract. I always keep my word, and I, I! am an honorable man. Welcome to the family. Now you'll have a cognac, and then you will casually converse with me for half an hour, no more."

"Bank President Thiel," Sven began but was promptly interrupted.

"You are grateful, Herr Lidman. But don't say so. You have reached the entry to heaven and forced your way in. Like a phallus. You have yourself to thank for your success. The rest is all a matter of contractual terms, like most things in life. Isn't that right?"

"Well, yes."

"And you have an admirable . . . well, what should I say. Resolve. Congratulations."

Everyone has his own *Lebenslauf*; some are written down, some are etched into suppressed memories, like frostbite in the soul.

Sven was one of those who later wrote his down. Not everything, but a great deal. Others, who came in contact with his fate, recorded other things. It's necessary to put them together. And all of them are now in God's acre, anyway; some under stones that are flat and identical, and with inscriptions that have been almost erased over time. And perhaps somewhere in the archives of God's acre there is a *Lebenslauf* for each of us that is visible for a few brief minutes, an inscription visible only in the slanting morning sunlight, when God, in His mercy, wants to give us access to the lives of those small creatures He has reaped and harvested.

But in one sense Bank President Thiel was right. It turned out to be an extremely impressive ceremony when the two young people were wed. And surrounding all this financial and intellectual radiance was the other Stockholm where Lewi lived, not yet illuminated by a slanting morning sun. Lewi still found himself far away from a union with his spiritual twin, who was now properly following the stipulations of the contract. Herr Thiel had been right: the rest, the outward conditions of love, so to speak, were a matter of contractual terms, like life itself. Sven recalled the terms; they had a sort of reassuring cynicism about them, which made it easier to bear the unbearable degradation that he now consigned to the heading: "Contract Provisions."

The stud fee, on the 22nd of each month, would no doubt make it easier to write. After all, that was the condition of art, and of artists.

But the young bride was a problem.

When the ceremony was over and the modalities associated with the wedding journey were all arranged (Sven preferred not to use the term "modalities," which his father-in-law loved, even though several years earlier Sven had learned from an elderly doctor what the word meant, but that was in a different situation, or perhaps not)—when they set off on their wedding trip, the conflicts began.

She was a problem.

Carin jumped down from the train compartment at Bahnhof am Zoo in Berlin without waiting for Sven. She left him behind with the vast piles of baggage and went on her way without heeding his call. Perhaps she did hear him but managed to elude him—that's one way of describing it.

She had an address in her hand, and she made her way through Berlin. She was looking for a hotel, or rather a pension, she wasn't quite sure; but at the front desk she asked in her correct schoolgirl German for "Herr Tor Bonnier," and then sat down on a sofa in the lobby and waited. And when Tor Bonnier, who was in Berlin on business, but not on this particular business, when he came down she was already sobbing and was quite beside herself.

He steered her to his suite, dried her tears, and asked her in bewilderment how she knew that he was staying there, how she knew the address.

"Ragnar told me," she replied. "In case something should happen."

"Ragnar?"

"Ragnar Östberg."

"Ragnar? Östberg? But aren't you on your wedding trip with Lidman???"

"Yes! It's too damned awful!"

Then she flung herself down on a divan and cried her heart out, clinging to Tor Bonnier's arm, but after a few minutes she pulled herself together and, sobbing, she said:

"I don't want to see that man ever again! He's stupid and wicked! He's stupid and wicked!"

Tor Bonnier, for the life of him, had no idea what to do: not that he wanted to question what she said, but the part about "Ragnar" presented an undeniable complication. He sensed that she was not an entirely compliant woman with whom to be sharing a wedding trip.

Under these circumstances.

"But you're on your wedding trip . . . and you're going to Italy . . . and what does Ragnar have to do with . . . I thought you and Sven were happy . . ."

"He's stupid and wicked!"

"But you can't really mean that . . . and Uncle Ernest tells me that you're with child . . ."

Then she stopped crying, dried her tears, and suddenly began talking in a low, intense voice.

"I think he's an evil man. I think he is. He says the most awful things about himself, as if he were boasting about them, or as if to make himself seem unusual. I think he's boasting, but you can never be sure. That's the worst part. He's a damned child, but he wants to be viewed as shocking! It seems he was just planning to use me for . . . well, in the best case I'll turn out to be a new poetry collection. But the most terrible . . ."

She fell silent. He waited a long time, and at last it came.

"He says that one of his old lovers has put a curse on our child."

"But . . . you can't possibly think . . ."

"On my, my!!! child. My my my my child! That damned wretch of a poet doesn't possess even one fingernail's share of my child! It's all mine! Mine through and through! I'm going to give birth like the Virgin Mary and . . . ohhhhh!"

She started screaming, and then the door opened and a porter came in with a bottle of champagne that Tor, in desperation, had ordered. The porter stared with horror at the shrieking woman with the tear-stained face, and when Carin caught sight of him, she snapped, although in Swedish:

"Stop staring, you damned German toad. Haven't you ever seen a poor defenseless girl before!!!"

"Well, defenseless . . ." Tor ventured. "You shouldn't swear so much, Carin, you should . . ."

"Should! Should should should! There's nothing at all that I should!!!"

"Think of your father! Imagine how unhappy he would be to see you now!"

Then she blew her nose, threw the napkin in the wastepaper basket, gave the porter a furious glare that made him slink away, and said, suddenly very composed and proper:

"Yes. We must continue on our wedding trip to Italy, where Goethe apparently said that the lemons bloom. Or glow. What was it he said, Tor? What do you think? Shall I glow or bloom?"

He smiled in the midst of all that misery, relieved that she now seemed to have recovered, more or less.

"You shall glow like the flower you've always been, Carin. But God save Herr Lidman."

"He doesn't believe in God."

"Then maybe he'd better start believing."

Sven couldn't figure out when the degradation started, what was the actual gateway to the hell he now found himself in, how he had entered, whether he had done it himself or had been driven through.

Everything was so dazzling and so terrible. He was envied. And he knew that people despised him.

He tried to imagine how he, at an early stage, might have gone on his way, said no! gotten to his feet and left. But he had slipped inside, been carried along. He thought about how, with his eyes completely clear, he had observed how his image of this dazzling world of admiration and intellectual phrases and receptions and money had gradually changed. The way that colors in a photograph imperceptibly fade, until only black remains, but no colors.

No life, just inner death.

And then the self-loathing. And being dependent. And the regular monthly stud fee.

And a woman who was as beautiful as a painting, but who now looked at him with her incredibly enticing, ice-cold wolf eyes, which no longer screamed and struggled but were silent. And sometimes, and this was the worst, she would smile at him, as if she were about to utter the decisive words: perhaps that he was no good, that he was nothing, that he was an onion, that he lacked substance, that everyone was laughing at him. That he ought to hold his tongue.

That he was an onion. And that was the worst.

At last they succeeded in tearing themselves away from awful Berlin to the equally awful Italy. Now they were sitting on the terrace at San Cataldo.

She gazed out at the sea.

Sven sat five meters away from her, pen in hand, the paper blank.

"Was this what it was supposed to be like?" he heard her ask.

He didn't reply.

He imagined an image of himself as frozen in a block of ice, like a million-year-old animal, dimly visible inside the clear ice. What kind of ray of fire would be able to free him?

He sketched this image on the paper. It was pitiful.

It would be incomprehensible to everyone, of no use. He then tried another image: a little spider imprisoned in amber. A black, insignificant little spider with thin legs. Imprisoned a million years, forever, in a piece of amber jewelry.

There it was. There they both were. Sven and Carin. There he had also captured her image. Petrified resin, great beauty, lethal imprisonment. He sat still. He did not touch his pen. No, not a spider, that was too hideous. But a little fly, imprisoned in shimmering amber.

It was unbearable.

4.

Sven didn't remember much of the period up until Crown Princess Louisa's Hospital, the maternity ward, but "suddenly," that's how it felt, he found himself in the corridor and was very confused. A doctor walked past him, then stopped and nervously said: "Herr Lidman, the child is in the wrong position and we're going to have to cut it up."

"Cut it up!?"

"That's right. That's right."

"But ... cut up ..."

"Yes, yes. We're doing our utmost, and Bank President Thiel is entitled, of course, to all the resources we can . . ."

"I'm not Bank President Thiel!!!"

"Of course . . . of course . . . but if we're going to save the mother's life, the child will have to be cut up and removed, and President Thiel said that we must at all costs save the mother's life, and . . ."

"What does President Thiel have to do with this???"

"Everything is going to be just fine. We have all the medical resources . . ."

"Of course. Of course."

Then the gurney was rolled past, and he stood there, as if petrified, or like a sheep, or paralyzed with fear, or shame, or something else that he didn't dare formulate, and Carin was still conscious and, dissolved in fear, she had screamed at him:

"Sven? Sven! What are they going to do to me?"

"There's no danger, Carin, my love," he told her. "There's no danger, they have all the medical instruments to . . ."

Then he couldn't think of any more words. To cut up?

"Instruments," she screamed. "Do they need instruments???"

"No, no, but Carin . . ."

"I'm scared! I'm scared!!!"

She screamed uncontrollably. Sven sat down on a chair in the corridor. The door closed behind her. He stared after her, as if he had seen his own past, or future, or merely the hell that was this very moment.

Late in the evening two days later, the hospital room was filled with flowers. Pappa had come to visit, and Sven had also come to visit, and was back again.

She was lying in bed, and he was sitting at the window and looking out at the darkness and thinking about nothing. Or everything all at once. And strangely enough it turned into nothing if you put it all together.

She was awake.

"What are you thinking about?" she asked.

"Nothing," he said without turning around.

"Oh yes. You know what you're thinking about. And I know. The curse."

Silence.

"That's just superstition," he said. "Madness. We have to keep the madness out of our life. Superstition."

"I can't," she said.

"Superstition. We're modern people, after all. We live in a modern age."

"Do we?" she whispered. "Do we?"

CHAPTER 9

The Children of Abraham

1.

LEWI OUGHT TO HAVE A WIFE, THAT WAS THE BROTHERS' OPINION, BUT he hadn't responded to them. Later he married; her name was Lydia, and she was Norwegian.

As for Lydia, she came from the same family as the composer Edvard Grieg. She was related to him, quite a close relation, though exactly how close no one knew, but all her life she refused to talk about it, refused to discuss his name. All her life she forbade any mention of him.

Many people were surprised by this, since he was, after all, a world-famous composer, and many people would have felt honored to be related to him. Yet Lydia forbade all talk of Grieg. The reason was that he had lived an immoral life.

That was her view. She was a fervent believer. Her mother was one of Norway's first feminists, politically active, and a Baptist.

They were married in 1913. That year the women of Norway won the right to vote. It would take eight more years before Sweden followed suit, and eighty years before women had the right to be congregation elders, deacons, or general overseers within the Pentecostal movement.

Lydia was, and on this point Efraim harbored no doubts, a splendid woman. That was his view.

Lewi had met his future wife Lydia in Norway. During those first years he didn't see her very often. They only spoke to each other a few times, but they got along well. Lewi knew her brother Georg quite well; they were close friends.

Later this would provoke a conflict between him and Lydia.

Apparently the young man named Lewi made an impression with his unruly lock of hair hanging over his forehead; it was always combed so that it seemed both unruly and controlled. Perhaps the same was true of his inner character, she sometimes thought. Or hoped.

Apparently Lydia became quite attached to him.

Perhaps "unruly" was the wrong word. Better would be "fiery" or "strong-willed" in a controlled sort of way. In any case, Lewi was easy to like, but shy, and extremely God-fearing. She herself came from a very fine Baptist family, and they gradually grew quite attached to each other. Lewi often emphasized that her family was a fine one, and Baptists. Then Lewi returned to Sweden, and they corresponded.

That was when the episode with the preacher in Bengtsfors took place.

It so happened—the descriptions of what occurred Lewi later gave a much different character in his sermons and memoir—that while visiting Bengtsfors, Lewi met a preacher from the Baptist movement.

This preacher—not mentioned by name—opened his heart to Lewi during the few days that they spent together, and he talked not only about the art of preaching (he was a great evangelist) but also about his atrocious marriage. "I never would have imagined that an evangelical preacher could get himself tangled up in such intolerable circumstances."

At a young age he had become a believer and started seeing a young girl and promised to marry her. She loved him dearly. She helped him financially while he was studying; then he moved to a big city, broke off the relationship. "The country girl probably seemed to him much too simple." He then began a relationship with a "big-city girl" and married her.

The marriage turned out to be hell. The big-city girl was not at all of a simple nature. Now, during their three-day conversation, he gave Lewi a good deal of sincere advice.

"Brother Pethrus," he said. "Don't ever get married. If you want to be successful in your mission as an evangelist for Jesus, then dedicate yourself to that and don't split yourself up. But if you ever do get married, don't marry for what is commonly called 'love.'

What people generally call by that beautiful name are feelings that come from various sources inside us. Sensuality and sexuality are often important ingredients in the warm and sometimes heated emotions that bring people together in marriage. A marriage can only be happy if you follow your reason. You have to take care and do what you think is wisest. If you base your marriage on a sensible and intelligent choice, then love will later have a good basis to build on."

So much for the anonymous benefactor.

His influential advice reappears in many sections of the memoirs. The conversation seems to have oscillated between two poles: the atrocious marriage, and the idea that love should not be mixed with the passion of the body. And Lewi goes on: "After that lesson, which I received from my friend, I wrote very serious letters to Lydia, and told her it was highly unlikely that I would ever marry. The specific reason I gave was the poverty that I felt would be my lot as a Swedish Baptist preacher."

There is no doubt that the economic argument was a pretext. He was genuinely terrified, or bewitched.

Yet eleven years after he first met Lydia, and six years after the meeting with the unhappy preacher in Bengtsfors, he changed his mind. He had become the general overseer of the Filadelfia congregation in Stockholm. Then, inspired by God, he had the impulse to renew his correspondence with Lydia.

At that time she was in America.

He wrote a letter, they renewed their contact, and they were married in April 1913. The episode with the preacher was thus closed. Much later Lewi wrote about the "harsh lesson" he was given by this chance acquaintance, who made such a strong impression on him and who almost seemed to have bewitched him, who in any case imprinted the lack of importance of physical love in the search for a life partner. This man who had promoted "reason," who had once rejected the love of his youth, who was now living in a hell, and who in such a distressing fashion depicted the desperate situation that was created if a man gave in to the birds of prey of his senses.

About this older colleague, with whom Lewi had spent such a brief but intense time, and who made such an indelible impression on him, about this man he writes: "Even though these predictions and apprehensions were not realized in every aspect, the stern advice of this wise and gifted preacher did do some good, because I developed a much greater respect for the matter of the preacher's position on marriage."

The latter passage, in its entirety, including the words "were not realized in every aspect," was deleted from later editions of Lewi's memoirs.

Perhaps they were merely rash remarks.

In the *Lebenslauf* no response. What conclusions did Efraim draw about Lewi's views on love and marriage?

None.

The marriage of Lewi and Lydia was exceptionally happy; that was the common opinion within the Pentecostal movement. From the very first moment. And it was confirmed by Lewi's own clear statements. It was blessed by God.

How did Lydia react when Lewi, after so many years of silence, proposed by letter? It was a rupture, and a silence, that was motivated by the impoverished circumstances under which a Baptist preacher could be expected to live. So! Not influenced by the awful preacher from Bengtsfors! No! Not at all! The friendship that Lewi had with her brother Georg, and with the awful preacher from Bengtsfors who had such an extraordinary power over Lewi, it was of the utmost priority in nature!

How did she react to this?

Efraim didn't know for sure. But one of Lydia's friends, Ida Knutsen, who had worked with her in the home of an American family, recounted to Efraim that on the day the letter arrived, Lydia was not at all herself. When she served breakfast, she burned one piece of toast after the other.

Later she explained the reason to her friend.

Was that all?

Yes, that was all.

After their marriage, which took place in April 1913 at Lydia's home congregation in Kragerø, and which Efraim attended as a witness, and the congregation surrounded them with their prayers of intercession, they all joined in to sing a song that Lewi had written two years before. It was printed in the first issue of *The Bridegroom's Voice*, in February 1911.

Lewi, twenty-six years old, had written both the lyrics and the music, in the classic Moravian tradition of wounds and blood.

The words were as follows:

A wondrous, wondrous refuge have I,
there safe from all dangers I dwell,
There cleansing I found, there peace have I
In the wounds of Jesus, my Savior.

A wondrous, wondrous refuge have I.
There I abide in days of storm,
Salvation's joys our tears will dry.
I found sanctuary in the Savior's wounds.

If your door is locked by human fear
And your heart now pounds with terror,
See, the One on the Cross stands with you here,
Take solace in your Savior's wounds.

The searing wounds your heart now holds,
Healing for them you shall find,
But the Lamb whom the heavenly host enfolds
Bears wounds eternal and deep.

When at last by life's crystal clear flood
My harp I will joyfully play,
My eternal song will be of the blood
That flowed from my Savior's wounds.

A wondrous, wondrous refuge have I.
There I abide in days of storm,
Salvation's joys our tears will dry.
I found sanctuary in the Savior's wounds.

* * *

It was a happy marriage.

But perhaps there is a contradiction built into the message that the preacher in Bengtsfors delivered, and in the songs that Lewi wrote. Because he was not only an ideologue, but also a song-writer.

Or became one.

Eventually everyone would witness the loving peace and warmth in Christ's name that blessed the marriage of Lydia and Lewi and their many children. But it was doubled-sided. The disquieting shadow of the man from Bengtsfors did not color the poems Lewi wrote, but it did affect the norms he preached. In the end he became the national standard for so many people regarding the question of love; for all those hundreds of thousands of birds in God's great tree of love.

What Lewi preached became the norm. But how did Lewi create this norm, which became the standard for so many, also for all those drops in the sea of women, perhaps even indirectly for my mother? How did Lewi create this norm? He, who for so many years had worked with the poor wretches in Stockholm's slums where the concept of a nuclear family did not exist. And where no core could be found. Merely single mothers and runaway fathers and children who died and women who gave up. Lewi, the gatherer of the shattered cores in the working class of the new industrialism where everything was in flux, and hope did not exist. And right next to this, the preacher from Bengtsfors, like an icy tone beneath the warm song of the sisters and brothers. The tone that took over the message of love and formulated the law.

And at the same time: Lewi the hymn writer who couldn't totally comply, but wrote in silent protest.

The hymns, the song, the wounds and the blood: that's where the other tone could be found in the Pentecostal movement's great love poem. Way up on the surface was the law, the chill from Bengtsfors: it spoke in the voice of the preacher with the horrible marriage, the nameless friend who "was a great evangelist," but of dubious character, the man who spoke of duty and withdrawal, and said that sensual love between a man and a woman should not exist.

And the person who had bewitched the young man with the unruly lock of hair.

Yet underneath this armor of ice there was inside Lewi the other tone: warm and forbidden, about resting in the Savior's wound, in the blood, the blood.

And the bridegroom who came toward you, with open arms.

It was as if Lewi were still hesitating between ice and heat, between organization and art. And it was only in the hymns and the music that the latter was allowed to exist.

But sensuality was not something to be talked about. Only sung. Yet it was there that the Pentecostal movement would live, in song, in sensuality and the warm blood. That was where the Pentecostal movement would shatter the stiff rituals and entice millions with emotions that were undernourished within Christianity all around the world; that's where the enticement lay, not in the ice-cold preacher from Bengtsfors.

But who was that man?

How did the six years during which love was absent, from the farewell letter to the courting, affect Lewi and Lydia?

There is no testimony about that.

Although sensuality could never be eradicated, not even by the terrible preacher from Bengtsfors and his magic powers.

It existed in the hymns, after all. That's where it was possible to hide, as in the wounds of Jesus. But how hard it was to make ice and blood live together! And how forbidden and harmful was the hymn singing about sensual love! Yet they were not allowed to speak of it! Merely sing!

But they could neither talk nor sing about Lewi's ingenuous and puzzling admiration for his friend from Bengtsfors: almost a different kind of love, the most forbidden of all, the kind that Sven had fallen for during his military service. But not even this was ever clear, no! Away with it!

He had written a letter to Lydia in which he renounced love forever. Later he changed his mind.

Sven was in dread of the inner death, and he dreamed of devotion. In his own way, Lewi did the same.

The ice-cold death, and then the other: the warm blood, the other tone, secretive and of the flesh and sensual.

It didn't make sense. Nothing made any sense yet for Sven or Lewi. Not for Sven in the café in Stockholm, on his way into the inner death. Not for Lewi, who was struggling with love, and his preacher role, and perhaps with sexuality too.

2.

The marriage of Lewi and Lydia was a thoroughly happy one.

A model for all Swedish Pentecostals, almost a political model for the nuclear family; but that came later, much later, when politics entered the picture. Although things threatened to go wrong, as Efraim pointed out. Very wrong. That was back when Lewi wrote his most famous poem: "The Promises." The one about "Heaven and earth may burn." Back then Efraim was there.

It was ghastly.

On November 8 Lewi and Lydia went for a long walk in the woods; an early snow had fallen. Lydia was very quiet, but then, in the middle of the woods, she stopped, turned to Lewi, and said in a low voice:

"I'm going to have a child, Lewi."

It was so quiet. Not a soul. A very early winter, vapor coming out of their mouths, a light snow cover. Just the two of them. Then they both fell to their knees, in the snow, and thanked God.

That's how they must be imagined. Dark little figures on their knees, in God's infinitely vast and good wilderness.

Barely a month later, in December 1913, she fell ill. Lewi was in Göteborg preaching, and Lydia was alone. He was in demand by many congregations; he was regarded as a great evangelist.

She woke toward morning, drenched in sweat. She drank a glass of water, and then another. She groaned and prayed to God, but she was sure that it was only influenza. But it was her stomach. Around six o'clock she took her temperature, and it was almost 104° F. Later that morning she sent word for Efraim, saying that she didn't want to worry Lewi, who was in Göteborg preaching; she would just drink more water, but she didn't have the strength to get out of bed to change the sheets.

Efraim wanted to call the doctor, but Lydia said no.

In the afternoon Efraim came back to see her and promised not to worry Lewi, but he did call him. By the time Efraim returned from the telephone exchange, she was practically hallucinating, and at eight o'clock the next morning a doctor came to see her.

It was Efraim who summoned the doctor. He didn't ask whether she thought it was necessary.

The doctor was a very young woman who looked worried. In the evening she came back, and then she said that the fetus was dead and that Lydia showed symptoms of cadaverous poisoning and the only way to save her life was through surgical intervention.

Efraim asked whether he should tell Lewi to come home, but Lydia urged him not to bother Lewi. In the morning a telegram arrived from Lewi, asking whether he ought to come home, and whether her life was in danger. Lydia sent word, through Efraim, that he should continue with the planned series of meetings.

Efraim was extremely anxious and, for the life of him, didn't know what he should do.

So what did he advise?

By telegram he advised Lewi to return home at once, but explained Lydia's viewpoint. Lewi completed the entire series of meetings, but then promptly came home.

How long was the period between the time she fell ill and Lewi's return home?

He doesn't mention this.

A couple of days? No one knows.

Lydia's condition had grown worse.

In the *Lebenslauf* there is a digression. Efraim feels a certain anxiety. He wants to defend his best friend.

In his opinion, Lewi often felt insecure, because "they" regarded him as an organizer and not a visionary. He never used the word "visionary" in conversation with anyone except Efraim. In a vague way he felt that "they"—meaning the brothers and sisters of the congregation—respected him because he could solve all the problems: in that area he was the master within the congregation. But he worried that deep inside they mistrusted him because he lacked fire, and the utmost faith.

The expression "the utmost faith" signified something that existed beyond reason.

Beyond reason was God. Spirit baptism and speaking in tongues signified reaching beyond the utmost boundary, where God was. Some people claimed to have reached that place. Others had reached God but had not, in that way, come through. There were many unclear points. It was impossible to know these things for sure.

Lewi did not know these things for sure.

And this had made him sad. Beyond the utmost boundary there seemed to exist an experience that he had been denied. That was a place reached only by artists and God's fools and those who spoke in tongues. He was no artist. Artists were people like Birger Sjöberg, who created poems but who could get into trouble and end up boozing or be deserted by God. Yet they were still in some sense chosen. God's fools were also chosen by God, in a way that was almost unpleasant.

Those who spoke in tongues! There was reason to be wary. Among them there were impostors, in truth. It was difficult to distinguish between God's fools and the impostors. If he followed his clear reason, which was not something he always did but instead controlled himself, he could have dismissed them all as babblers and impostors.

That was why he in some sense had enjoyed the conversation with Professor Gadelius. They had met to do battle, but in a rational way, He thought that he had also managed to play the role of professor in that battle.

But with the measure of reason that he undeniably possessed, what happened to the unreason of faith? Then nothing remained but the state church, career pastors, and spiritual death.

Yet he felt anxious. When the speaking in tongues broke out during the meetings, he often felt an almost insane desire to throw out the people who were babbling. He had no better word for it. Babbling. One time he focused on a man who began babbling over and over again. Lewi instinctively disliked him. He then interrupted him and told him to keep still. The brother responded indignantly that God's voice was speaking through him. From the pulpit, Lewi, in turn, replied curtly that God's voice was also speaking through him, Lewi, and that God's voice, through Lewi, was now insisting that he finish what he was saying so the other voice of God could be allowed to speak.

No one laughed. Instead, a ruckus ensued, and the man who spoke in tongues was thrown out. In this way Lewi had won even greater respect from the congregation. Later it also turned out that the babbler was a bad character. He was mixed up in crime and drunkenness.

Yet Lewi grieved over his reason. To Efraim he confided that the "gray reason" that seemed to characterize him might make him unsuited to be an evangelist.

He rested like a gray rock among the ecstatic children of faith.

That's why he sought guidance.

Lewi bought a copy of *Fear and Trembling* by the Danish writer Søren Kierkegaard, and in this book he read about a faith that was incomprehensible and paradoxical. It was willing to give complete obedience to God, willing to renounce even what was the most precious: in that case an only child. The only hope that existed. A faith that was prepared to set aside all considerations except obedience to God.

The book was very difficult. It was about Abraham.

God had commanded Abraham to sacrifice his first-born son Isaac, to prove his faith. In his readings of the Bible, Lewi had often paused at this chapter. What the Danish author Kierkegaard wrote about it was excellent, but difficult. Imagine sacrificing your own child! Killing your own child with a knife! Just to prove your obedience. The Danish author, Kierkegaard, had extensively analyzed this case of extreme obedience. The book was quite difficult. Lewi had bought the Danish edition.

God's fools, visionaries, and artists might possess this utmost faith. He himself felt much too insignificant.

But Abraham had raised the knife. If a person raised the knife and was willing to bury it in his own beloved child, he had crossed a boundary. Beyond that boundary was God.

He came home from Göteborg at eleven o'clock at night and knew at once that things were bad.

She was breathing heavily, lying there with her eyes closed, and sweating. At first she didn't recognize him, then she began to murmur, as if in a dream, that he shouldn't worry, and that she couldn't go to the afternoon meeting and that he should ask the brothers and sisters to forgive her for this. He asked whether he should send for a doctor or other help. She didn't understand the question but replied that the coffee for after the meeting was in the sink. He asked her, "Why in the sink?" She said that's where she had dropped the coffee sack.

He went into the kitchen.

There was no coffee sack in the sink. Nor were there any coffee bags made of jute, the kind that contained half a kilo and were usually used to boil coffee in the big pots of water for the congregation's coffee, which was very weak. When he came back, she had fallen into an uneasy sleep. He knelt down and began to pray.

He prayed loudly and fervently, but had a hard time concentrating. Lydia was muttering softly, and there was something about that confused mumbling that frightened him. It was almost like speaking in tongues. But this speaking in tongues he couldn't interpret, and he was certain that it did not come from God. And he didn't understand a thing.

"Lydia," he said. "What are you saying? Are you in pain?"

"Yes," she said after a moment of silence. "Forgive me, dear Lewi, I'm in such pain. But just think if the child has died inside me, like the doctor said. What should we do, Lewi? Can we trust the doctor?"

"We can trust only in God," he said then, almost out of habit.

"What should we do, Lewi?" she muttered over and over again.

Then he sat down on the edge of the bed and took her hands and looked into her face, shiny with sweat, and suddenly he realized that the hour was at hand. That this was a moment like the one with the boy named Enar, who had longed for Spirit baptism, and who had received grace through his hands.

Yes, this was the moment, Abraham's moment.

And he pulled up the damp sheet that had slid down from her breast and placed his hand on her forehead. That was the right thing to do. His hand on her forehead. Like the time when the boy received the power through his hands.

"Lydia, my dear wife, sometimes God tests us. Sometimes He has tested me. And I have not passed the test. And I have been struck with doubts about my calling. Whether I'm suited to be a preacher. But doubt is not sent by God. God demands unconditional faith. Then He tests us. That's what happened to Abraham, who was subjected to the most difficult test of all. But he passed it. We must put all our trust in God, and then He will grant us help."

"I'm in pain," she murmured. "Dear Lewi, what do you want me to do?"

"We must believe and trust in Him. Only He can save you. And me. Do you agree with me, dearest Lydia?"

Then she nodded vigorously, but since he wasn't certain that she completely understood, he asked her again.

"That only He can save you?"

"I trust in Him, Lewi. What should I do?"

He took a deep breath. He felt as if he were standing before a great precipice, like the one at Hunneberg near the orphanage, the steep slope at Mal-Ola's grotto, where he hadn't dared to climb, unlike his friends, and he knew he would feel the same fear before this daring act. But it was now inescapable.

"Lydia, we must not trust in the worldly power. You were right, Lydia."

"Was I right?" she murmured uncertainly. "What was I right about?"

"That God is the one who can save you. And not the doctor. You are strong and your faith is strong."

"Oh yes, Lewi."

"Will you, Lydia?"

"Oh yes . . . will I what, Lewi?"

"Trust only in the power of God?"

"Oh yes, Lewi."

"Do you wish it with all your might? To trust that God alone will deliver and help you?"

He felt strangely agitated, he was having a hard time breathing, the conversation flowed between them in an oddly breathless way, he was holding her hands in his, and he knew that the precipice existed but that he was supposed to leap, that he was not a stone but a flame, not a gray stone, there was a light all around her, he was almost certain of it, and he was supposed to take the risk.

"And then," he whispered, with his eyes shut tight since the light would surely be so strong soon that it would be blinding, "then, dearest Lydia, we will be joined in a new, a new love. A miracle will take place in God, a miracle between us, it will be . . . the miracle . . ."

"Oh yes, Lewi," she whispered. "Oh Lewi, I'm in such pain, but I'm so happy."

"Praise be to God," he whispered, closing his eyes tight. "God's power alone, not medical science."

"Oh, Lewi, I believe . . . a miracle . . ."

"... and the person who believes ... will find ..."

"Yes, Lewi ... but I'm so afraid of dying, Lewi ... is my faith too weak, Lewi?"

"The promises, Lydia. The promises, they still exist."

Around eight o'clock that night she fell asleep, or into a torpor.

He made up his mind. God would save her. It was decided. And it would be a sign. If He existed, and if He could do everything, and if Lewi was His instrument, then Lydia would be saved, and everything would be new.

And, he thought to himself again and again, she had insisted. I put the decision in her hands. It would mean so much if they could persevere. Also for him. To witness a divine intervention. Would God really crush this happiness that they had been waiting so many years for?

They had been waiting six years, six years. And now. The decision.

And later he wrote about it, in several different versions; he touched on the event cautiously, as if it were a painful topic, and occasionally almost with candor, *I could feel that there was something I loved even more than my wife and my happy family life and the future we had hoped for together: my faith in God and the work He had entrusted in me was something I regarded as even greater*, yes, everything on earth seemed small and insignificant compared to retaining faith in God, yes, it was almost with candor, and he was now very close to the book of the Danish writer Kierkegaard and understood, but ultimately it was in some sense Lydia's decision, that's what he quite clearly wrote, *I explained to her what grave danger her life was in, from a human perspective, and told her once again that she had to decide what we should do, she had her answer ready at once and said that the only way was to trust in the Lord.*

And retaining his faith in God suddenly became very important, and he made up his mind, and the sign would come from God alone.

When her condition grew worse, Lewi summoned Efraim.

Restlessly they paced back and forth in the kitchen, and Efraim may not have been much help, because he was furious.

Lewi spent most of the time on his knees with his eyes closed, praying with his hands tightly clasped. That's when, as Efraim writes, he "cursed" for the first time during their long friendship.

"Open your eyes," he said furiously. "Look me in the eye, Lewi, damn it!"

"Don't swear!" The response was almost automatic, without conviction, and in any case it made no impression on Brother Efraim, not that time, which was the first, and perhaps the last. No, Efraim was not of a mind to listen.

"I'll do as I like, Brother Lewi!!! And let me tell you! You're crazy! You have to take her to the hospital right now! She's sick. God created medical science! In truth! He did! And even if your faith is strong . . . Lewi! Lewi, in God's name, do you hear what I'm saying? Are you listening?"

"She said that she puts her trust in God," Lewi replied. "And she will abide in that trust."

"But you have to take pity on Lydia; she's sick and delirious." Efraim had "laid out the situation in the strongest terms" to Lewi, and then his dialect came through so clearly that he was almost ashamed, but Lewi seemed beyond reach. First he fell to his knees, then got up and walked around the kitchen table with his hands clasped, *and we knelt down together and enjoined our entreaty to God and we felt a wondrous abiding in Him*, no, that's not how it was, Efraim said, no, there was not wondrous abiding in God, only an agitated conversation interrupted by prayers, because Efraim was praying too, what more could he do? But Lewi was like iron. "If God wishes, He will perform a miracle," he said. "God has given me a promise, and His promises are firm and unshakable!" And in that way the night passed.

At last they were both sitting on chairs, silent and exhausted. At regular intervals they would go in to see to Lydia. She was breathing heavily, and her fever was rising.

It was the child. It was clear that if the child had died, there would be cadaverous poisoning.

Unless God had decided on something else.

"Are you sure this is right, Lewi?"

They were no longer screaming at each other.

"Do you have doubts?" asked Lewi. "If you have doubts, you have to leave, because your doubts are keeping out God's power."

"So if she dies, it's my fault!" said Efraim, and then he got to his feet and was completely beside himself, and Lord have mercy if he wasn't about to lay hands on Lewi. That was the first time; it would happen once again, thirty-four years later. But then Lewi realized his mistake and understood everything and stretched out his hand in apology, and he looked so miserable and pitiful that Efraim was filled with despair, and then the night continued on.

Toward morning they were asleep on the kitchen floor. When they awoke, there was no change.

Lydia was still alive, but unconscious. Lewi made a cup of coffee and then once again knelt down to pray.

There was nothing Efraim could do.

"You'll never change your mind," he said as he stood in the doorway, about to leave.

Lewi did not reply. But Efraim could see terror shining in his face, yes, it was terror, but he did not change his mind, because it was Abraham's moment and there was something that was greater than human beings and life; yes, everything on earth seemed small and insignificant compared with holding on to his faith in God.

Efraim carefully closed the door behind him, and the murmur of Lewi's prayers was cut off, "like the thread of life," he suddenly thought, so easily and so quickly. And what does that mean, other than that the sacred life ceases, or is brought to a close. And isn't the sacred simply what the one who is sacred does?

It was on the third day that Efraim said it.

"You're carrying out an experiment with her, Brother Lewi."

"God will save her," Lewi repeated, almost mechanically, as if he hadn't heard the unprecedented accusation.

"You're experimenting!"

"I'm trusting in God!"

"You don't really want . . ."

And then Lewi turned to face Efraim, as if he had suddenly heard and understood, and as if he were seized with tremendous anger, and he took Efraim by the arm and pushed him down onto the bench, and he did this with a contorted expression that Efraim had never seen before. And he screamed into his face:

"Brother Efraim! What do I really want? What don't I really want? Don't want!!! For her to live? Do you think I want her to die, Brother Efraim?"

But Efraim could not reply.

* * *

They had said too much.

Both of them knew that.

They calmed down, drank some water from the water bucket. Now they were both completely composed but couldn't bring themselves to look each other in the eye. And this was on the third day. Then they went in to see to Lydia.

She was sleeping calmly. She was breathing calmly. And it was at that moment that Efraim Markström, Lewi's best friend, who shortly before had almost raised his hand against him, it was then he realized that Lydia was going to survive.

By evening, no fever.

The next morning the fetus was expelled. It was a boy. A midwife was summoned. God existed, His mercy was great, He alone possessed the power and the salvation, the midwife took away the fetus.

"Forgive me, Lewi," said Efraim.

"What is there to forgive?"

"Forgive me."

And after a moment he added:

"You're so strong, Lewi. You're so unbelievably, terrifyingly strong."

"God is strong," Lewi replied.

"But sometimes," Efraim added, "I'm afraid of you."

"Afraid?"

"Yes. I'm afraid."

Then they said goodbye to each other. They embraced in Christ's name, they looked at each other with tears in their eyes; the moment had passed, the fear as well, but the memory would always remain with Efraim, as if those days and nights spent with the dying Lydia, who didn't die but would have a long life in Christ, were a tiny grain of sand that could not be removed, a very tiny pain, or insight, and nothing would ever, ever be the same.

When Efraim had gone, Lewi sat down at the organ. And then he composed the hymn that would be the most sung of all his hymns, and the most famous, perhaps the most beautiful hymn that a Swedish composer has ever created; and it was in the kitchen, since that's where the organ stood. In the next room Lydia was now sleeping, without fever, without fetus, without terror, and perhaps without ever knowing why she was so close to death or why she was saved, or by whom.

And he wrote the hymn that would make him famous:

The promises can never fail.
No, they are with us forever.
Jesus, with his blood, has sealed
All he has promised to us.

Heaven and earth may burn,
Heights and mountains vanish,
But whoever believes will find
That the promises are forever.

Do you as Abraham did,
Lift your eyes toward heaven!
As you count all the stars,
Your faith will grow, your hope.

Heaven and earth may burn,
Heights and mountains vanish,
But whoever believes will find
That the promises are forever.

He wrote calmly and quietly, picking out the melody on the organ with his left hand.

He wrote the first two verses and what would later be called the refrain, although that was almost a sinful word, but he wrote no more that night. Two years later, he would write four more stanzas, but on that night he managed only those verses, and that was enough.

It was the most beautiful hymn that a Swedish hymn writer ever composed, and it would always be sung with a strangely swaying rhythm, like a waltz. Yes, that hymn should be sung like a slow waltz, like oars stroking through the waves; no, that's not the right image, or perhaps, yes, like oars stroking and waves and a deep, swaying rhythm of faith and loyalty and hope.

* * *

But there was that line: "Do you as Abraham did."

Did anyone ever listen to that line? Or was everyone simply carried along by the song's great hopeful wave? Or were they supposed to keep in mind the whole time the book of Genesis, chapter 22, with its strangely laconic dialogue between God and Abraham, and that story so full of complications that even Kierkegaard was forced to capitulate to the paradoxes of belief; and yet the account was actually so clear and simple: *"After these things God tested Abraham, and said to him, 'Abraham!' And he said, 'Here am I.' He said, 'Take your son, your only son Isaac, whom you love, and go to the land of Moriah, and offer him there as a burnt offering upon one of the mountains of which I shall tell you.' So Abraham rose early in the morning, saddled his ass, and took two of his young men with him, and his son Isaac; and he cut the wood for the burnt offering, and arose and went to the place of which God had told him. On the third day Abraham lifted up his eyes and saw the place afar off. Then Abraham said to his young men, 'Stay here with the ass; I and the lad will go yonder and worship, and come again to you'"*; and still no emotions, still no fear, and he convinces his servants that both he and his son will return, but that is not the truth! *"And Abraham took the wood of the burnt offering, and laid it on Isaac his son; and he took in his hand the fire and the knife. So they went both of them together. And Isaac said to his father Abraham, 'My father!' And he said, 'Here am I, my son.' He said, 'Behold, the fire and the wood; but where is the lamb for a burnt offering?' Abraham said, 'God will provide himself the lamb for a burnt offering, my son.' So they went both of them together."* But the child had started thinking; wasn't that right? Wasn't there fear in his question? *"When they came to the place of which God had told him, Abraham built an altar there, and laid the wood in order, and bound Isaac his son, and laid him on the altar, upon the wood. Then Abraham put forth his hand, and took the knife to slay his son. But the angel of the Lord called to him from heaven, and said, 'Abraham, Abraham!' And he said, 'Here am I.' He said, 'Do not lay your hand on the lad or do anything to him; for now I know that you fear God, seeing you have not withheld your son, your only son, from me.'"*

Do you as Abraham did, lift your eyes toward heaven! As you count all the stars, your faith will grow, your hope.

No, Abraham did not use the knife. But he was prepared. Just like Lewi. Yet it turned out to be such a wondrous hymn, and perhaps that's what was important, the great wave, the hopefulness, the rhythm that would later carry thousands upon thousands of faithful forward, and he wrote it on that night after God had held back Abraham's arm, or however he now viewed it.

Perhaps it didn't matter. That's probably how poems come about, and faith.

CHAPTER 10

A House of His Own

1.

LEWI WAS MARRIED ON APRIL 13, 1913. ON APRIL 21 AT A CON-gregational meeting, Lydia was accepted as a member of the Filadelfia congregation, a branch within the Baptist Union.

On April 29 of the same year, the Filadelfia congregation was expelled from the Baptist Union.

That was the birth of the Pentecostal movement. It had happened fast. Afterwards many people had a hard time understanding what happened. They were expelled over the issue of the Holy Communion—they all agreed on this description of the dispute. But it was difficult to tell whether this was a big issue or a small one, or no issue at all.

Yet the result was that the small Filadelfia congregation in Stockholm, under the leadership of the young pastor from Lidköping, now stood free, and isolated. Lewi had his own small house, very small, but it was his. This Lewi with his clear, matter-of-fact, and plain sermons, this brilliant advocate of the welfare system, this Lice King who was constantly brushing off the little crawling friends of the tattered proletariat, this odd little man with his steadily thinning lock of hair on his forehead, he now stood quite alone at the head of his little flock.

How did this actually happen? And was it really necessary? In the *Lebenslauf* the expulsion is described very briefly. Efraim mentions it, strangely enough, in a text that covers only one page and is placed long after the episode with Lydia's miscarriage and the birth of "The Promises Could Never Fail."

Even though it took place before. First the expulsion, then the miscarriage, then "The Promises." Was there a connection?

It's possible that Efraim overinterprets the background. But he writes that it was the great ecumenical tradition from the ever-present Moravian spirit that had sprung the Pentecostal movement loose from the Baptist movement. And no doubt that was true. At least for him.

And he was a witness, after all.

It was the issue about the closed or open Holy Communion.

Lewi had practiced open communion within the congregation: non-Baptists were also allowed to participate in the Lord's Holy Communion, and that was against the principles within the Baptist congregations. It led to an exchange of letters; the central leadership began expressing itself in an increasingly sharp tone and finally threatened to expel the Filadelfia congregation if communion was not henceforth reserved solely for associated Baptists.

The letters are filled with theology, Bible quotes, forceful references to God's love, concern for the brothers' faith, as well as outright threats. It was a dirty conflict, as is so often the case within Christian factions, in which the question of power was the central issue, only scantily concealed behind assurances of Christ's boundless love and concern for the eternal life of the brothers.

People were a little afraid of the young man from Lidköping.

He was a bit too strong. He didn't know his place.

There were often private conversations with Lewi. "One fine day you're going to grow tired of standing in that congregation where you are now, and you will want to be called by some other congregation. But of course no one is going to call for you." Or references to Lydia; that was the most extreme argument during the last weeks of the conflict. "You're getting married and going to have a family. Have you thought about the financial side of this issue for your family members?"

Lewi's repeated response was that he could always return to his job at the shoe factory. In addition, he felt that he had the unanimous support of his congregation.

And he did.

2.

The Filadelfia congregation was expelled at the special annual meeting of the Baptist district on April 29, 1913. It was held in Eberneser Church on Blecktornsgränd.

Lewi was the defendant. He was soft-spoken, full of Bible quotes, and hard as flint.

Around six in the evening the chairman asked for a vote on expulsion. "With a resounding 'yes' the recommendation of the committee and work group was passed, and the decision was proclaimed unanimous."

The chairman pounded his gavel on the table. The Filadelfia congregation was cast out into the cold. Legend has it that one observer from the Filadelfia congregation, the tailor Oscar Rydberg, then said loudly:

"He just punched a hole in the bottom of the Baptist Union!"

Not a bad prophecy.

Lewi and Lydia were both present.

Lewi spoke, defending open communion. He was unwavering. After the fall of the gavel they left the room. Lydia cried almost without stopping for the two days that the district congress lasted. She had lived her whole life as a Baptist; her family was there, her friends, her faith. Everything was there.

Now they had been expelled.

Efraim was waiting outside the meeting room, and Lewi said tersely that now they had been excluded. Lydia didn't say a word, merely wept in despair. But when they reached Hornsgatan, she pulled herself together, stopped, and said:

"Lewi, I still believe that God has a mission for you!"

He did not reply.

It's with a peculiar matter-of-fact chill that Efraim writes about this upsetting evening which prompted the start of the most successful Swedish revivalist movement ever, and the other revivalist movement's incipient decline, not its extinction, though it came close.

A hole truly did appear in the bottom of the Swedish Baptist movement that evening.

And something was started. Was it a major event, or a very minor one? History is full of minor events that become great ones. On April 29, 1913: the expulsion of Filadelfia, a very minor event. It happened several weeks after Ivar Kreuger was appointed head of the United Swedish Match Corporation, the start of another empire, and a few weeks before the Swedish Parliament voted to institute a universal state pension of between 45 and 195 kronor per year.

What was major and what was minor?

Efraim notes that Lewi was very calm, not despairing, but oddly focused. Perhaps Lewi had achieved something he wished for: not to be the one who rebelled, a dissident who withdrew his little congregation from the big warm community within Baptism. Instead he was someone who was expelled, cast out, a victim.

As Efraim writes, he now had his own house.

It was not a big house, really no more than a little hut with only one room. But it was his. And that's why he was now walking along Hornsgatan, calm and meditative, but with a perfectly clear and determined gaze, an outcast but not someone who was destroyed, with Lydia weeping at his side. And perhaps he knew that this was not the end but the beginning.

Lewi had won a house of his own.

3.

In the *Lebenslauf* from this period only one mention of Sven:

"The young man named A. G. Jansson who, thanks to his experiences with speaking in tongues on Azusa Street where he listened to the one-eyed black preacher William Seymour, ended up being the one who brought the ecstasy to Sweden. And in 1907 he was the foremost babbler in the entire Småland region. This young Jansson, who was said to have lived an ungodly life before his Spirit baptism and had perhaps been a criminal, was working in 1911 with Pastor Axel Hammar at a small shelter in Söder, but under the name of Andrew Ek. I don't know why he changed his name, but it may have had something to do with the fact that he had been mixed up in crime. A year later he disappeared, and no one knows what happened to him. Whenever I think about his unhappy fate, Sven L. often comes to mind; I don't know why."

The foremost babbler! But Efraim detested speaking in tongues.

And Sven L. came to mind. Had he observed a person with many faces?

Yet Sven was a poet. Did that sort of person possess special qualities, perhaps granted by the Lord?

Efraim recounts a conversation with Lewi from 1914, seven years before Sven wrote his two articles defending the Pentecostal movement in *Morgonbladet*. This was right after the outbreak of the war. The lines in front of the soup kitchens were suddenly swelling, and Lewi was worried. The social work began taking up more and more of his time, and one evening he said to Efraim:

"We need a poet in our ranks, someone who could . . . sum up the yearning of these people . . . present a poet's explanation for . . . all of this."

"Have you forgotten that you wanted to be a proletarian writer? It's not too late. You could do all that."

But Lewi merely said, in a loud and annoyed voice:

"I know my limitations! I know my limitations!"

It was almost an outburst of anger, and quite inexplicable. Efraim realized that the topic might be much too sensitive, and he said dismissively:

"The great poets might not be accessible to us, and in any case, they don't sit in filthy little cellar rooms on Uppsalagatan, handing out food coupons and preaching God's word. They're too refined for that."

He had consciously chosen his words, intending to sound spiteful and contemptuous. But strangely enough, Lewi was once again in good humor, and he laughed for a long time and said that was probably true. They would have to make do without the great poets, although it was a shame, but under any circumstances it was God's will, whatever happened.

And an hour later he exclaimed, seemingly unprovoked but as if he had been brooding over it the whole time:

"In the body of Christ, all parts are equal!"

Efraim received his explanation at the evening meeting, "when I realized what turn Lewi's thoughts had taken."

That evening Lewi spoke from I Corinthians, chapter 12, the chapter about the body and its parts, the passage that says:

"To one is given through the Spirit the utterance of wisdom, and to another the utterance of knowledge according to the same Spirit, to another faith by the same Spirit, to another gifts of healing by the one Spirit, to another the working of miracles, to another prophecy, to another the ability to distinguish between spirits, to another various kinds of tongues, to another the interpretation of tongues."

Efraim had heard this text many times, and it could no longer fill him with either surprise or emotion. It had somehow become worn out because, he writes, it was the text used most often, perhaps too often, since in this passage Paul was very clear regarding the justification for speaking in tongues. But then Lewi continued reading.

And, oddly enough, his voice began to quaver.

Lewi's voice did not normally quaver. So they suddenly understood that this was something special: this was something he wanted to say from his heart, and then came the verses 12-27:

"For just as the body is one and has many members, and all the members of the body, though many, are one body, so it is with Christ. For by one Spirit we were all baptized into one body—Jews or Greeks, slaves or free—and all were made to drink of one Spirit.

"For the body does not consist of one member but of many. If the foot should say, 'Because I am not a hand, I do not belong to the body,' that would not make it any less a part of the body. And if the ear should say, 'Because I am not an eye, I do not belong to the body,' that would not make it any less a part of the body. If the whole body were an eye, where would be the hearing? If the whole body were an ear, where would be the sense of smell? But as it is, God arranged the organs in the body, each one of them, as he chose. If all were a single organ, where would the body be? As it is there are many parts, yet one body. The eye cannot say to the hand, 'I have no need of you,' nor again the head to the feet, 'I have no need of you.' On the contrary, the parts of the body which seem to be weaker are indispensable, and those parts of the body which we think less honorable we invest with the greater honor, and our unpresentable parts are treated with greater modesty, which our more presentable parts do not require. But God has so adjusted the body, giving the greater honor to the inferior part, that there may be no discord in the body, but that the members may have the same care for one another. If one member suffers, all suffer together; if one member is honored, all rejoice together.

"Now you are the body of Christ and individually members of it."

* * *

That's what he read. And there they had the explanation, Efraim thought.

With people it was often the case that the explanation had to be sought far in the past. Perhaps in childhood. But about Lewi's childhood he is still silent. Perhaps it was the idea of becoming a proletarian writer that was never born. "It was like a wound."

But in the body of Christ all parts, even the most disdained, have their justification.

Efraim noticed that Lewi spoke with great conviction, almost emotion, and for a moment Efraim grew uneasy, asking himself whether Lewi might be sick. But then he realized that Lewi had been thinking about their conversation that afternoon. And in some way wanted to give Efraim, and himself, a response.

Or actually a kind of thumb verse, that dealt with the equality and great significance of all the parts in Christ's body.

"It was certainly a roundabout way to take," thought Efraim afterwards. But things that are sensitive and cause pain always take a roundabout way.

In truth. But even if the Lord was tarrying, which He was, Lewi and Sven would soon meet.

And we are all parts of the body of Christ: preachers and poets, sinners and fervent believers, the good and the evil, and those in between.

We all have our value in the body of Christ.

Lewi and Sven too.

In 1916 Lewi travels to Berlin.

This is in the midst of the raging war. Lewi has taken the initiative and is leading a conference "with a large group of Spirit-baptized preachers."

This is the Berlin Conference. Afterwards he compiles a text, *Guiding Principles of the Pentecostal Revivalism*, which he largely wrote himself and which goes on to serve as the guiding principles for the international development of the Pentecostal movement. He presents a report and also places the movement within a tradition. He incorporates the Pentecostal movement into a great, radical history of revivalism: Zinzendorf, Spener, Francke, Wesley.

That is the Berlin program for the rebirth of radical pietism.

It's 1916. Lewi is now thirty-two years old. To him absolutely nothing seems impossible. He has caught the spark from the one-eyed black man William Seymour, he has created the Pentecostal movement, he is its international leader, he is writing guidelines, he has arranged the Berlin Conference.

There is a war, God's spirit lives, everything is blessed, everything is fateful, he is still young.

The Most Wonderful Fellowship

1.

YOU MIGHT SAY THAT CARIN AND SVEN SURVIVED THEIR WEDDING trip. They returned, the way people can return to a marriage that is over, though they keep on going.

They had not forgotten everything, but they continued to live.

It's also possible to survive a fetus that has been cut up. But forget? Later they had a child that lived, and then they had two more.

The metaphysical curse may have stopped working.

Brief notes about an episode from another Christian's journey, which was Sven's; from Stora Tuna, which was where Sven and Carin now lived.

One Sunday the master and mistress of the house went to church in order to demonstrate how to appear in public so as to astound the farmers, and for that reason they had put on their finest, or rather Sven had, since he owned a frock coat.

Tor Bonnier looked the same as always. Carin was very beautiful, and Tor's wife could only wonder what she was doing in that Protestant country church.

Sven and Carin had acquired a country house, and a country church belonged to a country house.

They had also aroused attention. It was quite clear that the farmers had been astounded, they thought afterwards. Then they strolled home through the wooded landscape. And Carin had time to hold a long monologue for Tor, since they lingered behind the others.

"I suppose it was nice of Pappa to buy Tuna for us," she said, "but I hate it. I'm no farmer's wife and Sven is no Almqvist. Or if he is, then God help us. I really don't know who he is. He likes furs and expensive antiques and wants to live as comfortably as the devil, and Pappa pays for it all. And yet, if I wake up at night, I can find him sitting in the kitchen, looking out the window, with his face as pale as death. If I ask him what he's thinking, he just says, 'Nothing.' He looks like a ghost. And sometimes he says that we ought to die together. I just laugh, but I'm scared, Tor. At least *I* don't want to kill myself. I want to move back to town. I don't know, but I think he's afraid of something. And what's scaring him is himself. But Tor, dear friend, there's one thing I do know."

"Yes, Carin?"

"I'm still young. But he's not. I think he's already dead, and he knows it."

"Why did we have to go to church today?" Tor then asked.

"Sven just wanted to show how foolish pastors are. So we can laugh at them. He has an odd view of religion. He both despises and loves it. If he's capable of love."

And Tor said:

"Why don't you come to visit us in Dalarö?"

"Yes," she replied, "why am I living this kind of life? Can you understand it? And while he's nothing but a walking corpse. Why do I do it?"

A week later Carin surprisingly insisted on going out to Dalarö, saying that it would be so pleasant and that Tor was still his publisher, after all, and that he could read something because Tor had said he was so curious and excited to hear what Sven was working on.

"He's an unusual publisher, in that sense," she added. And Sven nodded and finally agreed to go.

And that's what they did. They sat next to the open fire at lunchtime, because in the evening many guests were expected, and Sven had insisted on having peace for his reading. So it was just the four of them, and he recited, from memory, as usual.

He spoke well. Everyone thought so.

See, I have aged, Lord, I am so weary,
Everything is different from before:
So many candles whose lights have dimmed,
Such dear steps echo behind death's door.

A shadow crossing your sun so much conceals
of the brightness that enchanted our sight,
the rejoicing of youth will never suit
the fierce blows we dealt to kill and fight.

Our hands are steeped in blood,
and blood has stained our steps,
our souls endured a shameful flood:
We have aged, Lord, on our toilsome path
and will never find our way.

Our happiness has been a stolen joy—
we bore the yoke of day and weight of night,
we have tried it all, we have gone astray
and still in youth we delight.

Silence.

Then Tor, as if bewildered, looked at Carin for a moment and said, in a voice that was genuinely appreciative, but with an undercurrent of amazement:

"Well, that was excellent, Sven. It was so elegant and pure. Can we expect a poetry collection soon?"

Sven did not reply. But Carin, who seemed annoyed by Tor's tone of genuine appreciation, quickly said, as if teasing:

"At home he says that he can't write anymore, and wasn't that an old poem? Isn't it included in *The Springs*?"

And after an embarrassing silence, Sven merely said, in an increasingly loud voice:

"Yes. So it is. So it is, so it is! So it is!! So it is!!! So . . ."

"Stop that now, dear Sven," said Carin. "This isn't a play."

2.

The testimony about what happened is cautiously phrased, but there seems to be agreement that Sven was off balance. Actually, everyone was off balance.

Things were often like that at Dalarö.

Sven was off balance in a highly peculiar way. Afterwards everyone agreed that people with artistic natures were often off balance. The other guests arrived and found Sven already drunk. He spoke loudly and somewhat incoherently, almost aggressively, and when dusk fell he proclaimed that this was going to be an Italian night in the great theater tradition, in darkness with flickering lights, perhaps torches, but they would still spread a dark glow. He was mixing up his metaphors, and at ten o'clock he suddenly ran off and vanished into the woods.

Tor went after him and found him. "Night, shadows," Sven muttered, in explanation. It may not have been much of an explanation.

"Don't say a word, Tor," he said. "I have to calm down. I'm absolutely calm, I'm a whore who's being kept by a pimp in the Thiel palace and I dress in furs and jewels and I can't write and I'm utterly dead inside and also quite calm. Don't say a word. I don't want to disgrace you. I'm absolutely calm. Let's go back now. Come on. Come on."

They returned to the others.

The place was called "Nameless." There they all were, the beautiful and famous of Stockholm's intellectual world, which was also Sweden's: perhaps not the rich, but the extremely talented and seldom sober but without a doubt brilliant. That's exactly what they were, brilliant and well-known and very prestigious, just the way Sven always wanted to be. Not rich but esteemed. They had all been invited because the prestige of each enhanced the others. The guests included Hjalmar and Stina Bergman and Per Lindberg and a hated author whose name he didn't want to remember. But Ragnar Östberg was not there; that was something, at least. And Tor was there, of course, that gentle and ever-forgiving man. It was one of those August nights that was sultry and hot and the darkness quickly thickened.

That's precisely the way it was with the darkness in Dalarö: it thickened. It was fat. And for almost an hour now he had been aware that Carin had vanished.

Where was she? She hadn't gone down to the beach, hadn't plummeted off the quite flat rock that sloped down to the water, hadn't drowned. In all certainty, yes with great certainty! she must have gone for a walk! with Per. And he was quite certain where she was right now, and in what kind of situation: leaning forward, with her dress pulled up, and her naked behind offered to his filthy member.

Like a beast. Like a beast with two backs. That's where she was, in the dark, which was thick and fat. She was very beautiful. He was sure

she was whoring just to degrade him. He had seen her irritation when
Tor had genuinely liked his poem. He was certain his approval was
genuine. You could tell from the tone of voice. He longed for death,
but he was terrified of dying. He didn't know how everything had
turned out so wrong. What good did it do that Carin was beautiful?

Someone was playing a concertina on the pier. A fire had been lit
on the beach. He looked for them everywhere, he was sober now, he
was terribly pale.

He is searching. He finds nothing.

He should have looked in the attic; that's where they are, kissing
each other right now.

To Tor he muttered that now he was going to drown himself.

This was later at night, but Tor was preoccupied with something
else because his nighttime party seemed to have been derailed. He
asked Sven to look for Hjalmar Bergman, but Sven said that he wasn't
some damned baby-sitter for Hjalmar Bergman. Tor was worried and
practically on the verge of collapse.

"Dear Sven," he said, "help me. Please. I'm going to be ruined if
all my authors drown."

Later Sven found Hjalmar Bergman out on the pier. He looked
shriveled and very small, though fat; he too was jealous, and he too
wanted help.

"Have you seen Stina?" he said, slurring his words badly. "I should
kill her, wives are always running away from me, falling asleep, shouting at me, getting fatter, fucking, what was your name again, Lidman?
What was your name?"

"Sven," said Sven.

"Sven, you lucky dog, you're so damned rich. Going to inherit
from Thiel. It's good for poets to have money. Don't ever marry into
families that are poor and famous, it's a hell; do what you did instead,
well, you've already done it. Good job, Sven. Where has your own little sow gone off to? She's beautiful, what's her name? Carin? Hasn't
she been making eyes at Per? Oh yes, he's young and talented and a
theater prick and witty and interesting. Where is she, Sven? Shouldn't
you go up and get a drink, brother? She's probably lying there fucking
Per somewhere in the bushes."

"Shut up before I throw you in the lake," said Sven, though he didn't move but just kept sitting apathetically at Hjalmar's side.

"That won't matter! I'm too fat! If you throw me in the lake, I'll just float. Stina is too fat too! You can't drown Stina either! Plop! And she pops right up!!! Do you know what jealousy is? I do. It's like lying naked on an ant-hill. You keep thinking they're fucking everybody. Got a little lover hidden away! Under their dress! That she can fuck whenever she wants! While she's eating breakfast! With me! Then he crawls up under there, he crawls up between her thighs! right in front of my eyes! and can't see a thing! That's what they do!"

"Shut up and go to bed."

"Why do things like this happen to us, Sven? I like you. Put your arm around me. You're a handsome boy. But I don't suppose you have that kind of temperament. No. I feel sick."

"Go to bed."

Hjalmar then clambered to his feet and staggered toward the house, which glowed like a ferry boat in the dark. He looked terrible. He had thrown up.

"Supposed to be some damned boring novels you've been trying to write; at least that's what Tor says. Damned upper-class chronicles. Are you writing anything now, Sven?"

"Not really. No."

"No? You know I like you. A lot. Nothing at all?"

"Not really."

"Dried up. And so young. And handsome. But you've got your father-in-law's millions. Did you hear that he's about to go bankrupt? Then things won't be any fun."

"Haven't heard a thing about that."

"But I have. Then you'll have to get a decent job."

"Go to hell."

"I'm already there, my friend. I'm already there."

When Sven came up to the house, everyone had reassembled. It was dawn. Carin was there, and Per.

Everyone was giving him smiles of encouragement or scorn or innocence.

He knew their smiles were meant for him.

3.

In the fall he called Tor Bonnier and asked to see him at the publishing company.

He arrived pale and silent, no longer the slightest bit off balance, and he said that he wanted to ask a personal question.

"Tor," he said, "you're my publisher, you're a Bonnier. In many ways you have a responsibility for me, and for the company's authors. I trust you. In many ways."

"What is it?" Tor asked, since Sven seemed unwilling to come to the point and had fallen silent and was merely staring at the floor.

"Have you heard anything about Carin carrying on with Per Lindberg?"

"Carrying on?"

"Having a relationship. Having a sexual relationship. Fucking. It supposedly started this summer, out at your place in Dalarö. People are saying that it's been going on ever since. I mean . . . a married woman. And my wife. And everyone seems to know about it except me. I'm going crazy."

"I haven't heard about anything like that."

"Something like that would be utterly inconceivable. Utterly . . . improbable."

"Yes," said Tor Bonnier with only a trace of irony. "Although it does happen in the books that you authors write, so it wouldn't be completely inconceivable. Don't authors usually write about that sort of thing? Isn't it part of the profession that both you and I make a living from?"

He saw that Sven's reaction was inexplicably strong, and he hastened to add:

"But perhaps it *is* inconceivable. You're right. Well, I don't know, I'm just a simple book publisher and a bloodsucker of talented and pure-hearted authors."

"Are you insinuating . . . insinuating!!! something?"

"I'm not insinuating anything, because I don't know anything. I was just talking about literature."

Sven stared at Tor for a long time, without saying a word, and then he got up and dashed out.

* * *

He didn't punch her with his fist, he remembered that quite clearly afterwards; he only slapped her across the face.

She fell to the floor, her screams were furious or heartbreaking, maybe he hit her again, certainly no more than once, or twice, but she screamed so horribly that it was almost unbearable.

And so of course he stopped punishing her.

"Tell me! tell me! tell me the truth! You're going to tell me the truth and nothing else!"

"Stop it! I will! I will I will!!"

Then she stayed sitting on the floor and refused to get up, even though she undoubtedly could, and he didn't have the strength to persuade her to stand up, so she just sat there, as if to make everything even more awful than it was, he was certain of that, and she didn't speak, and he sat down on a chair in front of her, and finally it came, like one long monotonous stream of words.

". . . and I'm tired of you and your family and your forefathers that don't exist and your vanity and your uncles on your father's side and on your mother's side and your blood inheritance, it's sick, it's utterly sick, your whole family is sick, you're all preoccupied with the dead and your uncle Sam and his wooden leg and the Lidman family and the wolves, if they exist, but that's what you hope, that there's a wolf among all the sad wooden legs and all the ones who committed suicide, and by the way, more of them should have done that, why didn't you all take your own lives, by rope or drowning, or a shot through the heart I suppose, how damned elegant, but if only all of you had taken your own lives, and your astounding egocentricity and your wretched manor house novels and 'von' this and 'von' that, you can only see yourself, you don't see other people, you use them, but you're not interested in them, you're an utterly dead person who's looking for life in other people that you want to use . . ."

"Damned whore," he said very quietly.

"Well, that's preferable, at least I have feelings, in fact, I like making love . . ."

"Fucking."

". . . all right, fucking! But I don't fuck in order to write poems about it, but because it's the glue of life!!! the glue of life!!! it cements people together, but you don't want to be cemented to anyone, you get scared, and you're an unbelievable coward, you want to suck everything out and then drag the skin off with you, but I'm no snakeskin you can haul along on your little path, I'm . . ."

"Oh dear God," he muttered. "Oh dear God, save me. Save me."

"Don't talk about God! He's just as abstract for you as . . . women
. . . and people! You're an evil child . . . who died in life's . . . in life's
center. In life's center. In life's . . ."

"Womb?"

She wept quietly. And then he asked, without hostility, just because
he wanted to know:

"So are they going to cut up this evil child named Sven Lidman,
who's lying inside life's womb? And pull him out? Because he has no
chance of surviving? Is that it, Carin?"

"Sven, you make it sound so grandiose. But it's much simpler than
that."

"How is it, then?"

"Why can't I get away from you? Why can't I be free of you?"

"You will be free," he said. "There are just a few remaining troublesome . . . modalities. If you know what that word means."

He didn't know why he said that. He shouldn't have reminded her.

A long silence followed, since they both knew, because he had told
her about it, everything, including the part about the whore in Gamla
Stan. Why did he always tell everything? Why was it necessary?

"I know," she said. "Because you once told me about it."

"Did I?"

"Yes. About that too, and it didn't make you any smaller—or bigger. Which is probably what you thought when you told me."

"You're wicked," he said.

"Yes. You've made me wicked. And I don't want to keep being
wicked, because I'm still young."

To resolve the modalities Ernest Thiel and Carin called on Tor Bonnier,
who was a friend, and Carin insisted that he be present.

Carin still bore a faint bruise, which she refused to powder over.

"I thought," said Ernest Thiel in an almost surprised tone of voice,
"that there was something fine about his first books of poetry. And
those historical novels he churned out were boring as hell, but they
sold well. Nice for you, Tor. But there was something that has ebbed
away. He can be brilliant and witty in conversations. And Levertin proclaimed him one of the great innovators in Swedish poetry, which
means it has a dismal future, it certainly, certainly does, I must say . . ."

"Pappa!!!"

He did actually fall silent, and then very softly concluded:

"I suppose we should let it seep out very quietly, it won't do to hush it up, better to let it trickle out . . . very quietly . . ."

"I want a divorce!!"

Then she looked her father straight in the eye and said:

"Pappa, is it true that you're going to go bankrupt?"

He was sitting behind his desk with his back very straight, and seemed surprised by the question, but his expression didn't change; he fiddled with his papers and after a long pause replied:

"Dear Carin, my great art collection will never go bankrupt."

"What about you?"

"I feel most sorry for you," he said.

"Dear Pappa, money couldn't protect me from the filth of life. Not your money. Not all the money in the world."

"No," he said. "We know that now."

"Precisely. Will you speak to Sven?"

"Yes, I'll certainly warn him about abusing you again, my beloved child. And, in spite of everything, you do have three children. Who were not struck by his metaphysical curse. Is a divorce necessary, by the way?"

"Pappa," she said. "I. Want. To. Be. Free. Of. Him."

"All right, then," he said in a voice so filled with weariness, despair, and surrender that Tor, who merely listened, without being able to contribute or advise, would remember it for the rest of his life. "All right, then," he said, "you shall be free."

Two weeks later the author S. Lidman informed his publisher that he had stopped work for good on his novel *The House of the Old Spinsters*.

He had written six chapters, but they were terrible.

Sven seemed completely out of control. He wept and said he was on the verge of collapse. He started talking about his friend Pehr Norrman, whom he now claimed to love, almost physically, as well as Pehr's former fiancée, Marita; and as soon as the divorce from Carin was final, he would marry this Marita, but only so that Pehr would come to visit them, and Pehr could sleep with her, but then she'd have to come to Sven's bed, and all three of them would merge into a weird union, as if Sven were a Christ figure who could make those three merge into a strange love, and then he began babbling manically, as if he had lost his mind.

Tor Bonnier told him to calm down, but Sven merely continued, this Marita would give birth nine months later to twins, and no one would know who the father was, and all three of them would possess these twins, it would be the most wonderful fellowship.

He could not be stopped.

"Sven," said his friend and publisher, "Sven, I swear you're about to collapse!"

But Sven could not be stopped, he merely sobbed:

" . . . join in the most wonderful fellowship . . . the most wonderful living fellowship . . . the most wonderful fellowship."

CHAPTER 12

The Sea of Women

1.

AFTERWARDS NO ONE FULLY UNDERSTOOD WHAT WAS SO ATTRACTIVE about the movement, or what made it grow.

But it did grow. It wasn't just the tiny Filadelfia congregation in Stockholm that suddenly multiplied ten- or twenty-fold; it also sprouted offshoots. Small Pentecostal movements appeared all over Sweden, in Ervalla, Karlsborg, Hedemora, Järna, Kristianstad, Lundsbrunn, Norberg, Skede, Ståna, Tannåker. The Baptist movement, and the leading brothers, in particular, may not have imagined that's what would happen when they first allowed God's thumb verse to select the little preacher with the lock of hair from Lidköping, and then later kicked him out.

No, definitely not. With that act they had committed a catastrophic mistake.

Something seemed to radiate from this little Lewi, as if from a center of power; yes, radiate! No doubt the radiant grace of God and the Savior! No doubt! Although it was also something they hadn't expected.

Unfortunately, it still radiated after the expulsion. But what was it?

How could something radiate from a man who actually looked like a trustworthy little bookkeeper? With his lock of hair, and then a small mustache. But Lewi seemed to possess a capacity for work that knew no bounds. He was gentle and endearing in manner (Efraim in the *Lebenslauf*: "He was endearing but still managed to get things done"), and he traveled. He traveled constantly, organizing small cells in the Pentecostal revivalist movement. Each congregation was independent, in accordance with the idea of complete congregational freedom, but they seemed to form, strangely enough, an ever larger and more organic whole. The free particles fit together, miraculously, and were actually stronger than a societal structure.

The core congregation of Filadelfia, in Stockholm, soon achieved a stronger financial base, with its own newspaper, hymnal, book publisher, printing office, Bible school, mission, and large mission conferences. And the battle for souls was led by the gentle little invincible former shot-putter from Vänersborg. Or, as the early, perplexed religious historians were already writing in the middle of the 1920s when they thought themselves capable of placing what happened in perspective, though it was much too soon, it's true, yet it has a certain interest, considering what was to occur: "This congregation and its leaders possess an undisputed authority. Personal rule still dominates, exercised by the wise and gentle figures of Lewi Pethrus and his closest associates in Stockholm. The whole thing is reminiscent of the founding of Rome."

The founding of Rome? Were they already anticipating, after less than a decade, the fall of the Roman empire within the revivalist movement?

No, oddly enough, Filadelfia did not fade away. Although that was the intention of the expulsion.

They hadn't counted on little Pastor Pethrus and his strangely charismatic ability to organize cells in the body of Christ.

In 1915 there were sixteen new congregations in Sweden, in 1920 there were 129, in 1925 there were 298, and five years later 458. And the central cell, Filadelfia in Stockholm, grew during the first ten years from twenty-nine members, which was the small group that Lewi took over, to 1,830. The income of the small central cell, when he arrived, was 2,559 kronor; ten years later it was an unprecedented 340,809 kronor—and this was all from the offerings of the most impoverished people. Almost 200 kronor per member. This was an enormous sum during the war years, equal to one-fifth of a worker's annual wages per member. It was a popular movement that no one had foreseen, which outgrew the whole rest of the revivalist movement, and this aroused concern.

What was the secret?

* * *

It could have been the new and almost theatrical form of the religious rite.

There was a certain air of the theater about it. The Moravians once created a musical liturgy in which a hymn was never sung straight through. Instead they would skip around in the verses, in a constantly surprising leaping that was never planned. A section of the congregation or a preacher or an individual might suddenly point the way to a new song; it was the "never-finished" aesthetic, like Zinzendorf's Bible, a "work in progress," a song that was renewed as it was being performed.

And that created tension. Perhaps it was the tension that drove everything forward, also within the Pentecostal movement. The ritual dramaturgy was created under a type of breathless time pressure; it was urgent! How much time did they have?

It was the ever-present question about the return of Jesus, the reappearance of the Bridegroom and the final merging with the wounds and blood of Jesus: it might be very near at hand.

"If Jesus tarries" was the watchword.

It was under this time pressure that they worked, creating their ritual theater. "An edification meeting will be held in Fredriksberg, if Jesus tarries, during the Midsummer holidays," or "In Hässleholm the free friends will arrange, if Jesus tarries, a big edification meeting on Sunday, September 23," or "If the Lord tarries we plan to meet at the upcoming market in Lycksele on March 5-7 . . ." It lent everything a sort of inspiring uncertainty, like the choice between two wonderful alternatives.

The best, of course, would be for Jesus to return. The second best, though also good, was the meeting at the market in Lycksele.

As far as performances go, the blessed evenings were actually not bad theater. And once in a while the old Moravian inheritance would rise up in a manner that brought blessings. Perhaps not in the form of horn bands with lively melodies and tall top hats, which back in Christiansfeld gave me the feeling that life was a merry burlesque, a solemn and mournful procession on the road to God's acre; but in the very rhythm of the service. The shifting between prayers and songs and preaching and speaking in tongues.

And it was as if the revivalist movement had awakened from a hundred-year-long sleep. I remember that sleep: those two or three hours of immensely sleepy readings from the discourses of Rosenius.

That gloomy grinding, as if the sinful consciousness had to be forced
into every pore of the poor person, awake or asleep. In the end almost
everyone was asleep.

The Pentecostal movement was an ecclesiastical poke in the side.

No one knew where Lewi had learned this new revivalist rhythm.
"He was quite impudent in some ways," writes Efraim in the
Lebenslauf. "Occasionally he would interrupt the choir with a gesture
and start to pray. But if he felt that the congregation hadn't truly come
through then he would wave his hand again and resume the song;
everything was kept brief, but was quite long when all put together,
though we didn't notice."

One time he asked Lewi why he acted that way. And Lewi then
replied that the invocation and praise of the Lord required rhythm,
rhythm! And it was this rhythm that enticed many people in the
beginning, but then, after they were drawn in, they would start to listen to the Lord's words a little more closely. It was the anguish of sin,
and to some extent the rhythm, that brought the masses through God's
gate.

"Especially the sisters," remarked Efraim.

"Yes, praise the Lord."

"Aren't you afraid that it's merely a superficial seduction?"

"I'm not afraid," replied Lewi.

"In that sense, you're like God," Efraim then "jokingly" replied,
but Lewi sharply retorted that no one is like God. And the fact that
people came, and in droves, meant that there must be something
right about it. The Devil wasn't going to be allowed to keep all the
good melodies. And there must be something right if people
weren't falling asleep during the meetings, although this opinion
was apparently not shared in many quarters, especially within
the state church but also within other sections of the revivalist
movement.

That was the reason for the fury the Pentecostal movement
aroused, since it was difficult to fall asleep during their meetings.

No, they did not fall asleep. And there was something that drew
these crowds. It might not be God's dramaturgically innovative theater,
but at any rate there was a problem of space.

Lewi rented the Grand National, later on Nalen, which could hold
900, but they outgrew it. And the Auditorium with 2,000 seats was too
small.

There was something about it. And the Stockholm press was unhappy and took offense. And then came the lambasting columnists and satirical songs. The tone they took would endure like a shrill undertone for the rest of Lewi Pethrus's life: especially the image of the shepherd and his sheep! This shepherd who profited from shearing the sheep. The shepherd who became the coupon-cutter, as Sven much later would express it, and then took up an old tradition from the lambasters, which was given expression in poetic form for the first time in the tabloid *Fäderneslandet* in 1915:

"PASTOR" Lewi Petri
Address: Filadelfia congregation
Uppsalagatan 11

What a strange name, what a strange man!
How strong in faith, how strong in talk,
for no other shepherd could do as he can,
present a heaven to his gathered flock.

What a splendid heaven, yes, a wondrous land:
where savory dishes bedeck the table
and there both you and I may come, if we can
give all the treasure we are able.

But "pastor" Lewi gathers up treasures of his own,
and the "sheep" he shears as much as he can,
while those "sheep" submit without a moan.

Alas, how easy to deceive in Jesus' name.
All it takes is a sly and slippery tongue
and a wicked mind that knows no shame.

Wasn't that a perfectly formed sonnet?

In the press, that was the politically correct tone toward Lewi, and it would continue. As Sven would later say in 1948 at Rörstrandsgatan when everything fell apart in the movement and four thousand brothers and sisters breathlessly listened to him, and Lewi sat, his face expressionless, in front of them on the platform, and Efraim felt an absurd and thoroughly mistaken love for Lewi, "*The sheep could sit in the congregation and be sheared, while the swine interests sit up on the platform, leading the prayers, and shearing the sheep and cutting out coupons. Things go fine for a while. But when the swine have sat on the platform for too long, leading the prayers, the sheep start to get tired of being sheared. There's no wool left. And the revival grows cold, as the saying goes.*"

But that was much later. Although the tone was the same.

The question was whether what was slander back then in *Fäderneslandet* turned into the truth thirty years later. I actually think that was the question Efraim was trying to answer in the *Lebenslauf.*

2.

Yesterday I again read through my mother's diaries from the same time period.

She is still young. There are still happy references to "parties." She has just become an elementary school teacher, she is beautiful, admired, only nineteen. "Party in Gamla Fahlmark." "Party in Långviken."

Everything is so pleasant.

Later she will become a drop in the congregational sea, one of those who, with upturned face, looks at the figure of Jesus in front, the only one, the Bridegroom, while life flows on and the sea freezes over.

How did that happen?

It was always the brothers who wrote the history.

That was natural, of course. They were the leaders. Afterwards this often led people to forget one detail: that the Pentecostal movement was essentially a women's movement.

Take, for example, the Östermalm division of the Filadelfia congregation in Stockholm. At the beginning of 1915, it consisted of 729 members.

Of this total, 601 were women and 128 were men. This meant, in other words, that 82 percent of the congregation consisted of sisters and 18 percent brothers. And 75 percent of the total membership was single. Here the women also dominated, with 464 unmarried and 22 widowed. Consequently, 81 percent of all women in Filadelfia were single.

Almost all these single women were under forty. The average age was thirty. Nearly a hundred percent of these single women were employed in various types of service jobs: cooks, servants, seamstresses, clerks, or hospital workers.

Yet the leadership was one-hundred percent male (as it was in the rest of the Pentecostal movement around Sweden). The deacons, overseers, and elders were all men. On that point the registers are unequivocal. Men led women. The exception, in nearly all the congregations, was the "work and celebration committees," which repeatedly contained names like Anna, Ester, and Karolina.

That was the way things were, and would remain.

You might say that in the leadership, the Pentecostal movement was dominated by men, while the members were younger, single women employed in the service sector. The image of the Pentecostal woman as an older, care-worn widow with her hair in a bun at the nape of her neck did not hold.

She was not a housewife, in any case; it wasn't until much later that the movement would generate a political party that would take up the fight for housewives as one of its most important goals.

Or perhaps it had already started here.

Perhaps the ideology was born in that rapidly growing Filadelfia congregation during the years of the Great War. It was born under the leadership of older men who with alarm and anxiety watched the hosts of members who were younger working women, not married, not dependent on a man, and full of a passion that sometimes seemed difficult to interpret, but that, praise the Lord, was assuredly completely pious. Yet for safety's sake they wished the women to be in the security of a nuclear family, away from the temptations of sin in the work force.

There was something that was difficult to interpret in this Pentecostal movement.

In the 1930s, when the Pentecostals exceeded 100,000 official members, still with the same social structure, the same overwhelming dominance of young working women, Lewi was in reality the leader of Sweden's largest women's movement.

What was it that drew these young working women to the Pentecostal movement? It most likely was not a longing for the security of the nuclear family, or the state child-care allowance, or a desire to fight immorality in society, or an intense longing to

ban dancing, parties, movies, theater, sports on Sunday, or immoral
literature.

It was something else.

It seems only conceivable that Lewi had eyes to see with, and that he
was a man.

What was it he saw? He saw young women whose sexuality had
always been denied throughout the whole history of religion.

The denial of women's sexuality was the norm.

And besides, women's sexuality was the very linchpin of sin.
Women were the threatening element, temptation incarnate, the ones
who had driven the naïve men onto the path of sin. Which was sin
itself. The apple of desire in Paradise. And here, in the congregation,
Lewi could see with his own eyes the most peculiar sights. It was true,
of this he was absolutely convinced: it had nothing to do with sexuality. The shouting of these young women, their convulsions, their
hyper-sensual joy at the Bridegroom's open embrace, their happiness
at being united with Jesus—that love bore no resemblance to the filthy,
swift, brutal intercourse they could look forward to in the poverty,
unemployment, and crowded living quarters of Stockholm.

Juxtaposed to all of that was an alternative: this pure ecstatic love,
without children. This religious, desire-filled birth control. Everything
in Filadelfia was infinitely more pure and true than the sexual filth of
reality.

There, in Filadelfia, the time of rapture truly existed.

It was pleasant in Filadelfia. Somewhere in the *Lebenslauf* Efraim
describes how he saw a young woman, while speaking in tongues, rub-
bing herself against a pillar in the hall, "and one could only wonder
what some of these women were up to."

Efraim saw the woman in the sea of women. Perhaps her situation
was such that only there could she affirm her sexuality.

But what was it that Lewi, the man, saw? And what conclusions
did he draw? Some he might have drawn even if they weren't apparent to himself.

The Lewi who entered the 1930s as the leader of Sweden's largest
women's movement was not entirely the same as the young Lewi, with
his heart to the left. Sometime during the mid-'30s Lewi changed

tracks. "A change seemed to occur in Lewi when he took up the fight against immorality in society," as Efraim writes in the *Lebenslauf*.

This was not merely social involvement, dreams of proletarian novels, and charity. It became a moral battle. It lasted until the late '30s in Europe; in the end everything became difficult to interpret. What was pure finally became much too pure. The passionate young working women were dressed in clothing that hid their ankles, their lewdly billowing hair was bound in a Pentecostal bun, and they were stripped of jewelry and frivolity.

In this way the linchpin of sin, woman, was covered up.

She was also ushered into the security of the nuclear family, where her passions would not present as great a threat. There woman as temptation and seductress would be covered up. There heaven and earth would burn, it's true, but there her sexuality would to some extent be rendered harmless.

But that was much later on. For now the ranks of black-clad gentlemen were still sitting up where the congregational elders in Filadelfia had their seats, and they observed with benevolence, wonder, or uneasiness, the women down below: the murmuring, praying, speaking in tongues, falling to their knees, and shouting young women who in spite of everything found it more pleasant at Filadelfia than anywhere else, especially compared to the Swedish church. For a few hours they could forget the war and rationing and the cramped rooms and the men and the hands and the swift intercourse and the fear of pregnancy and the screaming children, and instead they raised their eyes toward the gentle Savior, Jesus Christ with his open arms. And without shame or fear they surrendered to the passion they possessed. Not wanting to deny anything, unable to deny anything.

And in spite of everything, the calm little man up there from Västergötland—Lewi with his mild gaze, his strong hands, and his now vanished childish lock of hair—let them keep it.

But with uneasiness.

Thirty years old, single with one child, working in the service sector. Yes, that was more or less like my mother. And for all of them there was ultimately that decisive question: What was the purpose of their lives? Was there a purpose? Did it all make sense, was there an answer up there, beyond the sea of stars?

3.

So what was it? Was it the opposition?

"There was always a problem with the police during those years," Efraim writes in the *Lebenslauf.* "If it wasn't the overnight shelters that we ran free of charge for the homeless, paid for by our poor brothers and sisters, then it was the faith healing."

That was certainly true. The police, who were the instruments of the reasonable and the unreasonable, presented a problem.

It wasn't hard to see why. As the Filadelfia's "charity" swelled, an ideological problem arose in the public debate. On one hand, it was clear that the Pentecostal movement's Rescue Mission, for instance, was truly saving lives. The misery and starvation in Stockholm during the Great War were getting worse and worse. It was evident everywhere. It became visible, the misery could no longer be hidden away. The unemployed could no longer pay their rent, and they wound up on the streets, roaming around or sleeping under tarps. The shelters, under the auspices of the Pentecostal movement, were also overcrowded. The Klevgränd shelter, which could house only fifty homeless, drew far more people than that every night. The space at Kindstugatan 4 was also quickly outgrown. The house on Didrik Fik Gränd was completely taken over for a shelter, but the need was still immense.

On the other hand, as their social efforts grew, especially among poor children, it also became clear that the activities of Lewi and the Pentecostal movement were a provocation against almost all the leading political forces of society.

From the Right to the Left, these efforts were viewed as—well, wrong.

What Lewi said was essentially true, that it would be right for society to provide for the poor, "but they aren't doing it." Yet wasn't this God's and Lewi's flypaper? Wasn't the ultimate goal God's Kingdom and not the physical rescue of the destitute? And didn't this charity merely serve to cover up the real problems, to protect the bourgeois under the veneer of nobility, when they actually ought to be strung up by their own guts?

The communist and Moscow-loyal paper *Ny Dag* launched a sharp attack on this business whose goal was salvation. But it was countered, and in this situation quite logically, by the competing communist but anti-Stalinist paper *Folkets Dagblad*, which thus, because of its view on the Soviet Union, found itself fighting on Lewi's side. The Social-Democratic press was also hostile to the charity activities, which were regarded as a bourgeois cover used to hide the real existing differences between labor and capital. And underlying everything was the old Leftist mistrust of the reactionary church, and the image of the charitable upper-class ladies with their little baskets in Vita Bergen, so brilliantly depicted by August Strindberg in his novel *The Red Room*. The state church, the free churches that had been left behind, the Left, the Right, and the police became joined in one large, deep, and concerned unit.

Business, that was the word for it.

And to top it off, not even a business run for profit. Rather, a nonprofit business run by poor sectarian schemers.

The criticism became more and more enraged.

The persecution in the press was finally intolerable.

A counterattack, thought Lewi, could come only from below. From the poor, though of course with certain help from God, though by way of Lewi's mediation.

On the evening before his decisive flank attack he prepared by reading for Lydia from Isaiah 58:6-8, where the prophet writes: "'*Is this not the fast that I choose: to loose the bonds of wickedness, to undo the thongs of the yoke, to let the oppressed go free, and to break every yoke? Is it not to share your bread with the hungry, and bring the homeless poor into your house; when you see the naked, to cover him, and not to hide yourself from your own flesh? Then shall your light break forth like the dawn, and your healing shall spring up speedily; your righteousness shall go before you, the glory of the Lord shall be your rear guard.'*"

The next evening Lewi spoke to four hundred unemployed.

They had gathered for a collective meal under the auspices of Filadelfia. Lewi presented the problem to them. He began with a brief prayer and then explained that he had carefully read what the newspapers that defended the rights of the poor and unemployed, meaning the labor newspapers, had to say about Filadelfia's social work. There he had learned that the relief work they thought they were carrying out was in reality merely a loathsome business. The food was inadequate. The rooms for the soup kitchens had poor hygienic standards. Aside from the food, the homeless had prayers and, in certain cases, hymns inflicted on them. And the fact that the Pentecostal movement's overnight shelters were free of charge and paid for by collections taken up among congregation members and the faithful had created an economic quandary for the shelters that charged a fee, since those who had no money preferred to come to Filadelfia instead of to the shelters asking for money. And the free food at Filadelfia took away the very economic base of those that charged fees.

There was no other way for Lewi to interpret the criticism on this point: the labor newspapers thought that the financial basis for fee-charging shelters was being undercut by the free Pentecostal operations.

This was what he had read in their newspapers, Lewi told the four hundred. He was now interested in knowing whether they shared this opinion with the newspapers that represented them. And, if that was the case, if they agreed with their newspapers, then he declared himself willing to close down the soup kitchens at once. And stop their activities. Which he regretted had caused so much suffering for them. Although this was not done with any ill intention on his part or that of the congregation.

He spoke in a calm but rather sharp voice, and after his presentation, he promptly opened the floor for discussion. The four hundred then unanimously appointed a deputation to handle the matter, to write up a resolution and force the newspapers to issue an apology.

But this did not stop the police from repeatedly cracking down on the Filadelfia free shelters.

The most noticeable attack by the police occurred at the shelter at Salviigränd 5.

At four o'clock on a Wednesday morning a cavalcade of eight police cars rolled across Vasa Bridge and into Gamla Stan. The cavalcade split up at Riddarhus Square, and cars took up positions on Myntgatan and Västerlånggatan at both ends of Klockgjutargränd, and twenty or so plainclothes officers attacked the shelter.

The homeless at the shelter were asleep. The police woke them up and made them, under interrogation, explain what their plans were. But the raid produced nothing other than the observation that fifty people were found sleeping in only two rooms. The reason for the action was the fear that among these homeless there might be former convicts who, if they ended up together, might be planning new crimes.

None of those who were interviewed admitted, in spite of a rigorous interrogation, that they were planning new crimes. In any case not at the shelter at Salviigränd. Afterwards *Dagens Nyheter* interviewed the head of the shelter, Pastor Lewi Pethrus. He said that if there were former convicts among the homeless, they still had to sleep and eat, and under any circumstances, they had served their time and it was their civic right, after serving their time, to carry on conversations with other people. He also said that the "warming hall" was a stumbling block for some people, since no fee was demanded, but he categorically denied that it was a question of a regular shelter. Rather, it was a warming hall where "the visitors are permitted to stretch their legs, to the extent that there is space. They make it as comfortable as they can with the existing resources, with pillows and scrap paper."

And nothing came of the raid.

But afterwards Lewi turned to Jakob Pettersson, the Minister of Social Welfare in the Ekman government, and requested a meeting. It was granted. He then asked when the police harassment of their activities was going to stop, and whether the Minister regarded the action at Salviigränd as justified. Shouldn't the authorities instead be protecting those who were trying to help the needy?

The Minister replied that he would have a talk about this with the police chief.

"But," he added, "I must tell the Pastor that it's no easy matter to punish the police."

Lewi said he understood.

The conversation was carried out in a calm tone. It should be noted that Lewi didn't seem hesitant to contact a cabinet minister to win justice. Yet he was still young, and the customs, like the respect for authority, were different back then.

After that no more police raids were launched against any Filadelfia shelters.

4.

The Pentecostal movement was a mystery.

It was not compassion that exalted the masses, or the battle for the poor, the most destitute, the lowly. If it were then perhaps even Jakob

Pettersson, the disillusioned Minister of Social Welfare in Ekman's cabinet, the man who didn't think he could easily punish the overzealous
Swedish police force, even he might have been able to fill the Winter
Palace to the bursting point if he had implemented, which unfortunately was not the case, a perfect social welfare policy that reduced the
number of the down-and-out, unemployed, and poor to zero.

Or if the state church had done this. No, it was something else.

Somewhere within the radical pietism there was an alarming core
that was not entirely theologically housebroken. At bottom lay a theological question, more controversial than most people realized. The
question was: Who was He actually, the one they invoked? Who was
this Benefactor, this Savior, this Bridegroom? Was He male or female?

Jesus was his name. And wasn't this Jesus actually God, the only
one? Was there a God besides the Benefactor, Jesus Christ?

Or was He all alone?

Had radical pietism quietly abolished God and the Holy Spirit?

"Jesus," they shouted at the meetings that were more and more crowded.
Jesus, a single, loving figure to be embraced.

Swedish religious sexuality had its disguises. But it was important
to uncover the beloved figure, to isolate him.

When Zinzendorf, during his endless private walks, carried out his
silent monologues with Jesus Christ, "often up to twelve hours a day,"
increasingly intimate, with Jesus as a constant conversation partner
who was more and more physically present, more and more freed from
the theological complications called God or the Holy Spirit, when he
talked about his revision of the Bible, rewrite! revise! start over! dear
Jesus, you are all!!!—then it was as if he had undertaken a palace revolution.

Included in this was the problem of too many gods.

God the Father, the Son, and the Holy Spirit. And two thousand
years of theology to establish the relationship among these three. There
was room for reduction. Less theological foolishness and humbug!

No one in the Pentecostal movement dared express it so clearly,
dared deny the first or the third of the dogma's divinity. But in practice it was Jesus Christ, soon only Jesus, who became the object.
Popular radical pietism created this solitary benefactor: Jesus.

Yahweh was a terrifying, avenging, and forbidding figure who could be reduced to something that theologians argued about. How liberating it must have been to suppress all the stories about this father of Jesus, whose bloody vengefulness they read about with wonder in the Old Testament. And who was most likely not entirely real. While the Jesus figure was so large and warm and loving. And through His sacrifice on the Cross, and through His blood, He cleansed the poor human being, that miserable wretch with all his flaws, from all sin.

Or the Holy Spirit! As an independent phenomenon! What kind of nonsense was that? Reductionism! Jesus Christ is the Spirit! Why this Trinity foolishness?

If Yahweh, God the Father, was quietly removed from the scene, and the existence of the Holy Spirit was relegated to something inside Jesus, everything became much more comprehensible. Then the Jesus relationship also became much stronger.

Christcentrism became the keyword.

Spirit baptism, speaking in tongues, and faith healing became easier to understand, and accept. At the core was the dream of coherence. That life had meaning. That human beings were not machines. That something separated us from the animals. That the misery of life had a meaning, a meaning, a meaning!

There was a meaning. Christcentrism within radical pietism simplified and clarified the dream of this meaning by giving human clarity to the ritual, and they had found a new God.

The worship of Jesus as God.

The *Evangelii Härold*, Lewi's little weekly newspaper, which he had now started with an initial investment of 1,000 Swedish kronor, and which in a couple of years would grow from a circulation of 2,000 to 18,000 and would become a very good business, praise be to Jesus, began to hint at radical viewpoints. Some were non-theological. For instance, the paper encouraged refusing to do military service. "God bless the young brothers who decline the service of the Beast."

But on the question of Christ's divinity, as the phrase went, they were without a doubt radical, and increasingly aggressive. Jesus was actually God. Not just God's son and messenger and the son of man. He was God. Period. Those who denied this, as for instance the entire Swedish state church did, found themselves in very very bad company. The *Härold* pointed out, with the help of John 8:42–47, that Satan was the first to deny Christ's divinity. *"Therefore anyone who denies the divin-*

ity of Christ ought to bear in mind that he is spreading the teachings of the evil spirit and doing the work of the father of lies. The devil has never denied God the Father, he has always acknowledged God; but he has constantly worked against Christ by undermining faith in his divinity and rank of king. The belief that God is one, and that the only True One is Our Lord Jesus Christ, has the support of the whole Bible, both the Old and the New Testament."

The system of salvation was thus quite clear, under the never wholly expressed assumption that there was only one God, Jesus. Salvation, baptism in water, baptism in the Holy Spirit, faith healing, and waiting for the return of Christ. He certainly was tarrying, but while they waited they could organize meetings, and even though the Lord tarried, His figure was now comprehensible and real.

Jesus Christ was the center.

All around him theological reductionism had taken place. He radiated alone. He was also very human, and He was a benefactor. He was physically comprehensible, simple, warm, and compassionate. He was no avenging Yahweh, the one who unfortunately had a terrifying affinity with the reality that existed all around them, in a decade when a shot was fired in Sarajevo, armies of millions were murdering each other in Flanders, starvation was spreading, hunger riots suddenly erupted even in little Sweden, hordes of unemployed roamed the streets of Stockholm, and everything seemed hopeless and filthy.

But not in the center. There stood the figure of Jesus.

The music, dramaturgy, ecstasy, charity, Christcentrism—they all played a part. But this was unnatural. Almost un-Swedish.

And that's why, during these war years, the outraged and sharply critical Swedish newspapers were filled with descriptions of the incomprehensible orgies of the Pentecostal movement. These vipers' nests! these vipers' nests! where people in distress and ecstasy threw themselves to the floor, whispering and shouting the name of Jesus. Because it was this name that became the great uniter. His blood, which was not the blood of soldiers at Flanders but of the Redeemer.

And His wounds, which were not death but life.

Lewi's mission, as Efraim writes in the *Lebenslauf,* was to create a well-organized popular movement out of these emotions.

5.

But the belief in faith healing presented a problem.

A succession of police reports began to come in, and accounts appeared of people who died or almost lost their lives because the laying on of hands didn't work and no doctor was summoned.

Lewi had undergone an experience that he refused to mention for a long time. It concerned Lydia, the child, and the background to "The Promises," the hymn that had now taken hold as the Pentecostal movement's *Leitmotif*.

Where did he actually stand on this matter?

Publicly, his defense was that all medical expertise was always called upon at the proper moment, that doctors and medicine were God's creations, and that everything was under control. Faith healing was solely an extreme and extraordinary supplement to the healing powers of Jesus Christ. At the bottom was traditional medicine, created by the Savior. Up above was faith.

But this was not exactly clear as a bell.

From one of the evangelist courses led by Lewi, a student took the following notes:

"We have to experience what we preach, otherwise we will be preaching lies. This includes, for example, faith healing. You can't stand in the pulpit and testify about the glory of the Lord's promise of health and then have pills or things of that nature in your suitcase. Or publicly talk about Jesus as the doctor of the congregation and then, for example, when your wife falls ill, even if she should be dying, you turn to earthly doctors. Brother Pethrus gave a gripping example from his own life. Let no one influence your conviction. And learn the most difficult lesson of all: leave the consequences to God."

Lewi had told them a story. And the students listened.

No, it was not clear as a bell. Lewi wrote a book about the matter, *The Pentecostal Movement and Divine Faith Healing*. Neither is this book clear as a bell in its view of the origins of illness; or, rather, the movement would later forget more and more about what was not clear as a bell in the text.

Though it was quite apparent.

Where do illnesses come from? he writes, and answers: It's instructive to see what God's Word says about this. "And then we discover that before sin appeared in the world, there were no illnesses. This means that illness is a consequence of sin." And suffering! What is suffering? "God's great brake on humanity's haste along the paths of sin. And it's good that such a brake exists. Glory be to God for that." "I am convinced that there are thousands of people in this city who would be restored to health if they were saved."

Many illnesses derived directly from the power of Satan. Sin creates illness.

Is there a cause-and-effect connection? The sexual temptation of woman created so much sin; yes, it was actually the origin of sin in Paradise. And sin created illness. And this could be cured by God, especially through the mediation of the men up on the platform, theocratically chosen.

No, that was too simple. He never expressed it in that way. But if you add it all up?

No, that was too simple.

It all culminated in the spring of 1921.

The Filadelfia congregation had called in an English faith healer by the name of Wigglesworth, and that spring a number of big faith-healing meetings were held in the Auditorium. The ill were exhorted to come up onto the platform. Each evening it was so crowded that Wigglesworth and Lewi were forced to hold back the throngs. On stage stood a square table with a pile of little white cloths. "The cloths had been blessed by the laying on of hands by the Englishman and Lewi P., which gave them healing powers, and they were later claimed by their owners," reported *Dagens Nyheter*.

These "sweat cloths," or veronicas, were more closely linked to a Swedish rather than an English tradition.

At the end of the nineteenth century, the Swedish "great miracle-worker" F. A. Boltzius from Glava in Värmland was active, and during quite extensive tours through central Sweden he cured the sick through "sympathetic magic methods." He took "sweat cloths," wiped his face with them, blessed them, and then placed them on those who were ill. Yet this was not an exclusively Swedish tradition: somewhere in the background there must have been Mesmer's *baqueter* and other sympathetic magic methods that he used. *Dagens Nyheter* continues its depiction of the meetings in this way:

"One by one they step before the faith healer: old bent women, young anemic girls, nervous youths, limping old men, and little crippled children: one person after the next. And Mr. Wigglesworth works with hand and mouth. He vigorously rubs the bodies of the ill people, pressing on their chests, running his hands over their arms and legs, all the while he and the men standing nearby repeat: 'Trust in God! oh, trust in God! oh, trust in Jesus!' He pulls canes and crutches away from those who are using them: 'Walk, just walk, walk, trust, trust in God, God!' And they stagger forward, most of them obviously in appalling pain, others radiant with religious ecstasy. A little boy of about ten has his crutches yanked away from him, and he is forced to walk, his body overcome with desperate sobbing and spasms that go on and on. A crippled little woman's suffering is terrible to watch. Here and there people can be heard saying: 'This kind of thing should be forbidden! This is criminal! To think this is allowed to go on!' But they are the exception. From many more directions can be heard: 'Thank you, dear Lord!'"

And it's as if a desperate procession of medieval flagellants were being described; not whipping themselves but being whipped, and now with one last frantic hope.

Lewi was immediately summoned to a police interrogation.

He was called in at eleven o'clock, and the interrogation was carried out by an Inspector Elfström. Lewi promptly asked him whether the Bible and all the Lutheran texts were not part of the constitution, since the state and the church were united. The inspector said that this was true.

"Can you then condemn a person or a congregation," Lewi went on, "for acting in accordance with the constitution of Sweden?"

"No," replied Inspector Elfström, "if Pastor Pethrus can prove that what you are doing is in the Bible, then no Swedish law can condemn you for it."

That's how they began.

To each question that was asked, Lewi answered with a text from the Bible. Jesus had performed miracles. He could be cited as the reason why people prayed for the sick. Inspector Elfström retorted that the fact that Jesus cured the sick was not reason enough for Pastor Pethrus to do the same. Or believe that he could do the same. Lewi countered this with John 14:12: *"Truly, truly I say to you, he who believes in me will also do the works that I do."*

And they went on like this for several hours.

Lewi denied that the meetings included hypnotic séances, merely persuasion, or attempts at religious persuasion. If such things were forbidden, all Swedish churches would be forced to close, since there too attempts were made to persuade people in a religious direction, although with miserable results. Persuasion could not be considered unconstitutional. Then what would happen to all of politics? Nor was it a question of business, since, unlike the state church, they did not receive money or other payment. The inspector wanted to know what the "sweat cloths" were about. Lewi replied at once with Acts of the Apostles 19:11-12, in which it says, among other things, that they even took handkerchiefs and aprons that had touched Paul's body and placed them on the sick, whereupon the disease left them, and the evil spirits came out.

The inspector then asked how this could happen today.

"The cloth itself," Lewi replied, "contains no healing power, just as the oil does not. But it becomes a means to help the faith of the sick person. As is often the case, people need something to help them in their faith, such as baptism and communion, because we generally have a hard time believing."

"Yes, you're certainly right about that," remarked Police Inspector Elfström.

After so many hours of interrogation, Inspector Elfström now seemed exhausted and dejected, and he said that since Pastor Pethrus seemed to have a Bible verse to defend and explain everything they did, and since it had been established in the Swedish constitution as true and just, no matter what kind of superstition and sorcery it might be, he could find no reason to forbid the meetings, since they were supported by the sorcery that had been established by the King and Parliament, which he essentially regretted, but such was the case, and he had found his conversation with Pastor Pethrus essentially interesting.

And that police interrogation too ended harmoniously.

Two weeks later Lewi was sitting at the kitchen table, reading *Svenska Morgenbladet*.

He was reading the second of two articles by a certain author named Sven Lidman who, using the confessions of St. Augustine as his point of departure, defended the Filadelfia congregation and the meetings with Mr. Wigglesworth. The headline was: "When Saint Augustine Was Healed Through Faith." The article was slightly humorous, but extremely logical. The reader learned what a toothache was called in Latin ("dolore dentium excruciabas me") and how Augustine, solely by means of his faith, was cured of it. Using a humorous tone, the article asked the question whether God's power over illness wouldn't be equally great in 1921 as it was in 386, and if not, when did the power cease? Had God transferred His power to dentists, and if so, when? And why hadn't we been informed! He caught the theologians of the state church in their own sorcery, so to speak.

But it was definitely a defense.

Lewi then urged Lydia to read it. She read it and asked:

"But who is this Lidman?"

Lewi sat in silence for a while and then said:

"I don't know him."

"It's well written," she said, "and so difficult and profound that it must have caused confusion among our opponents, since it's incomprehensible in an almost artistic way."

"So it is," replied Lewi. "But quite droll."

"But who is he?"

"I wish I knew," Lewi said. "I wish I knew."

CHAPTER 13

Meeting at God's Acre

1.

LEWI SAT AT THE BREAKFAST TABLE AND READ AN ARTICLE IN *SVENSKA Morgenbladet*, and afterwards Lydia asked him who this Lidman was who had written it.

And Lewi thought for a moment and said that he didn't know him. Although that wasn't exactly true. They had met very briefly at Didrik Fick Gränd 3 in Gamla Stan. It was during one of the free meals, at the time of Wigglesworth's series of meetings, and during the worst persecution by the newspapers against the Pentecostal movement. This Lidman came in, and there was a terrible commotion going on because food coupons were being distributed right then, and it wasn't a good time for intellectual conversations. Lidman was almost ingratiating and very critical of the newspapers, which was surprising. But Lewi didn't pay much attention to Lidman. Efraim was there, and he writes in the *Lebenslauf* that afterwards it was incomprehensible that Lewi didn't seem to notice Lidman, especially considering what would happen later on and what an enormous impression the two would later make on each other.

But Lewi was almost furious. Practically enraged.

Lewi asked—almost hostilely as Efraim recalls, though he may have remembered wrong afterwards—why Herr Lidman didn't write something about it, about the fact that the newspapers lied, "you who have access to the newspaper columns, and you can't say the same of us, the Pentecostals, who are always regarded as lice." And in any case, they would never dream of opening space in the columns for the lice. Which, by the way. They had plenty of. As perhaps Herr Lidman could see.

And Lidman muttered something, and "slunk away." Afterwards, surprisingly enough, he actually did write two articles.

But in a higher or deeper sense, Lewi was right. He didn't know this Lidman.

Who did know this Lidman?

The articles were published in the spring of 1921, which was six years after that unhappy night in Dalarö, and something had obviously happened.

What was it that had happened to Sven Lidman?

The day after the second article appeared in the newspaper, on March 22, 1921, the day when Lydia asked her question about who this Lidman was, Lewi ordered several books that Lidman had written and began to read them.

First there was a poetry collection that Lidman had titled *Primavera*, which contained poems about eroticism, but they were written with such artistry that no one could take offense if he didn't try too hard, and that wasn't something that Lewi cared to do. Later he started reading a novel called *Thure Gabriel Silfverstååhl*, which was interesting in its way, but the story upset Lewi because the hero was a young officer who raged against the policy of appeasement with Norway and wished instead for war before the union was dissolved. Lidman was obviously right-wing. There was a great deal about action, duty, and hero worship everywhere; but since Norway's cause was Lewi's cause, he took a strong dislike to the author. Regarding the Norway issue, Lewi had always supported peace and opposed the warmongers, and wished for Norway's independence, a point of view that he shared to a great extent with Lydia. And since he had always loved Norway and could never imagine a bloody attack on the Norwegian brothers, or sisters, he found this novel to be execrable to the highest degree.

It was obscene literature at its very worst.

Then Lewi read another book, *Child of Discord*, which was a historical novel and quite boring. And he still didn't understand who this Lidman was, or why he had written the articles, or even why he was thought to be a good writer. In one last attempt, he started in on the novel that was claimed to be Lidman's best.

It was called *The House of the Old Spinsters*.

It took all his will power to make it through the first hundred pages. The style was extremely wooden, describing four old noble-women living in a house in Stockholm. There was a great deal about the interiors and descriptions of how the women moved and walked among the furniture, although nothing happened except that the reader learned all about the furniture. This was all written in tremendously long sentences which the author artistically wove together so that they were practically impossible to read. And the greatest attention was given to the women's origins.

They had very long names, and their family trees were presented in detail, and it went on and on. It was undoubtedly about as exciting as reading a peerage book, Lewi thought, if a person were so inclined, which he was not. And he was about to give up without learning anything more about who this Lidman was.

But then, after about a hundred pages, it was as if a different writer took over.

It was as if an oddly vibrating beam of light broke through all that was gray and artificial. This part was about one of the old spinsters, Euridike Berg, whose father had been the proprietor of an iron foundry and owner of Ramsjöberg, the last descendant of the Huguenot family d'Estelle, who had immigrated to Sweden during the reign of King Karl IX (this was the type of information that almost made Lewi give up), and about how this Euridike became saved. And it was in the description of her salvation that the novel, suddenly, began to come alive. The writing became powerful and ecstatic and beyond all control. At times the reader might dislike the exaggerated tone and the way that Diken—as this Fröken Berg was called—became united in an almost sexual act with the figure of Christ:

"The trembling indescribable bliss of submission, surrender, immersion, and the annihilation of will had been hers, had thrilled her being in every fiber, every finger: 'A bride am I, the bride and property of Jesus Christ!' She fell to her knees on the floor, as if tossed by invisible hands, and with stammering, quivering lips she again and again whispered the most blessed of words—the most beautiful words of the human soul—the holiest sensation of the human heart:

"'I am your bride, Lord Jesus Christ—I am the bride of Jesus Christ—the bride and property of Jesus Christ!'

"Indescribable, strange, mysterious emotions—a quivering, trembling, ecstatic intoxication—which only the initiated can under-

stand—the perfection of the Holy Communion in a person's being:
"'My friend is mine, and I am his!'"

"Which only the initiated can understand."

Lewi read the novel with growing attentiveness. Something had changed. The ecstatic was often beyond control, perhaps loathsome in reality, although at times very vivid. He now saw that the author was describing a Moravian view of Christ, and that was surprising. But it was alive. It was not academic like all the other books he had read by Lidman, it was not fabricated, not dead literature; it contained a despair that made him feel oddly distressed.

He put the book aside and sat silently in front of it for a long time, trying to collect his thoughts. Perhaps he didn't understand who this Lidman was. But he was beginning to feel a certain respect.

He realized that Sven Lidman had many faces.

2.

What was it that happened?

The photo shows Alma Lindvall, a *Härold* newspaper seller. She appears to be in her seventies, with the Pentecostal bun, and wearing the usual round and unpretentious hat, the Pentecostal hat. The photograph was taken in a studio. She is holding a bag in each hand, and it's anybody's guess, but no doubt the intention was to imply that they contained copies of the *Evangelii Härold*.

She was photographed right before her death on April 11, 1939. The fact that the picture was taken, as a historical document of her, was due to her historical role.

She was the one who brought Sven into the Pentecostal movement. That's why she has a natural place in the history books of the Pentecostal movement. That's why she was photographed in a studio.

She met him on Villagatan in September 1919. She approached him and said she was selling the *Evangelii Härold*. Lidman didn't know anything about the publication, but he was friendly and fell into conversation with her. He was saved, he told her kindly, but not a Pentecostal. He had never heard of Filadelfia. She then told him about the Filadelfia congregation. She was very charming. She told Lidman about how she was saved, about all the abuse she was subjected to when she sold the *Härold*, and about her joy in Jesus Christ. Lidman then gave her a small contribution to the building fund of the

Filadelfia congregation, and took a subscription to the newspaper.

That's how it happened. That's why the picture was taken, that's why she was part of history.

Nothing else is known about her, other than that she was called home on April 11, 1939, and her membership number was 1,974.

It was the custom among sections of the Pentecostal movement—originally within the Methodist movement it was actually the indication and proof that a conversion was real and not pretense, that the Spirit had participated and that it occurred like a bolt of lightning out of a clear sky—that a person could precisely date his conversion to God.

John Wesley was converted on May 24, 1738 at 7:45 in the evening. The Pentecostal movement did not demand the same degree of precision, nor did Sven. He listed March 17, 1917 as his conversion day. No specific time. But no doubt he didn't have a time to record, nor any great moment.

No doubt he had given up.

The fact that he lists March 17, 1917 is due to his sense of resignation. On that day he gave up. He was now utterly alone. He had rented a fisherman's cottage outside of Rindö in Stockholm's archipelago. He was reading St. Augustine. Every night he had cramps in both legs; he blamed this on his former tremendous consumption of alcohol. He stayed on his knees for hours and tried to pray, but he achieved nothing.

Ever since he had given up his attempt to write his novel *The House of the Old Spinsters*, which he found sterile, he had gone back to writing poetry, and that winter he had completed a poetry collection. One night he burned the manuscript, which he knew was false and dishonest, although perfect in form.

It burned, brisk and clear, and he felt relieved.

On the morning of March 16 a haze hovered over the sea outside Rindö, and he felt no hope. He then decided to die. He felt no hope and his decision was firm. That night he prayed fervently to a God whom he assumed might exist, but the darkness was mute and he received no answer. He didn't know what existed out there in the dark. He didn't dare seek out the darkness, and he didn't want to remain in a light that tormented him to the point of despair. No one answered.

On the morning of March 17 he was saved.

He later often wrote about what happened. But he never could truly explain how exactly he conquered his former despair. In the night he wrote a poem, the first in several years, and it became a hymn. The stanza of a hymn! *Teach me, God, to humbly bend / knee and heart, mind and soul! / Let my will deep inside me / become Your will alone / that I might follow You / away from the stray paths of the world!*

Was that a solution? He could also take poison! He had some in his desk.

But he had written a verse. For the first time in a long time. Then he continued, and *as I wrote the last stanza, a strange transformation occurred: my entire being was transformed. My hands were bright, my fingers holding the fountain pen were like flames of light as I wrote the last lines of the verse, and when I got up from the desk chair and walked across the floor, I was nothing but light—clothed in light—transformed to light: a living light. And I was not at all afraid, no, I had a feeling that my being had been trans-formed, my blue suit was a light, soft, silver-shimmering fabric, my hands were light, my fingers were like flames of light,* yes, perhaps that was true, although afterwards he didn't know what part of the miracle was real, and who could possibly know! that which exists beyond the curtain of stars! that which cannot be sketched! not even on sandwich paper! *Yes, it was my innermost self that was lifted forth—something tender and soft—at once malleable and indestructible, that was lifted up and out from all the shells and ramparts and walls and trenches I had built, behind which, timid and frag-ile and unapproachable, it lived its secret life, a living substance, at once pliable and dirty, cowardly and treacherous, lame and cold, but it trembled in a dream of wholeness, purity, righteousness, light, and truth,* yes, perhaps that's where the secret was, perhaps it's there that he comes closer to himself, per-haps he is now very close.

Or did he merely realize that there is always something that is bet-ter than death? Perhaps there was a spirit that could also blow away the membrane of ice from around his face. Perhaps everything he had ever thought was wrong. Perhaps there was a possibility of starting over.

Perhaps he sat on the edge of the bed, with his bare feet on the wooden floor and dressed only in undergarments, and for the first time he looked at himself as he truly was. Noticed that his undergarments were filthy and his body was gaunt. That he was a poor, sinful person, that there were no longer any pretensions, no proud ancestors, no titles, that it was cold in the room, that he was freezing, and that he deserved it. And then, in spite of everything, that there is always something better than death.

That was the simplest: not some word from St. Augustine, but from a folk tale. That it was possible to get to his feet and walk.

That's what he thought. Get to your feet and walk. And then he did it, as a test. And he walked over to the window. And thought: Dear Jesus. Dear Jesus, I almost think I've been saved.

And then Jesus said to him: Dear Sven, you're right. You've gotten to your feet. And walked. And you're right, Sven.

You are saved.

That was the morning when he was saved. Two years later he met Alma Lindvall, who told him about the Filadelfia congregation. And two years after that Sven and Lewi met during Kölingared Week.

Then he arrived. That's how it happened.

3.

There is no photograph of them together during preacher week in Kölingared in 1921. But several photos show the external setting.

A large, two-story manor house with the Swedish flag flying. In the open courtyard, three tents. One that is quite small, capable of holding perhaps fifty people. A larger one, designated for meals. And then the big tent.

Stråken Lake nearby, not visible in the pictures. That was where the baptisms were performed. That was where Sven came to be baptized. Very tranquil, very Swedish images. This was a few years after the Great War. Bushes with currants, a field with rows of plants (potatoes? or strawberries?) and open fields of grain, as well.

It was here, after Alma Lindvall managed to "foist the *Härold*" on him, he came to join, at last, the Pentecostal movement.

Sven Lidman made an almost sensational impression. It was his frock coat.

He is not in any of the pictures from that week in Kölingared, nor is his frock coat, but the faithful are there. You can see how they were dressed. They are charming. The pictures look, in an endearing way, like all pictures from that period: the men are dressed in elegant suits, undoubtedly made of serge, with white shirts and hats or peaked caps, and they look happy and solemn. Although their happiness, you might imagine, was more of an inner joy, not frivolous, but you can tell that they're also happy at being photographed, and that's why they're making an effort to look serious and saved.

That was how men looked in Sweden at that time. All the pictures that I've seen of my own father are just like that. A few, from the harbor at Bureå, are work pictures that are different: in those the steamboat longshoremen are lined up, with the cargo ships in the background and enormous piles of mining props all around them, but their faces are happy. That's one kind of photograph I've seen of him. There aren't many. There are more of the other kind: countless pictures of Pappa and his friends wearing elegant suits and white shirts and ties and hats or peaked caps, standing on a lawn, or with the meeting house in the background; happy faces there too, and formal poses. And then the funeral photos, of course, when he lay in his coffin.

Photographs were taken only on special occasions, some of them with a waterfall behind, it might be Harsprånget before the power station was built.

When a photo was taken, it was important to look formal but happy, and the suit had to be clean and neat. During preacher week in Kölingared, they were also formal, but in a simple and dignified way that was customary. Clean and neat, and in a serge suit, and the women wore coats and hats, like Alma Lindvall.

That was how people looked in Sweden in those days, from north to south, if we're to believe the photographic documentation. In the photographs everyone in the year 1921 looked exactly alike, no matter where they were in Sweden, on the lawn at Hjoggböle or at a Bible study week in Kölingared. That's how Sweden looked to the camera, which was a solemn instrument. But Sven Lidman was different.

He wore a frock coat. More precise details weren't given by those who saw him, the witnesses, but he caused a stir. They weren't yet accustomed to the fact that he differed, but that would come; later on people were almost proud of the fact that he was so different. For the time being he caused only a pious murmur among those who were Spirit baptized and then spoke in tongues, who should have been used to almost anything.

The upper class made its astonishing entrance among them; because it certainly was the upper class, wasn't it? Surely this Lidman, the failed son of a toll collector, who groveled before the fancy titles of his ancestors and licked the ass of the upper class, who had grown up in impoverished circumstances in a tiny two-room house, with a mother who sold off their furniture to make ends meet, this frock-coat man couldn't actually be one of them, could he?

No, it was quite clear that the upper class had now come to pay them a visit, and had descended to the Pentecostal movement. A fallen angel, like Lucifer, but no doubt things would all go well. No doubt even Lucifer could be saved. If the message was powerful, anything was possible. No one was beyond hope. They should show Christian love and mercy to everyone. Even to those who were inappropriately dressed and didn't have the proper clean serge suit but appeared before the countenance of God dressed in a frock coat and vest.

But Lewi took him in hand, giving him the legitimacy of one of the saved who had come through. Lewi gave him God's accolade by slapping him on the shoulder. Lewi was the leading brother, after all, and surely he knew what he was doing.

Were there no objections? Not a squeak?

In one of his memoirs Lewi gives only a slight indication of what this strange bird was up against, this figure who made such an oddly dubious first impression, and what the objections would be later on. He writes, almost apologetically, not about his outward attire, but rather about the inner person, the sinner in Sven who still existed from heathen times. The Sven inside Sven. Or rather, the Lidman hidden inside Sven, who would in fact continue to reside, like an inner frock coat, inside Sven for decades.

Actually, all his life.

"The fact that even during the years he spent with us he often talked and wrote about his aristocratic ancestors and exalted connections probably impressed a certain type of person, but it aroused disagreeable thoughts in others."

In others? Who? Time would show.

But this was *adiafora. Adiafora! Lappri! Lex dura, sed lex!* There were many new words that the people of the Pentecostal movement would learn from this peculiar man in the frock coat. It chafed a bit in the beginning, arousing "amazement." But, on the other hand, God had created so many peculiar parts in the great body of Christ. And according to I Corinthians 12, once again, it was true that all the parts of Christ's body had worth. Each in its own way. So why not this man? Everyone had worth. And this peacock with his strangely warm,

humor-filled and observant eyes, he must also, in some way, be the
Lord's invention. And should be accepted.

And, as it would soon turn out, he had a great and inestimable
worth.

It had all been a great experience for Sven. And it had been Sven's own
idea to come.

He was not forced into it. But Efraim was not alone in feeling
almost terrified about how this Lidman would react to that first blessed
day with its cries of joy and speaking in tongues and prayers and songs
of praise. After all, they were used to the scorn of the so-called intellectuals, those who wrote for the newspapers.

But Sven fell to his knees like all the others and shouted along
with them, and prayed, and sang. And he didn't seem shocked or
embarrassed; on the contrary, he joined them in a manner that practically touched Efraim's heart. He was almost enthusiastic. So there you
could see! There wasn't a trace of snobbishness in the man with the
frock coat and vest, just a sincere, concentrated joy. And afterwards he
stood in the courtyard outside the meeting room, and the brothers and
sisters drank coffee and ate rolls, leaving a shy little space around Sven.

But then Efraim and Lewi arrived.

And apart from all the others, in a small but highly prominent
group, the three men stood there, a bit hesitant and yet rejoicing in
Christ.

Sven, Lewi, and Efraim. And Lewi, with his kind, tentative little
smile asked Sven how he felt after the meeting.

And then Sven replied enthusiastically:

"Well, from now on, this is going to be my music!"

Lewi thought that was both amusing and encouraging. But he
didn't comment on Sven's choice of words. Perhaps it didn't occur to
him, but those were the words of Karl XII upon landing on the island
of Sjælland in Denmark in the year 1700; at least as Voltaire represents
them in his not always entirely trustworthy book about the Swedish
hero king. And the music was the enemies' bullets whistling over the
Swedish king's head: this was going to be his music! And if Lewi had
known Sven, he would also have understood that the image and the
words were perfectly logical. It was Sven the young war-romantic and
reserve officer who had not yet adapted, was not yet adjusted to his

new circumstances. It was the reserve officer and conservative and Norway activist who was speaking, but who was on his way to becoming something entirely new.

Bullets and speaking in tongues, each a battle, a frock coat among serge suits, a soldier among conscientious objectors, not yet entirely adjusted, actually never adjusted; but with a tremendous joy at the fact that something new had happened, something that had destroyed the armor of ice and created a possible core inside the barren onion, which now felt great self-confidence.

He realized that the darkness out there did not contain implacable and inevitable death, that there is always something better than death, as it says in the old folk tale he had read as a child. Wasn't it "The Bremen Town Musicians"? Yes, it was. That folk tale by the Brothers Grimm, which his mother read to him, about the crippled and lame and useless animals who realized that there is always something better than death, and that's why they set off together, marching toward Bremen.

Surely God also had some use for a conservative reserve officer, a war-romantic, and failed poet. All parts of Christ's body belonged together, even those that were not perfect. Even the arrogant, aristocratic, and those with exalted connections. The Lord would ignore the frock coat. The Lord Jesus Christ tarried, but in the meantime Sven had found something that sent a ray of life into an existence filled with inner death.

Blood and fire. And music.

"Shall we take a little walk and have a chat?" Lewi asked, and Sven enthusiastically nodded agreement.

Efraim did not go with them. He instinctively understood that he should leave them alone, regardless of what they might "chat" about. He understood that something had happened which, much later, in a life that truly was a *Lebenslauf* and that ran almost all through the twentieth century in Sweden, would be decisive for him, as well as for Lewi and Sven, and for the Pentecostal movement. And that it was an important part in the *Lebenslauf*, which would be a strange sort of mirror on Swedish society, for better or for worse.

And it was, as he writes: "almost amusing to see them together."

Amusing? You had to imagine that it truly was in some way amusing. The march of the town musicians was in its own way an amusing story. The crippled animals organized a protest march against death, oompah oompah oompah, like the Moravians' brass band at the funerals in Christiansfeld, oompah oompah, on their way to God's acre. I suppose you would have to imagine that was how it started on that day in Kölingared, since the Lord tarried so stubbornly. A little oompah oompah, a tall man in a frock coat and a short man with a mustache, oompah oompah; now we're marching to God's acre and there is always something better than death. That's what you have to think, that's how it was; not gloomy but full of hope and controlled ecstasy: trumpets and top hats and joyous music on the way toward the gravesite that in the end awaits us all in God's acre.

Sven and Lewi looked at each other and almost saw each other.

There was something about that moment that Efraim would always remember. They were so different, those two, Sven and Lewi. And yet they looked at each other with an expression of curiosity, appreciation, kindness, surprise—and almost love. One of them, Lewi, was quite short, his hair now plastered down, without the lock over his forehead, and with a neat little mustache. And the other, Sven, was almost beyond description, but he was at any rate much taller.

And then they took their first walk together, to have a chat.

They followed a narrow pathway that passed through a field. The grain grew tall, the path was very narrow, they walked close together and chatted. Perhaps they looked slightly comical: the tall man in the frock coat, the short man in his dark suit. But that wasn't what anyone thought who watched the wanderers from the tent. After a while they saw Sven take Lewi's arm, as if for support, or to offer him support. The field of grain sank downward in a soft, billowing curve, down toward a valley. They walked farther and farther away through the field, until at last they disappeared from the view of the brothers and sisters.

First Lewi's head disappeared, since he was shorter, then Sven's. It was as if they were slowly descending into God's acre, which was not the final resting place of the dead, but truly God's acre, which was growing and still awaiting harvest, and which had now swallowed up God's twins, who were eagerly chatting with each other.

Then they were hidden by the grain. But soon they would rise up again from God's acre, still arm in arm, though it was impossible to tell who was supporting whom, or whether they were quite simply inextricably connected. And when they returned, everyone could see that these two who had descended into God's acre, but had now returned, that their happiness was almost complete.

BOOK III

June 1921–October 1930

CHAPTER 14

---·•·---

Uppsalagatan 11

1.

IT WAS THE BEST OF TIMES, AND THEY WERE ENJOYING THINGS.

In brief fragments in the *Lebenslauf* there are recurring scenes with the comment: "They were enjoying each other's company." From the very first moment. They stand in the coffee room and chat, with their arms around each other's shoulders, then suddenly, irresistibly both of them burst into laughter, louder and louder. Yet almost shy.

They seem, surprisingly enough, to have the same sense of humor. They enjoyed each other's company during this time.

Everything was so enjoyable.

Yet Sven Lidman's switch to the enemy camp was a media sensation, as it would later be called.

What he had switched over to, the enemy camp, was the side of the ecstatic friends. He switched over to enemies who were the enemies of reason. That was the general opinion. Lidman had thrown himself into their arms. It was an incomprehensible tragedy, perhaps not because this Lidman had ever appeared to be an entirely reasonable intellectual, but because he was, nevertheless, an intellectual.

He had betrayed his class, which was not the upper class but the intellectual class.

Zealots, people who spoke in tongues, adherents of religious sorcery, those who revived the dead and cured cancer through the laying on of hands—in short, the whole radical pietistic madhouse—that was the issue. Scathing articles could be written about them, preferably with elements of the comedy that the situation invited. In actuality, this was nothing more than popular reading material for times when there was no real news. But occasionally the tone grew sharper, also among the columnists. At first it was comical, later it grew sharp. Under the headline "Spreaders of Spiritual Contagion," the writer who signed himself "Fire" in *Dagens Nyheter* asked: "What should be done with a germ-carrier?" and answered: "He should be quarantined. There's nothing strange about that. He's a danger to national security. It is legally prohibited to walk around merry and free if you're infected with cholera, for example, or leprosy. Then you're taken care of and isolated in a hospital. But why do we merely cross our arms when the spiritual germ-carriers appear, and why do we let them wander freely among the public?" Later he writes about the Pentecostal movement's "contagion of the soul" in Sweden and the threats to "our ancient religion" by the lassitude the Pentecostal movement created.

And he concludes: "No, shouldn't we start thinking about the 'stamping-out' method?"

That was the tone, everywhere. Sometimes sharp and intellectually elucidating, as in this case, sometimes derisive, but there was great unanimity. It was important, at regular intervals, to emphasize that this religious ecstasy was harmful to the spiritual health of a nation, as well as an unsettling symptom of decay. *Dagens Nyheter* published the fiercest articles. They often made for exciting reading. The fact that Sven had crossed over to the madhouse sharply increased interest. In September 1921 the newspaper wrote about a meeting in the countryside of Småland under the headline: "Pentecostal Movement a Spiritual Black Death in the Countryside," and the subhead: "Speaking in Tongues of Religious Sensuality. Menacing Epidemic." It was quite a penetrating and popular article, which gave the reader a certain insight. "With the pronouncement of the prayer, the religious epidemic reaches its most repugnant forms. People lie down on the floor and crawl around each other, incessantly shouting for Jesus. This reporter will never forget the sight that presented itself when fifty individuals began crawling over each other in a mission hall, uttering completely incoherent cries. Having observed a revivalist meeting in that place, you can't help but have a feeling that something must be done to counteract any further spread of this spiritually impoverished and sick movement. Otherwise it threatens to become a spiritual Black Death for our nation."

But an alarmed older Pentecostal preacher later visited this place to find out if anything inappropriate or unusual was going on. "Not at all," was the reply. "It was an ordinary prayer meeting, the kind we used to have on Saturday evenings and after the public meetings."

An ordinary prayer meeting?

Yet the terms "decay," "the downfall of the West," and "decadence" were heard more and more often in the public debate; the Pentecostal movement was cited as an example.

The demand for purity. The battle for what was Swedish. Foreign influences that were much too great. Warnings of spiritual decay. These kept recurring. The National Socialist newspaper *Det Nya Sverige*, which carried on a fight for the preservation of Swedishness in Sweden, also printed an exhaustive analysis of the Pentecostal movement and summed up by saying that it was "an unhealthy deviation from the spiritual life of the time. By its very nature this phenomenon is un-Swedish."

Scores of articles in the same vein appeared on the editorial pages, with penetrating analyses: there are "weaknesses in the national character that make the mind gloomy and susceptible to religious excesses."

Which made the case of this Lidman all the more bewildering, and loathsome. Perhaps he was at heart a dreamer and charlatan, and then it wouldn't be so surprising. But he had prestige. And he was lending his good name to those who were weak in character, legitimizing them. This Lidman, who was well-known in wide literary circles, who was regarded as talented, and who had been married to a Thiel, had fallen! Of course there had been suspicions, for a long time, that everything wasn't quite right, either in body or soul, with this not entirely young poet and novelist. In his books he had also shown fanatical tendencies, and it was now clearly confirmed that he had never actually been an author of importance.

Yet this astonishment. A passionate erotic poet, who had once married into the financial upper class and was proclaimed a genius in *Svenska Dagbladet*, had suddenly thrown himself into the arms of the proletarian Pentecostal movement, that mob of speaking-in-tongues babblers, with their social welfare program that perhaps harbored ominous political intentions. A journalist recalled the hunger riots in Västervik only a few years before, and how easily the crowds had switched from ecstasy to violence.

Could the same thing happen here?

In the East, storm clouds were gathering. Was there a connection? The signs needed to be watched closely. Where was it all heading? That was the question they also needed to ask about the Pentecostal movement, no matter what quaint babbling it seemed to be.

Where was it all heading?

Lewi knew where it was heading.

He took Sven to the premises they had at Uppsalagatan 11, which in two months would be replaced by new quarters on Sveavägen. But as of now this was still the center where the great narrative of the Pentecostal movement was played out. He wanted to show Sven what it was like. He wanted to lead him back into history, in order then to move forward. Perhaps he wanted to revisit the moment that served as the starting point for their story, because he realized that this point was the most important of all and had to be as solid as the rock on which Jesus had built his congregation, the rock of Peter. It had to be identified if they were to reach agreement about the landscape of faith.

This was the first meeting hall of the Filadelfia Church.

There were three entrances down into the hall: the official one, directly from the street; the second one from what the brothers called the "first courtyard"; and the third from the "outer courtyard." The great stairwell seemed to break right through the hall itself; you had to go quite a distance into the congregation hall to be able to see the pulpit, to see who was preaching there. As a hall for religious services, the premises were genuinely impractical, although photographs present a more favorable impression than sketches or contemporary accounts.

The room next door was called the "little hall." It was actually a kitchen, created in accordance with the usual Moravian model: there was an iron range, on which stood a big pot used for making coffee. Nearby, neatly stacked, lay the small jute bags that, filled with ground coffee, were lowered into the boiling water to make what was called, within the entire revivalist movement regardless of sect, "meeting-house coffee"—sometimes in a pejorative sense. "His preaching was like meeting-house coffee," as they used to say about Pastor Lundmark from Skråmträsk, as opposed to Pastor Brimstone-Bryggman, whose sermons were like boiling oil cast upon those who were slumbering and those of little faith.

Lewi took Sven into the rooms that were the very heart of the Pentecostal movement.

From the little hall the preacher could not be seen at all. If, on the other hand, the preacher was positioned in the corner facing the little hall, everyone in there could both see and hear him, but then problems arose in the big hall. But those who stood on the stairs to the back courtyard could never see the speaker at all, no matter where he stood.

"So this is where we spend our days," Lewi explained. Sven merely looked around with a stiff expression, as if he were perplexed.

"I thought it would be bigger," he said. "And not below street level."

"No, this is how big it is."

"Well, I thought it would be bigger."

"No, this is how big it is."

"But in Kölingared it was bigger," Sven said, as if to explain, but Lewi simply replied:

"No, on a day-to-day basis this is how big it is. Praise the Lord. But in September we're opening the hall on Sveavägen, and then it will be bigger."

"Praise the Lord," muttered Sven. "But can everyone actually see the speaker?"

"They can hear him," replied Lewi.

A moment of silence followed, and then Sven said quite firmly:

"When *I* speak, they need to be able to see."

They went into the little hall.

That was where the congregational office was located, along with the deacons' room, and the dressing room for baptismal candidates. Lewi also pointed out the baptismal pool, and Sven studied it thoughtfully.

"It's awfully small," he said. "Can a person actually fit into that?"

"We Pentecostals aren't very fat," Lewi said in an almost cool tone of voice. He seemed annoyed or disappointed by Sven's lack of enthusiasm and the fact that he had so quickly expressed criticism about the cramped quarters that didn't look at all the way he expected.

"There are those among us who have little to eat," Lewi added.

There was now a peculiar tension in the air. "And that makes a person thin. But you're thin yourself, even though you probably didn't lack for food in the Thiel household."

The words came out by surprise. In reality they were almost malicious, if a person wanted to take them that way. Sven did not respond. Efraim writes that he "feared for a moment that a conflict had already started," but suddenly a crash was heard up above in the sewer lines that hung in full view along the ceiling.

There was a great roar, and it wasn't hard to figure out why.

A toilet was flushing. Someone had relieved himself.

"Can you hear that during the services, as well?" asked Sven with a little appreciative smile.

"Yes, you can," replied Lewi. "But we don't hear it because God's voice speaks to us so strongly."

"But just imagine if it's God's stomach that's rumbling up there," Sven said, and playfully poked Lewi in the stomach.

This was so astonishing that at first they simply stared at each other. God's stomach that rumbled and then let loose. Not amusing. And yet, in the end, Lewi started to laugh, and not in a strained or forced way; it was a completely genuine laugh, as if he found the joke utterly irresistible and was somehow relieved.

"Just imagine," said Lewi after he composed himself. "I've actually thought the same thing a few times. How strange. Praise the Lord. Blessed are His acts of charity."

"His is the power," Sven rejoined, and then the incident was over and they could continue to study the place that was the source of the Pentecostal movement's story, and which was now to be abandoned, including the much too small baptismal pool suited only for emaciated sisters and brothers, and the sewer lines and the ill-placed seats, and all the rest that had given them so many blessed meetings.

But which had now grown too small. And soon would be abandoned for something much, much bigger.

2.

Sven's first sermon was not perfect. Though it was not bad, either. But it stirred confusion. It was somehow a different kind of rhetoric.

The house was full, and the whole event was played out at Uppsalagatan 11, where a meeting was now held every evening. "Before the move, things were quite intense, as if they didn't want to abandon the old premises," as Efraim notes in the *Lebenslauf*.

Sven was intently scrutinized.

He gazed out at the expectant, saved faces in the hall. He picked up his watch. He wound it. He didn't say a word. He waited. Not a pin dropped. Then he began to speak.

"*Lex dura, sed lex.*"

Then he fell silent and looked out at the congregation. He repeated: "*Lex dura, sed lex.*"

By then the tension was unbearable. He said for the third time:

"*Lex dura, sed lex.* When I traveled here by train and looked at the faces of my fellow passengers, I thought that human beings are like tigers in a menagerie: woe to all culture and civilization if the animal tamer is killed by them. All tigers in the human heart are simply waiting for Jesus to be completely obliterated from the heart of existence. *Lex dura, sed lex.*"

That was how Sven began his sermon about the blackness in the depths of humanity, and how Jesus saves us. Afterwards the opinions were mixed, but they all thought it was interesting, in spite of the fact that he never explained that part with the Latin. Afterwards they gathered in the inner room for conversation and prayer, and Sven criticized himself, saying that he realized it might not have been very good. But he had pondered for a long time how to explain the religious experience. It was like music. How can you explain music, what the experience of music is like? Humanity has such a lack of words.

"How can we explain the religious experience?" he asked them.

"Give me time," he said. And they nodded and knelt down for a communal prayer, which was quite candid, and they praised God, who acted through Word and Spirit, and they trusted fervently in His promise of a glorious salvation and redemption through the blood of the Lamb, believing that the Spirit in a mysterious way would in rich measure come to the aid of our infirmity.

And afterwards Lewi and Sven walked through Stockholm, and Lewi said:

"It's going to be fine."

Woe to humanity if the animal tamer is killed by the tigers inside the human heart. Then all culture and civilization will be obliterated, and Jesus will be obliterated from the human heart.

There is something about this image that would echo throughout what happened later. The animal tamer. The driver of the wild ass.

What was that?

But it actually did turn out fine, and almost immediately.

Efraim was a diligent listener that first year, and he was astonished. He was not alone in his astonishment, he was almost bewitched. Efraim hadn't cared for Sven, not particularly, but he was won over. "Those first ten years it was powerful, and the fact that things later changed does not diminish it."

When the other person in Efraim's world, Lewi, spoke, he never used a prepared script, but spoke extemporaneously, following main points. Early on it was decided that if a parliamentary stenographer was hired to record the sermons, they could be issued in book form by the Filadelfia congregation's publishing company. As for Sven, it's true that he usually spoke extemporaneously, but he spent more time writing down outlines. Though he claimed to be lazy. He too made use of a stenographer.

But his sermons were published by Bonniers. And can still be read today.

If he was searching for a language for the religious experience, he very quickly came close.

It wasn't hard to understand Efraim: what an amazingly stirring boost Sven Lidman's preaching presented for the Swedish religious life.

When it was all over, when the conflicts reached their climax, the rupture was a fact, and the animosity had both come and gone, even Lewi could then rightfully conclude: Sven's sermons had meant a decisive breakthrough in the quality of Swedish religious preaching. "By virtue of his style and his manner of presentation, they are in a class by themselves among collections of sermons and Swedish religious literature."

That's how it was. And Sven seemed to find his voice at once.

If his novels, as Efraim claims—and no doubt Efraim was right— were sterile and wooden and had strained to win the love of the literary world, seeking legitimacy in the aesthetic values of his class, but in a disastrous way, as if his arrogance and inner death had indirectly also killed his writing, then his preachings, on the other hand, were sheer, unintentional masterpieces. As works of art, they were superior to anything he had ever done before, within the world of literature and art.

In a strange way he was like Hans Christian Andersen, who, with his convulsive ambitions to become very famous and recognized within the literary world, had written novels that were utterly dead while, on the other hand, his stories for children—which he himself practically scorned and which were written without specific intent, without literary dreams, almost in secret, and only "because they made him happy"—became literary masterpieces that changed all of Nordic prose.

Sven had found his artistic genre. It was storytelling as sermon.

Much later his narrative method would be exploited by his successors both within the Pentecostal movement and in the Swedish church, sometimes turning it to parody. The images and parables would overflow and fall flat. But during those years, in the presence of the astonished brothers and sisters of Filadelfia, his preaching was a leap upward. Sven could certainly tell a story, and his dramaturgical skill held his listeners in an iron grip. Even his erudition was no longer destructive. It's true that for a few brief moments of his sermon he might insert quotes from Alfred de Vigny, Hölderlin, and Shakespeare, but he found quotes that were simple and that opened the way to images and ideas they had never heard before.

The *Lex-dura* period didn't last long. It wasn't particularly necessary. Not anymore. He had once and for all established the notion of his bottomless knowledge, anchoring it deeply and firmly, and he no longer needed to seize hold of his irrefutably grandiose snobbishness about being an intellectual.

Then he seemed to turn downward, to greater simplification and depth, as if he had actually taken to heart the constantly repeated cry: "My friend . . . my friend . . . my friend." And looked upon all of them as friends whenever he now had to explain something very difficult, very astounding, and very exceptional in a very simple way.

The images, anecdotes, and quotations grew, one after the other, and it was utterly irresistible. He seemed to have an almost infinitely rich and terrible life from which to draw. The prodigal son returning from sin had baggage from his perdition, one tale followed the next. Best of all, many thought, was when he talked about something awful or incomprehensible from his life as a sinner, or presented some gruesome story about the way life was in the godless upper class.

Then it was almost breathtaking.

If the episode hadn't happened to himself, then someone else had told him something astounding, or shocking. The stories were about vain and successful people who were not saved and who were struck by horrible misfortune. Or arrogant people who were punished with death. It was Nemesis Divina as storyteller, like in the work of the gloomy and misanthropic flower king Linnaeus in the old days. Unpleasant people who persecuted the Flower King were always struck by righteous misfortune, breaking their leg on the slippery ice, and the avenging hand of God was behind it. But in the end there was still hope. That was part of the dramaturgy: it was possible to breathe freely.

Metaphorically speaking, and the images were numerous, Sven himself seemed to have been constantly on the brink of drowning, but at the last minute he was always saved by a crack in the smooth rock face and could haul himself up and find solid ground to stand on, just as Jesus is the solid rock, Hallelujah!

Or he had overheard an upsetting conversation in a train compartment that made him and his listeners shudder. Or he might report on the latest medical discovery, about the little gland that is the most crucial "not only for the harmonious development of a person's body, but also for the shaping of his soul," and which, if cut away, causes degeneration. "Those responsible for European culture have the same foolish view of Christianity and religion—a rudimentary organ that society no longer needs: cut it away!"

He was like an encyclopedia. A person could learn practically everything during his sermons.

And constantly recurring, like a menacing image that was not hell or the Devil, but something more earthly, was the state of spiritual decay in Europe. Europe was always present and in danger. Europe was disintegrating. A twilight land. It was as if Spengler had descended into Filadelfia's cellar premises and with his spirit permeated those strange years between the wars in Europe within the Pentecostal movement. Sven brought something with him, though it was unclear what that was. No one could match Sven in depicting the contemporary consequences of Belshazzar's feast, in which the feast signified "the squandering and misappropriation of the last remaining capital of love, veneration, and obedience, which was the sustaining force, *nervus rerum*, the blood in the body of European civilization."

Veneration and obedience as *nervus rerum*? Before whom? Oh yes, of course, before the Lord who was still tarrying.

It was "if the Lord tarries," but inserted in a European political context that seemed vast and ominous. Everyone agreed that it elevated the preaching.

Those were Sven's first ten years as a preacher, and quite splendid. He would never reach those heights again, not even in his memoirs. There was something utterly genuine underneath all of this. Something childlike, and utterly pure: as if the prodigal son had come home and was extremely happy and wanted to tell everything to his siblings, and it was all so pleasant.

And the dreadful experiences became an integral part of the pleasant, and the stories would never stop flowing.

Sven had come home and been given a mission. For the first time in his life he was allowed to compose stories right in front of his circle of readers. And it worked, the bridge held, they listened, and he knew that at last he was home.

Sven was a sensation, and everyone was overjoyed. What seemed strange to Efraim was that even Lewi appeared to be so unreflective and unequivocally happy.

Didn't he see anything disturbing in this breakthrough by a new figurehead? Didn't he see a play for power? Was he blind, or could it be true that the yin and yang of these two kinds of preaching actually complemented each other with no problem? Wasn't Lewi afraid that the strong storm Sven Lidman was now pushing forward and up through the Pentecostal movement might push him aside?

The *Lebenslauf* is filled with disquieting indications. For instance, after an evening meeting that was blessed but quite stormy because a woman spoke in tongues and at one point during the evening had almost shattered the unity. But Lewi sat up there on the platform, quite calm. And then Sven preached. And it was a good sermon.

It was very good and powerful—that's the word that Efraim always uses—but in Efraim's opinion a few of the thousand-headed congregation may have become rather thoughtful.

Sven spoke about John the Baptist, but began by talking about a

pastor he knew up in Värmland. He was a real pastor and not a career
pastor. And he almost came far enough along in his congregational
work for a revival to break out. Almost. Then another preacher arrived,
and when he preached, the revival did break out. And that shoved the
first pastor aside, the one who was wise and decent and no career pastor, but who had not been able to light a fire so people came through.

He was shoved aside. He was allowed to stand there and watch.

The same thing happened to John the Baptist. When Jesus Christ
appeared, he had to step aside. And Lidman spoke in a strong and
somewhat subdued voice, saying that was how it had to be. When
God's will has finished His work in us, then He takes another instrument. And Sven talked about that which is most difficult: to be diminished, to step aside, and the fact that God's work was more important
than personal pride. "God has set one to sow, and when the crops are
ready, then He sends another to harvest them."

And that's how it had to be.

For some reason this made Efraim uncomfortable. He glanced at
Lewi who was sitting on the platform, as he always did, and studied his
face, looking for a reaction. But Lewi was gazing out over the congregation with a perfectly pleased and very calm expression, and he
seemed to be squinting. No one could tell what he was thinking.

Sven was the great speaker, after all, and Lewi was the leader. But
was there room for both? Or what had Sven meant? Or did he mean
anything at all?

When the conflict arose, everyone claimed to have seen signs. But
there was actually only one sign of how things were during that time:
they both loved each other, and admired each other, and it was all so
pleasant.

After that blessed evening, which was only partially shadowed by the
story of the pastor in Värmland, the one who had to step aside, after
that Efraim sat with a cup of meeting-house coffee in the inner room.

And Sven and Lewi were there with him.

And they chatted for a while about the woman who almost went
crazy, and how that had developed. And then they talked about the sermon they had heard. And about being diminished and growing, and
relinquishing to someone else, and through all of this serving God.

And Efraim asked Lewi a question, though later he couldn't

remember how it was formulated. But it was about how Lewi now viewed his mission, meaning his collaboration with Sven. If it was a collaboration. Or was it a matter of leadership? Efraim chose his words carefully, since Sven was there too, and since both of them seemed so happy and seemed to enjoy each other's company. As if no one had noticed the undertone in the sermon that Efraim had noticed.

"You looked so strangely calm, sitting there on the platform, Brother Pethrus," said Sven, as if he understood the intent of the question but wanted to ward it off. And then Lewi looked at him, with a little smile, and said:

"You mean, how do I see my mission?"

"Yes," said Sven, "that must be what Brother Efraim meant by his question."

"My role in this fermenting revival?"

"Yes, your role."

Lewi pondered this for a moment and then said:

"When the farmers take water out to the cows in the field, they usually use a barrel. And they pull the barrel on a cart. And if the road is bumpy, a lot of water spills out. Then they usually place a piece of board inside and let it float on the water, to keep it from spilling out."

Sven didn't understand, but asked in bewilderment:

"What do you mean?"

"I'm that piece of board," replied Lewi.

CHAPTER 15

The Phosphorescent Cross

1.

LEWI SAID TO SVEN: "YOU BRING A GREAT DEAL WITH YOU; IT WILL BE a new life. Do you think it will be difficult?"

He didn't answer.

A recorded exchange of words after an evening meeting in September 1921.

An elderly sister in the congregation asked Sven:

"Have you received assurance of salvation and Spirit baptism?"

"Yes, praise the Lord."

"They say that you've written novels?"

Apparently he found the question a bit puzzling, perhaps insulting, since she didn't know him as an author and suspected his celebrity, but with a little smile he replied:

"Yes, I have."

"In our view, novels are the work of the Devil."

"I don't write anymore," he said after a slight pause, speaking in an odd tone of voice that surprised Efraim, though he couldn't interpret it.

"Why?"

"Why?"

"Why have you stopped?"

He was silent for a moment, then said in a very low voice:

"I don't regret having stopped."

"Are you sure?" she asked.

"No," he then said.

*   *   *

It happened so swiftly that he didn't even recognize himself; no one recognized him.

In July he took part in a summer excursion for Pentecostal youths. They set out in boats and headed for the archipelago. From that excursion Efraim recalls a conversation between Sven and a young girl of thirteen.

There were seven people in the rowboat. They had passed Djurgården, and the young girl pointed toward the thickly forested island, at the Thiel palace, and asked Sven:

"What's the name of the people who live there?"

"Thiel," replied Sven.

"Brother Pethrus has told us that over there they drink and dance and live an ungodly life and are enormously rich, but they haven't received grace."

"How strange," Sven said. "Why did Brother Pethrus say that about those particular people?"

"That's what he said," replied the girl. "They are infected with sin."

"But it's not contagious, dear child," he said as the boat slowly drifted forward with the strokes of the oars. He didn't look at the girl, but stubbornly kept his gaze on the house.

"It's the contagion of sin," said the girl.

"The contagion of sin?"

"And once you get it, it's like tuberculosis. Almost worse than tuberculosis. You can never get rid of it."

"Oh yes, you can. With the grace of Jesus," said Sven.

"Who was he?" the girl asked.

"Thiel? He was very rich."

"How do you know that?"

"He was once my father-in-law."

The words spilled out before he could think; they simply slipped out of him.

"Now you're joking," said the girl with a smile, and then added: "It almost frightens me to think about the people who aren't saved, those in perdition!!!"

"Me too," replied Sven. "But can't a person ever get rid of the contagion of sin?"

The girl now had the attention of the others in the boat, who evidently knew Sven better than she did. They were silent and embarrassed and kept gesturing to her; then she realized that he was not joking with her.

"But it probably doesn't infect anyone unless they want to be infected," she said, almost imploring, or as if she were suddenly afraid of him. "And it probably goes away, it's not like tuberculosis."

"You can never get rid of it," Sven then said in an oddly thick voice. "It's probably worse than tuberculosis."

The whole time he kept his eyes on the shore and the trees and the house with its stairs, which on this summer day were not shrouded or hidden by the Nordic evening light, and he didn't look at the girl who had plagued him with the question about the contagion of sin. Could a person ever be rid of it? Or was it even worse than tuberculosis or, in the best case, just as deadly as tuberculosis?

2.

It has to be assumed that Sven was a beloved concern for the Filadelfia congregation.

It was obvious that he could speak. And they had heard that he could write, although most of the congregation elders, in the strictest confidence, told each other that they wouldn't want to read what Lidman had written before he came through. Which in some cases was true. But Lewi, who was worried about his pet project, the *Härold*, called a meeting of the leading brothers and presented to them a plan for making Sven the editor of *Evangelii Härold*.

"The *Härold*," he said, "is part of what we expect from him. He's a celebrated poet and novelist, and he's a brilliant preacher. But he needs to be given a larger platform than the one at Sveavägen. The intellectuals, who control the newspapers and public opinion, hate us; it's pure class hatred. But with Sven and his pen we have a weapon they weren't expecting. I also think that Brother Lidman can open the eyes of many more people. He's a good writer. Sometimes his speeches are rather complicated; some people think he's speaking Greek. As for that, I say that we're used to speaking in tongues, and that too is foreign to many people, but it can be interpreted. Brother Lidman's writings are no more Greek than speaking in tongues; in fact, just the opposite."

He also said, "The Pentecostal movement plays many of God's melodies, and on many instruments. God chooses which instrument He, in His mercy, wishes to play. It is not the place of human beings to criticize Him. We play all too seldom the concertina, an instrument of the people, and related to the pump organ."

The pump organ, as Lewi pointed out, was the instrument that he himself had learned to play.

"The concertina is still an instrument of the dance floor, it's true, but the Devil does not have a monopoly on any particular instrument. Over time we will win back the concertina from the Devil, just as we did the fiddle.

"But Brother Lidman is a flute," he said, "on which God plays the strangest melodies. And we should make use of this flute."

We should make use of this flute.

After this speech all the brothers were utterly silent, almost taken aback, and Lewi then said he was pleased that everyone agreed with him. Which may have surprised the others, since he hadn't asked for their opinion, and in any case had not taken a vote. Which was something to which they had now become accustomed. They regarded it as a habit he had brought with him from his days in the trade union movement.

And then he went to Sven and presented him with his new assignment.

"Your sermons," he said, "are God's Word straight down to the stomachs of the faithful, and they satisfy better than the nourishment of any other preacher. But you reach only those who are sitting in the congregation. Through the *Härold* you can reach many more, and the circulation will grow. You will be the editor, and all your sermons will be printed, and that way we'll reach farther and to many more people." Lidman replied that his sermons were not written down but given extemporaneously, based on certain main points. In fact, they were created during fervent prayer and contemplation in the sight of the Lord, but he was lazy and didn't have the energy to write them down, and that was that. At first Lewi, displeased, let it go, but later he said that they would obtain a stenographer. He had contact with several who worked at the Parliament and who, in their dreary job and their spiritual need would no doubt wish for more powerful nourishment (the wording is Efraim's, there is always that word "powerful" recurring, but in this case he has doubtless reported correctly)—these stenographers would write down his sermon.

Then Sven could polish and perhaps delete whatever he didn't wish to include. Then it would be published. And this was crucial to the circulation.

In fact, they were in need of money, because Lewi had plans for a big new church building. He didn't want to mention it yet, but he was conducting negotiations.

These negotiations were, it was understood, with God and the Building Authorities.

So that's what happened.

Sven remained the editor-in-chief of *Evangelii Härold* until it folded in 1948. His sermons were published, and the circulation grew, and the money poured in, and Sven would become a very lazy editor, but that didn't matter.

He was the astounding face presented to the world. And Lewi was right.

His words would reach a long way, and they sowed the seed in many more people than those who listened to him in Stockholm. And the circulation grew. The *Härold* was part of what the Pentecostal movement expected from Sven; that was what Lewi had unanimously decided, in consultation with God.

Because it was between those two that a vote was requested and had to be carried out, and agreement was nearly always reached, with no opposition.

3.

When they walked off through the valley that first time, down through God's acre, Efraim noticed that they were walking arm in arm.

But who was leading whom? It was impossible to see or determine. That was just it. And the question kept coming up, as if it were important, though perhaps it was not.

In the *Lebenslauf* there is a peculiar account inserted about Sven's second marriage. It actually has to do with Sven and his second wife, Brita. But Efraim seems to have had a different purpose, as if he wanted to explain who was leading whom, and how difficult it was to explain, and that it was almost impossible to explain the problem with the walk that Lewi and Sven took through God's glorious acre.

Who ensnared whom? And how did they make use of each other?

The event took place several years before Lewi and Sven were united at Kölingared. Sven was newly saved and had started reading the marriage advertisements.

It was incomprehensible. The great author, who had brought down so many women and even at the age of thirty-five was in his prime, was looking through the marriage ads. For the most part not in the respectable bourgeois press, but instead in the revivalist newspapers.

What was he looking for?

Yet in the pious press the ads were sparse. He had the feeling that those who advertised there were certainly saved, and had come through, but were perhaps the kind who had ended up on the remainder pile and weren't particularly interesting. Now, in 1918, he was certainly saved, but he regarded himself to be more of a fundamentalist Catholic than someone who was ecstatically Spirit baptized. Yet he was looking for a sister in faith. He knew that this way of thinking, the passionate uniting of eroticism and faith, was part of his old life coloring his new life. And he prayed fervently for the Savior to free him from this sin, but at the same time he praised Him, in His mercy, for giving him this strong and clear awareness of sin. And he hoped that the virginal and pious woman he was seeking would actually possess the violent inner passion that he found so enticing.

But he couldn't free himself from the idea that there were few of that sort of women putting ads in the Christian newspapers, and that he ought to look elsewhere.

Finally he turned to the ungodly press, meaning *Svenska Dagbladet*.

There he found an ad that interested him. It seemed to have possibilities. It didn't sound quite so dull. His attention was caught by the word "cheerful." The girl from Malung, who in the past had helped him whenever he was feeling tattered and melancholy and in need of comfort behind the curtain, she had always called herself "cheerful." Sometimes he thought about her with regret, but he never used her in his sermons as an example. He had a kind of respect for her, although he wasn't able to explain why.

That was in a different time. Sven had many faces. But several of the old ones were starting to fade away. Or at least he was making an effort.

Then he picked up his scissors and cut out the ad.

It said:

"Young, educated, Christian-minded girl wishes, for the purpose of marriage, to meet a like-minded, good-hearted man, gladly a widower!

"Reply to 'Cheerful and musical'

"At Gustav Adolf's Square, Stockholm."

He sat in his room for a long time and stared at the ad. Then he finally picked up his pen and wrote a letter.

Brita Otterdahl was the one hiding behind the pseudonym "Cheerful and musical."

She was born on March 22, 1890 at the Tomteboda Institute for the Blind, where her father was a doctor, and at the time of her meeting with Sven she was twenty-eight years old, and a virgin.

She never wrote any memoirs.

Everyone else wrote; everyone else bore witness, or attacked, or polemicized, or wrote favorable accounts, or dissertations, or novels.

All around Sven and Lewi a choir of witnesses roared: opinionated, truthful, lying, curious, bewildered in the presence of the many faces of these strange twins, and everyone was eager to finally establish how things were. How they were! Conclusively, how they were. Brita Otterdahl, too, later wrote books, for children, as well as a particularly significant text for the Pentecostal movement: her ad in *Svenska Dagbladet*. That is her *Lebenslauf*.

The rest has to be reconstructed, with the help of others. Efraim describes her as a "strong and brave girl," and no doubt that was true.

The circumstances surrounding the courtship indicate that he was right.

Brita Otterdahl answered the letter, and Sven replied in turn, and quite a long time passed, their contact rising and falling like an ocean wave. But then he went to visit the home of this person who might wish to be his wife.

They carried on a rather strained conversation, but after a while she asked him, almost shyly, to come with her into the next room.

"Come, there's something I'd like to show you."

They went into the next room. It was almost completely dark. She led the way and then stopped, without saying a word. It was a bedroom, that much he could see. She had led him to her bedroom. Then she put out the lamp. She put out the lamp! No doubt this was what she meant in the ad by "cheerful," but he was still surprised.

On the wall hung a crucifix, over her bed. It was perfect, he started breathing hard.

She stood still and waited. Sven now felt almost confident.

Very cautiously he approached her, since he was now feeling almost confident. He crept close to her, and from behind, with a gentle, experienced movement, he placed his hand on her breast. He was now quite confident that this was what she wanted, and the room was in semidarkness. With the same movement, he kissed her.

She then, with a violent motion, tore herself free from his grip and, deeply shocked, she said to him:

"But what . . . how dare you . . . how dare you?!!!"

They were standing facing each other in the dark, and he suddenly realized that he shouldn't have been so confident. That she might actually be less "cheerful" and more "Christian-minded." At any rate, she was not particularly cheerful, perhaps not at all.

It was extremely embarrassing.

"Forgive me . . . I misunderstood . . . I . . ."

"Misunderstood what?"

"It's so dark in here . . . and I thought that . . ."

"That I brought you into a dark room to . . . to . . . to . . . ! I just wanted to show you the cross! It's phosphorescent! It glows in the dark!!!"

"Phosphorescent?"

He stared at the cross as if bewitched. It was hanging over the bed, and in the dark he could see that it quite clearly was phosphorescent.

The cross was phosphorescently shining at him. It was quite obvious that it was phosphorescent.

"Of course. I misunderstood."

She stared at him, dumbfounded.

"I just wanted to show you my phosphorescent cross! Absolutely nothing else!"

"I beg your pardon. Of course. A very beautiful cross. Actually quite beautiful."

Then she left the room and went into the little kitchen and sat down. He sat across from her. She merely looked at him and incredulously shook her head.

"Not a good beginning," Sven said, laconically.

* * *

Not long afterwards he proposed.

He regarded this as his duty, since he had nearly violated a pure Christian girl who had in no way enticed him into a trap, although this is what he implied for the rest of his life: that she had ensnared him, which she, over the years and whenever the marriage, at regular intervals, seemed to shatter, would persistently and with growing fury deny to the many friends to whom she told her story, and who couldn't understand her indignation after fifty years.

That was how the legend was born, about the one who ensnares and the one who is ensnared, the one who uses and the one who is used.

In the end no one could remember how it began, not even Sven, even though he transferred it to the other, larger event, and that's where it ended up echoing in the *Lebenslauf*, in a description of someone who never lied: a true story about the phosphorescent cross, that was turned into the legend about Sven and Lewi and in reality referred to a trauma within the Swedish Pentecostal movement: Who did the ensnaring, who was used, who was the parasite and who was the host?

"A strong and brave girl," Efraim wrote. Possibly it could be added that she was intelligent, able to distinguish the important from the unimportant and make decisions.

The events of the marriage proposal indicate as much.

During the proposal Brita sat in a wicker chair in front of Sven, who paced back and forth in the room. He had delivered a monologue that skipped all around, and since at first it wasn't easy to figure out where it was leading, though it was something about spiritual inheritance from an uncle he admired and who had a wooden leg, or had drowned, or was killed in a war, she started mixing up his ancestors.

Then she asked a question. She quite simply interrupted him.

"Sven, I have to ask you something."

"Yes?"

"I don't quite know . . . what your feelings are for me," she said in a low voice.

"No?"

"What your feelings are for me. Deep inside."

He then stopped his restless pacing, came to a halt and stared at her, saying:

"Shall I tell you?"

"Yes, but be honest!"

He gave her a sharp look and asked:

"Honest?"

"Yes, honest. I won't stand for anything else."

That's when a different kind of monologue began.

"When we first met," he said, and then hesitated for a moment before continuing in an even firmer tone of voice. "When we first met after I answered your advertisement, my first impression of you wasn't especially favorable. No, little Sven, I thought, this is a mistake. A delicate little woman with pious but for me strange eyes. With something about her being that I would call lamb's down. A gentle, fragile reed of a figure. Rather blond hair, a mark on her neck from an operation. White, elegant, but much too soft hands. Angelically sweet when she reads the Bible. Not as beautiful when she sings. She seems stupid and affected when she tries to make a joke."

"That's enough," she interrupted. "Shall I leave now?"

"But then—something good about her being. I would like to possess this soft, gentle figure. A feeling that she in some secret way would suit me. Not fond of amusements. But good. Possible to shape according to my wishes. I felt a deep sense of pleasure at the thought of a wedding night with her, a sudden excitement. Something soft, white, that became burned into me."

He fell silent.

"Yes?"

"But is this something," he added pensively, "on which a marriage can be built? I think so. I think so."

She stared at him as if she couldn't believe her eyes or her ears. After a moment of silence, since he didn't seem to have anything more to say, but was waiting, though she had no idea what he was waiting for, after a moment of silence she said:

"You're out of your mind! What an aria!!! Is that a proposal?"

"Yes," he said, "it is."

Then she started to laugh, almost in resignation, but at last she composed herself and said, in a very matter-of-fact tone:

"The answer is yes."

CHAPTER 16

A Man by the Name
of Franklin

1.

AFTERWARDS SOME PEOPLE CALLED IT A PURE BATTLE FOR POWER.

Others described the conflict as ideological, almost archetypal,
inevitable in all successful political movements. Or almost like the classic story about the struggle of a popular movement to survive in spite
of its success.

How to fight the inner death, despite success?

Perhaps it was simply inevitable. Perhaps the success was much
too great.

In the *Lebenslauf* there is a brief citation from one of the three books
written about the movement by the "dissident" (!) Adrian Holmberg.

It's a presentation in chart form of "the Filadelfia congregation's
development from idyllic movement to a democracy and then to a
bunch of incapacitated individuals ruled from the top," which is given
its "legal expression" in the bylaws of the congregation.

Holmberg's harsh summary is as follows:

Period I
August 30, 1910–March 27, 1916
No bylaws

Period II
March 27, 1916–April 6, 1936
Full democracy

Period III
April 6, 1936–July 1, 1946
Democracy reduced

Period IV
July 1, 1946–November 26, 1962
Democracy strangled

Period V
November 26, 1962—
Pure dictatorship

The chart was put together in 1980, two years before Efraim's death.

He copied it, then drew a wavy (hesitant?) line with pencil across the chart, and added the words "More like a theocracy."

That was it precisely. For safety's sake I looked up the word, and found the following definition: "God's empire. A form of government in which the person or persons in power derive their authority directly from God." In that sense there was hardly any difference between the absolute monarch, by the Grace of God, Christian VII—who gave all his divine power to Struensee, who then created the Moravian colony in Christiansfeld, where Efraim now rests—and Lewi. Except that Lewi believed that God had sent him, and that he was living in what used to be called the century of democracy.

It's obvious that a conflict had to arise.

2.

Perhaps the Franklin dispute was actually the cultural revolution of the Pentecostal movement.

Since everyone expected that the babbling idiots of this new Pentecostal movement would soon grow tired and the wave would subside, the stubborn and ever-growing success was deeply shocking. It just kept going.

It was utterly incomprehensible.

Whether credit was due to Lewi, or Sven, or the Lord Jesus Christ, who was tarrying so long in spite of that stubborn "Meeting at 7 o'clock, if the Lord tarries," who as if from compassion was tarrying so that Lewi and his brothers would have time to gather ever greater crowds, a token of Christ's love to allow as many saved as possible to gather in the wound in the side of Jesus before He returned; yet it was hard to say who deserved credit.

Why was this particular revivalist movement like an avalanche?

Did the Pentecostal movement grow during those early decades because the setting was so dark, the war so terrifying, the depression so deep, Europe so decadent, the unemployment so demoralizing, hope so meager, and the magical radiant force of the phosphorescent cross so irresistibly enticing in the semidarkness?

No doubt it was all of these things combined.

One fact remained: the Pentecostal movement just kept growing. All the other ecclesiastical communities in Sweden stood on the sidelines, gaping, and for the life of them had no idea what to do. In ten years the Filadelfia congregation in Stockholm had outgrown its cellar location on Uppsalagatan, and could now count 5,167 official members, which in Stockholm alone was six times larger than the Baptist Union that had once spit Lewi and his poor disciples out of its mouth. And all over the country this popular movement of Lewi and Christ had spread like a prairie fire; yes, the old image from the Enlightenment actually fit perfectly.

By the late 1920s there were "at least" 530 independent Pentecostal congregations around the country, with a membership that fluctuated, but from the viewpoint of the other free churches and the state church, it was presumed to be appallingly vast. It was also composed of—as an astonished editorial writer gloomily but quite rightly concluded in *Ny Dag*, making use of standard communist terms— "genuine cadre congregations."

Not something to take lightly. No career pastors and no nominal Christians. Devoted followers who had to endure a great deal of duress for their membership, but who stood firm. Many people wondered, with justified alarm, whether this lunatic sect was in reality even bigger than the Swedish state church. In any case it was bigger than all the other free churches combined. And it just kept on growing, with almost fifty new congregations each year. Not to mention its international development. It caused anxiety for everyone; the Pentecostal missionaries were terribly effective at spreading the contagion of the Pentecostal movement.

Where was it all heading?

The crux of the problem was indicated by the fact that the term "at least" 530 congregations had to be used. All figures were tentative, or rather minimum figures, and this had to do with the association issue. Lewi's basic ideology included a battle against the idea of any kind of association. All congregations were supposed to be independent. There was no central authority, no central administration except for the Bible, praise the Lord, and therefore no central statistics. Occasionally the *Härold* would write that it would be good if the congregations sent in reports to the newspaper; anything good should be communicated to the other brothers and sisters in faith. And many did write in to report on the creation of new congregations or the number of members.

But there were many others who didn't care to do so. If they were independent, then they were independent. And there was nothing in the Holy Scriptures, which was their guiding principle, after all, that spoke of statistics.

God loves human beings one by one. And not in bunches. Big or small bunches.

Yet it was here with the association issue that the whole conflict started, which would almost tear apart the Pentecostal movement and annihilate it.

Perhaps it was old Zinzendorf's fault.

No, fault isn't the right word. He had been right in his remarkable antifundamentalist view of the movement, and the expression "old Zinzendorf" is used with great love by both Lewi and Sven, praise God.

Yet Zinzendorf is not always used in the same way.

Early on, during Sven's heathen period, which could now be used in such an exciting way in his sermons before the amazed brothers and sisters in faith, Sven found the mystery of the blood to be the religious gateway to his sexuality. In one of Sven's historical novels the soldier Silfverstååhl washes his lover in his own blood—as a sexual rite of purification. "His young pure blood was what would wash away all her stains—the blood, which was mysterious and sweet, the gift of his strong, young love. His blood he gave for her salvation and liberation, and she would receive it in humble, ecstatic adoration. Each hot red drop of blood that caressed her cheek bound her to him with unbreak-

able bonds—for the eternity of all eternities: the sacrament of blood—
the sacrament of union."

This may not have been so far from Wigglesworth's "oil on the
forehead of the sick," although Sven wrote his novel in 1910. But Lewi
was a bit concerned that this blood cry from Sven the heathen had
ended up echoing through his pious sermons. That could be too much
Moravianism.

Of that type, anyway.

In a sermon toward the end of the 1920s, when Sven reported that
he was working to create a concordance of all the places in the Bible
in which blood was mentioned, Lewi confided in Efraim and asked for
his advice on how "the blood could be calmed," as he expressed it,
straining for a jest.

Yes, "old Zinzendorf" lived on in Sven and Lewi, though in different ways. For Lewi, distrust of the association idea was a tradition
from the history of the Moravian Unitas Fratrum congregation: the
very deepest root fibers. This would have consequences in the darkest
hours of the Swedish Pentecostal movement.

It was actually before Zinzendorf that it all started. There was also
something about Zinzendorf's predecessors, and spiritual forefathers,
that had set the direction. It was necessary to disguise yourself outwardly if the inner flames were to be kept ablaze. Disguise! How clear
it was that the inner flames had been extinguished! In the Papists! In
the theological careerists! In the church builders! Protectors of the
absolute truth! The designers of associations! Yes, above all, the theologians! Those men who rattled off questions that led only to disputes
and war. They were the real rattlers, babblers, much worse than those
who spoke in tongues!

Yes, there was something inherent in the academicization of the
experience of faith that was the sickness itself.

A strategy had to be worked out.

This was practiced by the very first brothers of the Unitas
Fratrum, the spiritual forefathers of Moravianism, who, when it was
founded on March 1, 1467 by the persecuted followers of Jan Hus, set
the tone. Their founder was burned at the stake, but the movement had
to live on. It was not practical to continue to be tortured and burned
to death. Perhaps they could put on a mask? Could they assume an
outer disguise, and in that way conceal themselves? The important
thing was Christcentrism, the internal union with the Savior. The

external, what they called themselves, which group they belonged to, was of less importance.

If an association: great risk of being called a traitor, followed by torture and death at the stake. If in disguise: survival while waiting for the return of Jesus.

It was noted that people were seldom burned to death for devotion to the Savior, as long as they enthusiastically accepted the outer mantle of the various church associations. If a person crept inside this disguise, he was hidden from the normally intolerant, ruthless, and bloody face of the various churches.

This became the ecumenical idea, actually created and perfected by the Moravians. The brothers could enter any group, be it Protestants or Catholics or Methodists or, later on, practically any other type. Perhaps not devil worshipers or cannibals, but almost anything else! almost anything else!

An individual's personal relationship to Christ: that was the important thing.

Lewi's basically Moravian point of view may have been a thorn in the side of all those who embraced church and free-church organizations, who found joy, order, and career opportunities in the idea of creating permanent organizational models according to prevailing Swedish models. Or, as *Ny Dag* spitefully but with scarcely any self-awareness described it, keeping "the sorcery alive" through a strong central committee and clear hierarchical lines of command, in which the principal comrades guided and allocated the work of faith.

Or was it, in fact, the same thing as the parable about the piece of board in the barrel? What kind of centralized management actually corresponded to the persistently tranquilizing piece of board in the barrel?

The complete independence of the congregations was possible only thanks to the charisma and authority of the piece of board. The charisma of the piece of board, meaning Lewi, held everything together; that was a rather vague image, but true. And it was there, somewhere, that the problem was formulated.

For Lewi it became a life-long battle against the idea of an association.

If they compromised on this issue, the Pentecostal movement would soon be dead, like the other dead associations he saw all around in that apparently dead Christian Sweden. Association enthusiasts within the Pentecostal movement, as it became more successful, also seemed to sprout up like mushrooms.

But Lewi had the Bible indisputably on his side.

The original Christian congregation was the model; nothing was mentioned about any association. "We don't need to have any union or administration over the congregations. Everything can function in the same free manner as it did during the days of the Apostles." And Sven, who on this point was in full agreement with Lewi, formulated it in political terms that sound almost relevant today:

"Even a revivalist movement can become afflicted by hardening of the arteries. The vital flow threatens to deposit harder and harder material at its edges. The joy and satisfaction that I myself have found in the Pentecostal movement originated in the fact that there was a flow from a living Spirit. And so my hope is that the Swedish Pentecostal movement will not become hardened into a bureaucracy, an institution, or a new free church, but will continue to be a revival, a living flow of spirit, without human offices or human boards of directors. We Swedes have a weakness for wanting to organize and form bureaucracies. But the Pentecostal movement is at its very core anti-organization, and that is how all brothers who fight in its ranks will keep it."

The ideological guidelines were clear, and were consistently carried out. All dogmas, except for the Bible and belief in the all-encompassing presence of Jesus Christ, should be opposed. This meant, among other things, that Lewi also effectively prevented the use of a creed within the Pentecostal movement.

A creed came from human beings and not from God. It was something that a group of people pulled out of the Bible and that would basically cause nothing but division. The clear words of the Bible were sufficient. The word "creed" was always spoken with the underlying connotation of "academic theology," which sounded like "Antichrist" and in any case reeked of the state church.

The section about the Franklin dispute is quite extensive in the *Lebenslauf*. This was, after all, the Pentecostal movement's cultural revolution, as Efraim would later characterize it with a not entirely apt anachronism—and this battle included Lewi's battle against the preacher schools.

Lewi himself had once almost lost his faith. This happened during the year he spent at the preacher school at Bethel Seminary. That was when he wanted to become a proletarian author.

Perhaps the experience had lingered with him more intensely than anyone could imagine. Afterwards the training of preachers came to represent for him a cancer to the life of faith. At the schools the religion of revelation was transformed into an intellectual matter. This did not mean a contempt for book learning. Preachers should read. By all means read.

But true faith is not! not! born through theological studies!

"Because of the preacher training system, we are in great danger of making God's cause into an intellectual enterprise, while God's kingdom, on the contrary, is something that surpasses all reason." The Pentecostal movement ought to be liberated from all career preachers. These fault-finding specialists who came from the preacher schools with their authorized and standardized messages—how could they act as intermediaries for the divine secret and the mystery of faith? Preachers then became, in a certain sense, "professional," which led to spiritual death.

Lewi wrote an entire pamphlet on this issue.

Better than this training at preacher schools would be "if the preacher devoted himself, at least partially, to a worldly occupation, but if he has received training at a preacher school it is difficult for him to tear himself away from the idea that he ought to spend all his time on spiritual work." Also, those who were "trained" often assumed a "misguided pastoral dignity," which cut them off from human experiences. You only have to listen to the trained preacher for a few minutes, he wrote, and the picture becomes clear. "The tone of voice, a constantly recurring gesture, or the way he stands are all like factory trademarks in the industry of religion."

But—"what God does, He always does with a free hand."

He wrote this in 1919. There is a phrase that, considering what happened, is very strange. "Trademarks in the industry of religion." Very precise, a very astute observation.

Could it be that all along he was extremely frightened by this industry of religion, since one of his own faces was that of the brilliant religious industrialist? Or was this merely a defense against all the slander, which loved to describe him that way?

And he did want to defend himself.

* * *

Defense, and personal experiences.

He seemed to be speaking about himself, and his own life, and drawing logical conclusions from it. A preacher shouldn't go to preacher school, but instead devote himself to manual labor in order to "strengthen his body and especially his nerves." That's good for both his health and his finances. "A preacher who wastes his time on chatting, sleeping, and going for walks is a heavy burden for God's congregation." These trained preachers were largely, according to Lewi, "semi-skilled gentlemen who think they're too refined to do ordinary, honest work. And if it turns out that the congregation's finances are not sufficient to provide this kind of preacher with the required allowance, then he would rather starve than go out and find himself a proper job."

Lewi's pamphlet has a peculiar undercurrent of restrained fury.

The message is that it's not possible to produce revivalist preachers through study. Books are fine, especially the Bible, but theological studies are bad if they're not called Bible studies. Every preacher can best be taught through hard manual labor. And pride, particularly of the theological sort, is a mortal sin. As an example of the kind of commercial occupation to which a preacher ought to devote himself, Lewi mentions the model of Hans Nielsen Hauge, a Norwegian! "who built flour mills, spinning mills, pulp mills, salt mills, etc." He also referred to the commercially quite far-sighted brothers in Christiansfeld, who did precisely that.

Perhaps they were the ones he actually had in mind. It was, as in so much else, the tone from "old Zinzendorf."

No hardening of the arteries because of cathedral building through the establishment of associations. No written declarations of creed. No central preacher training.

The ideology was consistent during those spring and summer months of 1929 when the conflict exploded. And the ideology had to be put to the test, in what Efraim in the *Lebenslauf* called "the Pentecostal movement's cultural revolution," and what everyone afterwards mainly described as a power struggle.

It's clear that it was a power struggle. If Tabor and Smyrna hadn't joined forces in a competing Pentecostal movement in Stockholm, none of this would have started; at least that was the analysis of those who hated Lewi.

Yet all great ideological disputes are power struggles. Including those that have to do with revivals that suffer from hardening of the arteries, and dreams of liberation as opposed to bureaucracy, and cultural revolutions, even in God's acre, and laymen versus professionals, and academic dogmas as opposed to incomprehensible religious experience, or sorcery, or babble, or what Sven called the painfully difficult task of finding words to describe and understand the religious experience.

There was a man named A. P. Franklin.

Efraim begins a chapter about him in the *Lebenslauf* by recounting two episodes. The first deals with him directly and is easy to interpret. The second seems more puzzling. Yet for Efraim it seems to have had significance.

The first episode occurred in the winter of 1929, in January.

Stockholm had been struck by the first wave of crisis and was a city of people looking for work and starving. On that day a light snow had fallen, and Efraim was standing in the sleet on Götgatan with a money box in his hand, collecting funds for the unemployed, or rather funds for the Filadelfia congregation's soup kitchens to feed the unemployed. Franklin came past, stopped, and greeted Efraim in a friendly manner, since they knew each other slightly, and Franklin was the leader of the Swedish Free Mission, which was a cooperative organization of the Pentecostal movement for missionary work abroad.

"I don't suppose you were ever this cold when you were a missionary in India," Efraim said to Franklin in jest.

"No," he replied with a smile, "those were seventeen warm years."

"And you probably didn't see this much distress, either."

"Oh yes, I did."

"When do you think all this misery will end? Do you regret coming back home?"

"No," Franklin replied with a bright smile, "it's odd, but I've never been as happy as I am right now, since God called me home to lead the missionary work of the Pentecostal movement. To gather all the missionary friends in the whole country into one organization."

"Gathered into one organization? Lewi wouldn't describe it that way," said Efraim.

"He says a lot of things," replied Franklin, and was about to go on his way, but stopped and added:

"I don't think he truly understands the missionary organization."

"Lewi is a remarkable man," Efraim declared. "We should be glad he exists. I'm glad he's my friend."

A strange expression flitted across Franklin's face, but he stayed where he was, as if he wanted to say something, or a thought had crossed his mind. And after a long pause, when Efraim had almost forgotten what they were talking about, Franklin said:

"Yes, be glad that he's your friend. Because as an enemy, I think he'd be terrifying."

The second episode doesn't have an obvious connection to the first. We have only Efraim's insertion of the event to indicate that he interprets it as a comment on the Franklin dispute.

It took place in August 1928. A widow, active in the Pentecostal movement, had asked to meet with Lewi regarding spiritual guidance for herself and her twelve-year-old son. By chance, Efraim happened to be present, and Lewi asked him to stay for the meeting.

This is what happened.

The woman was in her fifties, perhaps younger, and wore her hair in the customary so-called Pentecostal bun. She wore plain-looking glasses, no jewelry, dark clothing, and sturdy walking shoes. Efraim noted that "she was beautiful." That is the only remark about a woman's appearance in the entire *Lebenslauf*.

She looked frightened.

The boy was thin and pale and kept his eyes lowered the whole time, looking down at his hands that seemed clenched rather tightly.

The problem was, the woman explained, that the boy was being bullied at school because his mother was a Pentecostal. And since the woman knew that Lewi always responded to these kinds of matters and was ready to come to the defense of congregation members who were persecuted because of their faith, she had decided to contact him.

Lewi said that was fine, and wanted to know more details about this religious persecution. He asked the boy to tell him about it.

The boy's name was Lucas.

"Well, we have gym class in school," he began in a low, quavering voice, "and there was a teacher who wanted to teach us folk dancing. And then Mamma went to the principal and put her foot down."

He fidgeted nervously and seemed unwilling to go on, but then, after direct urging from Lewi, he explained how his mother had "put her foot down." His mother had said that since dancing was a sin for a Pentecostal and one thing could lead to another, she had to put her foot down.

As yet no one understood the point, and so the boy continued: "And then the others got mad."

The woman went on to say that as she saw it, dancing was offensive to a Pentecostal—for a child to learn any kind of dancing. And even though the principal had professed surprise "and didn't think it was so dangerous," she didn't stop there. She contacted the chairman of the school board, who was a pastor in the Katarina congregation. And this man had then talked to the principal because he, although not a Pentecostal himself, understood the woman's feelings. And so the dance instruction in gym class was canceled, instruction that the rest of the pupils hadn't been especially interested in before this happened.

But afterwards it was a different story.

Why was it a different story?

Well, then his classmates found out that he was a Pentecostal.

And what happened then?

She nodded to the boy, whose name was Lucas, and he looked up at Lewi with such an odd expression on his face that Efraim would never forget it.

"Well," said the boy, "at first they refused to talk to me during recess. And I wasn't allowed to join in when they played soccer."

Lewi didn't seem to understand. "But," the boy went on, "then a classmate named Håkan came over and began babbling and speaking in tongues to the others and scoffing . . ."

The boy named Lucas then fell silent and didn't want to say anything more.

"And then what happened, Lucas? You have to tell us . . ."

The boy burst into tears, and sobbed:

". . . and they kept at it . . . and kept at it . . . and kept at it for months . . . and they keep on even . . . and then they babble . . . and pretend that I speak in tongues . . ."

"But my dear little friend," said Lewi, "you know that sometimes we have to suffer for the Savior's sake, and I know it's upsetting, but you're a saved boy, aren't you? You have given yourself to Jesus Christ, and you know that . . ."

"No," the boy said.

They all looked at him in surprise, but the mother had also started to sob, and she nodded, as if it were only now that the real tragedy was going to be revealed to them.

"Lucas, what do you mean?" asked Lewi. "What do you mean by 'no'?"

"I'm not saved," the boy said and stopped crying. "And I don't want to be saved. And I think it's unfair that I still have to suffer."

"But aren't you God's child? You don't want to be condemned to perdition, do you? Answer me—don't you have a good relationship with Jesus?"

"No," the boy repeated quite stubbornly and almost with a hint of rage in his voice. "No."

"Don't you want to be saved?"

"No."

The woman was now sobbing in utter despair.

The conversation lasted for over an hour. Without making any headway. The boy named Lucas merely repeated, with increasing obstinacy, his "no." The woman then left, still sobbing, with the boy in tow. He was only twelve years old and seemed small for his age.

"This conversation," Efraim writes in the *Lebenslauf*, "evoked in me the strangest emotion, or rather several emotions. I saw in Lewi a harshness that I hadn't seen before, a much too stern attempt to force from that young boy an awareness of sin, or rather a sense of submission that was impossible to obtain. When he didn't succeed, Lewi seemed in an inscrutable way embittered. I suppose that was natural, because he was undoubtedly filled with sorrow that a child's soul would now be condemned to perdition. I felt the same sorrow. But there was something about that little Lucas that greatly agitated me, even though his stubborn and spiteful 'no!' struck me as unreasonable, and yet, considering his difficult situation during that conversation, and the force that all three of us exerted under that 'interrogation,' his 'no' gave the impression of a strong although sadly misguided character. Or perhaps I should say: a great personal courage. I often ponder this event, which seemed to me lacking any element of compassion. Especially when I recall the future conflicts with Franklin, and particularly his wife, when in spite of my agreement with Lewi regarding the actual points of contention I found this same lack of compassion."

This passage in the *Lebenslauf* is written in a different, almost formal style. There is a strange tone to the story, as if Efraim were writing about himself, and he was the boy.

4.

There was a man named Anders Petter Franklin. He was born on November 14, 1877 in Harlatorp, Slättshög parish, Kronoberg County.

He was saved at the age of fourteen, pursued his studies on his own, attended several courses in Sweden and England, and in 1900 went as a missionary to India, where he worked for seventeen years before he returned to Sweden, due to illness. In 1919 he earned a doctorate in theology from Oskaloosa College in America. After returning home to Sweden he was appointed secretary of the Swedish Alliance Mission, a position he held until 1923, when he became a member of the Pentecostal movement.

Within the Pentecostal movement he was regarded as a gift from God and a man sent by God. He was thought to possess an immense capacity for work, and he had a talent for leadership and making decisions. In photographs he makes a powerful, manly, almost charismatic impression.

It should be noted that he was a doctor of theology. That came to play a certain role in what happened next.

In June 1929 *Svenska Morgonbladet* published an article under the headline: "Major Schism Brewing in Pentecostal Movement."

Something had apparently happened.

Efraim had seen it coming for a long time. On June 3, 1929, the merger between Tabor and Smyrna had occurred "like a whack on the head," as he, with misplaced humor, expressed it.

But it had been under way for a long time.

There was something in the air. There was something in the tone that hinted at danger, even though the brothers in the leadership assured one another that the presence of the Lord was "like a refiner's fire" or that He "let the turtle dove coo and the grapevines blossom and spread their fragrance."

Yet a threat existed. There was something beneath the harmony that indicated something threatening was in the works.

Because otherwise harmony was the norm; it was as if the images had been fertilized with an almost erotic grape juice. There was something jubilantly tropical about the parables. The Swedish pine trees were replaced by cedars and grapevines. If the terror of getting mixed up with booze hadn't existed, it might have been possible to sense an almost Bacchanalian life. But in general the tone was sensually divine, praised be the name of the Lord. In the descriptions, great sinners were constantly bathed in tears and were miraculously saved. Adversity too was clothed in the new language, for adversity did exist. Even the heavenly Bridegroom sometimes had to stand outside the heart's gate of the congregation and knock in vain, while lamenting: "My head is full of dew, my locks full of nighttime drops." But the river of benediction flowed onward, for the most part, abundantly overflowing. They praised the precious blood of Jesus, the field grew white in a glorious way for the harvest. The word "glorious" was always included, that was the rule, and people urgently testified about "inexpressible joy" and unceasing "glorious" successes—with the exception of a few backward parts of Sweden, and in particular the coastland of Västerbotten, which "belonged to the most conservative and prejudiced regions of our country" and where the rural population was "almost as prejudiced against the preaching of baptism in water and in the Holy Spirit as the followers of Schartau," which was due to the lack of understanding of those "backward and narrow-minded members of the Evangelical Homeland Mission."

Still that disquieting undertone. Where was it coming from?

In December 1924 a conference was held in Stockholm. A missionary organization had been created within the Pentecostal movement, the Swedish Free Mission. Lewi called the meeting "historic" and "marvelous," although some brothers had asked him, in confidence, whether the free Pentecostal movement congregations, through this centralized collaboration within the missionary field, would now have to give up the freedom they valued so highly.

That was not the case, Lewi told them. They would keep their Biblical and original freedom.

But the man who was put in charge, a doctor of theology named A. P. Franklin, had in practical terms begun to take liberties, even though he accepted the fact that he was not supposed to govern the free congregations.

Efraim was sitting in the editorial room at *Evangelii Härold*, talking in peace and quiet with Lidman, when Lewi came upstairs on the afternoon of June 4, 1929.

Lewi was in a strange state of distress, his voice almost shaking when he talked, which was most unusual. He came right to the point and said that he wanted to discuss Franklin with Sven.

Efraim then stood up and asked if he should leave, but Lewi merely replied with an impatient gesture, as if ordering him to stay. And Efraim stayed.

Lewi was "agitated," as Efraim writes.

"It's happened," Lewi began. "It's not a rumor, it's not slander, it has actually happened, and we're going to be forced to take a stand. You know . . ." (he seemed to be speaking only to Sven, as if Efraim weren't even in the room)—"you know that I've had my suspicions for a long time. Tabor and Smyrna have now joined forces. It's true that these Pentecostal congregations of ours in Söder are not big. But we wanted them to become part of Filadelfia, to avoid competition in Stockholm. They have refused. Now they've established Södermalm's Free Congregation, and the man behind it all is Franklin. And on top of that, he's in charge of the whole centralized missionary effort of the Swedish Pentecostal movement. It's an abomination. Now he's starting a faction in Stockholm. This is just the beginning. This is a declaration of war. I want you to realize that this is war, Brother Lidman."

Sven glanced up at the word "war," as if with newly aroused interest. Lewi was by turns sitting down and standing up; he seemed extremely restless.

"You have to write about Franklin," said Lewi. "He's dangerous, he's scheming behind my back. He's a snake. For the sake of unity in Christ, he has to be exposed."

"But you yourself have said that he's a gift from God . . ." said Sven with surprise, "that he's the Pentecostal movement's greatest . . ."

"You're so naïve, Sven. You're so naïve. But you're a terrific polemicist; you have to write."

"If I want to," said Sven with a gentle tone. "If I want to."

"You will want to, Sven. You will want to. Södermalm's Free

Congregation wants an association. Now a centralized countermovement is being formed. Division! Division and death!"

"But surely they can be free in relation to . . ."

"A faction!" Lewi snapped.

A long silence ensued. Then Sven said "in a honeyed voice," as Efraim writes:

"And this is in spite of the fact that you expressly told them that their congregation should be completely independent under your leadership?"

"Yes! And I'm going to ignore your irony!"

"So what are you thinking of doing?"

It was very unpleasant. Efraim would have preferred to leave, "because I didn't recognize Lewi's voice or manner of speaking and everything seemed so strange. But I pulled myself together, since with his gesture Lewi had expressly ordered me to stay, and listened to the rest."

After a long pause and after giving Sven a long look, Lewi said:

"I want to know where you stand. I want to know if I can trust you. I know that you're one of God's soldiers. But if you share my view, you have to tell me. If you're not on my side, say so now."

Sven looked at him for a long time, as if he knew that this was a decisive moment, "and that was true, because this conflict would weld them together," as Efraim writes.

"Lewi," said Sven, "I admire you. You know that you saved my life. No, you don't know that, but I do. And I won't ever tell you how, but you saved my life, with God's help. I don't truthfully know what that is. I have to confess that. But I trust you. I will stand by you, like the soldier Lidman that I'm not, though that's what I previously wished to be. I will write."

"Stand by me, one hundred percent?"

"A Lidman is always one hundred percent," said Sven with a little smile.

An extraordinary thing happened then as Lewi, as if in an instant, changed his demeanor. The tension slipped away from his face, he smiled his gentle, almost boyish smile, and said:

"Then that's what it will be! One hundred percent! Well, Sven, you're used to percentages. How much of a percentage do you actually get from Bonniers for your sermon collections? I'm sure it's quite good, isn't it? The Pentecostals represent a big group of readers, after all."

This almost seemed to take Sven by surprise, as if he suspected some hidden venom, or perhaps a threat. As if Lewi, after this troublesome but decisive negotiation was finished, and he had won, wanted to say with a little hint: praise the Lord who gave you the inspiration of the Spirit to stand with me, and not against me, because then you might have risked losing considerable income. Which, of course, for a man of your character is of no importance. And yet, and yet. And how clever of him to wait with this until afterwards, because it was still impossible to tell how Sven would react to a direct threat. "Sven was truly pig-headed and, if threatened, might have shown his stubbornness."

But it came afterwards.

Just as a reminder. A hint about the financial wisdom in the wise decision the Spirit had made through Sven. And Sven gathered his wits almost at once, pulled himself together, and with a teasing smile he said:

"I had a talk with Tor Bonnier about the matter. I told him that I spoke to God about the percentage for my books. And God told me that, considering the circumstances, and the vast number of readers anticipated, God thought a twenty-five percent royalty would be reasonable. But then Tor said that he, in turn, had also spoken to his God. And his God suggested fifteen percent."

"And what did you end up getting?"

"Fifteen."

And Lewi then turned to Efraim, as if he only now had noticed him, and was overwhelmed with love for his old brother and comrade-in-arms over the past twenty-five years, "my one true friend," as Efraim often writes, and said with a radiant smile:

"He's an amazing preacher, isn't he, Brother Efraim? But he's a miserable negotiator and strategist. We have to thank our Savior for the fact that in this way we complement each other. Let us kneel down and thank the Savior for his guidance and for allowing us to place everything in his hands and for giving us this sanction of the Spirit."

And they all fell to their knees.

5.

It's true that Sven didn't really understand what this was all about. But he began to investigate. And he saw what it was about. And he began to realize that Lewi might not have such a bad starting position.

Perhaps Lewi was right. It made the problem simpler. In the end it became much simpler, or just plain simple.

In the end, of course. And then it was possible to close your eyes to the one detail onto which Efraim seemed to have fixated.

That little word "compassion."

Franklin was truly an enterprising and capable man. That became quite evident.

He realized that the missionary work of the Pentecostal movement was a rapidly expanding effort. In 1929 there were more than 125 missionaries in over thirteen countries on four different continents, and this required a strong governing hand. This hand was a troika, though excluding Lewi, with Franklin in the lead. That was the most effective way. The Swedish Free Mission was led by these three or, to be honest, mostly by Franklin or, as described in the bylaws in strictly legal terms: "The Swedish Free Mission is a free entity and represents the legal name of the spiritual office for missionary efforts abroad, which the undersigned have received directly from the Lord. The congregation may send out their missionaries and provisions through us, and various believers may also send their offerings to be conveyed to the missionary field."

Directly from the Lord. That meant theocratically chosen.

The fact that Lewi had been chosen as the leader of Filadelfia was one thing. But for Franklin to be chosen for all the missionary efforts of the Pentecostal movement? "Received directly from the Lord" was partially unconditional, partially rather vague. How was it received? And was it actually legally binding? Were there witnesses? How many of the brothers were authorized to receive direct assignments from the Lord, and who selected these brothers, if not the Lord?

On the other hand, this was not unusual. It was actually a common expression. Every time an important decision was made on a central level, this was the conventional phrase used within the Pentecostal movement. Sometimes it was "through the wondrous inspiration of the Spirit," which was not at all curtailed by "if Jesus tarries," though it was fairly inevitable for this to be included. It felt greatly reassuring, although no one thought about what the words meant, just that it was reassuring. And extremely odd if they were not included. There were various phrases that everyone knew how to interpret. Such as "inspired by God's guidance," which was the slightly freer and not as strongly legal phrase, not as strong as "received directly from the Lord."

But what it said in the bylaws was perhaps not as important. If the Swedish Academy could elect its own members, then surely the Pentecostal movement could too, and it created a great feeling of security. But it was the change in activity that was the problem. Not the points of departure. The change, and in a certain sense the leadership's interpretation of how things ought to be.

The missionaries had to be trained, of course. This training was so necessary! But wasn't there something about this that resembled ... the preacher schools? Yet it was true that the missionaries had to learn languages. Languages were not theology. They contained no risk of dissemblance or of a spiritual hardening of the arteries. But wasn't it sliding toward dogma?

Wasn't it sliding over into ... theology?

A missionary school was started in Högsby, and this too came under Franklin's control. Later it became clear that Högsby was rather remote. The school was then moved to Stockholm. This move was a "step taken on faith" and "inspired by God's guidance." Yet there, in addition to language studies, "starting with the spring courses and for a period of 2 or 2½ years, if Jesus tarries, students would seek to make their way through the Bible and strive for Biblical knowledge of important related topics."

This was now almost bordering on preacher training. And they were almost certain that Jesus would tarry so the school could be established, in spite of Lewi's singular and more emotionally based opposition.

It was also natural, after a while, for all of the missionary movement's property, all the mission stations and their premises in Sweden, including personal property, etc., to be assigned to Franklin and the two other individuals in the troika. Franklin was a doctor of theology, after all, and a learned man, and so there would be no risk. And the Pentecostal movement's offerings from all of Sweden were enough for the purchase of two properties in Stockholm, necessary for the administration, and also put under the charge of the troika.

Who was governing the troika? Upon closer examination of the bylaws, there is a paragraph 4, also inspired by God, that read as follows:

"The council replenishes itself. All members must be in agreement in order to admit a new member to the council. The council's decisions, in other instances, will thus have a unified basis for determining matters. In the event of a tie vote, the side supported by the chairman shall prevail. The council shall hold a regular meeting once every quarter upon summons by the chairman, and otherwise according to need."

Regardless of what the Lord may have intended when He gave the official position to the troika, it was clear that a new branch of the Pentecostal movement was now on its way to seizing power from Filadelfia. Quite honestly a faction. This was what Sven began to realize when he chose sides, and understood what he had chosen.

Sven and Lewi found themselves in the midst of a classic factional struggle. Sven the soldier, one hundred percent, and Lewi the empire builder threatened for the first time, stood side by side. In this way too the Holy Spirit had revealed its judgment by giving Sven the inspiration to say yes.

Yet in this struggle all of them, good and bad, both the hostile factions, had been theocratically instilled by the Holy Spirit, inspired by the Savior. They had received their assignments from God, and so in some sense these authorizations neutralized each other and canceled each other out. Stripped of the escutcheons of faith, they could take up the battle.

And then the thoroughly naked battle for power could begin.

6.

Sven had always been fond of war.

"In his honorable and esteemed true-hearted German autobiography *Aus meinem Leben*," he writes, "the great General von Hindenburg attempted to characterize and evaluate the many years of collaboration between himself and Ludendorff, his chief of staff: 'Solidarity in thought and deed would unite the two of us from that moment and many years forward.' That is actually the precise and most appropriate description of the collaboration and way of life that united Lewi and myself, from the moment that we met—because of the decision of a higher power."

Sven was quite enchanted with this image. Lewi was the general, Sven his chief of staff. The friends in faith were the troops, who had to be taught enthusiasm and a willingness to sacrifice.

This was at the very beginning of the Franklin dispute, and it had a powerfully stimulating effect on Sven. For the first time in his life, he heard the battle horns sound, which were part of his blood inheritance, tones from the dead, both near and dear, about whom he so often had thought: the officers and sea captains, those he had betrayed in a sense, though not entirely, by his wandering into poetry, art, and later evangelism.

It would be a blessed battle.

Yet at the beginning of this struggle he had an awkward encounter with Carin.

He was walking through Gamla Stan, and there she was, coming right toward him, and she stopped and called to him in such a loud voice that everyone nearby was startled.

It was awkward.

"You have to stop ruining our children!" she said furiously. "The girls seem completely changed after they've stayed with you. They rattle off litanies about how they've sinned! Confessions of the most bizarre things! And whenever I offer to take them to the theater, they have a breakdown and start sobbing about the horrors of 'theater and dance and other such entertainments' . . . other such! And what kind of damned words are you stuffing into them! The awareness of sin for children! And they cry at night because Ragnar and I are going to boil in the oil of hell, and whatever else you've thought up or duped them into believing. It's madness! You can't keep on like this. It's sick! It's sick!!!"

Everyone nearby had turned to stare. Sven made an effort to stay calm, and he also managed to speak in a low voice:

"If the girls have heard about salvation and grace in Brita's and my home, I don't find it so . . ."

"It's sick!!! You're harming the children!!!"

Then she left without waiting to hear his explanation. It was awkward. By no means had he tried to influence the children to feel in any inappropriate fashion the guilt of sin, or blamed their mother because she was not saved. His concern for her lack of faith had been justified. He couldn't help it. As for the issue of theater and dance, he and Lewi were in complete agreement. There were borderline cases.

Dancing around the pole at Midsummer could be discussed. But, as Lewi once said to several Pentecostal youths who asked him about this: "How would you feel, my young friends, if Jesus returned to earth and at that very moment found you dancing?"

And the youths then fell utterly silent and still. And in a low voice he repeated:

"And found you dancing."

Yet Sven felt upset by his meeting with Carin.

It wasn't easy to be a sinner, a prodigal son who returned to the home of his parents. And at the same time know how thin the line was that divided the pure from the filthy.

And the attraction.

Did he have to be the holiest of the holy? he asked himself. Or was there some mercy, and exceptions? Theater was not always the work of the Devil. Sometimes he felt completely torn apart. Sometimes he thought he was trying to repent for a sin that was not his own. Sometimes his faith felt overwhelmingly heavy. Sometimes he thought he could hear a voice from the Lidman he had left behind, like a distant voice from a lost sinner who had drowned, who had gone under, who lay there beneath a transparent covering of ice and was dead but could still speak to him. They were words he didn't want to hear, but they called to him, about something distant that he would have preferred to forget, like siren calls through the ice.

Carin had left, and the awkwardness was over, but the anguish was still with him. Then he pulled himself together and went home and returned to the battle, armored against the siren's call, but with anguish, with anguish.

What about the children? What about his girls? What if they weren't happy?

Those secretive siren calls. That time when they had passed Djurgården, and the young girl asked him about the Thiel palace, and about the contagion of sin—back then he had felt the same way.

The contagion of sin, the attraction. Was the only answer the utmost purity?

Efraim had a brief conversation with Sven about which side he should take in the Franklin dispute.

Everyone began to realize that it wasn't at all clear who was stronger. Franklin had powerful friends within the movement.

"Are you thinking of writing something against him?" asked Efraim.

"Yes," replied Sven without hesitation.

"Are you sure?"

"Lewi says that those who are not with him are against him."

"And what do you think? Franklin is, after all, a very capable man."

Then Sven said very quietly:

"You don't understand. I have lived a very lonely life. To write means to live in solitude. I hated it. Now I've become part of the movement. I'm floating, surrounded by brothers in faith, like in a river. I have a feeling of solidarity. In some sense I've ceased to exist as an individual, which means that for the first time I am a human being. It's been like coming inside from a great loneliness. I have no intention of going out into that loneliness again."

"Is that why?" Efraim asked.

"Yes, that's why."

7.

At first it was commonly thought that Franklin would be quickly crushed, and that it would happen at Kölingared.

Lewi seemed frightened and dejected. Lidman discussed various "methods of attack," but decided that he would have to appeal to the people, since it was only the masses, as personified by the brothers and sisters in faith at the Kölingared week, who with their power, instilled with God's Spirit, would be able to triumph against this organization that had already grown so strong.

Lewi would turn to the masses, writes Efraim. His report was written down much later. His use of the word "masses" might seem surprising. It has an anachronistic tone, as do his discreet references to the cultural revolution.

"Only by means of the power of the masses will we achieve victory," was not something Lewi would have said. He would hardly have used those words. Yet, in fact, that was what he meant. The question must have arisen during the Kölingared week. "And there, he no doubt thought," writes Efraim, "that we would have control, by means of various impulses from the Spirit, God's grace, and Lewi's experience."

It sounds ironic, almost malicious. He doesn't explain his malicious tone. But there was something about the Franklin dispute that wounded Efraim's love for both Lewi and Sven.

Four days before Kölingared, they summoned Franklin to a preliminary meeting in order to scrutinize the strength of his opposition. Efraim writes in the *Lebenslauf* that "afterwards I wished I had been spared that role as witness."

Franklin had requested to be heard at a meeting of elders and deacons, but was refused. Only three people were present: Lewi, Sven, and Efraim. By all accounts, Franklin seemed to have understood the desperate nature of the situation and his face was an ashen gray. Several days before, in the *Evangelii Härold*, an accusation against Franklin had been published. The main point was that he had plagiarized several foreign books and published them in Swedish under his own name.

Franklin felt this had been done deliberately. Someone had planted the story. Who had investigated the matter, and for what purpose, was not apparent. But the plagiarism story would eventually grow and seriously hurt Franklin, who declared himself to be mostly innocent, but only mostly.

It was the nature of his "adaptation" that was unclear.

He had now been summoned to be given the opportunity to defend himself, though not regarding the accusation of plagiarism. Lewi explained at once that they were not going to discuss this matter, which was certainly a serious one; it would have to wait until more investigation had been done regarding the degree of truth. It was the other matter, the accusation of a schism, that was central. Franklin then took a letter out of his inner pocket. Efraim noted that he did this "with hands that were shaking hard."

"I received this letter from Brother Pethrus last year . . . I'm going to read . . . I want to read what you yourself wrote . . . I . . ."

"Get to the point."

So he started reading in a strong but quavering voice.

"'Even before we were united in this way in the same work,' my beloved Brother Pethrus wrote, 'I had a feeling that a deep harmony existed between us, and I'm glad that the closer we get to each other, the more this feeling of harmony and concord has been confirmed. Our mutual sole desire to serve Jesus and to be as useful to His cause as possible, unites us. Hallelujah! It is the will of the Holy Spirit! Hallelujah!'"

"Hallelujah," said Lewi without expression.

"Hallelujah," echoed Sven from his corner of the room.

Franklin then stopped reading, threw out his arms, helplessly, and said in an almost childish voice:

"But what have I done? You told me that I was your closest colleague, 'my closest friend,' as I remember your words, perhaps 'my only friend,' and now these attacks. And I understand, I've understood that Brother Lidman has also . . ."

He turned to face Sven, who was sitting like a statue.

"Let's not drag in Brother Lidman," said Lewi, obviously annoyed. "Lidman is a true friend. He hasn't gone behind my back. You have."

"I have???"

"You've used my name to further your own purposes both with the Bible Institute and the Swedish Free Mission, and you've created the embryo of an association that has grown into a monster and that intends to destroy Filadelfia. A center of power. Directed at me! Here I've worked for almost twenty years, and now you want to create a faction, a competing enterprise of the faithful. Yes, I'm actually going to use those terrible words, God forgive me: a competing faction. But the Pentecostal movement can never become an enterprise!"

"But I've never . . ."

"But I'm going to crush that enterprise. In God's name. Crush!!!"

Suddenly Lewi pulled himself together and clasped his hands, as if in prayer. The silence lasted for a long time.

"Yes," Franklin said at last, "you're a strong leader. Who would dare defy you?"

"The vulnerable Pentecostal movement needs a strong leader. We're being attacked from all sides. And now also from within. Strength is required to withstand all this."

"Yes," said Franklin. "You are strong. Incomprehensibly, terrifyingly strong."

"God gives me strength. And this conflict needs strong men. You shouldn't underestimate me."

"I don't. I truly don't."

They were silent for a very long time, and then Franklin again began assuring them that his despair was genuine. That the mistakes he had made could easily be corrected. Yet suddenly a tone of rage crept into his plea for forgiveness, and Lewi then interrupted him and reminded him that he had publicly, in front of the brothers, exhorted them to rise up as one man against Lewi, the dictator. The dictator!

Franklin did not speak for a long time.

The conversation lasted nearly two hours. Then it was over. It was as if Franklin realized that there was no longer any point in continuing the discussion.

Sven was silent. Efraim had not said a word.

"And now," Lewi said, "let us pray together. In silence. Kneel down."

Efraim, Sven, and Franklin knelt down, and Franklin suddenly said, with tears in his eyes:

"I have a family . . . if you throw me out . . . my wife is in despair and I'll lose all my friends . . . my wife . . ."

"Let us pray," Lewi repeated. "Let us pray."

And so they prayed. But Efraim noted that Lewi, alone among them, did not kneel down but merely clasped his hands and fixed his unwavering, thoughtful gaze on Franklin, and he was no longer as nervous or uncertain as he had been at the beginning of the meeting. Instead, he had now received grace and guidance from the Spirit, and was so overwhelmed by this insight and clarity that he had forgotten to kneel down.

8.

At first everyone thought that the victory during the Kölingared meeting in the summer of 1929 was absolute, and that the matter was closed.

And the victory was absolute. The general meeting agreed. Franklin had admitted his errors. It was inevitable, since he was easy to convince regarding the plagiarism issue, which they did by assigning an overwhelmingly qualified language group to study the original texts and "the adaptations." Yes, Franklin was certainly in a bad position.

And he was forced to concede.

The mood was also such that if he was wrong in one area, then everything pointed to him being wrong in all the others. And the general meeting recommended dissolving the Swedish Free Mission and replacing it with a more biblical institution under Lewi's supervision.

That was not how it was formally expressed. Formally it was unanimously decided on August 19 by Filadelfia in Stockholm, "without a word being uttered that might indicate any divided opinion, and to which a wondrous sanction was given by God's Spirit," as Lewi declared to the *Härold*.

Lewi was the one who took over control.

The "foreign, dangerous organizational plan," which had been rejected by God and through the prompting of the Holy Spirit, and which was threatening to destroy the spiritual life that had until now "so gloriously pulsed beneath the simple forms allotted by the Bible itself," this plan had now been averted.

But it was not over. It was still going on. And why did it keep going?

It kept going because Franklin was not destroyed and because he wrote to brothers all around the country. And the brothers (always brothers) were alarmed. He made them alarmed. And that was why he now had to be expelled from the Filadelfia congregation. A process that began on September 24 when he was stripped of his title as elder in the congregation, which was the first lash of the whip. He was stripped of this sacred and Spirit-inspired office with sixteen votes in favor, and three abstentions.

But that was not enough. He had to be conclusively expelled from the fellowship of brothers.

There was a risk, said Lewi, that he might not stop his factional activities. "There is a great deal of evidence that his pleas for forgiveness are not supported by sincerity or true remorse," as Lewi emphasized to the board. A viewpoint that was unanimously confirmed by the board. "Be it resolved that we unanimously recommend to the congregation that he be expelled; this should be presented to the congregation on October 14, provided Franklin does not before then appear with a true confession, based on remorse for his sins."

And it went on and on.

When is a person sufficiently destroyed? How is it possible to measure, within the world of politics or religion, the moment when a faction is no longer dangerous, but destroyed, so that compassion and the Spirit's grace and blessing may once again embrace the sinner? And when can he, as a harmless plasma aware of his sins, once again take part in the warmth and grace that are the divine trademarks of compassion? When?

*   *   *

He tried to seem despairing and contrite, but as Sven, with his academic wisdom, so rightly concluded, "In a footnote you can reveal chasms of ignorance, and in a well-formulated confession of sin a lethally poisonous snake can be hidden."

On October 11 Franklin read aloud a letter addressed to the elders and deacons of the Filadelfia congregation, which to a certain extent reflected the tone of voice that, assigned by the Holy Spirit, was used by the combatants:

Dear Brothers!

In reply to the document which I received last Friday, I wish to express my gratitude to the brothers for this opportunity for atonement, which it offers me. It would be a great joy and relief to my heart if a settlement could be reached so that we might come together in Christ's love.

I ask your forgiveness for the injustice I perpetrated by giving the appearance of being the author of the books that were not original and collecting the same fee for them as for an original.

In Norway I have already returned what I received from the publisher there.

I ask Brother Pethrus to forgive me for my suggestion that the sermon he gave in the Auditorium about Christ's divinity originated from Dr. Torrey, and for my statement that we ought to rise up as one man against his dictatorship, as well as for any other suffering I may have caused him.

I also ask all the brothers to forgive me for making them suffer for my sake. I wish to clarify matters with both God and my fellow men.

As requested, I have written to cancel all the arrangements in the places where I was supposed to preach during the month of October.

Both my wife and I have spent a great deal of time praying to the Lord during these difficult trials, and calling upon Him, that in His great mercy He might allow a sweet "southern wind" to blow after the "north wind" that for a time has so distressed us. So help us God.

With heartfelt greetings to all the dear brothers, with whom I have had the pleasure of working for six years, and in the hopes of a favorable reply.

Fraternally yours,

A. P. Franklin

Aside from the greetings of peace and the submissiveness, the letter is clear. That was what Sven meant by the poisonous snake.

If the letter were published, Franklin's accusations against Lewi would be made known to all. Meaning that Franklin, before the elders and deacons of the congregation, had accused Lewi of plagiarizing a sermon, for which he apologized, though without discussing the extent to which this was true, but with the tone that "one man is as good as another." And behind this lurked other accusations against Lewi about copyright violations in the hymnal *Triumphant Tones* (as nasty as everything was getting, even the songs were now besmirched) as well as charges of dictatorship and autocracy. He had exhorted the leading members of the Pentecostal movement "as one man" to rise up against Lewi's "dictatorship."

Which was also the fraternal subtext to this confession of sins.

And where was Sven in all this?

There is testimony about how he reacted to Franklin's letter. Like the others, he listened as it was read aloud. Then he swiftly rose to his feet, grabbed the letter, crumpled it up, threw it to the floor, and shouted:

"What hypocrisy! What hypocrisy!"

Franklin merely stared at him, without understanding. But he did understand that the door had been closed and that the two leading brothers were in agreement.

And who could stand against them?

The question as to where Sven stood was actually superfluous.

Sven was happy, and had made up his mind. Efraim met him after a blessed meeting at the Auditorium where Sven had spoken. He pulled Sven aside to ask him what the congregational leadership was now intending to do. Sven said that he wasn't sure what was going to happen. But Franklin had to be destroyed.

"Is that truly necessary?" asked Efraim.

"Yes, it's necessary."

"But you were at the meeting. You saw how despairing he was."

"Brother Lewi rebuked him."

"And you sneered at him. Was that necessary? Why so . . . uncharitable?"

"This is a matter for the inner circle."

Efraim looked at him in surprise.

"And the other brothers and sisters and I don't belong? Then who does belong to the inner circle? Is it just you and Lewi? And what do you mean exactly?"

"I don't want to cause any division," replied Sven is a strangely stilted tone of voice.

"Sven, my brother," Efraim simply said. "Sven."

Lidman then launched into explanations, visibly upset. They had to do with the fact that Sven owed Lewi tremendous gratitude and that in this situation indulgence was impossible and that a certain harshness had to be demonstrated and that he was now thinking of writing something, clearly and firmly, in the *Härold* to bring the victory to a definitive conclusion. When none of this seemed to make any impression on Efraim, he added:

"Franklin is truly taking treacherous paths to reach his goal."

"What kind of treacherous paths?" asked Efraim.

"He's making his wife beg and beseech my wife, in the belief that this might move me."

"Has he succeeded?" Efraim asked.

Franklin's wife had, in fact, paid a visit to Brita.

They had gone for a walk in Vasa Park. Brita was expecting a child, in her ninth month.

Franklin's wife wept in despair, and they sat down on a park bench. Finally Brita put her arm around the despairing woman, bent her head down to her huge belly, and stroked her hair for a long time, though without praying.

Neither of them had prayed.

It was late autumn, with a few yellow leaves in the park. With one hand Brita stroked the other woman's hair, and her other hand she placed on her stomach.

The next day she spoke to Sven. She told him that Franklin's wife had come to her in need. His wife said that if they were expelled from the congregation, this would be in effect a bull of excommunication. No one would want to have anything to do with someone who was expelled. No one would want her husband to preach. After almost twenty years of hard work in the missionary field, he didn't have the strength to go out again. The years in India had impaired his health. Besides, who would summon a man who had been expelled?

"And this is only the beginning," Brita added.

"What do you mean?" asked Sven.

"It will happen again. And in the end, you're going to be the one who will be purged, Sven."

"I'm not that weak," he said. "My position is strong."

"But one day it will happen," said Brita. "When you too are weak."

"I'm not weak."

She kept on appealing on behalf of Franklin's wife. Sven listened, but he finally interrupted her, apparently furious, and asked:

"Are you going behind my back? Are you with me or against me? This is a crossroads; I have to know!!!"

"Yes, Sven," she said, "it's a crossroads."

Then she went back to her work in the kitchen.

9.

There was an uproar in the press.

No one had expected anything else, but there was an uproar, and it was not God's roaring voice that was heard. There was malicious joy and scorn, as if it had finally been demonstrated that the words of the spirit babblers could be interpreted in plain language, and that it was a hate-filled, scheming, rash voice that spoke of division and treachery.

The newspapers loved it. The headlines got bigger and bigger. "Schism in Pentecostal Movement More Acute" and "No Prayers Help Against Pethrus" and "Authority of Lewi Pethrus Shaken" and "Pentecostal Movement Fears Organization"—the latter clearly expressed the frank astonishment of organization-minded Sweden at the true core of this conflict, meaning the question of an association.

There were hints that this was not merely a matter of ordinary intrigues. The battle was between a Swedish principle of organization that was healthy, and one that was not.

Pethrus was fighting against what was healthy.

Yes, there was a healthy, Swedish in spirit, almost nationalistic and well-tested for centuries, primally Swedish means of creating clarity and order through solid organizations and distinct lines of command. Opposing this were the odd guidelines taken from the Acts of the

Apostles, with spirit tongues and personal relationships to Jesus and chaos and speaking in tongues and claims that faith could only be made to survive through organizational chaos.

Or "the independence of the congregations," as the babblers, strangely enough, called it.

Why then this nostalgia for chaos when stability and great organizations since the time of Gustav Vasa had proved to be the Swedish means for resolving questions of community and faith? And! and!!! when it had also been demonstrated that this Pethrus was a demon at organizing.

What were they making such a fuss about? It was impossible to comprehend a single word. But the tumult was magnificent and, above all, it made for magnificent reading. And now Sven went on the attack.

It was as if Franklin, as an individual, seemed to him too small and weak, unworthy of the great battle's more meaningful words. But now the unified persecution in the newspapers had aroused his attention. The opponents were in agreement. The task was heroic. A new and militant dimension appeared.

Sven returned to the dream of his youth about a battlefield that was intended specifically for him. He reacted in the same way as he had once obeyed "like a war-horse," at the outbreak of the Great War, back when he experienced the initiation of hostilities as "a decree from God. Like lightning that slices through the thunderous summer heat of a sultry idyll. And brings with it destruction and the rain of renewal."

But he was not the same person now. Something had happened. He was not the activist and arch-conservative Lidman, the one who in the spirit of self-sacrifice had contributed the considerable sum of 3,000 kronor to the collection for armored ships, and who in the role of editor of *Svensk Lösen* had advertised for a "leader" who would be able to pull the sluggish populace up by the hair. A chieftain. "Those who have gathered around *Svensk Lösen* all have this in common: they are waiting and hoping for leaders who dare to think Swedish, and fellow citizens who will feel and believe Swedish." Later he would distance himself from this "hysterical Kaiser cult and love for the Germans." Yes, he had changed.

And yet he hadn't.

Something was still there, something from which he could never free himself: the cheerful eagerness to fight, images of the intellectual struggle as a bloody battle and of following in the footsteps of his illustrious ancestors in this way. There was a sub-lieutenant, eager for a career, hidden inside the poet and preacher, and this could be gleaned from his polemics.

And Sven truly was a brilliant polemicist. He was not only precise and ruthless, he was also something that was much worse for his opponents: he was entertaining. When Franklin refused to die, expelled or not, and was accepted into the Södermalm congregation and from there continued his sniping, meaning his preaching, Sven launched a deadly attack in a long series of articles in *Evangelii Härold*.

He scoffed at "this salon of rejects," meaning Franklin's supporters, who "at most numbered 1,000." Those who belonged to "Franklin's fraternal union," largely consisted of "deposed preachers." But these misfit individuals lacked all support. "In a travel account from Haiti it was said that the army consisted of 1,600 generals and 60 privates, and the situation is the same with this newly formed faction."

Otherwise the tone was charitably bloodthirsty. "In this struggle we are now undergoing, all hypocrites, all secret sinners, all sham Christians are joining up as one man against us. For that we praise God. It is a glorious schism—a schism for which we have always longed."

Lewi was at first upset by the ferocity, but he mustered his courage, and in the end perhaps he too praised God for this longed-for schism. In any case, he praised Sven. Because Sven was now the one who, better than anyone else, and far from the blessed sound of the battle trumpets, could formulate where the fundamental problem lay.

"The Pentecostal movement has been criticized in sharp terms for not wanting to organize. This shows that people have no knowledge or understanding of the fact that the Pentecostal movement is a living revival, a living source, that will not and cannot have any cemented wharves or wide bridges. It is a movement that cannot be exploited, that will float onward like a living stream. In this revival individuals mean very little, but the movement will no longer have any justification for existence if it becomes organized. It will not, under any circumstances, erect great churches or fortresses that can be seen. We do not build walls, we live in tents. Freedom and independence from all restraint is the life-blood of this movement."

One sought control. The other freedom. And yet they seemed in complete agreement.

* * *

It often got extremely nasty.

That was what Efraim remembered best afterwards. Everything was dug up—everything. Precise charts showed how much the main players earned from their work as preachers and authors. In the years 1924 to 1929, Sven earned an average of 15,991 kronor per year—though this did not include income from his sermon collections that were published by Bonniers. Lewi earned an average of 11,870 per year. Franklin 7,854 per year.

The average income for a Swedish factory worker in 1927 was just under 3,000 kronor. An associate judge made 11,000 per year. A person may not have become rich by holding a central position in the Pentecostal movement. But he wasn't poor either. And yet it was not money that was important.

What was important was ideology, faith, and power. And that's why, at regular intervals, there was systematic assassination of the enemy's reputation.

Franklin's plea for forgiveness was "a document dressed up in common phrases and religious terms that in no way bears any evidence of true contrition of heart or any genuine remorse for sins." Certainly this conflict was about spiritual decentralization, so to speak. But the mobilization against Franklin and the Södermalm Free Congregation (which Tabor and Smyrna were now called) was administered on a national level and strongly centralized, and it became the model for many other, and in the future thoroughly worldly and political, organizations.

Each congregation was centrally exhorted to write, from a completely decentralized and spontaneous position, a call for support, which was then centrally published in the *Härold*. Anyone opposed? No. The spontaneity was organized by telephone, which meant it could not be traced.

The appeal campaign against Franklin was the first small step against centralized administration of the Pentecostal movement, Efraim writes. He is undoubtedly wrong. There were earlier indications. But if the young Lidman in *Svensk Lösen* had called for a chieftain he might serve, he had now found one. The question was whether Lewi realized this.

But serve he did. And Brita was quite right: he found himself at a crossroads and had made his choice.

* * *

Why did it have to get so nasty?

But it was not so much this, not the nastiness, that makes the *Lebenslauf*, almost with fear, record the conflict as a weak but extremely unpleasant tremor in the earth's crust, a faint rumble that portends something else that is even more painful.

Efraim constantly repeats, in spite of his anguish: "But Lewi was right." It was in fact true that Lewi was right in the Franklin dispute. And if he had lost the battle, his prophecy, with great certainty, would have been proven right: the Pentecostal movement would have organized itself into an inner death, and would have been struck by efficiency and hardening of the arteries, and then gone the same way as so many other revivalist movements. And it was actually true, as Efraim in his anachronistic remark about the cultural revolution, had hinted: the battle to keep the movement alive had cost blood.

In the end there was only that small question left, which seemed to echo through the story about the boy and his "no."

Wasn't it each person's calling to think for himself?

More and more filth. No compassion.

Lewi was right. But there was something else that made Efraim afraid. Otherwise why would he preface his account of the Franklin dispute with the story about the boy who said no? Why? The fact that this lengthy Franklin dispute, which lasted five years before the enemy was finally obliterated, in reality could also be viewed as a dress rehearsal for future purges, including one that would strike Sven and another Efraim, was not something that Efraim could have imagined.

Nor did Sven. The battle right now was so glorious, the unity so great, and the camaraderie of the soldiers on this battlefield of God was so inspired and enclosed by the Spirit.

A brief note in the *Lebenslauf*, underlined: "It was probably at this point that Lewi learned to fear Sven."

Efraim has underlined the sentence with a different pen than the one he used to write it, as if he had read through it and only afterwards found it to be an important truth.

The birth of fear. Lewi was starting to be frightened. And the fear would practically fling him out of the Pentecostal movement and away, far away to the foreign country where strong leaders and empire builders also try in vain to hide from God's countenance, as well as their own fear.

10.

Whatever rises up can be destroyed. And that's what happened to Franklin. He was destroyed.

He disappears from the story several years later. The Södermalm congregation enfolded him in its embrace for a few years, but the Södermalm congregation could not hold out against Lewi and Sven. It stopped growing, and in 1935 they had to crawl to the Cross.

Although that wasn't the image they used. Not the Cross as the image of the utmost humiliation. Even though that was exactly what happened.

There wasn't much of a life left for Franklin and his wife. The decades out in the missionary field had taken a toll on their strength. He was sickly. That's often what happened to missionaries: they died. But Franklin died a broken man. No one wanted, or dared, to engage A. P. Franklin as a preacher. And it didn't help matters any that his wife had wept at Brita's knee.

Great, successful popular movements always leave many people destroyed in their wake. There would be more, also within the Pentecostal movement. Especially there. And sometimes Efraim, who writes about those who were destroyed and takes a great interest in them, thought that he saw the movement as a great procession of singing, happy, saved, and ecstatic people marching along a seashore toward a light far away, led by their leaders, who were successful and strong and charismatic and who refused to be destroyed. But he hoped that the people in the procession would sometimes hear the faint, almost imperceptible sound of seashells being crushed under their feet, an almost inaudible sound of those being destroyed, and that they would then think about the situation of those who were crushed. Not in order to judge them or to state whether those who were destroyed were right or wrong, but simply because they were once human beings; no, because they were still human beings. And because Jesus Christ was love, and that was the important thing about the procession; the happy migration along the seashore, toward the light, which in spite of everything was love, God's love and God's forgiveness, and this applied to both those who were happy and those who were destroyed; yes, also to those who were destroyed, who vanished from the story and now existed only as a faint, almost inaudible sound beneath the marchers' feet.

11.

But it's easy to forget the other part. The part that continued in spite of everything.

The Franklin conflict was a dispute that was almost ideological in character, but this battle between the leading brothers was barely noticed by the rest of the members.

Most of Lewi's time was spent on other things. This also included the incident with the Senegalese plate-lipped natives, which occurred in the midst of the Franklin dispute.

What happened was that in the spring and summer of 1932 a group of Senegalese plate-lipped natives performed at Gröna Lund amusement park in a so-called freak show. They didn't use that term, but it was implied. The plate-lipped natives had been transported to Stockholm by an impresario who toured with them in a number of European cities. The plate-lipped natives danced, or at any rate moved their bodies and legs in a way that was characteristic for plate-lipped natives, and put on a show. They were called plate-lipped natives because they were considered to have bigger lips than normal. They were actually monstrously big, at least if they were compared to the thin-lipped Swedes. And many Swedes had never seen a black person before. The plate-lipped natives had some sort of wooden discs inserted in their mouths to enlarge their lips, and they had been instructed to stick out their lips, to practically flap their lips, to give the audience something for their money. But after a while the word spread widely that their lips weren't actually so big that the plate-lipped natives could be labeled monsters. The crowds then diminished. This might also have been due to the fact that there was great unemployment in Sweden, that the crisis during these years was the worst of the twentieth century, and that the social misery was formidable. This meant that the working class, or those who theoretically belonged to it even though they didn't have any work, couldn't afford to pay the entrance fee to see the plate-lipped natives. In the upper classes, many had already seen blacks during their travels, and besides, they seldom went to Gröna

Lund, and so they stayed away. At this time the intellectual class was quite small in Stockholm, and in the long run couldn't have provided a vital and stable audience for the plate-lipped natives.

So after a few months the enterprise was forced into bankruptcy, and the impresario and his ensemble of Senegalese plate-lipped natives disappeared very quickly, and unexpectedly, from Stockholm.

During their time in Stockholm, the troupe had taken lodgings on a barge that was owned by the amusement park Gröna Lund. According to a report in *Dagens Nyheter*, the barge had been outfitted with woven mats and other tropically themed furnishings to make the plate-lipped natives feel at home. Yet the barge was very primitive, but this also contributed, as intended, to making the plate-lipped natives feel at home.

Now the barge was vacant.

Since it was known that the Pentecostal movement was looking all over Stockholm for premises for its work with the homeless and its soup kitchens, Lewi was contacted by Gröna Lund. He promptly declared his interest.

The very next day he and Efraim went to inspect the barge, which was moored at Torsgatan, below the old gas works. Lewi felt that the barge could become part of the solution to the desperate need for accommodations for the poor and homeless.

He purchased the barge.

A collection among the faithful brought in 8,000 kronor, and the barge was furnished. The Public Health Department inspected and approved it. Fifteen dormitories held fifty-eight homeless, who were given shelter for a maximum of ten days. They received food and lodging, free of charge, and the food was served at Tegnergatan. Those who could provide a certificate of having been deloused were given a separate dorm, with sheets and pillow cases. The others were placed in bunk beds of the standard regimental type, purchased from the Göta Life Guards, with mattresses covered with Pegamoid.

Over the course of a year the barge, which was called the Ark, took in over 3,000 homeless. Yet this was, as Lewi pointed out, a mere drop in the ocean. An ever-growing part of the Filadelfia budget was now being used for such social work, in which the Ark was just a little cog, though it was often written about in the media because the fact that the barge had been abandoned by the Senegalese plate-lipped natives seemed fascinating, and in any case attracted plenty of readers.

But the Ark caused a long series of conflicts, though of varying types. A faction within Filadelfia disliked the so-called philanthropic work, since those who were unemployed and down-and-out had surely to some degree, through a disgraceful life, created their own misery.

And there was plenty of work for those who were truly willing to work. Those who were unemployed had probably not taken proper care of themselves.

Lewi noted that this undoubtedly expressed a common feeling within the movement. Whenever collections or campaigns to raise money were organized "for those in need and distress within the Pentecostal movement"—meaning for their own members—it seemed jinxed. Almost nothing was collected. On the other hand, this movement of essentially dirt-poor members was willing to sacrifice almost anything for those in need who were not Pentecostals. The idea was, somehow, that a Pentecostal, by definition, could always take care of himself and therefore didn't need help. If people were in distress they were not, in some way, Pentecostals. That was quite clear. Lewi had trouble with this notion of "those who did not take care of themselves."

His view was that need had nothing to do with taking care of yourself.

And since Lewi's position during these years, due to the Franklin dispute, was vulnerable and threatened, he had resorted to using his authority to the utmost. Which was intimated to be practically dictatorial. In order to keep their work going.

The Ark also prompted a conflict within the leftist press.

The communist newspaper *Ny Dag*, which was loyal to the Soviet Union, accused Lewi of merely using the less fortunate as advertisement and flypaper. It was true that during the course of one year 39,000 poor people had been fed, but at the same time they had been forced to listen to hymns and prayers, and the pea soup was often poorly cooked. The anti-Soviet communist paper *Folkets Dagblad* had then harshly attacked *Ny Dag*. This was repeated with the regularity of a metronome. It was just as in the past with the raid on the Salviigränd shelter. Lewi became the communists' spiritual punching bag in their internal conflicts. For the brothers and sisters in Filadelfia it was very difficult to follow the communist intrigues; they felt slightly uneasy. But it had something to do with the view of the Soviet Union, a factional battle, as Lewi reassuringly explained. Yet Lewi said that he was glad for any support, regardless of origin, and that's why during a prayer hour they also thanked God for *Folkets Dagblad*.

For these communist supporters of Lewi, the idea was that the Moscow lackeys in *Ny Dag*, through their persecution, were taking bread out of the mouths of the starving, and *Folkets Dagblad* exhorted the unemployed to rise up against the communist backbiters in this newspaper that was a traitor to their class.

Efraim followed Lewi like a shadow, and he saw everything, everything, and acted as witness.

He followed him to the Ark that had been abandoned by the plate-lipped natives and saw how Lewi laboriously wrote down his long list of what needed to be done: the toilets that had to be renovated and the floor that had to be scrubbed; how Lewi squatted down and sniffed, as if he were a dog, making his way to the place where dividing walls would be put up; how he "jokingly" hinted that Christ's miracle of the loaves and fishes certainly pointed the right direction, but that for practical reasons it would be necessary to anticipate this miracle through other financial means. And Lewi asked about the hours when the army's surplus warehouses were open and whether there might be a brother who could get a discount. And how Lewi without expression had read the headline "Lewi Pethrus & Co. Sharper Businessmen than Negro Impresario." And how he threw out what he called "a Bolshevik lout" who was demonstrating at another soup kitchen. Outside the premises he grabbed this fellow by the lapels and said that "the rights and welfare of the people are for me not just a social matter but also a Christian demand," which sounded impressive but made no impression on the youth, who said: "You give them delicacies, we give them revolution." And how Lewi, with an almost astonished and childlike smile, then said: "Delicacies? Pea soup?"

But the youth was thin and pale. And afterwards Lewi was pensive and untalkative, almost upset, even though Efraim had commended him for his resolute action. And all of this took place during the Franklin dispute, this too—but there was so much, as Efraim writes, there was so much and Lewi had so many faces.

Perhaps that was what Efraim meant when he writes in one place with great love:

"When God created Lewi Pethrus, he undoubtedly broke the mold afterwards."

Much later in the *Lebenslauf* he repeats this phrase.

When God created Lewi Pethrus, he undoubtedly broke the mold afterwards.

But then, much later, he adds a question: Why?

Why did God do that? And it's as if he fearfully and yet "with great love" wanted to intimate that there are two answers to this question.

As of 1935, Franklin disappears almost completely from the story.

Almost no information about him or his life after the expulsion can be found in the movement's extensive and fact-filled archives. He seems to have been removed from the course of events, as if the history of the Pentecostal movement were a group portrait of the leading brothers in which one face has been erased and a mysterious empty space remains.

He became persona non grata, and silence descended around him, although it is possible to map out his last years. After the dissidents in the Södermalm congregation were defeated, he moved in 1935 to Göteborg, where he formed a very small Pentecostal congregation under the name "God's Congregation."

It had a short life, and then became part of Smyrna.

But Franklin was very frail and sickly, and during the last years of his life he couldn't work. He was called home to his Savior on March 19, 1939, at the beginning of a conflict to which his own purging was merely an ominous prelude, or a dress rehearsal.

BOOK IV

November 1930–February 1941

CHAPTER 17

Meister Eckhart's Student

1.

IN THE MIDST OF THE FRANKLIN DISPUTE, ON NOVEMBER 1, 1930, the temple on Rörstrandsgatan was consecrated.

It could hold 4,000 sisters and brothers, and had cost in the currency of the day over 1.5 million kronor, most of which had come from collections. It was a miracle, as well as a great feat. The times were not good. Lewi had come up with an idea—and here too he was an entrepreneur far ahead of his time—of "selling" pews in the premises to the members. They would have their own place, so to speak, in the sight of God. A whole pew cost 250 kronor, half cost 125, and a fourth was 62.50.

No one would have his name on a pew, but he would know it was there.

It was a Colosseum to God, the press declared. *Svensk Kyrkotidning* wrote that there was reason for alarm. "The situation in coming decades will be grave for the Swedish state church." The communist paper *Folkets Dagblad* concurred and stated that it was high time for "other associations to take up competition against the Pethrus group. But they will have to stock up on all the same strong spices that they use to stimulate the souls: speaking in tongues, Spirit baptism, crawling on the floor, exorcising the Devil, and the like. It won't be enough to have sewing circles and ruminating cowards. Even the expectations regarding religious enticements have been terribly intensified. That's why the state churches are empty, while kilometer-long lines (mostly women!) wind around outside the Filadelfia congregation's cellar of horrors."

The fact that the cathedral could be financed by the dirt-poor Pentecostal movement was generally regarded as incomprehensible. Was everything truly legitimate? Surely some shady business was behind it all. Yet that was not why a time capsule was bricked into the foundation, containing documents about the creation of the building, the financing, and the genesis of the Filadelfia congregation.

Brother Pethrus spoke at the ceremony, bricked in the tin box, and said that "if Jesus, as we hope, returns soon, it's possible that this document may be found during the millennium when the church comes to be torn down."

It was not crystal clear. Pride over the cathedral, hope for the swift return of Jesus when the cathedral would be torn down, yet faith in the future. That was a lot to swallow all at once. In his statement, Lewi united what was for him a characteristic belief in the necessity of practical action while awaiting the inevitable miracle. In this case, the return of Jesus, who, praise God, no matter what happened, perhaps would tarry.

The church was always full. The Pentecostal movement was now a powerful force that could not be ignored.

But what was the position of the Pentecostal movement going to be in relation to the political powers? Lewi and Sven were leading Sweden's strongest, fastest growing, and politically least defined popular movement.

The question once again was: Where was it all heading?

These twins of God had power. Might it also be political power? The genuine love, which over time would include elements of terror, this love that Lewi felt for Sven Lidman, who had long ago resigned as editor of the arch-conservative journal *Svensk Lösen*, was not marked by any political solidarity.

On the contrary. But while Sven, almost fleeing, had now shut himself inside a newly purchased apolitical ivory tower, a villa called Stora Vilunda, surrounded by a Gunnebo barbed-wire crested fence, Lewi was spending more and more time wrestling with the problem. It had to do with political involvement in the service of Christ.

If that was even possible, or desirable.

It had been a long inner battle for years. "I come from the working class," he wrote much later, "and have always regarded myself as belonging there." Never a bad word from him about the trade union movement, as opposed to the other leading brothers. Always taking a stab at the lack of social involvement on the part of the established churches. "Why does the world church never take the side of a party when it's weak? This groveling before and flattering of those who hold power in the world is characteristic of the world church and her prelates throughout the ages, and no one should be surprised if those in power despise them in their hearts. If you want to do anything good in the world, you have to take the injustices in hand and dare to speak the truth."

But he is balancing on the edge of a knife.

Those first years in Stockholm he takes an active part in the political battle. In 1914 he supports the liberal Staaff against the conservatives and the king. He is upset about the farmers' march, and he joins the rally outside the Parliament building when Branting speaks to the 50,000 participants in the workers' march. "It was fortunate for Sweden that the leader of the great labor movement was opposed to any sort of violent measures. His speech at the Chancellery against the government seemed as menacing as a lion's roar, but the indignant crowds who listened to his words knew that he didn't want a revolution. And no doubt we have him to thank for the fact that the day turned out to be as peaceful as it did."

The question is not where his heart belongs. The question is what he is going to do with his beating heart.

On the morning of the workers' march in 1914, he paces back and forth in his room. He has no appetite. He is afraid. That evening he is supposed to preach.

The issue is not where he stands. He stands without hesitation on the side of the workers. The issue is whether it's possible to unite political conviction with the religious battle.

The Pentecostal movement is still small, but he is farsighted. "That morning I had a great battle with myself. Was it right for me to pay so much attention to what was happening around me? There was a feeling of reproach trying to force itself upon me because I was devoting so much time to reading the newspapers in the morning. Finally I flung the newspapers aside and told myself that I had to stop taking such an interest in societal matters. Yet, on the other hand, it was in this society, in which these events were occurring, that I had my work. Wouldn't the political situation's course of development in Sweden have an effect on our spiritual work? One fine day we might end up under a regime which forbade us from conducting spiritual activities, and we might even be stripped of our personal religious freedom. Should I, as a Christian, stand by, indifferent to these matters?"

He walks through the streets toward the Parliament building, aware of his own insignificance, and that of the Pentecostal movement. "The relatively small groups that gathered for the various worship services exerted an inconsequential influence on their surroundings." But his conclusion must still be that "we Christians have a role in connection with the critical situations that are brewing."

He was "Staaff's man," and quotes with approval Staaff's governmental declaration from 1911 which says that "this government was a leftist government, not a moderate party government. Its program was to bring about the transformation of our political life, which was the dream of the decades: a transformation that would make Swedish politics a popular politics, which more than ever before devotes itself to the common man, those who have been relegated to the shadows in our society."

At the time when the farmers' march and the workers' march intersect in Stockholm in 1914, Lewi is thirty years old. He regards himself as a member of the working class and the labor movement. He is hardly a socialist. In his youth he certainly was "deeply gripped by the first assembly's community of property," and never let go of that idea. But socialist: no. There was a Bolshevik threat in the East. His heart is leftist, but turning around in confusion, seeking allies. Over time he will see how the Social Democrats come to view his beloved Pentecostal movement as a hotbed of the plague, something the cat has dragged in onto the carpet.

That was often how things went. The same was also largely true of the attitude of the Social Democratic Workers' Party toward the Pentecostal movement. This was what Efraim started to talk about when I once asked him about the circumstances behind the musicians' procession on the Västerbotten coastland. The spiritual dimension of life was not of interest to the ideologues of the labor movement. At the very least, it was uncomfortably vague. In the worst case, threatening. Especially as it was expressed in the babbling of the Pentecostal movement.

Spiritual matters were not the strong suit of the labor movement. What the hell was that all about? Especially this Pentecostal movement. A bunch of old ladies rolling around on the floor. It was obvious what they really needed.

Even though Lewi's heart beat for the left and would continue to do so, he could find little support in the political branches of the labor movement. And definitely not in their newspapers, with the exception, as mentioned, of the anti-Stalinist communist paper *Folkets Dagblad*, which during the 1940s and under the management of Nils Flyg slid into Nazism and swiftly died a dishonorable death.

Perhaps Lewi felt a bit lonely, in a political sense.

And something else occurred which, in the long run, may have been just as important. This was the influence of the views held by the Pentecostal movement's leadership. Those who surrounded him.

The fact that the foundation of the movement came from the lower class, often purely from the tattered proletariat, was one thing. But the leadership was another matter. When Lewi arrived in Stockholm he "entered an environment that was hostile to workers," as Efraim expressed it. The circle around Lewi in the Filadelfia leadership consisted of shopkeepers, small businessmen, and civil servants; many of them had been caught in the middle between trade unions and capitalists and chose to regard unions as Beelzebub. Lewi was all alone with his views, even though in the autumn of his life he wrote that "the view of society that I had from my childhood and which later took on a certain theoretical form, I have preserved through the years."

It became very lonely for Lewi in this massively bourgeois group of gentlemen. He could stubbornly carry out social involvement by referring to a wealth of Bible quotes. But he had to keep quiet about his political sympathies.

They became watered down, blunted. And slightly cautious.

His heart was beating, but he was sliding. In the end the question was more tactical: Which party would benefit the Pentecostal movement most?

No one thought of the Pentecostal movement as Sweden's largest women's movement. No one, as yet, viewed the movement as the roots of a great Swedish bourgeois party.

It was still only the 1930s. And the way of thinking in the '30s would turn out to be a problem.

Efraim writes in the *Lebenslauf* that it wasn't easy to understand certain words in the '30s. It's easier now. Back then it was thought that "certain words seemed to have a false or evil light to them. You can see if a word is wicked."

Perhaps this can be translated as: malevolent, ominous.

When the conflict between Sven and Lewi exploded in the 1940s, the wicked words of the '30s played a certain role.

Guilt by insinuation, guilt by vilification. Sven gathered up his accusations against his friend Lewi in a terrible document that he called the "Journey to the Court of Justice," and of all the charges, most of which turned out to be weak or groundless and were forgotten, only one remained in the end and proved to be lethal.

It was the wicked '30s that rose up from the swamp.

"During a summer vacation in Dalarna, Sweden in the late '30s," Sven writes, "Lewi Pethrus borrowed his host's copy of *Mein Kampf* by Adolf Hitler. It caught fire like tinder. The book revealed and proved to him the nature of his own talent and possibilities in life. Upon returning from Dalarna, he was fired up with enthusiasm when he came to see me at Stora Vilunda.

"'You should read Hitler's *Mein Kampf*—can't imagine that you haven't read it—oh, that's quite a book—what a genius—oh, what a book—that man, you understand, true genius—no one has realized, as he has, how to lead the masses—believe me, that man—he's a leader of the people—it's obvious that he's going to end up conquering the world—because you see, he truly knows how to lead a nation—he knows how to make use of everything, let me tell you—every trick and gimmick—he knows how to lead the masses.'

"During the next few years the name Hitler was often on his lips during our conversations."

This conversation was impossible to verify, or deny.

Lewi protested furiously, and he succeeded in proving that he didn't read the book until 1942, after his trip to America; no doubt that much was true. But how does a person deny an enthusiastic outburst that occurred in a private conversation? It had to be a resilient defense. Lewi stated that reading biographies was a great hobby of his. He had read biographies of Stalin, Churchill, Eisenhower, Mannerheim, "and various other great leaders of the present day. Would it, in fact, be considered an advantage for someone who is the leader and preacher of throngs of people, not to know the great leaders of his day and their work? I have not read any of these books without learning something, be it positive or negative, but I don't think I was bewitched by any of them. And surely no one would believe that I was as intoxicated and dazed as Lidman says, in 1940, when I resigned my position and went to America, by a book that I didn't even read until 1942!"

The phrase "the great leaders of his day" was perhaps not particularly well chosen. But then, even those who were evil had pervaded the twentieth century to a certain—great—extent. More interesting is the implied identification between Lewi himself, "the leader and preacher of throngs of people," and "the great leaders," whether they be evil or good.

People learned from others; that was the idea. At that level. Though it was unclear what was learned. But the masses were the common denominator.

And the rest?

Lewi was certainly aware of how the "great leaders" of national socialism were persecuting Pentecostals in Germany during the 1930s.

That was something he might have mentioned.

They were persecuted by Hitler; in fact, they found themselves in the situation that Lewi had predicted in 1914: "One fine day we might end up under a regime which forbade us from conducting spiritual activities, and we might even be stripped of our personal religious freedom." This was precisely the situation in which the German brothers and sisters in faith now found themselves. Could the victim move the executioner? At the end of the European Pentecostal conference at the Karlberg tent, several weeks before war broke out in 1939, it was decided "upon the recommendation of Dr. Pethrus" to send a telegram of gratitude and congratulation to Adolf Hitler—in the hope of "thereby arousing the love and good will of *der Führer* toward the people of the Pentecostal movement."

A great deal might be said about the naïveté of this telegram. But they did know how the German Pentecostals were being treated.

Could the Pentecostal movement actually be interpreted as political?

Many people asked themselves this question. Was there some way of using these floor-rolling seers of visions who at the same time! at the same time! seemed to be such decent, industrious, frugal, generous, sober, and respectable people, who seemed able to conquer all opposition, who from their empty pockets conjured up the most astounding sums of money, and who seemed so full of contradictions?

Would it be possible to undertake an ideological invasion, so to speak, of the Pentecostal movement?

When the conflict exploded in 1948, Sven would pull the Hitler card out of his sleeve in order to annihilate Lewi.

Perhaps he was trying to forestall something.

On one of the first days of May in 1926, Sven found himself taking a springtime walk along Strandvägen when he suddenly met an old friend.

He wasn't sure that the man was still a friend. Not since he had joined the speaking-in-tongues babblers. But before that, he had been a friend: Fredrik Böök, a member of the Academy and literary critic.

Sven recognized Böök from far away, and began to feel nervous or uncomfortable or frightened, and for a moment he considered crossing Strandvägen—in the beautiful spring sunshine—to go to the dock and from there observe, in a completely natural fashion, the glittering sun on the waves and thus avoid a meeting. But he pulled himself together and kept walking. As they approached each other, Böök greeted Sven in a friendly manner, and said:

"Lidman, old friend. I think about you so often."

"You do?" replied Sven. "Yes, well, quite a few things have happened to me, praise God. But maybe you don't know that."

Böök laughed heartily, asked Sven whether he thought he had given up reading the newspapers, and then added:

"I've written several articles about you, for *Svenska Dagbladet*. Quite extensive. The first one will be in Saturday's paper. You'll find them interesting."

Sven looked at Böök in astonishment.

"I didn't think I was of any interest anymore to . . . well, to critics."

"Oh yes," said Böök in a friendly voice. "You'll see."

"To be honest, I expect something very bloody. You don't like the fact that I've changed. And switched sides."

At first Böök looked at him kindly, and in silence. Then he shook his hand and said:

"The point is that you haven't changed at all. And I like that. But you'll have to read the article."

Then he went on his way.

Sven did read it. It was, in some sense, an attempt at annexation.

It turned out to be an examination of Sven Lidman's writings from a literary criticism point of view, and a tribute. And Böök was right in terms of his conclusion: Lidman may have hidden himself in the wounds of Jesus, rolled in the blood of Jesus, and babbled with the babblers. But he was the same person, though disguised. There is reason in the irrational. The political beast never loses his stripes.

And Böök is fond of stripes.

It is a brilliant analysis. Böök is skeptical about the early poetry collections while, on the other hand, praising the historical novels: "He dreams of the intoxication of the human will, of the ecstasy of war, the way the saint dreams of a martyr's death." Böök calls *The House of the Old Spinsters* Lidman's great masterpiece. "Among all the works that have been created in Sweden during the last twenty-five years, very few can be called outright brilliant, but *The House of the Old Spinsters* is one of them." He ignores the undercurrent of Moravianism, nor does he note that "Confessions of a Beautiful Soul" in Goethe's *Wilhelm Meister's Apprenticeship* might have been a direct inspiration (the portrait of the Moravian woman). Perhaps Böök the atheist wasn't especially interested in the various factions of radical pietism.

But for Böök, Sven's collections of sermons stand far above his literary works. This is where the "stripes" become visible, the ones that Böök is so fond of. In the sermon collections he rediscovers the young Lidman, and a familiar although disguised political attitude.

It is not until these collections that Lidman becomes cast in one piece. That is the reason behind this tribute to a revivalist preacher who was otherwise generally scorned as an intellectual defector.

It is an attempt at staging an occupation.

He is writing about a religious leader in an ecstatic revivalist movement, but at the same time this man is a political model who talks about the principle of sacrifice, and submission: submission under a single lord.

This was the era between the wars, and Böök was a conservative ideologue and friendly to Germany. This was still long before the Second World War, when Böök would quite openly side with the Nazis and Hitler, and in this way commit the intellectual suicide that would forever after remove him from his position as a leading arbiter of taste.

But the hearty friend that Sven meets on Strandvägen is then at the height of his power. And he is fond of Sven. He has known him since his days at *Svensk Lösen*. He believes that he is speaking to an ideological kinsman who has chosen a strange path, and defected to the Pentecostal movement.

Though he doesn't seem to notice the defection, but rather the consequences. And the watchwords are flashing.

Sven read with amazement, and growing delight. Yet there was something about Böök's enthusiasm that he didn't understand.

"It should be possible to create a concordance of the places where blood is mentioned and its meaning in Sven Lidman's writings. He has always coveted the full-blooded reality. In his early youth he wrote poems about blood; it blazed in his limbs, pounded in his temples, sang in his rhythms and shone in the feminine flower: 'What a mystery was your womb, which in sweet nights / opened its secret of blood and darkness.'

"Then came a different time, when he dreamed of the blood that is shed on the battlefield in the service of a noble cause, to protect a beloved woman, for the honor and salvation of a beloved homeland.

"Finally there came a time when the blood became a great mystery that wipes the soul clean of sins and guilt, the emblem of the pact between man and God.

"Blood is everywhere the immediate, overwhelming experience, the complete devotion, the warm and irresistible, the ecstasy of lover, soldier, and saint.

"Sven Lidman has never doubted his conviction that blood solves all the mysteries of life. Absolute devotion, valor: those are the keynotes that resound through all the melodies of his life. In this last stage, it has become a spiritual wholeness that knows neither doubt nor tribulation.

"Sven Lidman is a lucky man. He has made heavy sacrifices, but he has also reaped rewards. The others, the children of discord, who have not been able to sacrifice ideas and reason to the blood, have every reason to envy him. Perhaps he looks down on them with sympathy. Things aren't always so easy or comfortable for them. They too might want to be brave, but it is more difficult for those who do not have a single lord for whom they can live and die. They too might want to be true, but it is difficult to balance what is proper as long as they doubt and fumble. They too might long for humility, but where is the great and sacred, before which they might fall to the dust? They too make sacrifices, but this is not done in jubilant certainty, for they have no guiding principle, and with anguish they question the purpose of the sacrifice. They live in the world of relativity, which robs our strength with hesitation and deference, confuses our feelings, paralyzes our will. Sven Lidman lives in the world of absolutes.

"Between these worlds lies a real gulf, and it would be futile to attempt to minimize it. The bridge will not hold up for just anybody. Yet they do have something in common. A person doesn't have to share Sven Lidman's faith to see that he has found a berth for himself and his true nature. An honest, brave, warm soul: that is Sven Lidman. In the world of relativity, that is an absolute value."

It was a strange text.

The man who wrote the article has found a phenomenon that he in reality dislikes, a revivalist movement, the Pentecostal movement. He himself is an atheist. But he wants to see something behind it, and what he wants to see, he likes. The watchwords from the world view of fascism occur frequently: sacrifice, devotion, blood, will, the great and the sacred, the absolute, to die for a lord. And opposing this is the world of relativity, which means hesitation, deference, doubt.

It is the world of enlightenment that is the enemy, and the weapon against enlightenment is unrestricted devotion, sacrifice, the world of the absolute, and the will to live and die for a single lord.

He talks about religion, but refers to politics. He describes Sven as a model. The model is not theological, but political. This is a long way from Immanuel Kant's fundamental idea of the enlightened human being, which says that it is the calling of every human being to think for himself. For Böök doubt is an abomination. Submission and sacrifice in jubilant certainty a virtue.

A text that is both brilliant and extremely frightening. But he has seen something. He has seen in Sven something very frightening, something that he likes a great deal.

He makes a transference that is dizzying. To make it work he has to ignore a great deal, including Moravianism's character of a Christ-centric rebellious movement. He forgets about the red thread going back to Hus. For Zinzendorf "blood" had another meaning; here it is a different blood than Christ's warm amniotic fluid. Blood is inheritance, or race. Whatever is difficult to interpret in the Pentecostal movement opens doors, some of which he steps through, others he does not. Since he is writing an unjustified tribute—which does, nevertheless, express a truth in its way—he should have been able to describe the nightly ecstatic homoerotic naked dances which occurred in Christiansfeld at the beginning of the nineteenth century, and were precursors of the German nudist culture of the 1930s: The Bridegroom was transformed to sun worship, the naked male body gazed straight up toward the swastika and the sun.

Yes, what is the actual meaning of the very strangest forms of the religious rite?

Could it, in fact, be subject to ideological attempts at staging a takeover? Could the long arc of the history of ideas in radical pietism be bent so that the Moravians and the pietistic men of the Enlightenment in Halle and Altona, those who once inspired one another and for whom rationalism and ecstasy went hand in hand, would now seem to oppose each other as enemies, between whom "lies a real gulf?"

Was that the Zeitgeist? The blood no longer warm and life-giving, but rather the blood sacrificed for a lord, perhaps divine, perhaps earthly—who knows, who knows? Fredrik Böök seems to see a man "able to sacrifice ideas and reason to the blood," and he applauds him because he thinks the next step is political; yes, it certainly is. Perhaps the step has already been taken, perhaps these peculiar babblers within the Pentecostal movement can be used as an illustration of trends that Fredrik Böök, more sensitive than most, had read during that spring of 1926. And he was pleased, and that was why he praised Sven, or at any rate the ideas and the religious leaders who were the opponents of reason and enlightenment, this enlightened reason that "confuses our feelings, paralyzes our will."

Fredrik Böök had seen something.

Sven liked the articles because they contained such strong praise.

Yet he might have felt himself used.

Sven Lidman is a lucky man because he has submitted to the sacrifice, the blood, the anti-rationalism, the Lord for whom he would die. He has taught himself not to doubt. His obedience to the Lord is absolute. He is lucky. Go thou and do likewise.

It's clear that Böök was using him. But he had seen something. The question was whether this applauded attitude toward life could be transferred from the arena of faith to that of politics. The '30s were filled with anti-rationalism, both within politics and philosophy. The symbols flowed easily together, and there were plenty of lords. If a divine one was described, it was easy to see behind the contours of an earthly one, even if a person was an atheist—especially if he was an atheist. The watchwords were the same.

Blood, submission, obedience, sacrifice, devotion. Several years after Böök's articles appeared, the National Socialist chief ideologue and philosopher, Alfred Rosenberg, mounted in *The Myth of the Twentieth Century* his own takeover of Meister Eckhart, the ancient fourteenth-century mystic, and it was the same type of effort; the book was printed by the millions, seducing and confusing.

This was the era between the wars. It was the last time that Sven met Fredrik Böök.

But the congregations!

Those throngs far below and beneath the cries and prayers of the leaders, those without hope who had learned to find faith and hope under the benedictory hands of Lewi and Sven; they were still the same shabby, limping, crippled, and useless creatures who, like the animals in the Brothers Grimm story, full of hope and defiance set off on the road to Bremen to become the town musicians. Because there is always something better than death. There were fallers and those who spoke in tongues, and the unemployed housed on the barge belonging to the Senegalese plate-lipped natives, and those who sought a prayer corner in the stables if they found no peace in the kitchen, and those who purchased a quarter pew for the temple on Rörstrandsgatan.

And they gave hardly a thought to the fact that the combination of Lewi and Sven might be impossible.

Or dangerous. Depending on how you looked at it.

Organization and ecstasy. The combination might have become catastrophic if the conflict had not arisen. Lewi, the empire builder, with his heart to the left, in combination with Sven, who had been praised by Fredrik Böök with such icy sharpness, perhaps a scurrilous portrait, perhaps with a streak of terrifying truth, this combination of reason and "unrestricted devotion" might in the long run have turned ghastly.

If the life-giving conflict had not occurred.

It would come soon. And perhaps it was necessary.

3.

The year before Efraim died and I walked behind his coffin to God's acre in Christiansfeld, accompanied by the merry oompah-oompah of a brass band, I met with several Baptist families in Riga, Latvia.

This was in the early 1980s, during the time when the Baptists were the most forbidden group in the Soviet empire. They refused to register; they seemed to create secret underground channels, linked by faith, but never in society, never controllable.

That was probably the closest anyone ever came to the Pentecostals in the Soviet Union at that time.

Most of the families were undoubtedly being wire-tapped in their miserable little rooms. No Baptist academic was allowed to keep his position. They were mostly assigned to cleaning jobs. Their humble natures made them improbable overthrowers of society.

One chemical toilet in the attic, used by eighteen families.

We knelt down in the corner of the kitchen and prayed, loudly, so the microphones wouldn't miss hearing God's Word. Two hours after I returned to my hotel, I received a call from an "official" who nonchalantly seemed to assume that the wire-tapping was necessary and didn't need to be kept secret, and he pointed out how improper it was for me to be visiting Baptists. It involved risks, not only for me, but also for them. So I didn't visit them again.

I assume that the KGB was attempting to interpret the political content of Baptism. Why else such fear of these destitute but fervent brothers and sisters? What was it that was so frightening? Their opposition, their reckless will not to conform under tyranny? Or was it merely their chameleon-like, elusive nature, and the difficulty of interpreting the political aspect? What did this fervor mean? How could it be used? Was a political application under way? Something subversive! What did it mean?

Yet there was no ready interpretation, no ready answer. Nor was it possible to invade the Swedish Pentecostal movement. Not yet. That would take some time, if it ever succeeded at all.

If clarity could ever be found.

CHAPTER 18

The Battle for the Minds

1.

ONLY SIX MONTHS BEFORE THE CONSECRATION OF THE TEMPLE ON Rörstrandsgatan, Lewi went to Brazil.

Brazil had always been Lewi's favorite in terms of the mission. It had become the largest missionary field, and there were now 160 congregations in Brazil.

Unrest had sprouted. The local pastors felt they could take over the work, and that Brazil should no longer be run by Swedish Pentecostal pastors. Lewi shared their view, and in order to put this declaration of independence into force, he was compelled to travel to Brazil, in the midst of the Rörstrand construction.

During a round-trip journey that lasted twenty-two days, the transfer of power was executed in the states of Amazonas, Pará, Maranhão, Ceará, Rio Grande do Norte, Paraíba, and Pernambuco. Everything was turned over to the local pastors and congregations. "It became so clear to me," Lewi writes, "that a mission, no matter where it is established, must have as its goal to make itself superfluous as soon as possible. The old missionary approach of building mission stations and the associated institutions and then remaining in the same place for decades, even for centuries, is wrong. Many difficulties could be avoided if more of the missionary work were left to the countries' own sons."

By the year 2000 the Pentecostal congregations of Brazil had 30 million members.

After visiting Brazil, Lewi then returns to Sweden and the consecration of the Filadelfia church.

* * *

It's difficult to follow Efraim's own life in the *Lebenslauf.*

He seems to hide behind Lewi and Sven. Maybe he doesn't think he's very important. A person shouldn't put on airs.

We get information indirectly: He has left Västerbotten, he has left Vänersborg, he is continuing his studies in Stockholm, he has passed his exams as a privately tutored student, and for a while he makes his living as a longshoreman. He becomes an elder of the Filadelfia congregation. He has never visited any other country except Norway. He lives for thirty-five years on Hornsgatan. He marries, and his wife is the daughter of a Baptist from the "Demolition Battalion," a faction of the Salvation Army.

He has no children. He and his wife are both old by the time they marry. He is God's child. He says that he met Prime Minister Erlander and talked to him "for several hours."

I meet Efraim for the first time in 1972.

At that time he mentions practically nothing about everything that dominates his *Lebenslauf.* Nothing about the Unitas Fratrum congregation. His wife is not buried in Christiansfeld; I don't know where she is buried. No explanation is given. He works almost his entire life within the Pentecostal movement. In the 1940s, before the conflict, he works at the Kaggeholm folk high school.

He mentioned little about this on the occasions when we met. Maybe I didn't ask him about it. He may have mentioned it, but when he saw that I wasn't interested, he talked about what he thought would interest me.

Who was actually interested in the Pentecostal movement anyway? I wasn't, at any rate. That was doubtless his assumption. I was interested in the birth of the labor movement, especially back home in Västerbotten. What did the Pentecostal movement have to do with me? What could it tell me about twentieth-century Sweden? I received answers according to what I asked. I asked about Nicanor, though that was not his name, and about my mother's brother, Aron.

It may not have been so strange that I didn't ask the right questions, and didn't see things right. What is right? Who sees the Pentecostal movement? Although I should have realized that what I didn't ask about ran parallel to the rest. Perhaps it's sorrow that I feel. If I had asked, I might have seen fallers and babblers and the others in Lewi's army, and realized that they too were musicians marching toward a hopeful town beyond the clouds, like the animals in the

Brothers Grimm story. A gigantic, expanding procession of limping, mangy, sick, and hopeful wretches who understood that there is always something that is better than death.

Yet what I asked about, the birth of the labor movement, and what I didn't ask about seemed to Efraim, at least, to go together. Why didn't he say so? But in all fairness he did invite me, from his heaven, if it exists, to his funeral and gave me his chronicle of what was unimportant, what I had not asked about. Perhaps he was hoping that the slanting morning light would reveal this epitaph he had left behind so that I would understand at least something of what had happened in this God's acre, which was also Sweden.

Efraim was the one who told me about Uncle Aron's death. Did I mention that?

One of Efraim's uncles had gone out to find Aron on that winter day on the ice of Bure Fjord. He found the hole he had cut and finally managed to make big enough. They found the crowbar, the second one, the one that didn't slip into the hole during the first unsuccessful attempt. They saw the spots of blood and above all the potatoes that lay scattered all around. Efraim's uncle gathered up the potatoes and took them back to Josefina, who boiled them because she was in such despair and couldn't think straight. But later, when she came to her senses, she threw out the boiled potatoes. That was the first time they ever saw Josefina let food go to waste, his uncle said.

The crowbar belonged to Hedman and had to be returned.

Efraim talked about Aron's last night on Bure Fjord as if it were a hero's death. But Aron was a sinner. If Aron wasn't a sinner, then who was? Yet this admiration, almost love. Like for Lewi, although Lewi could not be compared to Aron. But this love! Efraim was obsessed by this story of Aron who squeezed himself down through the hole, which he finally managed to make big enough so he wouldn't get stuck, and at last he was able to squeeze down into the enormous black hole that was the deepest darkness of the sea. And eternity. He thought there ought to be salvation for Aron too, and grace.

No one knows what happened in that icy water, during the half a minute it took for him to die. Perhaps Aron spread out his arms and called to the Savior for forgiveness and compassion. And if he did so, then there was compassion to be found, in truth. And then Aron would sit beside the Lamb. Because what he did to Eva-Liisa was certainly terrible. But forgiveness could be found in abundance. And surely there were worse sinners than Aron.

Efraim was almost positive that grace was also given to Aron, and that he did in fact receive this grace, that there was only a brief time from the moment he pushed himself down through the hole in the ice to the moment he was extinguished, but it was enough. And that Jesus could have been found down there with his arms open, in the darkness, because Jesus can be found everywhere, in places where human beings would least expect; yes, in truth, he was almost positive about that.

Compassion.

2.

There are very brief remarks about Lewi's personal life in the *Lebenslauf*.

Yet the personal life of Lewi and Lydia seems well organized, and happy. At first it's happy in private, later in public. They had a few children, then more, and at last they bought a house north of Stockholm, in Bredden.

Lewi was not a confessor, like Sven. Nothing said about personal matters; he did not seem happy about his remorse for his sins, if it existed, if any sin at all existed in Lewi. It would take a great deal of searching.

But his was an ideal family life. Pastures and fields belonged to the house in Bredden, and Lewi decided that the children would learn to do hard physical labor, and that farming and raising livestock would be the right thing. Some of the pictures from the '30s indicate the tone. In the photographs that he selected for his autobiography, there are often horses. "A leading principle in the raising of so many children was that early on they should participate in the farm work." In one of the photos Lewi stands alone, wearing a hat and shiny leather shoes, with a horse. "Farmer Lewi Pethrus in Bredden." In another one from the early '30s, with Karl-Jakob, Dora, Oliver, and Mirjam in front of a mowing machine and horse, Lewi has taken off his hat and is standing there in his shirtsleeves.

A photo from 1939 shows all nine children.

It presented the image of the nuclear family as the center of earthly life, and the worldly bastion of defense for faith and morality, which were slowly becoming political.

At stake, Lewi confided to Efraim, was the battle for morality, meaning conscience.

One of the few conflicts in Lewi's marriage had to do with the family's visibility in public.

It so happened that Lewi was contacted by a reporter from *Husmodern* who wanted to do an article about this embattled, hated, admired, and always controversial Lewi Pethrus in his home.

That wasn't exactly how she phrased it. But that was the assignment, from the magazine's point of view, and so she called Lewi, without hope but simply because she had been given this hopeless task.

Lewi Pethrus in his home setting was the assignment.

It was an unusual assignment. This type of article had never before appeared in the Swedish press; people were still remarkably deferential. The leading figures in politics, business, and religion were to be referred to with the proper language and only as public officials. They existed in their professional roles, and "the home" was still only a vague notion that disrupted and erased their authority. It was assumed that a wife and children existed, and that was enough. And especially regarding Lewi! Surely his speaking-in-tongues babblers provided enough material for a journalistic experience. A home wasn't necessary. But perhaps *Husmodern* had grown tired of these endless articles about Hallelujah and ecstasy and the laying on of hands and babble, and had heard that this obviously remarkable high priest lived a perfectly normal life in a house with horses and children and a wife.

And this in itself was astonishingly interesting.

To the immense surprise of the journalist, Lewi agreed to the article.

But Lydia was furious. She stared at him for a long time and then started to cry, asking him if he had gone mad. Were the persecutors and scandal-mongers now going to be allowed inside their home? When he chose a thumb verse for her, it was unfortunately Revelation 2:26–28, which says: *"He who conquers and who keeps my works until the end, I will give him power over the nations, and he shall rule them with a rod of iron,*

as when earthen pots are broken in pieces, even as I myself have received power
from my Father, and I will give him the morning star."

That was the thumb verse he read. And then he fell silent and
looked at her. And then she said that this, in any case, told her nothing, nothing! And then, furious, she had gone to get a bucket and mop
in order to start cleaning up, because she refused to be shamed by a
home that was not tidy. That evening, after she finished and had still
not uttered a single word of remorse, and Lewi was practically in agony
and kept wandering around, she slammed the mop and bucket down
on the floor and said:

"Well, at least it's clean. But you'll have to receive that reporter yourself. I refuse to make an appearance! I'll go out in the woods and hide.
And you'll have to sit there with her, and have your picture taken."

Lewi could tell that she was unusually angry because the water had
been sloshing out of the bucket all afternoon in an almost uncontrollable way. But then he calmly and without getting carried away
explained that the battle for morality in society had to be fought by
every means possible. It was immorality and the wretchedness of the
dance floor and the tabloid press and the way children were subjected
to Nick Carter. This battle for purity had to start with the family. And
the young needed role models. And so they shouldn't be afraid of pre-
senting a model, and she, as a housewife and mother of nine children,
was just such a model.

She had to participate.

She merely sniffed, and by evening was almost hostile. Lydia simply continued with her stubborn sniffing. The day before the journalist was supposed to visit them, Lewi managed to get her to relent, even
though she felt it was shameful.

When the journalist arrived, Lewi was very straightforward and
friendly and talked a great deal about Lydia and the children. Lydia was
calm and quiet by nature, he said, and when the reporter asked her
whether Lewi was right about that, Lydia hesitated for a long time and
then sternly nodded, but with such a fierce expression that the reporter
didn't dare ask her about anything else.

Lydia didn't utter a single word during the whole visit. But with
her nod she had undeniably confirmed that she was calm and quiet by
nature. The photographer took pictures, and everything looked very
plain and comfortable, and then they took a picture of Lewi and Lydia
sitting on the good sofa, and Lewi told her to smile.

"Come on and smile, Lydia!" he said in a simple and humorous way.

And then she smiled.

The article was an enormous success, and a positive breakthrough for Lewi in terms of the public. One phrase, in particular, lived on from the article. It was Lewi who thought of it.

The journalist had thanked the family for so generously putting themselves at her disposal for this . . . well . . . what should she call it . . . that they were doing a . . . a . . .

"An At-Home-With report," Lewi said with a smile.

The reporter made a note of this, and it was included in the article. That's how the phrase originated. This was another way in which Lewi was unique: this article in *Husmodern* was the first at-home-with report in the Swedish press, and it was Lewi who coined the phrase. It would, of course, be used by many others later on, but this was the first time. And perhaps Lewi was right in his thinking: that in the battle against sin and evil, it was important to present a model, and the happy nuclear family in Bredden, with the horse and the wife and the nine children, was an important part in this Jesus-ideology production, part of the moral battle, and part of the battle for the minds.

In Efraim's presence, Lewi had early on developed his ideas about the role of the family in the cultural battle.

Efraim was astonished that he viewed it, to some extent, as a political battle. He knew where Lewi stood politically, after all. He had known this ever since they met in Vänersborg, and in spite of everything, Lewi had never changed. But as the leader of the congregation, Lewi had always said that politics did not belong with salvation and sanctification through the Spirit.

"The battle against immorality," he told Efraim, "must be the great political mission of the Pentecostal movement. And we have to take it seriously."

Efraim was astonished.

"Is it Lidman who has put those political notions into your head?" he asked.

"Lidman?"

"You know that I don't really trust him," said Efraim.

"Lidman is one of the God-given evangelists," Lewi then explained, "and I love him dearly. But he doesn't have a single decent political opinion in his poet's head. Can't even think a straight political thought. Or a crooked one, either. And if he does, it sounds like an article in *Svensk Lösen*, and we have to pray to God to save the Pentecostal movement from that. But he keeps quiet about politics, praise the Lord. And as for the battle against immorality in Sweden, he undoubtedly has nothing to contribute."

He said this with an undertone that surprised Efraim, though much later he understood why. It had to do with the story about Aina. But then Efraim asked:

"You're not going into politics, are you, Lewi?"

Lewi just smiled and shook his head, though what he was driving at wasn't quite clear. A moment later, after Efraim had already forgotten what he had asked, Lewi said in a very matter-of-fact and curt tone:

"We'll see."

3.

The story of Lewi's visit to the newspaper office of *Dagens Nyheter* may have been wrongly interpreted. It has been recounted as if it were proof of the little pastor's comical lack of common sense.

People have talked about Lewi's ingratiating attitude.

Yet it may have been an early contribution to the battle for the minds, a failed attempt, and therefore, as things later developed, a significant and decisive one.

This is what happened.

Lewi went to the editorial offices of *Dagens Nyheter* and told the receptionist that he wished to speak to Editor-in-Chief Dehlgren. He was kept waiting for forty minutes and the cigar smoke was quite annoying, but finally he was admitted to the holiest of holies, the office of the legendary Dehlgren. Dehlgren's name was on the door.

The legend said, "Good day, Herr Pethrus, to what do I owe the honor?" And he said that he didn't have much time but that he was curious. If Pastor Pethrus was planning on faith-healing the circulation of *Dagens Nyheter*, he was willing to listen, but Herr Pethrus shouldn't try any speaking in tongues, because *Dagens Nyheter* had no translators. And please be seated.

By then Lewi had already sat down and was listening calmly to this introductory jesting.

"Herr Dehlgren," he said, "we Pentecostals are used to being insulted, so nothing bothers us. And I've already sat down. As you can see."

"Yes, well."

"And I'm not here to speak in tongues. I'm here to talk business. And I don't think I can make the blind see. That is reserved for the Lord Jesus Christ and, by the way, He doesn't care about the circulation of *Dagens Nyheter*."

"A pity," said Dehlgren, a bit subdued.

"But if He did care about *Dagens Nyheter* . . ."

" . . . things would probably go to hell for us. Get to the point. What do you want, sir? Do you want us to print a retraction? We've written a lot of dirt about you, and now you want a retraction, but you won't get it. Was there anything else?"

"I don't want a retraction," said Lewi. "I want to have a discussion with you, and ask your advice. Do you think the Pentecostal movement could start a national newspaper? And if so, how should we go about it?"

Dehlgren was undeniably disconcerted.

"Of all the nerve. Why in hell would you come to a future competitor to ask for advice? Of all the nerve."

"Yes, Herr Dehlgren," replied Lewi. "Jesus didn't even have a waiting room outside the door. But I asked Him for advice and He thinks it's just as well to come to you directly because you're the best—and the worst."

That was how it began. Yet with these powerful words, Dehlgren suddenly seemed more interested and offered Lewi coffee, and then listened. After listening, he grew thoughtful. He advised against the plan. Without hesitation he advised against it, but for a long time he discussed newspaper finances with Pastor Pethrus.

It wasn't until the end of their conversation that Dehlgren asked the decisive and simple question that he should have asked in the first place.

"But tell me, Pastor . . . if you're not going to start a newspaper in order to make a hell of a lot of money—which you'll never be able to do, by the way—why the devil do you absolutely have to have a national newspaper?"

"We don't want to make money," said Lewi. "We want to preach God's glory."

"But don't you have that poet Lidman for that? I've heard he draws a crowd."

"God's voice does not speak through Lidman alone!"

"No?"

"No. And we need to have a voice. Right now we're being locked out. If we have a voice, we'll have a counter-force. Then *Dagens Nyheter* won't keep lying about us without restraint. Then we'll have some control over the press."

"Control? Over us? But my dear pastor . . ."

"It's easy to lie if no one protests. If people protest, they gain control."

And with that the peculiar conversation with Dehlgren came to an end. Dehlgren had no more time. He seemed irritated and pensive.

Pethrus thanked him in a friendly manner and said that he had gained a great deal from their conversation, and that he could now proceed. Dehlgren then looked at him in confusion and said:

"You must be out of your mind."

Efraim said almost the same thing to Lewi.

"You're out of your mind," he said. "Why did you go there? What good would it do?"

"People often think," said Lewi, "that the big newspapers are governed and managed by people who are bigger than the rest of us small creatures. That we're helpless, and incompetent."

"And?"

"It felt good. It wasn't that remarkable."

4.

Hovering over all of this was the mysterious glow from the phosphorescent cross.

Brita had gotten rid of the cross almost at once. Yet in some way it was still there, with its extraordinary, ambiguously shimmering glow, which was supposed to arouse hope and suffering and evil and good.

Perhaps it ended up shining over the entire Pentecostal movement, while the movement continued to grow and grow.

* * *

It was quite obvious that most of the people who came to Lidman's meetings were women.

That's the way it was in the whole Pentecostal movement.

It was women who sat there and sobbed and testified and were silent and pale and joyous and despairing and entertained, but sit there they did. They were the faith-bearing layer, never part of the leadership but always the reliable foundation, and they made coffee and trudged home through the slushy snow and offered support to the movement. Not by sitting among the congregation's elders or as part of the leadership, but by being the body and soul of the movement, though not its head.

There was a women named Aina.

She was Brita's cousin. The photographs show a very round and full face above a plump body. She might be described as sweet. It's possible. At that time she must have been in her forties. She worked as the family's housekeeper. Efraim had observed her many times at the meetings. She looked happy and devoted, and occasionally Efraim spoke to her because he knew that she was a member of the family, so to speak.

He noticed that she was carried away by the songs and preaching. She was charming. She sat with her eyes fixed on Sven as he spoke. Everyone did the same, though Efraim didn't actually understand why. He was pleased by Sven's preaching, for the sake of the Spirit and the message, because the message was powerful, but why was everyone so fixated?

There was something about Sven that made them fixate on him.

He couldn't exactly be called handsome.

Afterwards Sister Aina said to Efraim:

"The way he speaks makes a chill run through a person."

"Is that right?" he said.

"Yes, that's right."

"Well, not me," he said.

"Oh yes, it makes a chill go right through a person."

"Not me," he repeated, feeling almost hostile at her insistence.

Then she seemed to hesitate for a moment, as if not quite sure that she dared, but at last she asked:

"Efraim, you've said that you know Zinzendorf. You've read so much; do you know if he has any particular ... views about family life?"

He didn't understand what she meant.

"Any unusual . . . ideas?"

"What do you mean by unusual?"

He wasn't aware of anything like that. She didn't ask any more questions. And since he hadn't understood her question, and she didn't want to help him understand, the matter was dropped.

What had happened did, in fact, have something to do with Zinzendorf.

One afternoon when Sven and Aina were home alone and she was just walking around and humming, Sven came over and stood quite close to her and began talking about spiritual matters. About how they were different for different people. About the nervous strain for those who were chosen by god as preachers! And having to keep yourself free and open to receive God's voice. And that this was different than for ordinary people, and the circumstances weren't the same. And how great spiritual men had dealt with this.

Then he happened to mention Count Zinzendorf.

For his part, Zinzendorf had written somewhere about the unusual burden that religious evangelists bore, and how it created an unusual strain. Sven seemed to be talking in circles, but he came back to the point that spiritual leaders were different, and that according to Moravian teachings, it might be justified for a religious leader to have two wives, also in the flesh, or one woman for the spiritual and one for the flesh. It was quite difficult to follow his reasoning.

He stood close to Aina but partially turned away.

She asked him what he meant. Did he mean that other rules applied in the sight of God when it was a matter of preachers? According to the Moravians?

And, with his back turned, Sven nodded vigorously.

"Aina," he said, "things are often so difficult for me."

It was an autumn day, and the sun was out, and afterwards she recalled that an extraordinary light had played over the room. It was so beautiful and at the same time so mysterious that she could hardly breathe.

"I know," she said after a long pause.

"Aina," he said, "I've often thought I could sense a certain closeness to you."

She hardly dared breathe. It was both terrible and incomprehensible, and she could barely understand what he was saying, but then he began talking about Zinzendorf again.

"Things are so difficult for me, Aina," he said once more.

She waited until the silence was almost unbearable. He was still standing with his back to her, looking out the window, and she would always remember the yellow leaves and autumn sunshine and the extraordinary light that made it nearly impossible to breathe, and then the fact that he finally stopped talking about Zinzendorf and fell silent.

"Yes?" she said.

And then he turned to face her.

This was the way in which he initiated the sexual relationship with Brita's cousin. After a year it was discovered, and Aina had to move out. Several years later he resumed the relationship, but this time, too, it was discovered, and that was the end of it.

The second time Brita suffered a nervous breakdown. They found her out on the balcony, in convulsions, and had to carry her inside. The children helped her. No one understood why she had this breakdown, except Sven. At first it seemed as if her breakdown had made her "withdraw from" the family group, because the children didn't understand the situation. She had somehow failed the test. But after only a year's convalescence she was again completely healthy in body and soul, as the saying goes. And it turned out that her brief advertisement in *Svenska Dagbladet*, in which she was cheerful and musical, was not the last thing she would write.

She got back on her feet and began writing children's books which, by the way, were translated into many languages.

What made her pull herself out of her degradation, no one knew, or at least Efraim didn't in the *Lebenslauf.* But one of her books depicts the happy family life at Stora Vilunda. Perhaps not as it actually was, but as it ought to have been.

And it ought to have been very, very pleasant.

Within the Pentecostal community, the marriage appeared happy. It was the way a Pentecostal movement marriage always should be, closely connected and firm in principle. By no means a hell. And it was also extensively covered through an "at-home-with" article and photos, including the picture on the stairs when Aina was present, looking so healthy and short and plump. The article, which now could be said to be a regular part of the battle for the minds, especially after Lewi's at-home-with article was generally declared a success within the movement, became part of the movement's general ideological training.

There was almost a sort of competition between Sven's and Lewi's happy families, and it was doubtless the case that back then Sven's happy family was the victor. In the pictures his family was often gathered on the stairs of the manor house, Stora Vilunda, which Sven had bought. The picture in which Aina is present is the best. It's a completely ordinary picture of a Pentecostal family, except for the size of the stairway. The family radiates great happiness, and later on so many people would write about this family. The children would write, testifying to what it was like to be God's grandchild, which was also the title of the most well-known novel by Sam, one of the sons.

The family ended up being meticulously documented, as was the estate, Stora Vilunda.

But there was something about the photos that wasn't quite right. There is a note of discord in Efraim's *Lebenslauf*, as if he is growing more and more restive about his relationship to Lewi and Sven and these family pictures.

Was there something that didn't quite fit?

Sven had written so beautifully about the Pentecostal movement's character of nomadic faith: "Under no circumstances will it erect great cathedrals or fortresses that will be visible. We do not build walls, we live in tents. Freedom and independence from all constraint is the lifeblood of this movement." Yet almost at the same time the gigantic and not at all tentlike temple on Rörstrandsgatan was consecrated, with room for four thousand people. And even though Sven so poignantly described the Pentecostal movement's tent existence and inviolable determination, in all simplicity, constantly to strike camp again, he wrote these words in a very private stronghold, hardly tentlike, and preserved with very little seasoning of Christian love.

At the time he was formulating his statements about the Pentecostals' nomadic philosophy he had just won a court case which granted him the right to enclose Stora Vilunda and cut off traffic along the road that passed through his property.

He could then surround the land with a Gunnebo fence crowned with barbed wire. In addition, and this was the most important result, the very poor and large families of the tenant farmers who lived on the neighboring land—and did not have access to their own water or well and were therefore forced to use the only well around, which was located on Sven's property—were now allowed to come to God's well, so to speak, only during certain brief periods in the early morning and late evening.

These were the periods when it was thought they would not disturb too greatly preacher Lidman's need for solitude with his God.

Sven has described it so well: "Out there at Stora Vilunda I live a most delightful and comfortable country-house existence. Occasionally —at most a couple of times a week—I go in to the office and cheer up the church members with merry conversation and witty ideas. My life is actually a Sunday life, and I've become a figurehead on the vessel of the Pentecostal movement."

The tenant farmers' access to water is not included in his confessions, as Efraim briefly notes, remarking that: "Lidman never confessed to this sin, although he admitted to so much else that made a good impression in his books, but this was no doubt too minor."

It was as if Efraim wanted to say: "Why doesn't it all make sense any longer? What was it they had done? Why was the gap between reality and their language so great, when everything, without interruption, was through the grace of God, the inspiration of the Spirit, and through the consoling mercy of Jesus, even the discussions about interest rates on loans and wage negotiations. Why had the language turned so mute, and the Spirit so mechanically present, and the tents so few, the temple so great, and the barbed-wire-crowned Gunnebo fence so evident, although thoroughly invisible?"

That must have been why Efraim began to miss more and more the testimony of the children of grace. The way in which they had gone out to the woods to pray. They knelt down amid stones and stumps and prayed to Almighty God, *and the whole forest was filled with the murmuring of prayers. And the Spirit fell. And understand! that before it all becomes as it should be, we have to go back to that, when there were prayers even out in the barns. If someone prevented them from going to the prayer corner inside, they would go out to the barns and pray to God there. That happened often. People never parted without a prayer and an invocation; no, never. Before they parted, there had to be a prayer meeting.*

That's how it was, wholeheartedly. But for some reason all of that was lost. Yes, things were different back then, weren't they? Not that the prayer meetings vanished altogether, but something was lost. And that was somehow the beginning of what happened later, the fact that something was lost.

For whom was it lost?

Those who sat close, along with cousin Aina, may not have thought that it was lost. Perhaps it was mostly lost among the leadership. There it was noticeably absent, as Efraim writes. He is still writing mostly about the way in which Sven held the congregation under control. Every minute, every instant. And how Aina, leaning forward, kept her gaze fixed on him, and later asked that peculiar question about Count Zinzendorf's view of marriage, and whether it was true.

The question that Efraim could not answer.

What about Lewi and the women?

Nothing. Almost nothing.

An intensive search was made, but little was found. One rumor was widely spread and caused distress and alarm among the brothers and sisters of faith: that on his trip to Palestine Lewi was accompanied by a Pentecostal's wife. It turned out to be a retired Pentecostal, and a man. To everyone's relief.

The second rumor was the story of the actress. In his old age and with a certain pride, Lewi recounted that a rumor had spread that he was having a relationship with an actress. Several Pentecostals called on Lydia regarding this matter, and she had thrown out the delegation and "in resounding Norwegian" declined to have any part in such mudslinging.

The actress was Anna Larssen. At the turn of the century she was Denmark's most celebrated actress, and she played all the great roles—from Nora in Ibsen's *A Doll's House* to Fröken Julie in Strindberg's play of the same name. She was forced out of her acting career because of a strange story. A spiteful female colleague spread the rumor that Anna Larssen was having a sexual relationship with her dog, a dachshund. When Anna appeared on stage, several members of the audience began shouting: "Woof! Woof! Woof!" and general merriment broke out. It became intolerable, it ruined everything, and she had a breakdown and left the theater. Then she became saved and a Pentecostal.

For several decades she was one of the Nordic Pentecostal movement's most beloved evangelists and speakers, and she also toured in Stockholm.

In countless interviews she is described as delicate, beautiful, and charming, in a Danish sort of way. It's possible that Anna Larssen and Lewi might have discussed what it was like to be the object of mud-slinging. Lewi never sued any newspaper for libel. His principle was: A Pentecostal never prosecutes.

Perhaps that was wise. Yet in the 1940s, when the mud-slinging subsided, he would lament that the publicity was diminishing and the attention paid to the movement was declining.

5.

It's unlikely that Efraim invented the expression "battle for the minds."

It was probably taken from somewhere else. But he became more and more obsessed with the expression. Editor-in-Chief Dehlgren at *Dagens Nyheter* had, in a way, asked a relevant question, the one concerning the battle for the minds. If they still had Lidman the poet, did they need anything else?

But Lewi had said: control. The control that Lidman the poet had over the minds was undeniably great and astonishing, and sometimes frightening. With or without the help of Count Zinzendorf. But there was another kind of control over the minds.

And for that Lewi needed a newspaper, a daily paper that could voice opposition. Lewi's faith in the power of newspapers was so firm that he was certain no one would then dare lie, and through this threat the minds would be brought to accord and the Pentecostal movement would continue its triumphal march, not just among all those calm women who listened in fascination and formed the foundation of the faith, but among all of humanity.

Lewi seemed to have two ideas. This was one of them: the battle for the minds. But when that battle was won, then they could ease up on the organization. Then it would be, as he had written in his big keynote address for the Pentecostal movement's world organization in Berlin back in 1916, "*collegia pietatis*," or germ cells, as old Zinzendorf said; that was the small circle. Then the human being was alone with his God.

Two ideas, but they seemed to fit together.

The germ cell was silence, together with God. Alone with God.

That was the ideal congregation. Then there was the larger one. But to achieve the small one, the so-called decentralized presence with God, they had to organize centrally.

But the goal was the small one. Independence.

If they succeeded with the central organization, their goal would be near. The goal was the germ cell. Then they could more or less hand over everything to the local population. Meaning to the individual. Just as it occurred in Amazonas and Pará and Maranhão and Rio Grande do Norte, when Lewi went there and turned everything over, because he didn't want to be an imperialist of God, just a creator of germ cells.

And then, through God's inspiration and grace, along with Lewi's resolute mediation, a way of thinking would emerge which many people might not yet understand but which had its basis in the Bible, as well as in what was very modern.

CHAPTER 19

Modernity

1.

LYDIA HAD TOLD LEWI THAT THIS LIDMAN, THIS LIDMAN! HE WAS SO wonderful. But she didn't trust this Lidman for a second.

Then Lewi grew quite upset and rebuked her. But she wasn't about to be rebuked.

"You're blind," she said. "Blinded by your love for him."

In the *Lebenslauf* a brief reflection: "Brita undoubtedly said the same about Lewi. But they weren't blind."

Efraim went up to the *Härold* on a March day in 1937 and, as usual, did not find Sven there.

He expressed his displeasure.

To the brother on duty, whose name was Lundgren or Lundberg, he said that with Brother Lidman, the editor, things were such that he only made a brief explosion of effort each month, and then only by proofreading a sermon that had been taken down in shorthand. It would be a blessing if he devoted more time to his editorial duties. But the brother on duty replied that Brother Pethrus had not expressed any sort of disapproval, so things should stay the way they were.

Brother Pethrus loved Brother Lidman, and was completely satisfied. He was satisfied. The movement was very grateful to Brother Lidman, after all. There was great unanimity that he had been sent by God.

Then Efraim replied that there was no lack of gratitude. The congregation's sisters, in particular, were grateful. And sometimes during the meetings he had the feeling that they not only believed that

Lidman was talking about the Bridegroom, but that Sven himself was the bridegroom, and that this caused an almost unhealthy feeling.

The brother on duty, who probably was named Lundberg, then expressed his displeasure at Efraim's remark, but said that he had another problem of a more controversial nature.

This too had to do with the women.

Now it was true that the women formed the very foundation of the Pentecostal movement, and in so many ways. The leadership, meaning the leading brothers and congregation elders, was aware of this. The battle over societal morality had begun to move more and more into the forefront. It was not just the entertainment industry that was the enemy. It was in a sense the pleasures themselves that threatened morality. And a woman's morality, in particular.

If a woman was subjected to, or created, immorality, this would also affect the man. The source of immorality was, of course, the enticement of a woman's body. That's why it had to be concealed. A woman must not be enticing. And the battle against sin, against frivolity, and for the protection of family unity and discipline had become increasingly important in the battle against immorality.

European decadence! which Brother Sven also so clearly used to describe in his sermons. Decadence!

Hadn't Sven seen it for himself?

One time when his two oldest daughters, nine and eleven years old, came to visit, and they jumped out of the carriage and ran toward their father, he saw it in their clothing! and! as he later wrote, he saw decadence in their "slack, pleasure-loving faces." And he shouted: "You're going to end up as harlots!" But the Savior had prevented that; His grace was great. The children had stopped, as if turned to stone.

And they were now saved.

In short! Woman was the weak point of morality. The protection of woman as the pure center of the family was part of the battle. That's why it had become increasingly important for women in the Pentecostal movement to dress and to conduct themselves outwardly with a special kind of respectability of the highest order. The sight of ankles drew the gaze up toward unshielded legs! Pulling the hair back into the so-called Pentecostal bun prevented the loose tresses of a harlot! As well as the general decree that women should not wear emblems of frivolity or sin.

Which included jewelry.

That was why, at *Evangelii Härold*, they were having certain problems with the photographs in the newspaper. Occasionally the photos printed in the newspaper showed women who were wearing jewelry, and so, using technical means, they regularly touched up the photos to erase the jewelry.

But on this particular morning a problem had come up, Brother Lundberg reported.

They were going to include a photo of the Swedish queen. In the picture she would, without a doubt, be wearing a necklace. The question was: Did they have the right to touch up pictures of the queen? Might this be regarded as an insult, or in any case a definite criticism of a member of the royal family?

Efraim writes that as a republican, he doubtless recommended that they should also touch up the queen. He says that he wasn't entirely certain that this ban on jewelry was wise, or served any purpose. And in any case he later came to doubt this principle. But he felt that from a democratic point of view, "and the Pentecostal movement was by all means democratic, I would think," it was appropriate for the *Evangelii Härold* to apply the same rules to queens as to poor Pentecostal women.

And so they touched up the queen's photo.

They could erase sin from photographs. But the Pentecostal movement was growing within Swedish modernity.

When the new temple on Rörstrandsgatan was going to be built, Lewi showed a great interest in the architectonic design of the building.

He was especially concerned with the acoustic problems.

The first drawings were delivered in 1926 by the architect Birger Jonsson, and over the next few years Lewi rejected fourteen different designs. One day the architect came to Lewi with the building trade journal *Byggmästaren*. Printed in the journal were drawings for the famous Paris hall, the so-called Salle Pleyel. The owner of a French piano company had built this Salle Pleyel, inspired by his interest in acoustics and his experience constructing pianos, and—of particular interest to Lewi—designed on the basis of new research into the effects of various materials on tone quality.

The temple on Rörstrandsgatan was to house four thousand people, and it was Lewi's firm resolve that it should be a model of the most advanced technical innovations of the day.

At that time acoustics was an often neglected issue. The concert hall in Stockholm was an example of such a failure, in Lewi's opinion. He was fascinated by the drawings in the journal *Byggmästaren*. He gave the architect the assignment, at Filadelfia's expense, to travel to Paris to study the Salle Pleyel. There he was to pay careful attention to various listening distances in the room, as well as inspect the material and design of the hall. All specifications—the type of wood and the structure—everything that might affect the design of the temple was to be meticulously recorded during his visit. The temple was to be a model of the finest leading technology. In this way Jonsson, the architect, was commissioned to create a building in which the most modern ideas in the field could be put to the test.

And that's what happened.

The architect returned from Paris with all the necessary information. Only a month after his visit, the Salle Pleyel burned down and could not be restored until several years later. Speaking before the congregation, Lewi thanked God, who in His mercy had expedited the architect's journey, so that the temple could now be said to represent the most modern advances within architecture and acoustic research.

In this functionalist temple, basically created by Lewi, admirably designed and a model of Swedish twentieth-century modernity, would sit the thousands who had pulled their hair back into a bun and were not allowed to wear jewelry. In this way, at Rörstrandsgatan, twentieth-century Swedish modernity and ecstatic anti-rationalism were gathered in one congregation, in one image, in an optimistic waiting for the return of Jesus, when everything would be torn down, and the millennium would be inserted into and merged with Sweden's twentieth-century irresistible faith in development and optimism about progress.

2.

Perhaps Lewi had at last found his ideal writer, his Birger Sjöberg, but this Birger Sjöberg who was saved, meaning Sven, might not have realized the complication: that Lewi still had a Birger Sjöberg inside himself, very well hidden, like a secret dream.

And this was a problem.

* * *

For fifteen years they truly loved each other.

They were such a fantastic pair. A kind of joy spread within the movement over how much Sven and Lewi loved each other. And how they complemented each other: preacher and poet, administrator and author.

No one actually knew what happened when the chill set in. They had worked together so brilliantly and didn't seem to interfere in each other's areas. The resolute respect they felt for one another was part of this. They basically never competed.

Yet there was one area that was a minefield. The fact that Sven was an idiot about practical and financial matters and a miserable organizer was something about which they both agreed. Cheerfully and merrily agreed. It was quite obvious: Sven was a poet. It was a poet's nature to be a financial idiot. It practically reinforced his authority. But, on the other hand, he was a true poet.

Lewi was not. That was the understanding.

The fact that Lewi had once had a different dream was not something that Sven knew anything about. Or that the dream could still be found deep inside Lewi, perhaps no longer the dream of the proletarian author, but the dream! the dream! Who would know this?

Although as it turned out, Lewi too began to publish books. They were real books, with covers and everything. Of course they were sermons, but several received surprisingly favorable reviews. His travel books were, in reality, brilliant journalism. But they were journalism. And Sven always nodded at them benevolently. But they didn't add up to a real body of literary work.

It was nice for Lewi to have something published. "Have something published" was the expression.

But it was a matter of books that were in a different class. He was not an artist, after all. Finally irritation arose. Lewi had entered Sven's territory, and then there was suddenly a new tone of voice. It came from slightly above, in the midst of Sven's tribute to Lewi's fantastic talent for organization.

Sven himself would later record and revise it. Wasn't it a little pretentious of Lewi to claim to be a great preacher, and on top of it all, an author, an author! What was he thinking, anyway? "But," Sven writes, "then I always thought about what Plutarch has the great Spartan king say about the lion skin that was his royal cloak and the symbol of his power:

"'If the lion skin isn't big enough, you have to lengthen it with fox skin.'

"I'm sure I've thought more than once, whenever I found him much too short in the coat: The sad thing is, of course, that sometimes deep inside you're nothing more than a shrewd little peddler from Västergötland."

There it was.

That was the tone that appeared and crept in, and it always had something to do with situations when Lewi had ventured across the territorial boundary, which was the realm of art. It got even worse when Bonniers Publishing Company—Sven's own publisher! Bonniers!!! —made Lewi an offer to publish a volume of his discourses in a series of three volumes. The two others would be works by Thomas à Kempis and John Bunyan. With a radiant expression Lewi had told Sven the news and said—words that he would eat for many, many years, and which, when the conflict culminated, would become the very symbol, the emblem! of the arrogance of the shrewd little peddler from Västergötland who now thought he was an author:

"Imagine," he said, beaming at Sven, "it's just going to be Thomas à Kempis, John Bunyan, and me!"

It was unbelievable. At Bonniers! It was obvious that the little peddler from Västergötland had lost all sense of perspective.

Close to boundaries there are always desires—and conflicts.

On another occasion, Sven read through a text that Lewi showed him. Kindly and imbued with Christian love Sven had told him that the profundity he was trying to display was much too superficial. That it would be better if he wrote in a simpler and more concise style, since he would then do greater justice to his ideas. Lewi had listened, and in this way improved his text. And afterwards he thanked Sven for his collegial criticism.

But it stayed with him like a thorn.

Of significance was the incident that both Sven and Efraim witnessed, and about which they both testified, but perhaps in slightly different ways.

It was the story of the pious female student and the galley proofs.

Lewi had taken a journey to Palestine and written a travel account which he called *In the Land of the Bible*. A young university student had been hired "from a genuine, deeply Christian family of Methodist persuasion" to proofread the book. Then a "furious" Lewi came into the office and had a fit that shocked everyone.

"Sister may think that she can write Swedish because she's a university student. Isn't my Swedish good enough for you? How dare you correct my manuscript in this manner!!!"

The outburst shocked the girl, who afterwards "went into Filadelfia's bathroom and sat and sobbed out her sorrow and despair," as Sven notes in *Journey to Judgment.*

It was embarrassing, even though Lewi later calmed down and apologized and tried to gloss over his outburst.

The passage in question concerned Lewi's visit to the catacombs in Rome. In these catacombs, Lewi wrote, they had made such good use of the space for the burial grounds that they had placed the bodies head to tail.

He had used the expression "head to tail."

Those were the words the student had deleted. She thought the phrase was poor Swedish. It meant, of course, that one body was placed with the feet in one direction, and the next with the head in that same direction. Surely this was a provincialism? And provincialisms shouldn't be used.

Or else you weren't a real author.

It must have felt like a slap in the face. He wasn't a real author, he was a provincial author. Actually, not an author at all. He had taken the image from his childhood, when children were packed head to tail in the beds, to make enough room. Lewi had slept head to tail all his childhood. Could this image be used about the dead in the catacombs of Rome? No, Lewi had made a mistake that revealed his social class.

He had stepped forward with pretensions but had exposed himself.

Efraim, who made note of the episode, pauses for a moment at the image of the dead resting in God's catacombs like children in God's crowded bed, and he thinks the phrase is wonderful, and that the image is actually quite beautiful. Actually tremendously beautiful, almost like a poem, like a very fine poem captured in a single phrase, and he doesn't understand why Lewi should be ashamed of that poem.

Which was one of the finest he ever wrote, though it was only a single phrase.

* * *

Yesterday I sat and wrote down, on a piece of paper, the last words that Lewi uttered on his deathbed regarding Sven.

I added my mamma's last words. Her name was Maria, but she was called Maja.

Three lines, like a little poem, or a rebus that could be solved and would then explain how everything fit together.

3.

The same day that the Winter War broke out in Finland, on November 30, 1939, a big revivalist meeting was held in the Filadelfia church on Rörstrandsgatan.

It was a full house, but the mood was not particularly strained because the news about the outbreak of war hadn't yet reached everyone, and those who knew about it didn't fully understand.

Sven Lidman was preaching.

This was not something he did very often at that time—it depended on his work load, as he put it—but when he did preach there was great excitement, and the church was always full. As usual, he barely used his script as he spoke. He simply held the Bible in his hand and looked out at the crowds. It was a lovely evening. He knew that he had everyone with him, and there was laughter at regular intervals, which was the best evidence that the emotion would be high when he pulled everything together.

Pulling everything together was an art.

It was "magic," as he used to say, to pull things together and then let go—that rhythm. Just as he raised his eyes after having read I Corinthians 1:13 and the following: *"Is Christ divided? Was Paul crucified for you? Or were you baptized in the name of Paul?"* and then, just as he raised his eyes, he saw Margot.

Margot was there. She was sitting in the third row. He froze.

It was impossible to mistake her for anyone else. She looked different from the others. She wasn't dressed as they were.

What was she doing there?

Afterwards he didn't know how he managed to complete his sermon. There was a pause in his speech, then he pulled himself together. Several people speaking in tongues had interrupted with shouts and long strings of words, but he succeeded in calming them. It was a very tranquil evening.

Perhaps many had heard the rumors from Finland after all.

The woman next to Margot was weeping. Margot sat rigidly. She was wearing a hat, which clearly set her apart from the others. Lewi was sitting on a chair behind and slightly to the side of Sven, and he had undoubtedly noticed her too, but he may have been merely surprised.

So many sinners came to the congregation. Sometimes they looked sinful. Later they melted in better.

What was she doing there?

When the meeting was over Sven went backstage, meaning behind the platform, and drank a glass of water, telling himself to stay calm. There was no reason to be upset. Margot looked much older than he remembered her. He remembered her as being beautiful. In fact, he remembered her quite clearly because she was like a cloud of sin in his sky—that was the image he used in his mind—and she was always beautiful. And sometimes naked. Maybe she was still beautiful. He hadn't looked at her very closely during the rest of his sermon. He had talked about Jesus Christ as the one who, solely and undivided, represented change.

At least he thought that's what he had talked about.

About Jesus Christ as the benefactor, and the very instant that he said the word "benefactor," he thought it wasn't a very good word. But he couldn't change it. The benefactor who had made Sven get up and walk.

Jesus was the one who made people rise up out of sin. Or something like that.

Everything was like a fog.

Afterwards, backstage, meaning behind the platform since they didn't use the worldly term "stage" even though it was a stage, Efraim appeared and talked about editing the *Härold* and Sven replied in a slightly distracted manner. They went out the back door together, and Efraim was still talking about editing and proofreading.

That was about how it was. Still as if in a fog.

Then they reached the street, and there was Margot coming toward them, wearing a very beautiful coat, which set her apart, and a hat that was not at all the usual Pentecostal hat. She was wearing makeup "like harlots," as he usually thought, and she held out her hand to Sven and said:

"Finally the poet has a great audience. Congratulations, Sven. You've always taken unusual paths."

He took her hand. Efraim stood nearby—that was the most embarrassing—and looked surprised. Sven now saw her quite clearly. Her coat was not a cheap one, but it must have been a long time ago that it was expensive. There was something shabby about it. Not a shabbiness that could be washed off, but an inner shabbiness. She refused to let go of his hand, and she was wearing nail polish and some of the polish had chipped off. He was suddenly seized with immense horror.

"Well, I'll call you tomorrow," said Efraim after a pause that went on too long.

"Do that," replied Sven.

"Then we'll . . ."

"Sven is an old, intimate friend of mine," said Margot with a smile that was not as warm as it could have been, but instead rather menacing. "We haven't seen each other in a long time, so you never know whether we'll be done catching up by tomorrow."

"I understand," said Efraim.

"You have no idea," replied Margot.

Then Efraim went on his way.

"Sven the poet boy," she said. "So you've become a sectarian schemer. Did the poems stop coming? And what the devil are you doing now with all the whores you were always yelling about? Do they have whores here, Sven? Where have you hidden the whores? Did you hide them in the cupboard backstage, or where did you put them? You can't fool me, Sven. Where do you keep them these days? Sven."

She made an effort to talk softly and clearly and in a friendly voice, but Sven could smell the odor since he was standing so close.

"You've been drinking, Margot," he said.

"A person has to fortify herself to face the great experience of meeting you," she said.

At that moment Lewi came out, paused for a second, and looked at her in surprise. Margot recognized Lewi at once, no doubt from his photographs in the newspapers.

"Your theological Highness, forgive me, I didn't see the bishop. Delighted to make your acquaintance."

"Sven," said Lewi, "are you coming?"

"Not yet," Margot said. "Not just yet."

It was terrible. Lewi promptly left. And at last they stood there, completely alone.

* * *

That was the night the Finnish Winter War began, he thought afterwards. That was the horrible night the war began, and that was the evening when Margot came to see me for the last time.

But he never wrote about it.

"What do you want, Margot?" he said. "I think you should go now."

She had aged, that was evident. But she was still beautiful. He had the intense feeling that she was still beautiful. The words coming out of her mouth that were not beautiful could not entirely cover up the fact that she was still a very beautiful woman. Whenever she appeared to him in his dreams, or in the consciousness of sin, like a cloud, and it happened almost every day and at night, she was often naked, as well as beautiful. Now she was clothed but he knew that he could not move or leave, though he ought to. She held him there with her eyes and he remembered precisely how it had been, and he couldn't move.

"I've read the newspapers, you know," she said. "I saw that you were saved. And married. And married again. And I was just a little curious. About how you would look with a halo."

"What do you want?"

"Or a crown of thorns? You've always been deceitful, so you probably wear a crown of thorns too. So how are you, Sven? The last time we saw each other you sent me off to have an abortion while you went dashing after a whore, but how did it all turn out? Did you write a poetic masterpiece about it, full of self-contempt? And then I suppose it was celebrated in *Svenska Dagbladet*. Doesn't it always require a lot of self-contempt to get good reviews? Sven. Sven. I've had nothing but troubles with my womb, and I got divorced and I didn't even get a crown of thorns. Have you found yourself a new career now, Sven? Do you know what you do with people? No, you don't know, little Sven."

He waited. Nothing but silence.

"Surely you have something to say."

"I deserve this," he said at last. "I have prayed to God to forgive me for what I did to you and . . ."

"Shut up, Sven."

"I've prayed and prayed and . . ."

"Shut up, Sven, you and your empty phrases. You make me sick."

And he didn't say a word.

"Have you been giving sermons about me too? The female sinner! Oh yes, you know all about female sinners. I suppose it's rather exciting for them. Tickles in the crotch. It was strange to see you there with all those women, Sven. Do you understand what it's like for them? Do you know anything about the people you talk to?"

What was he supposed to say?

"Do you know who you're talking to?"

"What do you want, Margot?"

She was taking slow, deep breaths, as if it were a strain to speak, or as if she had just done some hard physical labor, and they were standing very close to each other in the dark street, and suddenly he saw her eyes fill with tears.

"Oh Sven. I wanted to have your child, Sven. Oh dear God, how I wanted to have your child, Sven. I've grieved so much about it that I almost went mad. Oh Sven, you big goddamned swine . . . oh, how I wish we could have kept our child."

"Even though I'm such a swine," he said in a low voice.

And then she looked at him, and he could clearly see that she was crying, and suddenly her voice was almost tender and that was the worst of all, he thought afterwards, and she said in a low voice:

"I've always loved you, Sven. In fact, I thought you were so wonderful. And worst of all was . . . seeing you now. I had revenge in mind. But then I saw you as I sat there and listened. And Sven, it was actually a shitty sermon, but at the same time it was quite fine. Quite a fine sermon. That was the worst of all."

"Thank you," he said.

"I was actually planning to stand up and testify."

"You were?"

"Yes, that's what I was planning. Because you do testify, don't you? The other women, do they do that? And then I suppose the little whore Mary Magdalene could also testify about her relationship to Jesus, couldn't she? About how it was? I could have testified too, couldn't I? Although it would have been extremely unpleasant."

"Yes."

"But then I realized that I was actually so enormously fond of you. Even though you're such a shit. And I thought that maybe he . . . well, had changed. That maybe it was possible to become someone else and still hold on to what I loved so much. And that made me hesitate."

"Yes," he said. "It might be possible. Sometimes I think so."

"So I didn't stand up to testify."

"No."

"Because I didn't think you deserved it, after all. I thought that maybe you . . ."

"Maybe God has . . ."

"But I beg you," she then said with renewed vehemence and in a voice that almost rekindled his fear. "But I beg you. It's the only thing I beg of you. Don't talk about God. Or salvation. Or grace. Don't try to save me. Don't give me any of your goddamned nonsense. Because then I might get angry again. And I don't want to be angry."

"Then what do you want me to say, Margot?"

"Just say that it's possible to become a different person. That people can get back on their feet on their own. And walk. All on their own."

"Is that what you want?" he asked.

"Yes, that's what I want, Sven. It's rather important to me."

"It *is* possible, Margot," he then said, not trying to hide the fact that he was crying.

"And don't talk about God or Jesus or salvation or the Holy Spirit. Don't talk about any of that, because then I'll have to hit you, Sven, right in the face."

"I won't talk about any of those things, Margot."

"And I just want you to know," she said, "that I think about you all the time, and I'm glad that things are going so well for you."

"Thank you."

"And it was nice that you said it was possible to become someone else, to get up and walk. Is that what you've done, Sven?"

"I think so."

"I'll remember that," she said. "And then you have to remember how much I loved you, and I promise that I will never, ever testify. But I wanted to see you one more time."

And then she turned around and left. And he never saw her again.

The next day he met Lewi and made an attempt to explain, but Lewi seemed merely annoyed or embarrassed and said that he didn't want to know.

"Sven," he said, "you've made a journey from one class to another, out of the realm of sin, though in some sense it was in reverse, and the sins of the upper class don't interest me much. But it's still a journey from one class to another. Although not the usual one. Provided, that is, that you've actually done it. That you've left everything behind, and a small part of you isn't, in fact, still there."

"Isn't there any part of it that a person should keep?" said Sven.

"Why keep any of it?" Lewi asked in surprise.

But Sven couldn't explain this thought, even though he felt that it contained a truth, some sort of truth. But perhaps something could be kept, not merely forgotten in shame, as a humbling experience, perhaps secret, but kept, even though the duty of a human being was to get up on his feet and walk.

And yet keep part of it. But he wasn't able to explain this to Brother Lewi, or to anyone else, and they never discussed this incident again.

CHAPTER 20

The Suitcase

1.

"WE DON'T BUILD WALLS, WE LIVE IN TENTS," SVEN ONCE WROTE
during the Franklin dispute.

That was beautiful. Wasn't it also enticing for Lewi? Wasn't there
also a wild ass, and not just a driver, living inside of him? Could that
explain his imminent flight into the Forest of Despair?

A brief note about a previous, but canceled, exodus.

In March 1922 Lewi travels to Palestine. This is almost a year after
Wigglesworth's stormy visit to Stockholm, which in a sense resulted
in Sven joining the Pentecostal movement. Wigglesworth was subse-
quently deported from Sweden, the storm in the press was fierce, and
Lewi was exhausted. A new preacher had certainly stepped in, and
Sven loved the storm and the slander, but Lewi, for his part, was
"broken down."

That was the term. Broken down. It would return twenty years
later.

He leaves. He spends four months in the Holy Land. And suddenly
he wants to stay there. When he "saw this country, which in many
places had such an abundance of flowers, with its man-made irrigation
and numerous gardens, and when he also learned about the particularly vigorous Zionist movement promoting the return of the Jews to
their land," he was seized with a yearning to leave Sweden and, with
his family, settle in Palestine as a colonist.

"Oh, if only I might stay in Palestine and for the rest of my life hide somewhere among the mountains of Judea or Galilee."

He wanted to become a colonist, cultivator, journalist, and with the help of his loved ones, plant a garden. At the same time he would work as a missionary and newspaper correspondent. "Many newspapers in Europe would probably appreciate getting direct reports from Jerusalem during these eventful times," he writes, with great foresight. And: "How glorious to be rid of those voracious shark swarms of slanderers back home in Sweden!"

But he pulls himself together. When he, riding on a donkey (!), catches sight of the Mount of Olives "it was as if I had risen up from the valley of temptation."

He pulls himself together. He returns home.

2.

Margot had asked whether it was possible to become a different person. And Sven had said: yes.

It was possible. And perhaps Sven actually had become a different person. Perhaps that was exactly what she saw when she chose not to testify, not to destroy him.

There were two episodes that might have indicated a change.

Lewi had composed a song about "The Promises," that time when he prayed so fervently to God that Lydia might regain her health without the help of a doctor.

Now "The Promises" was sung constantly. Sven had also undergone a similar experience. He had joined the side of the Pentecostal movement as a defender of the faith healer Wigglesworth, and he too believed strongly in the healing powers of God.

In February 1929 Lill-Carin, who was his youngest daughter from his marriage to Carin and who was now living with Sven and Brita, cut herself with a cheese knife. After a few days she became feverish; blood poisoning had set in. They prayed and sang for her, but at last were forced to take her to the hospital. There she died, trusting in her Savior.

They took the coffin home and placed it on the veranda, with the lid removed so that the deceased could take part in the morning and evening prayers.

Perhaps she might have been saved if her parents had put less faith in God. No one knows. Sven and Lewi never talked again about what happened. Sven never wrote a hymn in memory of the girl. No one ever knew whether the delay or their faith was directly responsible for the girl's death.

She was fourteen years old.

The other episode took place in May 1940, almost a year before Lewi's flight into the Slough of Despond.

Together they were building an empire of faith. Both of them had also built their families as solid bastions in this empire. From the outside, and to the public eye, their families seemed quite similar, yet they were very different.

Lewi's solid fortress, his family of nine children living in the house in Bredden, had no cracks. There may have been some, but no one ever knew. Sven's family, over time, became the most intensely portrayed family in Swedish literary history. In the end the house seemed so full of cracks that it was a divine miracle that it remained standing. All the testimony quite simply could not express the whole truth. Something must have held the Lidman fortress together.

If one of the families seemed much too cast all in one piece, the other was too decrepit and dilapidated. But something changed. Perhaps it was God's terrifying tolerance that began to break through in the Pentecostal movement.

Or the onset of modernity, which Lewi didn't know how to handle.

Here's what the second episode was about. Sven was talking to Lewi on the phone, and it had something to do with a personal matter. Maybe it was the fact that Ulla Lidman, Sven's daughter, had christened her firstborn as an infant. Maybe it had to do with the rumors in the congregation that Lidman's children were accustomed to dancing at home. It was something personal. And Sven, in a fury, had hung up on Lewi and then gone outside to take a walk on the lawn.

He was not happy.

That's why he ordered his son Sam, who would later become a writer, to rake the yard. It was supposed to look nice for springtime. Sam, who would later become a writer and therefore hated yard work,

grew tired after only half an hour and was leaning on his rake, medi-
tating. Sven, who was already a writer and therefore entitled to wander around in contemplation, discovered this and furiously made his
way over to his son.

"Are you loafing, you rascal?" screamed Sven. "You're spineless!
Spineless!!!"

"No, I'm not, Father," his son replied.

"Don't you think I saw you loafing? You're spineless! I'll teach you!
I'll teach you!"

Sven tore the rake from his son's hand and hit him hard on the
backside. His son was then seized with great anger because he thought
his father was being unfair. He yanked the rake from his father's hand,
swung it in a wide circle over his head and yelled furiously:

"Get out of here, you damned tyrant . . . or else I'm going to kill
you! Get out of here!!!"

At first Sven Lidman stood there as if turned to stone, but then he
countered:

"How dare you call me that? How dare you???"

Then he turned on his heel and went inside the house, walking up
the wide front steps with the pillars which were so often photographed
in the weekly papers.

Ten minutes later a cab drove up. Lidman was supposed to be
picked up for a meeting where he was going to preach. He was now
dressed in a dark suit, the one he usually wore for his sermons. It was
his preaching uniform. With firm steps he walked over to his son,
stopped in front of him, and said:

"I'm asking you for the last time. Do you realize what you did?
Are you planning to apologize? Are you?"

And then his son, in a low voice, almost as if in a trance, said to his
father:

"Father forgot to button his fly."

His father's face, which had been suffused with anger, then relaxed,
like the face of a child who has been rescued from the greatest misfortune, perhaps from deadly danger. His hand fumbled with his fly.
Yes, it was true, he had forgotten to button it.

"Thank you, my beloved son, thank you!" he bellowed. "Thank
you! It would have been terrible if I arrived at the meeting like this,
you know . . . stood there in front of the congregation with my fly
unbuttoned . . . I was so upset! Thank you!"

The next second he spread out his arms and went over to his son to embrace him.

"Oh, my beloved son . . . we love each other so much, don't we . . . thank you!"

"Yes, Father . . . forgive me . . . forgive me . . ."

"No, you must forgive *me*, my beloved son. You see, a public figure like myself, if I had stood there with my fly open . . . if I had . . ."

They stood there, embracing each other, for a long time, and both of them were breathing hard.

Then Sven left in the cab. He had tears in his eyes. Before he opened the cab door, he turned around, waved the Bible he was holding in his hand, and shouted:

"Thank you, my son! Thank you, my son!"

Then he got into the cab. But publicly, scenes of this nature were never the standard for the Pentecostal movement's view of families.

3.

The gap between Sven and Lewi was growing deeper and deeper.

In only one place in his writings does Lewi mention Efraim directly or indirectly.

It has to do with the mystery of Lewi's exile. "Over time my decision to leave the congregation and Sweden began to ripen inside me. I never told anyone the reason for it. I went to America with this secret hidden deep inside my heart. In the twelve years since then, I have never spoken about this to anyone except for one person. After returning home in 1941, I revealed to an elder who later left the congregation and who was one of Sven Lidman's foremost defenders, the reason for my journey to America. But he clearly didn't understand the matter, because I've never heard any more about it."

Efraim quotes this passage in the *Lebenslauf*, with a penciled remark in the margin, obviously added later. "We actually had this conversation earlier, in the fall of 1940. At first I didn't believe him, though today I do, but I found it best to keep quiet."

It's true that there weren't many who believed Lewi back then. And the mystery is still a mystery, as true mysteries ought to be. Efraim at first thought: no, that can't be true, and later: yes, maybe it is.

* * *

In the fall of 1940 the baptism numbers were declining, and Lewi was worried.

In the *Lebenslauf* several pages are devoted to the tragedy surrounding the arson fire that burned down the Norrskensflammen factory and in which one of Efraim's uncles perished. There was apparently strong indignation in his family, because the police investigation came under criticism. This is abruptly followed by a more coherent depiction that shifts the main focus back to the Pentecostal movement.

The title is "Crisis."

The baptism statistics were poor. You might say that the world was on fire. Norway and Denmark had been occupied for the past six months, the "strong leader" Churchill had become prime minister, and the British had retreated from Dunkirk, but the great catastrophe within the Pentecostal movement seemed to be that the baptism numbers had declined.

Or perhaps Efraim was alluding to another crisis, which may have been a personal matter for Lewi.

Everything had been going upward, but then started to stagnate. One afternoon in October Lewi was sitting in the office when Efraim came in for one of his regular visits. Lewi was sitting there as if asleep, with his head resting on his arms on the table. He gave a start at the sound of the door opening, leaped to his feet, stared at Efraim, and exclaimed, almost in a rage:

"The baptism numbers are dropping! Everyone is scared!"

Efraim calmly sat down at the table and replied that things probably weren't that bad. Norway and Denmark had been occupied six months ago, that was something they needed to keep in mind, and these were not normal times. Everything was abnormal. It was understandable that the baptism numbers had gone down. Half of all the men had been drafted.

The women had to work hard.

"I think they're afraid to register," said Lewi, "because they think Hitler is going to occupy Sweden. And then Pentecostals will be on the death lists. They're afraid of him."

"Or Stalin," Efraim added calmly.

"Or Stalin. Just as bad."

Then Lewi, sounding aimless or confused, began talking about the conflicts within the movement and the fact that the elders, especially Lidman, were opposing his plans to start a daily newspaper. And it was impossible to work with Lidman.

There seemed to be no coherence to Lewi's thoughts.

Finally he pulled out several issues of *Svensk Lösen*, the journal that Sven had edited during the First World War, and began to read some quotes that he had come across. It was something that Sven had written. It had to do with "the enlightened minority" that Lidman purported to represent, as opposed to "the thoughtlessness and selfishness of the millions." The opinions of the masses were "commonly vulgar."

Had he made a terrible mistake, Lewi asked in a flat voice, by allowing this man of the elite to become a leader within the movement? The contempt that Sven showed for the sisters and brothers and for the revered king—had Lewi made a mistake?

And Lewi went on and on.

"Why are you doing this?" asked Efraim. "We both know what Sven is like. We've known that for twenty years. Why are you dragging up old sins? Let them lie. You know that Lidman has always been and still is a political idiot."

"He hates me," was Lewi's surprising reply.

Efraim merely looked at him in astonishment. Lewi was obviously off balance.

"I know that he wants to destroy me. He's been trying to do that for five years. And he's a terrifying enemy."

"Lewi," said Efraim, "are you frightened? Don't you love Lidman?"

"Yes," said Lewi. "That's why."

"What do you mean?"

"I think he despises me," said Lewi in a low voice and with an expression of such great sorrow that Efraim couldn't say a word.

"That's why?" What did Lewi mean by that?

Efraim suddenly realized that Lewi, perhaps for the first time in his life, was afraid, but also felt great sorrow. It was incomprehensible. There was no reason for this. But there was something about the word "love" that might have explained it, or was it "admiration"? Perhaps tremendous admiration, which was also love, and in some way was connected to fear and sorrow over a much beloved brother and model, and poet, who possibly now despised him.

Things were no longer pleasant. That's why.

Twelve days later Lewi stopped his brother Sven as they were on their way to a meeting of elders and deacons. He pulled Sven aside and said, strangely enough with his face averted:

"There's something I need to talk to the brothers about this evening. I'm going to America in the new year."

"But why?" asked Sven in amazement. "In the middle of a raging war? It's dangerous."

"May God protect me," Lewi automatically replied, though without looking at Sven.

"For how long?"

"For good," said Lewi.

And only then did he look Sven in the eye. And Sven realized, to his enormous surprise, that this was not a joke. Lewi was going to give up everything, leave behind everything he had built, and his decision was irrevocable.

Then they went in to join the brothers.

The *Lebenslauf* is not always chronological.

A brief note much earlier may give an explanation for this. It had to do with the newspaper dispute.

A meeting was held to deal with the newspaper question. After two hours of discussion Lewi left the meeting. "His face was almost white," and he shut the door behind him with a hard bang that was almost unchristian.

Efraim was among the last to leave.

Sven seemed so triumphant that he didn't want to leave and was eager to talk.

"I suppose congratulations are in order," said Efraim. "There won't be any newspaper. There will be no *Dagen*. This is the first time Lewi has lost, but you succeeded in persuading all the others."

"It's best this way," said Sven with a smile.

"Your position is strong within the movement," said Efraim.

"It's best this way."

"And you spoke well."

"It's enough having the *Härold*," said Sven firmly. "And the publishing company is doing a good job putting out books. We don't need to get involved in the newspaper world. Our faithful will listen to our voices, and then they can buy my books. I think everyone realized it was best this way."

"Yes, you spoke well."

"God's spirit seized hold of me. God's spirit seized hold of me."

Efraim was then "seized" by a feeling of irritation that was difficult for him to explain.

"In terms of the politics of newspapers, I'm afraid that God's spirit is mistaken, and we really ought to have a daily paper. Now it probably won't happen for years. And by then it may be too late."

"Praise God. Lewi wants to build a worldly empire. He wants to be the head of the movement. But only Jesus Christ can be the head. Didn't he say: 'I am the vine, you are the branches'?"

Then he was about to leave the room, but just as he reached the door, Efraim said:

"But this means war, doesn't it? And you're a warring man, aren't you, Sven?"

"I'm a soldier of Christ," Sven explained. "And Lewi knows that."

Then he left, but without slamming the door as Lewi had. It was the gentle exit of a victor, although that's not how Efraim expressed it, saying merely "now Sven seemed to be in charge of the offensive, and Lewi simply had to follow along."

I recognized the image of the offensive. He had once used it about Nicanor and Elmgren. It's all a matter of being in charge of the offensive. The others simply have to follow along.

Now it had all come back. Although this was a different kind of popular movement, but the issue was the same.

4.

Everyone found it completely incomprehensible.

The official explanation was that Brother Pethrus had been summoned by the Filadelfia congregation in Chicago and would now travel to America to spread the Pentecostal movement in the American field.

Of course no one believed this. It was clearly nonsense. Brother Lidman had confided in everyone, in the deepest confidence, saying that his head was actually spinning. Why leave everything behind? And to whom? It's true that Lewi had said at the deacons' meeting that Brother Sven could now more wholeheartedly devote himself to the congregation and to his preaching activities in Stockholm, and that it was not necessary, with regard to the public, for a "real name" to take the lead after Lewi. He actually said that.

Sven thought this was, in fact, quite friendly. But his head was still spinning.

After the meeting, which had practically paralyzed everyone, Sven went into the elders' room, and in bewilderment called upon God, taking the Bible out of his pocket. As a thumb verse he chose Nehemiah 6:8, in which the prophet says:

"No such things as you say have been done, for you are inventing them out of your own mind"; and those words were quite clear.

Yes, that was God's message. It was very clear. Lewi said one thing but meant something else. What he said was quite clear. He was leaving the movement he had built, leaving everything in Sven's hands, and fleeing. But what did the prophet Nehemiah think was Lewi's reason?

Could it be contempt from the one he loved?

Sven later writes that he at this point—at this point—began to despise his friend. Sven was convinced that it was fear of the Russians that made Lewi flee. And that was worthy of contempt. The Bolsheviks had not, in fact, been very successful and were no longer at war after making peace with Finland. Hitler was the one who possessed Europe. Norway and Denmark were occupied. But wasn't Lewi at heart terrified of the Russians? Sven, in his memoirs—and these twins of God would come to write memoirs about each other, which were entertaining in their own way but rarely came particularly close to the truth about each other—Sven would truthfully describe his reactions to Lewi's incomprehensible capitulation during that gloomy European winter, as well as his contempt!

"I was seized with tremendous contempt for Lewi Pethrus—I saw his cowardice, his mad arrogance. He thought he was called to become some sort of world evangelist, and for egotistical reasons he was going to secure his own life and livelihood while he left high and dry the congregation and the revival which he had built and which had given him love and sacrifices! He had not just built this revival; the revival had also built him and created his position and in this manner provided him with a livelihood for more than thirty years. And now he was going to leave it high and dry, leave his homeland to its fate as a sacrifice to Russia—out of sheer terror, out of a childish dream of becoming great and famous as a world evangelist. But I myself had neither the stomach nor the power to try to stop him in his panicked, mad desire for flight, like a wild animal. Yet now I remember all too clearly how occasionally, when I saw him from a distance hurrying through the corridors of the Filadelfia congregation or saw him on the lawn outside Rörstrand Castle in loving conversation with some elderly sister or brother, how this echo resounded deep through my entire being:

"Oh yes, that's what the first rat to leave the sinking ship looks like!"

Yet this was not at all close to Lewi's truth, in any case not what Efraim came to perceive as the truth. And Lewi was not afraid of the Russians. Perhaps he should have been afraid of the Germans. In the winter of 1940-41 there was good reason for this, but that wasn't it either.

And yet it was peculiar, at any rate, that the rat left the ship but did not take his family with him.

No, there was something else, and no thumb verse could explain to them what had happened. God did not cast slanting morning light over the flagstone on which Lewi's name was carved so the script would stand out. But Lewi did flee, and he tried to explain to Efraim why. If he stayed, the movement would fall apart. He was doomed to lose, and the movement was more important than Lewi himself.

Yet this was so peculiar and unrealistic that not even Efraim believed him. But flee he did.

What he was fleeing toward, he had no idea. He did not harbor any fear, yet he was terrified. Lewi had suffered a breakdown, in a controlled form. Now everyone began to arrange the farewell ceremonies and farewell parties, and they made a gramophone record, a farewell record, with Lewi's farewell speech on it, as well as Einar Ekberg's heartwarming song of gratitude, which would end up selling over a hundred thousand copies. Nothing was supposed to indicate that it was a breakdown, but all the while Lewi was slowly sinking down into the incomprehensible and, for everyone else, inexplicable depression and despair that were as dark and deep as the hole that Uncle Aron once fought his way into, that night on Bure Fjord when he chopped a hole in the ice and finally, with a soundless roar, opened his arms to his Savior, and sank down into the deepest darkness of the sea.

5.

Never has a depression, a flight in the name of sorrow and desperation, been given such perfect and opaque organizational form.

Sven was installed in all the leading positions. He was already editor-in-chief of the *Härold*, and now he also became chairman of the board of Filadelfia. The congregations in the rest of the country were free, of course—that was constantly repeated—yet it was obvious: Lidman was now going to be the leading light.

This too was organized by Lewi.

One evening Lydia had an outburst that surprised even her. Lewi was harping on the fact that he and Brother Lidman no longer had a loving relationship. The situation was intolerable, and he wouldn't want to split apart the Pentecostal movement with a dispute that might annihilate it. Later he would come to get his family. After he was settled.

Finally Lydia couldn't stand it anymore and began almost shouting.

"You've built a cathedral in God's honor," she cried, "and now you're turning it over to that Lidman, and you know what he's like. Everything will be ruined!"

"That's not certain," he said feebly. "You shouldn't worry about it, my beloved wife."

"I shouldn't worry about it?" she screamed. "You can't treat me like this, you have to tell me what's going on!!!"

He was utterly shocked.

"But you know that we have outside worries and troubles . . ."

"Yes, that's all in the newspapers when they write about us, and you say 'we've kept away the outside worries and troubles from our inner community,' but I'm sick and tired of you not talking to me and . . ."

A long silence followed.

"Have you no respect for me, Lewi?"

Then he went over to her and patted her cheek and said:

"Things are difficult for me, Lydia. And no matter what a preacher I am, I find it difficult to speak."

After that neither said much. But in the dark, when she realized that he couldn't sleep, she whispered:

"I've never heard you talk about giving up before. No matter how unbelievably strong that Lidman must be. I don't understand it. He has power over you. I hate it."

He did not reply.

*   *   *

There was a long series of farewell events.

Lewi spoke, and Sven spoke.

There was no end to the sorrow and the tributes. But it was irrevocable. At the very last meeting, at Rörstrandsgatan, the house was full, and there were songs and tears. Sven held a great farewell speech for his friend, brother, and admired predecessor.

"My friends," he said, "Lewi Pethrus, the man who created the Pentecostal movement in Sweden, is now leaving us, and we feel a sense of loss and despair. Allow me to say one last personal word to him. I have sometimes had a terrible feeling that he was a treasure we did not value.

"A treasure we did not value. Allow me to quote a poem:

But value the treasure
that God sends you
gently it slips
from your hands
not to be seen again
until its value you confess.

"We're going to miss you, Lewi! I'm going to miss you. And when the train slips out of Central Station, the treasure Lewi Pethrus will also slip out of our hands, and one day we will have to answer for how we valued him."

They embraced, and Efraim saw that both men were weeping, and that it was sincere.

They wept and embraced and no one understood a thing, and at that moment everyone knew that these two men truly loved each other. This was a true moment, the only true one. Everything from fifteen years of sincere love and admiration was found in that moment; the last five years of frost and mistrust no longer counted.

Then Sven presented his personal farewell gift to Lewi.

It was a knapsack. And they both smiled happily, and then Lewi could go home and Lydia would pack Sven's gift full of clothing and sweaters, because it was supposed to be so cold in America. The next morning Lewi left from Central Station on the train that would take him to Bulltofta. And everywhere in Swedish Pentecostal homes, at any rate where they had a gramophone, Lewi's farewell speech was played, along with Einar Ekberg's song, and everyone cried, but no one knew why this had happened, and everyone asked where it was all heading, where it was heading, where it was heading.

Efraim was not at all happy and didn't want to have anyone's company after the meeting. But as he was leaving, he was stopped at the door by a young man.

At first he didn't recognize him. But suddenly he knew who the man was. It was the young boy who once, along with his mother, had visited Lewi at the beginning of the Franklin dispute.

He was the boy who had said no.

"Do you know who I am?" asked the boy.

"Yes, now I do," replied Efraim. "How are you?"

"Good."

"Are you still saying no?"

The young man didn't reply to the question but merely pulled out of his pocket a piece of paper on which a text had been written in pencil.

"I was thinking of giving Lewi Pethrus a farewell present," he said, "but I couldn't catch him. And maybe it doesn't matter. I suppose Lidman is the one who's going to be in charge of everything now?"

"Yes," said Efraim. "That's the idea."

"Well, I happened to come upon a couple of verses from Job that might serve as a guide. They were important for me, and then I thought I ought to give them to someone else. But I don't know whether Pethrus or Lidman should have them. It seems rather unclear."

"What's unclear?" asked Efraim.

"Who needs them most," the boy replied. "I've only met them once, and people change."

"Which verses are they?" asked Efraim.

"I'll let you decide who should have them," the boy said.

Efraim took the piece of paper. At the very top it said "Job 39:5-8."

"Should Lewi or Sven have them?" said Efraim, as if to himself.

"I don't know," said the boy. "If one of them has changed it might be of some support."

"Changed?"

* * *

It was incomprehensible. But since the boy, who was now a young man, couldn't give him any clear answer, Efraim read aloud from the paper:

> Who has let the wild ass go free? Who has loosed the bonds of the swift ass, to whom I have given the steppe for his home, and the salt land for his dwelling place? He scorns the tumult of the city; he hears not the shouts of the driver. He ranges the mountains as his pasture, and he searches after every green thing.

When he looked up, the boy was gone.

But Efraim would wait to give anyone this thumb verse; then he gave it to both Sven and Lewi, though it was for Lewi that the thumb verse came to play a decisive role. That was later. But the piece of paper can still be found in the Lebenslauf. It has been there the whole time. A thumb verse for a wild ass who sought other wild asses, and for a driver with the dream of a wild ass, and perhaps the boy himself had found a pasture in the mountains, or on the steppes, where the cries of the driver or the preacher could not be heard. But it was a good thumb verse, no matter how it was interpreted.

On the evening of February 23, 1941, Lewi Pethrus departed from Stockholm's Central Station. Then he took a plane from Bulltofta, with a stopover in Lisbon.

He was ill. He had to take to his bed in Lisbon. The doctors didn't understand what was wrong with him. He lay quietly and submissively in his hospital bed, and they examined him but found nothing wrong.

He told them that he felt broken down, but that was not a diagnosis they could accept.

Eventually he got better, but still felt broken down. By the time he arrived in America the planned seminar in which he was supposed to participate was already over.

He had begun his long exile, and he had no hope.

BOOK V

February 1941–October 1948

CHAPTER 21

The Preacher's Progress

1.

ON JULY 12, 1941, EFRAIM SENT A LETTER TO LEWI, ADDRESSED CARE of a Pentecostal congregation in Chicago. It reached him on the morning of July 22.

Efraim had enclosed a piece of paper from an individual who had contacted him, and he said that he now wanted to send it on, after thinking about it for several months; until now he wasn't sure that Lewi was the proper recipient. "But since you now find yourself, like Christian in Bunyan's book, in the Forest of Despair, maybe this thumb verse will be of some guidance to you on this, your preacher's progress."

It was a thumb verse. Lewi read it.

Why had Efraim waited so long, almost five months? And why did he at last decide that Lewi should have this thumb verse?

It turned out to be important. No doubt that's how things were with God's thumb verses. Some of them He held back for a while, so that they might appear at the right time, and become time itself.

In his billfold Lewi kept a picture of Kristina.

She was his mother. She was the Kristina who was not allowed to emigrate. In the picture she has her hair parted in the middle and she is looking solemnly straight ahead. Lewi thought she was very beautiful, and upright, but in the picture she doesn't make any special impression at first. You have to look at the picture for a long time before she makes a special impression.

Then it doubtless appears. Lewi thought that she made a special impression and was beautiful, and he had probably looked at the photograph for a long time, so what was special became clear.

2.

It had rained for two whole days, and there was nothing to do.

When he first arrived in Chicago he made a point of walking a couple of hours each day, for his health and in order to get acclimated in Chicago, but he didn't have the energy to walk very far. And it was all so dirty. This was his third trip to America, but the New World had never before seemed so dirty! Why was it so dirty? When Lewi's uncles had written to his mother Kristina about how things were in America, they had never mentioned this either.

Lewi still felt broken down.

He had difficulty breathing, and he took this as a sign that he was broken down. The doctors in Lisbon, who had not understood him, said that perhaps he had a slight cold, even though he hadn't coughed at all, and they didn't think that he was broken down. There were whorehouses everywhere in Chicago. Such filth. If freedom was going to be created for the congregations, a strong center would have to be established to defend the freedom on the periphery. That was his view. It was the same thing in politics. If there was no strong leader at the center who could defend the freedom of the parts, then the parts would be inexorably sucked into a giant vortex toward the middle. As in a centrifuge. A maelstrom. Then the only power would be in the middle, and the parts would die. That was why he had transferred the missions in Brazil to the local population. In the midst of the Franklin dispute. Because he was serious about the matter, even though some people claimed that large financial assets were involved: houses and churches, and the like. But all of it had to be transferred. They had to make themselves superfluous. Otherwise there would be nothing but associations and petrifaction. Lidman didn't understand that. He just *talked* about freedom. He wasn't able to defend freedom.

They had to make themselves superfluous. Become nothing, a nothing in God's hand. But it hurt terribly to become a nothing.

Sven had become an enemy. Why this animosity? Just as an iceberg cools the sea all around it, though only an insignificant part is visible, this coldness was invisibly spreading. Why such coldness from Sven? Lewi had resolved to believe that Sven's animosity stemmed from the fact that Lewi had criticized Sven's daughter Ulla. She was a missionary in China but had broken off her engagement. That was bad. That was why Sven had ended up being so hostile. That's what Lewi had decided to believe. But was it true? It had to be something very personal.

He decided not to brood over it, but he still felt broken down.

The brothers and sisters in Chicago had given him a warm welcome, but maybe not as warm as he had hoped. Booze and women were openly sold on the streets. He didn't have the energy to walk as far as he liked, which had to do with the fact that he was broken down. And the customs among the saved were also strange. A Pentecostal congregation in America was accustomed to arranging dance evenings in the chapel. Everything was falling apart. Where were his enemies, where were his friends? He tried to write a song but couldn't. His hotel room held an iron-framed bed and a desk and chair, so that he would be able to write.

He couldn't write.

Surely everything would be resolved for the best, praise the Lord, but the days seemed very long. It never stopped raining. It was wintertime in an earthly hell. He had brought along John Bunyan's *The Pilgrim's Progress* and was diligently reading it. It was possible that he now found himself in the very middle of this journey. The Forest of Despair. The dark woods of despondency. Wild beasts were threatening.

By the fourth day he had already preached before the congregation, but it was not like in Filadelfia on Rörstrandsgatan. He knew that it was necessary to build things up. He had to build up interest in the congregation, but also in himself.

And he *had* been building. For thirty years he had built things up.

He had now left all of that behind. He was fifty-seven years old and was intending to start over. But to his great surprise, he had ended up feeling broken down.

He recalled what it was like when he arrived in Stockholm from Lidköping and the brothers met him at the Central Station, and Brother Efraim was among them. The simple two-room lodgings they gave him were not elegant. But he could feel the brothers' love. Here in Chicago he felt lonely. There were few people to talk to, except for the Savior, though He too often seemed absent. If was as if the

Benefactor no longer had time. Why didn't He have time? And not many in the congregation were present when he gave his first sermon in Chicago. It wasn't even half full. But with time, the Lord would undoubtedly gather the flocks here too. The American pastor spoke first and then turned to the congregation and said:

"And before we adjourn, I would like to ask our Swedish guest, Pastor Johannes Pethrus, to say a few words of greeting from the brothers in Sweden, and then Pastor Brown-Boysen will lead us in prayer. I also want to remind you about our wonderful congregation meeting on Thursday at 7 o'clock. I give you, in God's name, Pastor Pethrus."

Pastor Johannes Pethrus, without pointing out the little misunderstanding over his name, then got up from his seat, went to stand behind the pulpit, and noticed that at the same time some people in the congregation got up and left.

Yet everyone had smiled kindly at him. Then he began to talk, trying to conquer the feeling of being broken down. He was certain that no one noticed it. His English was excellent, although he spoke with a Swedish accent. He was glad he had read so many novels in English, and he especially remembered *The Grapes of Wrath*.

The evening could not be called a success.

A collection was taken, and the evening was over. He wasn't sure whether he was going to speak on Thursday as well, but he didn't want to ask.

I'm nothing, he thought. I'm nothing, and everything that I am, is in Christ. As the psalmist says, I have based my cause on nothing.

He had this same thought over and over again. I'm nothing.

It didn't help. He lay down on the bed and stared at the ceiling and thought about the fact that he was nothing, and kept on thinking that, and finally he simply lay on the bed and stared straight up and watched light and shadows dancing along the ceiling and thought about nothing.

He had brought along his portable gramophone, and occasionally he would play the farewell record that was made to commemorate his departure from Sweden.

The best thing on the record was not Lewi's farewell speech. That wasn't what he wanted to hear. He felt phony whenever he listened to himself saying everything he had said in farewell. Phony was the word. No, the best part was Einar Ekberg singing "Wherever I Go." It was the poem by Rosenius, and he had always thought it was the best one in Västerbotten Moravianism: *You loyal and pierced heart, follow me / through the desert without cease / Let my faith, in joy and misery / in your wounds find lasting peace.* And then this solace:

Wherever I go in woods, mountains, vale
A friend follows me, His voice I hear,
Invisible is He, but His words never fail,
A warning He speaks, or comfort so dear.

But when he listened to the words, he felt bewildered.

The invisible was still invisible. Einar Ekberg was in Sweden now. He was singing on Rörstrandsgatan. Lewi could imagine Einar, whom he loved and whose voice had brought joy to so many brothers and sisters, singing at this very moment. He could picture it all quite clearly. First the way Lidman stood there, alone on the podium, swinging the Bible, and with everyone's eyes on him, and saying, as was his custom, and perhaps at times he also meant it: "Just think, my dear friends—just think, and this is reality—just think that for every poor, ragged, ousted, demeaned, and despairing human soul there is an immortal message of peace and freedom promising salvation, victory, strength, and grace." And then that swinging of the Bible. But after that, Einar Ekberg's mighty voice would chime in to sing "Wherever I Go."

Maybe they also sang "The Promises." It was impossible to know. Now that Lewi was gone, they might not want to sing "The Promises."

Occasionally when he lay in his room to gather his strength, he would have the urge to break that record. He didn't know why. Not because of Brother Ekberg's singing. He had a glorious voice. No, it was something else that he wanted to break. But he would pull himself together. He knew he had a bad temper. It had gotten him in hot water all his life. He had prayed to God for forgiveness so many times. He had been hot-headed ever since he was a child. Why was he so hot-headed?

Why this feeling of being broken down? He didn't understand. Was it from his childhood? Or from his life?

What was his life?

He had always known, throughout his childhood and youth, that those who could not fit in, emigrated.

Lewi's mother was named Kristina, and she was the one who did not emigrate.

She was born at Faxen, in a smallholder's hut outside the gates of the Nygård Estate in Västra Tunhem parish. Her father was a groom and her mother did the milking on the estate. Her mother's parents had never succumbed to drunkenness. This was almost certain, although at Christmastime her grandfather gave Christmas aquavit even to the children. In the records of the parish catechism meetings, it states that one of the children, a boy, had learned thirteen hymns by heart. Lewi's maternal grandmother had a stern demeanor. She died in 1862. Five years later Kristina found her father lying dead in his bed. The children were then auctioned off. It wasn't easy because 1867 was a famine year. The children were all registered as "paupers," and every year there was an auction. It was difficult to find any buyers.

What kind of life was that? And so it had to be America.

The first one to leave was her brother Anders, and that was in 1872, when nearly sixty thousand people emigrated from Sweden to America. He became a gardener in Chicago. After several years he managed to save enough for a ticket for the next brother, Johan. He began working at the Steinway piano factory in New York. Then it was Carl's turn. He succeeded in obtaining an emigration certificate even though at first Colonel Nils Eriksson, the railway builder, refused to grant permission. But at last Carl was released.

In the end all the brothers except for one were in America. This brother's name was Svante. He would end up fundamentally changing Swedish Christianity, although it would be through Lewi's mediation, if you want to look at it that way, but that was pride.

The one who did not receive money for a ticket was their only sister, Kristina. They all wrote to her and told her about America. Kristina was Lewi's mother. She used to read the America letters aloud to her children, and then she would always cry.

Lewi's mother was named Kristina, and she was the one who did not emigrate.

Lewi read his Bible, but all his thoughts ended up circling around John Bunyan's *The Pilgrim's Progress*.

Suddenly he saw that Chicago was like the City of Destruction in *The Pilgrim's Progress*, and that Chicago stretched over the entire world.

The people were thin and dressed in shabby clothes and were always alone, but in *The Pilgrim's Progress* it was clear what this was all about. It made sense. It was a journey and it had to be undertaken, but the temptations were many. The temptations themselves were not the sin. The sin was surrendering to them. And then God would mete out His punishment. Lewi had always been terrified of God. Not of being punished, but of the fact that God was just. That was what was terrifying, though it did not contradict the New Testament. Bunyan understood. Lewi had discussed this book with Efraim many times. It was the revivalist movement's equivalent to Dante's *Divine Comedy*. Lewi had always thought the revivalist child was given his own Inferno legend, and his own morality, on the way to Paradise. Christian's journey was the lens through which the child of the revivalist movement was supposed to regard his own life.

Lewi had read the book as a child. He had brought it along, and it was this book that now, in his hour of need, in the Forest of Despair, made him turn his face to the past and try to understand how it had all begun.

Turned away from 1940s America, he sees only Västra Tunhem.

The Bible and Bunyan, those two.

Lewi once had a friend whose name was Daniel Högberg. His mother, whose name was Rika, owned a copy of Bunyan's book. Lewi read it for the first time when he was nine years old. He read about Christian who had to leave the City of Destruction and then met interesting sinners. The most amusing was Obstinate. And Christian wandered into the Slough of Despond, which nearly endangered his life, but it was a matter of fighting his way up, not being like the cowardly Pliable, who turned around and went back to the City of Destruction. But Christian came to Mount Sinai. He met Evangelist. And Christian was spared from the lion, went into the Interpreter's House, to the Enchanted Ground, and to Vanity Fair. And everywhere there was danger. Everywhere were drawings illustrating the story. And Christian always looked so gaunt and miserable that it was quite distressing.

But the book taught Lewi not to give up, and he began to understand what the world was like. It was evil. And sin was everywhere. He began thinking about his own early years. They were like in Bunyan's

book. But salvation was possible, even for those who had gotten mixed
up in boozing.

That was the case with Lewi's father, Johan, who was mixed up in
boozing before he was saved. He was an orphanage child; his father
was unknown, and he was the son of a maid.

He was illegitimate. There were many children who were illegitimate, but for him it still felt like a wound. Lewi's father never spoke of
his mother, Lewi's grandmother, who had ended up pregnant.

3.

For two weeks Lewi lay apathetically in his cheap hotel room in
Chicago and for the life of him didn't know what to do until several
brothers in the congregation made arrangements for him to move on.

It was a small town in the Midwest. He didn't make note of the
name. But there was a forest.

He went into the forest and his face was now turned completely
toward the past, toward what might offer an explanation and coherence.
Yet he could see no coherence, though he unceasingly saw Kristina's
face, the face of his mother. She was the one who did not emigrate to
America, like her brothers, and like he was now doing in her place.
How terrible that she wasn't allowed to experience that happiness! that
dream! for which she had shed many tears. But the memory!

The memory from his birthday in 1888.

How clear that memory was! now that he was making the pil-
grimage that had been denied her! *There was a chair next to the sofa-bed
where I was lying, and a coffee service had been set on the chair, and I don't
remember what I was dreaming, but when I woke up I found a vase with flowers. Where Mother had found them in early March, I can't explain, but who
can explain motherly love? She may have cut the flowers from a potted plant.
My mother and I were alone in the room. Father had gone to work, my siblings weren't there; they had gone to school. It was my fourth birthday, so I
hadn't yet started school. I had apparently slept for a long time. My mother was
caressing me so I would wake up. I can still remember seeing her smiling face
framed by the sunlight that filled the room. Mother was forty-six years old at
the time, and I still remember the warm words she said as she wished me happy
birthday. It must have been almost summer, even though I was born in March,
because I remember the warm sunshine, as if it were a summer day, and how
the light encircled my mother's face when she caressed my cheek, my hair, and*

smiled at me, and at that moment I understood the power of a mother's love, and the memory had never left him, nor did it now in this valley of despondency.

But it didn't make sense. That's why he was in despair. That's why the image of his mother appeared so strongly in his consciousness.

But it didn't make sense.

When he built God's cathedral, and God's empire took shape— what Lewi himself had never called a cathedral or empire because they were the last words he wanted to have on his lips—then everything had made sense. Then he never felt any fear of becoming broken down. Yet now it had happened, without warning. It had to be Sven's influence. A person was not allowed to love anyone as much as he loved Sven. And if it so happened that the person you loved despised you, then it was practically a mortal sin. It turned your face away from the love of Jesus. And Jesus alone possessed the power of unconditional love toward those who felt contempt. But to be despised by the one you admired and loved, that was painful. It was painful. Of course he also despised Sven's bewildered lack of financial understanding, but that was only natural. It was actually rather humorous. He was a poet. Lewi was not a poet. That was the difference. But the contempt! The contempt! How painful!

But was Sven the real cause?

He began to compare Sven to the old memory of Mal-Ola's grotto. No doubt there was some connection—Sven and Mal-Ola's grotto. He began investigating. He had admired Sven so much. Why did he admire Sven? Nothing seemed to make sense for Sven, and yet it didn't worry him. He was utterly unafraid of the black precipice. Maybe that's how it was with artists. It was their prerogative not to make sense, and yet they were happy and admired. That was the reason Lewi was not one of those who wrote. He was from the provinces. What were the provinces? The provinces were where he had started.

Had he forgotten where he started? Was that why nothing made sense? He should have played a pump organ and not this gigantic organ that was the Pentecostal movement.

It was important to start at the beginning.

His mother's face, radiantly encircled with sunlight, when she woke him, was always present. It was a constant. But it had to be supplemented. She had to be sketched into a landscape. Then it might all make sense. He understood that sketching himself into his own landscape was the only thing that would save him from insanity or suicide. He had to make a sketch. Not a great cathedral, like the one on Rörstrandsgatan that was larger than the Salle Pleyel in Paris and more modern than the Concert Hall in Stockholm, and had better acoustics.

But rather, the most simple of all.

The house came first.

He had to start with that. So first he thought about the little hovel in Västra Tunhem where he was born. In his mind he called this hovel "the house." He thought about the house because he knew that it was the only thing that could save him from being forever broken down. The house was a memory that was solid. In the house he could start, or start over. That's why, when he came back to his rented lodgings, he began to draw a floor plan of the house, in the same way he had made sketches for the temple on Rörstrandsgatan, though that was much bigger.

But the house in Västra Tunhem was still intriguing. As a child, he had measured it. It was 7 meters by 4.25 meters, measured on the outside.

The two rooms were quickly sketched. There was a kitchen and a small room, and behind the stove, niches had been made in the wall where the little children could sleep, and it was nice and warm. That's where two adults and nine children had lived in perfect harmony. No one complained, at least not after their father stopped boozing. They lay head to tail and listened to the other children breathing. It was like a rush of breaths.

He sketched the stove and the kitchen table and remembered how many straight-backed chairs there were. How had they slept? He made several changes to his sketch as things became clearer. When the oldest children got bigger and started working at the age of ten, which was the proper age, the smaller children were by then on the way. Had all eleven of them ever slept in the two rooms at one time? He decided that they had.

They had lain head to tail. Like in the catacombs.

That was how he would one day rest in the arms of the Savior Jesus Christ, head to tail with the Savior. But when this thought occurred to him, he regretted it and found the idea childish, perhaps an expression of his broken-down state.

To rest in eternity, head to tail with the Savior, that was how he imagined the eternal life. He pushed the idea aside, though it came back, because to lie head to tail was warm and secure, and that's how the Savior was when he dreamed of Him, as a child, and also as an adult, although he had never used this image in any sermon. Yet he almost did in his Palestine book, and then the student changed it, and he was so incomprehensibly furious, and he had many times prayed to God to forgive him for that.

This was the house he grew up in. There were nine children. He was happy as a child. He had a thoroughly poor but happy childhood, even though it was crowded. But it wasn't happy until Johan, his father, stopped boozing.

It wasn't so strange that his father got mixed up in boozing. Nearly everyone did. Those who were mixed up in boozing had no morals; liquor robbed people of morals. This was something he had talked about many times, using an example he took from a statistical book he had read. Lewi used to preach that of all the children born in Stockholm the same year that he was born—and the total number of children was 2,746—1,100 were illegitimate. It was the booze. This had to be understood. It was poverty, drunkenness, and loose living. George Scott, who became a famous preacher of the Evangelical Homeland Mission and yet was often quoted by Lewi, was shaken to his very core when he came to Sweden. "Ever since my arrival in this in many respects charming country, I have with sincere distress observed the sad truth that Sweden, more than any other European country, is marked by a copious use of alcoholic drinks which have a highly damaging effect. No other country in the world consumes so much aquavit per capita. There is no other country in which the burden of drunkenness, with its innumerable consequences of crime and misery, is so widespread or so destructive. Sweden is the capital for the manufacture and consumption of alcoholic drinks; yes, it's the capital for drunkenness."

This had to be understood. His father had started out as a boy driver for the famous railway builder, Colonel Nils Eriksson, who owned a distillery. Eriksson was a swine. The wages and food were awful, but the drivers were allowed to drink as much aquavit as they liked, free of charge. They were especially encouraged to drink when the colonel signed contracts with his subordinates, and then the contracts always turned out bad. They were given a few coins and they signed their names in a haze of liquor, and ended up in poverty.

This is how Eriksson held on to his slaves.

As a ten-year-old, Lewi's father drove loads of limestone from the quarries near Västra Tunhem church to Vargö where this Eriksson had a cement factory. On this stretch of road, which was ten kilometers long, the child Johan drove in all kinds of weather. The worst was during winter storms. The countryside was flat, the snow piled up in drifts, and he had only thin clothes to wear. Then it was booze that warmed him, though some of the other child drivers died. They simply froze to death. Later Lewi's father became a sheepherder. And then he was a driver for Bojson the brewer, who was also a swine, and completely sunk in booze. Bojson also beat his animals, and that was the worst, especially when he was practically dead drunk. It was understandable that Lewi's father had gotten mixed up in booze. He took part in drinking bouts and dances. Later on he married, but he was still mixed up in entertainments and booze.

No doubt it was the booze that made his father sick for a time, so he had to stay in bed with nerve fever. Everyone agreed that it was nerve fever, a type of breakdown. Then Lewi's mother had to provide for the nine children. This too she managed, and they were generally a happy family.

Then one Christmas a relative came to visit. His name was Svante Nyman, and he was a brother of Lewi's mother. He was known for getting mixed up in drunken revelry and dance parties, and Lewi's father had placed bottles of aquavit on the table, as was the custom. Then this Svante confessed that he was saved. And that's why he no longer drank.

"Go ahead and have a drink if you like, Johan," he said freely. "As for me, it's over!"

The next day Lewi's father carried the liquor out of the house and put the bottles in the woodshed, though he made many trips out there, but always alone. Later this relative had a long talk with Lewi's father about revivalism and Christ and C. O. Rosenius, who had now completed his life's work in the service of the Evangelical Homeland Mission. And together this Svante and Lewi's father went around to the houses and invited everyone to prayers on the day after Christmas.

Most of them had known Svante Nyman as a wild and boisterous youth who frequented places of entertainment in the region. Now he spoke of Jesus, and together they sang songs, also Sankey's songs. He had a very good singing voice. Then he read chapter 15 in the Gospel according to Luke and chapter 3 in the Gospel according to John.

This Svante had a spiritual discussion with Lewi's parents, and they then decided to give up sin and live their lives in the righteousness and holiness of God. They knelt down and placed their lives in God's hands. That very evening Lewi's father threw out his supply of strong drink, which signified his farewell to liquor for good.

But later three of Lewi's brothers got mixed up in boozing. And that's where they stayed. It was a great sorrow. It was especially a great sorrow for his mother, whose named was Kristina and who never emigrated to America.

Booze was the sin. It was booze that prevented her from going to America. In a sense. But Lewi, who loved her, knew that she had always dreamed of getting away. It was the Savior who became her salvation from misery when she was left behind, yet she still wept whenever she read the much-thumbed-through letters from America.

It was America that in some sense was heaven. That's how she had always imagined it. A person left the earthly world, which was liquor, and went to heaven, which was America.

Yet Svante Nyman was the first preacher in the family. With his own hands he cast Lewi's family into the arms of Jesus Christ, except for the three brothers, which was a great sorrow. Then he disappeared from the story.

4.

In Filadelfia they heard how things were going for Lewi, that he was still broken down, and that's why they wrote to friends in America. One of the friends was dispatched to Chicago.

He was supposed to find out how bad things were with Lewi.

The friend, whose name we don't know, found him weak and apathetic. They sat in Lewi's lodgings with the radio turned on. All the news was about German victories. Lewi lay stretched out on his bed, dozing.

"Lydia ought to come here," the friend said. "Wouldn't you like her to come here?"

"No."

"Why do you seem so lost, Lewi? Have you given up your faith in your Savior?"

There was no answer.

"What's wrong with you?" the friend stubbornly asked.

"The last time I was in America," Lewi finally replied, "I had Einar Ekberg with me, and that was much appreciated by the Pentecostals. He's a great preacher in song, after all. But I don't think it was just the songs, do you?"

The friend couldn't find an answer, but merely repeated his question:

"Lewi, how are you, actually? Do you feel forsaken?"

"He who has his Savior," Lewi replied almost mechanically, "is never forsaken, never alone, though he wanders through the valley of despair and despondency."

"Yes, the Savior," replied the friend, "yes, that's right."

And then Lewi finally opened his eyes, looked at him, and said:

"And I pray to God that Lidman won't ruin the finances of Filadelfia and the *Härold*."

Then they traveled south together, to the southern states and to New Orleans.

"John Bunyan and I," Sven had scornfully quoted him.

But wasn't he, too, a Pilgrim?

Yes, shouldn't people be regarded as Pilgrims? And wasn't he himself a Pilgrim on a journey? Couldn't this way of thinking give everything a sense of coherence?

He tried.

Who were these people he had met on his life's journey, the ones he might call Faithful, Discontent, Shame, Hypocrisy, Adam the First, or By-ends? Or did they exist inside himself? He was now reading *The Pilgrim's Progress* with such intensity that it had almost replaced the Bible. By-ends, yes, he knew him. "How loathsome it is to use the Lord Christ and religion as an excuse for seeking wealth and prestige in the world."

That was comrade By-ends.

He certainly had met him. That was true. Was it Sven? Or was it Lewi himself?

Sven had occasionally hinted that Lewi also had a By-ends concealed inside him. But was it true? He wasn't seeking wealth, in any case! He would regard it as shameful! shameful! to die a rich man, no, never, never.

But prestige? Prestige?

And he had met so many named Hypocrisy. He began to write them all down. There were many names on the notepad. But what was it he sought?

He sought the Plain of Ease, which would give him peace. But he knew that he was imprisoned by the Giant Despair; the giant had imprisoned Lewi in his den. And the Giant Despair consulted his wife, whose name was Diffidence, and she had told her spouse the best thing would be to strip the Pilgrim Lewi of all hope, so that the Giant Despair wouldn't have to kill him, but instead Lewi would take his own life. And like Christian, meaning the Pilgrim, he would be forced to think: "No, I would rather suffocate now, rather die than become nothing but bones."

But then the Pilgrim remembered that he possessed a secret key. That released him from the imprisonment of Despair.

Do I have such a key? thought Lewi.

Lewi's thoughts circled more and more manically around his childhood.

He reconstructed their house, in every detail, on the drawing paper, but it didn't help. The sketch had to be expanded, surrounded by a landscape so that there was also room for people. Then he could populate the drawing with people. Include them so that the Pilgrim's encounters became comprehensible. Yet this assumed that he also drew in the landscape. Otherwise it would seem jinxed.

Then they would have no landscape in which to move.

The landscape slowly began to materialize.

The area of Halleberg and Hunneberg was a wilderness. There were only five little houses with great distances between them, and then forests and lakes. There were pine forests and mountains that towered like mighty ocean liners above the wilderness, and Storgårdskleven and Draget up near the highest peak of Häcklan, which was Ättestupan, which meant suicide precipice. That's where they had lit the defensive beacon when the enemy approached, in the past, or "in bygone days" as his mother Kristina said when she told stories. And there, beneath the gigantic Atlantic steamships, lay the deep valley, and the forests that stretched for miles. And off to the south Trollhättan was barely visible, where the North Sea had once reached, and where foreigners had appeared.

Below Ättestupan was Odin's pool, which had once been used for something, perhaps blood sacrifices, although someone had said that it was there the bodies of the old people were washed after throwing themselves off Ättestupan.

They had wanted to end their lives.

It was a mortal sin to take your own life. But that's how things were in the past: when someone knew that his days were over, he would take his own life. A moment might come in a person's life when everything was over, and before, in ancient times, when only the belief in the Æsir gods existed, then those individuals whose strength had run out would make the long climb up the cliff and bravely stand on top. And think about how things had been and what the meaning of it all was. Whether there was any meaning, and whether what they had done made sense. And since they had not put their faith in the Savior Jesus Christ, they decided to take their own lives.

With a certain courage; yes, that was what Lewi had thought when he was a child. It occurred to him that he had thought of it as "courage."

He thought about this again as he reconstructed what the landscape had looked like. They had no faith, but they made a decision. Their incomprehensible courage might seem surprising since they had no hope and no faith and no Jesus. Wasn't that courage? They didn't know the Savior Jesus Christ, yet they dared to make that long climb up the mountain, which was an end point, of sorts. And then they flung themselves off. And fell. With their arms open wide. Into the deepest darkness of the sea. And perhaps during the fall, before they were crushed to death and were washed into Odin's pool, they understood how it all made sense and what the meaning of life was.

They knew nothing about the Savior and his wounds. Did anything exist beyond Odin's pool? What did they think about when they stood up there? What was the answer?

Were they broken down? Or did they have strength, for the first time, to stand up and step into the darkness, which was the only thing they knew?

What courage they must have had. Without Jesus, without hope, yet daring to step into the darkness.

* * *

The landscape was becoming clearer.

On the slope beneath the cliff, or rather in the middle of the cliff, ten meters up but far below the crest, there was a cave. The grotto was called Mal-Ola's lair. History tells us that in bygone days, in ancient times, when foreign armies pushed northward and the inhabitants of Västergötland were the barrier to the enemy, a man by the name of Mal-Ola hid himself in the grotto. His role was to act as scout and keep the defenders apprised of the enemy's movements. He was supplied with provisions for several months. If enemy soldiers tried to force their way into the grotto, he would knock them down with a long cudgel. The grotto was practically impregnable.

All of Lewi's friends had succeeded in entering Mal-Ola's grotto. A difficult, dizzying path led up to it. You had to climb. It seemed to threaten mortal danger. Lewi had never dared go there. And this had made him greatly ashamed.

He had never entered Mal-Ola's grotto. Later he grew up and turned away from such childish games, but the fact remained. He had never dared go up to Mal-Ola's grotto, and then he left and became the man that he was and built his congregation—no, God's congregation—but the fact remained. He was the only one who had never made it up to Mal-Ola's grotto.

He had talked about the grotto to the friend who accompanied him to New Orleans, and whom he now thought of as Faithful. The friend was interested but didn't understand why Lewi had told him the story. It certainly wasn't any major defeat, the friend had said, with a smile. Lewi then developed a theory: If a person constantly gives in to cowardice and fear and dangers, then a yearning arises inside of him for this capitulation. But if he constantly fights to conquer all obstacles, this is what he becomes accustomed to instead.

"It reminds me," he said, "about the parable of the buried talents. The person who buries his talents doesn't seek out Mal-Ola's grotto either."

The friend then gave him a long look and said:

"Lewi, you're now fifty-seven years old. And you've made use of your talents all your life. Why have you now decided to bury your talents at the base of Mal-Ola's grotto?"

At first there was no reply. Then Lewi said:

"I'm afraid that God is punishing me, and that He is just."

Two days later the friend departed. Lewi said that he was going to preach to a congregation in New Orleans. Lewi didn't think there was any reason to worry.

He was now utterly alone.

5.

He started taking a great many walks.

There was no longer anything wrong with him physically.

He had been a good ice-skater as a child. That was when he was a sheepherder, before he started at the paper mill, where he did his job well, as it stated on his work certificate, which he oddly enough had brought with him on his trip to America. According to the certificate, he had made use of his talents and that's why he brought along the certificate. He had worked "at first as a messenger, then in the chemical factory, and finally as a mesh belt operator in the paper mill," and, according to the certificate, he was "willing and conscientious at his work, and demonstrated very good conduct."

But his days of ice-skating were before the period at Vargön, when there was not as much time for games or sports. Earlier there was a great deal of running and competing. He was very fast. And in the wintertime, they had skates made from blades fastened to wood. He was small but fast.

They would go to the pond. Below the pond was a waterfall where the water flowed in the summer, falling freely 1.5 meters. As a ten-year-old Lewi had made a water wheel and placed it under the falls, but to make it stable he needed a flywheel. One of his friends then took from the Vargön factory a discarded flywheel that was approximately 25 centimeters in diameter. It worked, and Lewi set up a whole mechanism with cotton spools and lines and wheels, and in this way created a little power station.

And everything worked.

His mother often came down to the falls to look at his machinery. Then she would pat his head and say that he was probably going to turn into a little power station himself. She said kind words about the structure, and declared that it was good he was building machines, so that he wouldn't succumb to temptations like his friends.

Then came the worry about sin. It destroyed his joy in being an inventor and possibly an engineer.

He began thinking about the flywheel and worrying about sin.

Wasn't that theft? His friend said that he had taken the flywheel from a scrap heap, but that might not have been the whole truth. What if he had stolen it? Then Lewi was an accomplice. Lewi became terribly worried about sin. But without the flywheel his hydroelectric power station wouldn't work.

He prayed hard but found no peace of mind. Finally he tore off the flywheel and carried it the whole long way back to the Vargön factory, where he threw it on a trash heap.

After that he felt a spiritual peace.

Now, in America, when he so surprisingly had become broken down and completely incapable of fulfilling his mother's dream of the glory of American heaven, he thought, "I've torn off a flywheel from my life, and the machinery has stopped, but this time it hasn't brought me peace." He thought this was a good metaphor. If he had still been in his former life, before he was broken down, he could have used the story and the metaphor in his preaching. Lidman would have undoubtedly done so. Lidman was a poet, after all, and he was always using metaphors like this one, taken from real life. But Lidman's true metaphors were often made up. This one was not made up, but true, although Lewi couldn't make use of it because it had played out in bygone days, because everything was now in bygone days, because he seemed to be standing on his own suicide precipice and staring into the dark, with Odin's pool far below, and with the grotto in the middle of the cliff wall, the place where he never went because he was a coward: the grotto and the pool right below.

And far off in the distance the house hidden in the dark forest, and no hope, and the metaphors now utterly useless.

In Bunyan's book there were many evils that he now with dread tried to incorporate into the landscape.

Mr. Blind-Man, Mr. No-Good, Mr. Malice, Mr. Love-Lust, Mr. Implacable. He drew them on the map. Had he met them? And not seen them? When he was fifteen, his worry about sin was at its peak. But now there was a different worry, which was almost worse than worry about sin. Why didn't he have anyone to talk to?

Someone like Georg.

When he lived in Kristiania, he met a young man who shared all his interests. His name was Georg, and he was the brother of Lydia, his future wife. He met Georg before he met Lydia. They took walks and conversed, and Lewi had never met anyone who, in a purely spiritual sense, embraced him with such love. He had a marvelously life-giving effect on Lewi's way of life. The time they spent together was never enough. It was nothing like an impure relationship between men. It was simply a great love, like between Christian and Faithful. This new type of impurity was not something he had even heard of at that time. Such thoughts were also completely foreign to him. It was a Christian brotherly love, but also a great deal of genuine friendship in its purest and noblest form. During the entire time he lived in Kristiania, he never spent any time with a girl, but this young man, whom he regarded with such great and pure love, was Lydia's brother.

One time he said to his wife, as a joke:

"I think I ended up falling in love with you because of your brother!"

It was said in jest. But Lydia took it wrong, and that night he heard her crying. He asked her why, and she told him that she was unhappy because of his joke. It was incomprehensible. He loved Lydia deeply. What would he have been without her? he asked.

She didn't reply.

Now that incident had come back. He walked and walked through the streets of New Orleans, and his friend Georg, whom he hadn't seen for many years, returned in his memory, along with Lydia's tears, and then, strangely enough, the tears of Franklin's wife. It was as if they had all gathered together: those whom he, out of Christian love, had left or been forced to destroy because they were stones in his path; they were now crunching like shells under his roaming feet.

Those he had left behind. And those he had loved, like Georg. In that case with an utterly pure love, but it may have been stronger than anything else he had ever known, either previously or later in life. Why was Georg not here in this deep forest of despair? But then he pulled himself together and thought about his mother and her smile when she stroked his hair, radiantly encircled by sunlight, and also about that time at the waterfall when the flywheel was in place, before his worry about sin forced him to destroy his dream, and later, now, before the great darkness descended upon him, the darkness that might be a feeling of being broken down, but might have resembled his father's nerve fever. And then Hunneberg's gigantic dark ocean liners loomed up in his memory. But now the mountain was not enticing or irresistible or an enormous Atlantic vessel in a fairy tale that could be climbed and explored, but instead something darker and more menacing.

Was it the Mountain of Clarity, or the Mountain of Judgment?

He was alone in the wilderness, once again, no Companion in sight, and no Benefactor. Making a sketch no longer helped. He had finished drawing the landscape of forests and mountains and outlined paths, but this mapping out of how it had all begun didn't help him.

And he had no idea how to go on.

6.

In May he returned to Chicago.

Three months had now passed since he had left Sweden for good. He received assistance from the Pentecostal congregations for life's essentials, and occasionally he would preach.

He was one of many. It was not like in Sweden. But this was not what weighed on him the most; no, that wasn't it. It was possible to start over. His mother's brothers had traveled to the new land and started from scratch, and one of them was hired by the Steinway piano factory.

So why couldn't he do the same, since he had God on his side?

But that was just it: Where was God to be found? What made him feel broken down was the fact that he received no guidance. God's voice had fallen silent. He shouted and shouted, but God did not answer. Though he did receive letters from Sweden. He read them many times, and wept. It was strange. His mother had cried over her letters from America. Now he was crying over his letters from Sweden.

The turning point came on July 22, 1941.

That was when he received a letter from Efraim. It was written in almost a bombastic style, and Efraim called him "Pilgrim." It included a thumb verse, one that had been chosen by a young man who had once said no, Efraim wrote, and this young man said that it should be given either to Sven or to Lewi, but Efraim had now decided that God meant it for Lewi.

The thumb verse had been jotted down on a piece of paper. It was not in Efraim's handwriting. It was from the Book of Job, chapter 39, verses 5-8.

*Who has let the wild ass go free? Who has loosed the bonds of the swift ass,
to whom I have given the steppe for his home, and the salt land for his
dwelling place? He scorns the tumult of the city; he hears not the shouts of the
driver. He ranges the mountains as his pasture, and he searches after every
green thing.*

He read the thumb verse with a peculiar agitation. What was it
that God was trying to tell him? Was he the wild ass or was he the
driver?

Or was he both?

And had he been thinking wrong?

There was a morning meeting at the Philadelphia Church in Chicago,
and not many were present because that was just how things were and
besides, it was in the morning, and afterwards Lewi went alone into the
congregation's prayer room.

This was what he told Efraim later. It was a summary of the conversation in the prayer room. But he told it to Efraim. And this was
what Efraim wrote down in the *Lebenslauf.*

Lewi was alone during the conversation.

He fervently asked God why He had been so silent, and if this was
fair. He didn't think he deserved this. After so many years of conversation: now silence. And he was almost desperate. And he found himself
in the Slough of Despond, or the Forest, but why this silence right
now when he was so alone in America?

Yet God then broke His silence and replied.

"Lewi," said God, "I have followed you through the years. And
sometimes I've been amazed how much that little peddler from
Västergötland managed to do." Yes, God had almost in jest referred to
what Sven had said about Lewi, that he was basically just a little peddler from Västergötland, but God had done so in a kind way, as if He
were fond of Lewi. "Yes," God told him, "don't despair. I have given
you only one talent, but you have used it well. I have watched with
surprise at how you have used this one talent that I gave you. Maybe
I gave you two, I don't remember, I'm old, my memory often fails me,
but you have used it well. And I give you my blessing. But I don't
understand what you're complaining about. Can you explain why you

actually fled from the congregation? You have never been a coward. Although I've heard your moans about a grotto you never managed to reach, Mal-Ola's grotto I think it is. What are you moaning about? That's not like you."

Then Lewi said that the situation had seemed desperate. It became inevitable that he would have to leave. He didn't want to cause division and discord within the Pentecostal movement, and that's why he had gone into exile, leaving all power to Lidman.

But then God started talking in earnest. "Lewi," said God, "is that really the truth?"

"Yes," said Lewi. "Yours is the truth, yours is the power."

But God interrupted him and said, "Don't blame me, and the truth is respectable, and this is not the truth."

"Then what is the truth, dear God?" whispered Lewi.

"The truth cannot be pinned up on the wall of your conscience like some *mene tekel*," God replied. "The truth is as manifold as the drops in the sea and the grains of sand in the desert. The truth exists inside of you, and you are avoiding the truth. You say Lidman; in truth, I say to you that Lidman is not it. Not it! You have fallen apart, and now put the blame on others. Think about your mother and what she sacrificed for you, and now you're burying your talent and not speaking the truth and you say that you're afraid of Lidman. I've never heard anything more ridiculous." And God said, "No, something has broken inside you, and you think that you'll never reach Mal-Ola's grotto, but you can. I'm telling you that you can. You have weighed yourself on a scale and been found too light, but in truth, in truth, I say to you: Yours is not the power to weigh. That power is mine, and I weigh you, and you are not yet too light, but right now you are diminishing the talent that I gave you. To succumb to despair," God said, "is like getting mixed up in boozing. It's like a nerve fever."

"A nerve fever!" Lewi said. "A nerve fever, like my father! Then what should I do?" And at the words "nerve fever" he was seized by great alarm and terror, and he whispered half-aloud: "Nerve fever! What should I do, dear Lord God my Savior? Have I somehow gotten mixed up in boozing even though I don't drink? What should I do to get out of it?"

"What should you do?" replied God. "You think that a person can come before the sight of God and ask what he should do? But in truth, in truth, I tell you, that decision is yours alone, and you should not shift the blame to someone else. You have labored as a loyal worker in my vineyard, and now you're running around in America as if you were crazy, and you're constantly praying for my voice to guide you and complaining about my silence, but you should know that I have heard your prayers. And God's voice is never silent. He merely holds it back from a person. He doesn't allow the person to hear the voice, but it is still there. You are the one who is spiritually deaf, and you shouldn't shift the blame to God, because God is never silent. The deafness is yours, Lewi, yours alone. Mine is the voice, yours is the deafness."

"How have I sinned, dear Savior?" Lewi then said.

"Don't ask me how you have sinned. Instead, ask yourself what you should do."

"Yes, but this Lidman," Lewi began again, but then God sternly interrupted him.

"You must learn that the thread of sin can ensnare in many ways. You must fight the enemies who are also my enemies."

"How do I know who they are?" asked Lewi.

"That's the trick," said God. "That's the trick! To choose the proper enemies, but in my name. Is Lidman an enemy? You know," God said, "that Lidman is, in his own way, a sinner."

"But I love him dearly, and he is, in his own way. He is, in his own way. In truth!" Lewi replied.

"But Lidman labors in my vineyard in his own way, and you know what I allowed to be said through my disciple Paul, who in his letter to the Corinthians spoke of the body and its parts. You are all Christ's body and his parts, each in his own way. The hand is not the eye, the ear is not the foot, Lidman is not Pethrus, but all of you are equally important, and when I put together the body, I did it so that a division would not occur in the body, but so that all the parts should, in harmony, take care of each other."

"Dear God," replied Lewi, almost impatiently, "I know this is true. You don't have to tell me this, and I have preached about this, but I'm worried that he will destroy Filadelfia's finances, and he's not really much of a newspaper man. How will things go for Filadelfia and the *Härold*? And he's against my idea of starting a daily paper, and he's against the idea of using the *Härold*'s printing presses for *Dagen*, which would mean sheer waste of capital, not to mention the need for our own radio station, which we really do need to make Your voice heard amid this buzz of sin."

"Lewi," said God, "you're not as small as you think. I have given you a mission, and you're misusing your talent."

"I'm broken down," Lewi replied. "All energy seems to have left my body. I feel myself standing at the very top of the cliff, and I'm looking at the precipice before me, and down there is Odin's pool, and there's a tremendous longing inside me, like in the old heathens, to throw myself out into this darkness, as if it were a dizzying black hole that is the deepest darkness of the sea, and eternity. I'm stating the facts. I have given up, dear Savior, and for the life of me I don't know what to do."

"Then I can give you only one piece of advice," said God. "You must stop thinking so much about your insignificance and about the division that is going to come and about everything terrible and about how old you are. You're not old. God grants you life, God gives life. God is the Sovereign of the Universe. I am time, I am all time. And now I am giving you time. Listen to what I tell you and stop moaning so miserably. Your time is not up. I am time. I am giving you time."

"But then what does the thumb verse that You sent me mean?" said Lewi. "The one from Job, as You may remember, the one about the wild ass and the driver. Am I the driver and Sven the wild ass? But how much I would have preferred, once in a while, to be a wild ass searching for everything green. And this driver, doesn't he have a whip in his hand? And I don't want to be the one wielding the whip. No, in truth, in truth, I tell You, my God, how much I would prefer to be a wild ass, because those are the ones that have much greater prestige with us."

"You're seeking prestige!" said God in such a stern voice that Lewi almost gave a start and felt contrite. "But don't you remember the Apostles' message about the entry into Jerusalem, especially John, chapter 12, or Mark 11, how the words of the prophet Isaiah would be realized, which said: 'Fear not, daughter of Zion; behold, your king is coming, sitting on an ass's colt!' Did I send my son to enter Jerusalem on a wild ass? No, in truth, I did not. An animal that might grow restive and kick and pitch my only begotten son headlong to the ground? No, in truth, this ass was not a wild ass. A tamer had disciplined her so that she would not throw off my only begotten son, the world's savior. And why do you think this driver did not have a mission that was equally important to that of the wild ass? And it is true that these wild asses find their green patches of grass and are much esteemed by the ones who have dreams and who write, like this Lidman you are constantly complaining about. But the driver and the tamer are also parts of the body of Christ and should not be scorned. I know full well that you wish to be a wild ass, but I have appointed you as a driver, and as such you are an important part of the body of Christ."

"But what should I do?" said Lewi in the same whisper of a voice.

"Get up on your feet and walk," replied God. And after that God had nothing more to say.

And that was the final word.

7.

That very day, in the afternoon, Lewi went to the Clipper office and bought passage for his return journey to Sweden.

He booked passage for September. But now it was decided. And that's how it happened. On the advice of God, he had gotten to his feet, in the same way as he stood up from a kneeling position in the prayer room of the Philadelphia Church in Chicago. He stood up and walked, and he came home, and everyone asked but no one received an answer. Only once did he say anything to Efraim, who back then did not understand.

But later he understood.

Lewi was back. The journey through the Valley of Humiliation and the Forest of Despair was over.

He would never again be broken down, never be struck with nerve fever. He came back as a different man, and opinion was divided as to whether this was better or worse. But as a different man. What had happened was something he would never explain. But perhaps it was true what God had said, that there was no one *mene tekel*, that the truth is as manifold as the grains of sand in the desert, that it serves no good purpose to brood over it, that he was now standing on his own two feet, and that he was walking. Lewi was back with a small sharp crease between his eyes, a little more resolute.

Lewi had returned, and he did not intend to allow himself to be destroyed. The map he had drawn was now complete, with hills and valleys. He had descended from the enticing precipice of Ättestupan. Kristina's hand had blissfully caressed the top of his head so that his father's nerve fever would never again strike him, and so that his fear of Mal-Ola's grotto was now gone for good.

And now whatever happened would happen.

Lewi had returned. God had given him time. Now whatever happened would happen. He was the same man, yet different. He knew that the time of strife might come, but so be it. God had given him time. And he was standing on his own two feet. And he could still walk.

CHAPTER 22

The Battle at
Mal-Ola's Grotto

1.

MUCH TO EVERYONE'S SURPRISE, THE EAGLE HAD LANDED, AND
Efraim was present at the press conference that Lewi held upon his
return to Sweden.

Things were not crystal clear.

Everything was, in fact, quite hazy. Lewi tried to explain what he
had been doing in America, but no one understood. He spoke of God's
calling, partially to America, partially back home, but this too was
vague. The journalists were not accustomed to interpreting this voice
of God. God had clearly spoken, calling Lewi first here, then there; no
one dared question too sharply what God had meant. The follow-up
questions were hesitant, not at all pointed. No doubt it was all, well,
unfamiliar.

The reporters seemed unfamiliar with God.

But Efraim noted that Lewi was very composed. One thing was
quite clear: He was not broken down. He was absolutely determined
to resume control of his empire, and he was a different man.

The question was: Who was he?

It was like coming home to icebergs floating all around. Not much was
visible sticking above the surface. But the water was ice cold.

Late in the fall Lewi gave his first policy speech at the Filadelfia
church on Rörstrandsgatan.

Efraim is the one who uses this much too modern expression "policy speech" in the *Lebenslauf*, perhaps to mark the fact that something new had arrived. A political dimension, or rather the fact that the Pentecostal movement's old battle, scorned but well-known, against worldly sinners had been revitalized. And politicized. The battle whose goal it was to reinstate the family and the relationship between man and woman in purity and respect, to keep filth away from children, meaning certain children's books that were not of an edifying nature. And of course the misery of the dance floor, and obscene literature in general. And the theater, and movies. All these old well-known things from the '30s were now brought together and armored and given a weightier, more consciously political content.

It was a full house at Rörstrandsgatan when Lewi gave his policy speech.

These days it was almost always a full house, and everyone seemed curious about what was going on, and who Lewi was. The returning Odysseus! Would the suitors be annihilated? And would the congregation, still eighty percent women, be restored like Penelope to the embrace of the scarred returning traveler?

Sven was the one who expressed it in that way, in a brief, acidic remark to Efraim. He had found yet another apt metaphor from the classics. The return of Odysseus. Odysseus, who draws his bow against the enemies. The congregation as the threatened wife.

Yes, the eagle had landed, and it was no broken-down man who spoke. But the community that surrounded him was quite clearly ailing.

"The nation," he said, and that same year he expanded this policy speech in the book *Today We Play—Tomorrow We Cry*, "the nation that shuns healthy, joy-evoking work in order to throw itself into the arms of pleasures and enjoyments is not worthy of life, and will inexorably head toward defeat. The current generation has sunk to a position where even marriage is regarded as a means for pleasure and enjoyment and is recklessly exploited to that end. Recently Marshal Pétain—after the military collapse of France—gave one of the mightiest revivalist sermons ever given in Europe during the last hundred years. He spoke of the craving for pleasure. About contraceptives. About what a crime the moral decay is, undermining the morals of a nation and thereby its viability. This is no time for games, frivolity, pleasure, or enjoyment. This is a time for responsibility, self-sacrifice, a sense of service. A Christian does not go to the theater or the movies;

he does not dance, he does not live an immoral life. People ask: Why
is the world being afflicted with these bloody wars in which millions
of people are swept away? I tell them: The wars are blood-lettings that
are necessary so the world won't become completely poisoned. When
putrefaction threatens to take the upper hand, these kinds of catastro-
phes descend on the world. It is a discharge that will restore the balance, a cleansing that prevents the utter extinction of the human race.
God does what every foresighted planter does: He rids His fields of
weeds. He sweeps them away."

Both Sven and Efraim were sitting up on the platform among the
elders. For the most part it was a blessed evening, but Efraim was feeling out of sorts. Lewi was no longer afraid; he could see that. But
Efraim didn't really care for what he heard, and strangely enough the
same seemed to be true of Sven, even though he had spent the '30s
preaching the collapse of the Western world into moral decay.

No, Sven didn't care for what he heard either, although in many
ways he was actually listening to an echo of his own sermons from the
'30s. In the prayer room Efraim witnessed a brief but chillingly hostile
conversation between Lewi and Sven.

"I was surprised," said Sven, "when you quoted Marshal Pétain.
Some people call him a Fascist and the Quisling of France."

"But he's right," replied Lewi, "with regard to these issues. Not
regarding others."

"You have a rather unusual, and exciting, but strange view of war.
War is a blood-letting that is necessary so the world won't take sick?"

"So it can recover!"

"Quite a peculiar idea."

"Do you think so, Sven? I recall that you wrote in Svensk Lösen
that God sent war like a bolt of lightning that sliced through the summer heat and brought devastation but also a rain of renewal. I've always
thought that was peculiar."

Sven then looked at Lewi with a little, perplexed smile, as if he
heard an echo from something he had almost forgotten and only with
help could remember.

"I didn't know that you had read the old sins of my youth. But a
person can change his view."

"Yes, he can."

"Well, I'm glad that God didn't cleanse away such a valuable
weed-ridden person as Sven Lidman when he was young."

"You know that wasn't what I meant," said Lewi in an ice-cold tone of voice. "I don't think of people or sinners as weeds."

"But?"

"I meant sin!"

"Difficult to separate the two. To separate sinners from sin. Difficult. And my poetry collections . . . no doubt they're obscene literature?"

"Yes. As you yourself have said."

"And they should have been part of the book burning?"

Lewi then gave a start and said furiously:

"I deny what you're insinuating. I deny it! Deny! And I've never used the phrase 'book burning.'"

"You're right. I'll make a note of that. Praise God."

The two men were standing far apart from each other in the room, standing utterly still, as if frozen. And Efraim would always remember the moment because he had previously witnessed quarrels between them.

But this time it was different. Everything was clearer.

It was as if they had both said: I'm not afraid and I defy you! And both were aware that they could no longer revert to the usual biblical rhetoric of love, praise God, brotherly love, with the tenderness of Christ, praise the Lord.

It was a moment of pure speech, free of rhetoric.

"Well, I hope," said Lewi after a very long pause, "that in regard to the issue at hand, you essentially agree with what I said!"

"Essentially?"

Sven waited a few moments and glanced at Efraim who was sitting on a chair and not saying a word. Then Sven turned to Lewi and said with an almost teasing smile:

"No."

"I knew it," said Lewi, and left the room.

Efraim is the one who, at the beginning of the *Lebenslauf*, uses the image of Sven and Lewi as two planets.

He imagined them approaching each other in a gigantic circular movement. Being drawn to one another. Being sucked toward one another, until at last they were united in one enormous and sensual planetary embrace, the chaste and yet erotically pulsating galactic intercourse of the Pentecostal movement.

But perhaps the image was incorrect. Perhaps their paths merely crossed. Perhaps they only lay very close to each other for a couple of decades, like two strange prehistoric beasts let loose in space who rubbed up against each other in love and hostility up there in icy space, which had once filled my own childhood with the song from the telephone wires attached to the distant stars. And then they drifted apart, although the pelts of the prehistoric beasts brushed against each other, picking up dust and straw and thoughts and ideologies.

Not a pretty picture. But it must have been something like that. Lewi's policy speech—and this, too, undeniably contained many watchwords. He just didn't have a Fredrik Böök to analyze them. And if Sven Lidman recognized the words, he never mentioned it.

The prehistoric beasts brushed up against each other, which resulted in a number of ideas. They exchanged places, including several watchwords. Or else they merely spoke and thought, these twins of God as Efraim loved to call them, they spoke and thought as the times required.

The times required. And finally it was time. Did they trade roles with each other?

Perhaps Sven had grown tired of sanctity.

Gradually the memory of his youthful sins may have dimmed; they were no longer as enticing or as terrible, praise God. He had loved the radical deviation, from the greatest sin to the greatest sanctity, but he was also a restless man. Lewi was not restless. Lewi might fall apart, but he was not restless. Sven was restless. He was, he once admitted, tired of his new role as the Poet Prince of the Pentecostal movement. He now knew all the catalogues of sin.

There was actually something comical about them.

Not to mention Lewi's increasingly fiery talk about obscene literature and the horror of dancing.

The peddler from Västergötland and his sins. Rather comical. Swedish modernism of the Pentecostal movement type, thought Sven, contained a basically comical and not up-to-date peddler from Västergötland syndrome. It didn't work. Sweden was a new society, after all. Lewi was both a forerunner and outmoded reactionary in this society. Family politics and birth control and functionalism and Pentecostal buns and a ban on going to the movies. But Sweden was no longer an impoverished country in the third world where fifteen people lived in one room and the promiscuity was shocking. If sin existed, and it did, it was of a new type. Sven was starting to think that Lewi was an anomaly. There was something generally irritating about Lewi. He was the master entrepreneur and organizational engineer of the new age, a man of modernity.

But he never seemed to have pulled his feet out of the mud of his childhood.

He was stuck. He didn't make sense. He was, in an almost perfect sense, the symbol of twentieth-century modernity in Sweden: a master engineer, but his soul was stuck in the mud of the nineteenth century.

The morals of the new age were not those of the nineteenth century. Sven had experienced the ecstasy of the Pentecostal movement's speaking in tongues as a liberation. But the Pentecostal buns! And the battle against jewelry!

Furthermore: the Lord was tarrying, and time was passing, and Sven's own children were grown up. The movement's children were grown up! And there were talented people in the Pentecostal movement. An extraordinary number of the young people became doctors or bank officials. The practice of faith healing and the laying on of hands and the idea that sin caused sickness were all troubling when the young people became doctors, which was in essence wonderful, praise God, but they did have their own opinions. And objected.

The children were shrewd educators.

Perhaps Sven and Lewi were starting to trade roles.

2.

No, Lewi never got mixed up in boozing. Instead, he fell into despondency, the nerve fever with which fate had finally struck him.

Fate had caught up with him; it was booze in the form of despondency. And then he had come out of it. He got to his feet and came out of it. Never again despondency. Never. Never. And with an almost furious resolve he now went on the attack against the arch-enemy: not only the social injustice he had learned to despise as a child, but above all the sin he had learned to hate. It was a battle. Once again he enjoyed the battle. He was fortified by the solid resistance which now, as in the past, met the Pentecostal movement. And now he loved the adversity, the persecution, the hatred.

And Lewi was, as mentioned, a different man.

So who was he?

One hundred and seventy years had passed since the day when the German man of the Enlightenment and—to use a modern expression—"cultural radical" Johann Friedrich Struensee, as his last deed before imprisonment, as a sort of final act of reform in a two-year Danish revolution, drew up the concession for the Moravian colony in Christiansfeld. There the Enlightenment and radical pietism found their almost symbolic shared memorial: God's acre. There the flat stones, with their inscriptions that became increasingly blurred over the years, grew in number. There, one day in 1982, the oompah-oompah band and I had buried Efraim.

There was something about this cultural radicalism that touched both Struensee and Lewi.

Lewi had now designated cultural radicalism as his arch-enemy.

No one within the Pentecostal movement was exactly sure what the term meant, or what it stood for. But they would learn, from sermons and books. "Entertaining movies, theater, and dances in schools are weapons that are part of the war plans of cultural radicalism against living Christianity." That's what was constantly repeated. But if so much of Lewi's own ideology, his political radicalism, had its roots in the Enlightenment, which was the prerequisite for cultural radicalism, how did this change in course occur?

Or was it a change in course?

Many hundreds of years of rain and snowstorms had worn down the inscriptions of God's acre in Christiansfeld, but in some sense they were inseparably associated with the Pentecostal movement's twentieth century, which was also Sweden's century. Perhaps that's why Efraim had chosen God's acre as his resting place, his grave affiliation.

Puritanism and cultural radicalism: they had started out as twins, they belonged together. The basic texts of the Enlightenment and radical pietism were at times the same. Even in their way of thinking. When Ludvig Holberg wrote the books that would become the canonical writings of the Nordic Enlightenment and cultural radicalism—*Moral Thoughts* and *Peder Paars* and his plays—then it was quite evident that he had read, and based his work on, Bunyan's *The Pilgrim's Progress*: the same ice-cold irony toward hypocrisy and double standards, the same kindly scorn, the same form.

Bunyan, Holberg, and Kant. And then they drifted apart.

Lewi had certainly never read about Struensee; no, that's not certain, since he did read an enormous amount. His education in history was particularly substantial. But there is no doubt that he knew nothing of what finally caused Struensee's downfall, meaning his admirable, almost poignant, political naïveté. He was much too idealistic and refused to execute his opponents, or exile them. He did not reinstitute censorship, even though this did him harm. And he also lacked interest in the power structure of the political arena: he did not understand how to choose his enemies.

He was able to see far ahead, but was incapable of seeing close up.

Lewi knew nothing of Struensee's blunders, or what made Struensee a good revolutionary, but an unsuccessful one who in the end was decapitated and dismembered on the wheel.

Yet it was as if Lewi were now drawing conclusions from Struensee's defeat. The sharp crease between his eyes, which Efraim noticed after Lewi's return—it truly did exist. Lewi had no intention of allowing himself to be destroyed, even less to be executed or dismembered on the wheel. God had said that He loved Lidman, as did Lewi. But God had also spoken in a tone of displeasure on that afternoon in the Philadelphia Church in Chicago, as if God wanted to say: "You should not yield to that upper-class dandy. It doesn't become you, Lewi. In truth, in truth, I say to you, you are no less than that dandy."

Lewi was almost convinced of this. There was something about God's tone of voice.

No, he no longer possessed Struensee's naïveté. Maybe he even liked power. Enemies existed, and they had to be dealt with. Some could be persuaded, others cast out. Even the Pentecostal movement was a power play. It wasn't enough to give talks. Power had a structure. Dissidents existed. Forbearance toward them was not acceptable.

The dissidents would kill the revival. The dissidents were careerists. The name of the dissident was Comrade By-ends. The battle against the dissidents was a game.

Possibly he even liked the game.

If Lewi had, in some sense, been a Struensee of the revivalist movement, he was now more and more like Struensee's adversary, Ove Guldberg: the pietist with the sharp fingers, unforgiving and possessed of a comprehensive feeling for the power structure of the political game. It was as if Struensee and Guldberg had merged in Lewi, dividing him up between the two of them.

And as if this symbiosis were the explanation for what some called the final victory of the revival, and what others called the inner death of the movement.

The battle was also exciting. If Lewi was once broken down by it, he was now galvanized.

God had galvanized him—that's what he thought. God was the galvanizer.

Lewi increasingly seemed to seek out and identify with revolutionaries and persecuted figures in history, as well as some who were contemporary. If anyone tried to create a complete and consistent ideological profile of Lewi, the task was now growing more difficult. It may have been imprudent of him to applaud Marshal Pétain. But he was measuring with his own particular gauge. He wrote furious editorials about apartheid and the oppression of blacks, especially in Africa, but also in his beloved America, and he found a symbolic figure to applaud: the bass singer Paul Robeson.

Robeson was certainly a communist. That was a problem, but not a big one. Lewi notes with concern that Robeson all too often interrupted his huge concerts to hold political speeches, but it was necessary to understand Robeson. His fight for the rights of blacks, his "declaring the equality of the colored race to the white," and the fact that this battle "had become for him a passion, or maybe a calling of conscience."

"Calling" was the word, the decisive word.

God had called the communist Robeson to preach for the equality of blacks, and Robeson was a revivalist. A descendant of the Pilgrim fathers, even though black, a black Wesley, perhaps. He was what the black race had been waiting for, "a capable leader." Robeson preaches "what was actually the view of the pilgrim fathers regarding the equality of all human beings, both before God and within human society."

Robeson is an evangelist. And he's right. "Rather, we should be surprised that the blacks, who so often feel humiliated because of their skin color, could be held down in this way until the present times." Lewi himself, during his countless travels through the missionary fields of the Pentecostal movement, had seen terrible things, especially in Africa. "In the interior of Africa you can see how whites treat the native population worse than their dogs." But, he writes, "Africa is swiftly awakening." The methods of imperialism are intolerable. "In its day black slavery was a small and rather innocent enterprise compared to all the slavery and oppression that large parts of humanity are subjected to today. In particular the spirit of ruthlessness, cruelty, and oppression that is spreading more and more among peoples and nations, which is a blatant threat to the very existence of the human race."

"Africa is swiftly awakening." There were few Swedes in the 1940s who saw this so clearly. On the other hand, it was only natural. The hundreds of preachers in the Pentecostal movement had used their eyes and ears, and had been doing so for decades. Why shouldn't Lewi see?

Paul Robeson was a communist, Lewi was not. It was something else that struck a chord. Robeson was, he repeats time and again, "an evangelist of the Puritan Pilgrim fathers' belief in the equal worth of all people." If this view is regrettably on the retreat "among the Anglo-Saxon nations," Lewi writes, they are faced with a problem that is represented by Paul Robeson.

Who is Lewi's man, aside from the communism.

Robeson was subjected to political persecution, abuse, and police brutality. But he did not yield. Lewi recognizes this persecution on his own skin. It is the same as Robeson experienced. The identification between the people of the Pentecostal movement and blacks is clear as a bell for him. Quite clear, encouragingly clear, cannot be avoided. "For years we too, here in this country, have been subjected to an intense persecution against the Pentecostal movement."

"Thomas à Kempis, John Bunyan, and I" he had once delightedly and almost childishly intoned. Now he added Paul Robeson. The children of the pilgrim fathers were few in number during the great, terrible transformation of the twentieth century.

But the children of the pilgrim fathers recognized each other in the face of adversity.

* * *

But was it truly adversity?

What was Lewi actually complaining about? From the outside it looked like a saga of amazing success. The finances were incomprehensibly strong; there seemed to be no limit to the willingness for self-sacrifice among the Pentecostals. In 1942 they bought Kaggeholm Castle and turned it into the Pentecostal movement's folk high school and spiritual center. The textile manufacturer Ottosson—who would play a decisive role in the finances of the movement and who either profited from it or was ruined by it, opinions varied—proposed in 1944 that 50,000 Pentecostals should each contribute 200 kronor toward sending out hundreds of new missionaries when the war was over.

And they did! It was unbelievable!

And they started the daily paper *Dagen* in 1945, the newspaper on which Lewi had set his heart and which gave him a national forum. They opened their own bank and bought real estate. The whole worldwide missionary work grew and grew, as well as the social welfare organizations under the protection of the Pentecostal movement. Especially alcohol treatment centers. Booze! Always booze! Those who got mixed up in boozing were Lewi's special responsibility! He would never abandon them!!! And later there would be a radio station, IBRA radio, which was the free voice on the air, which from Tangiers once and for all would break the Swedish monopoly of the airwaves. And the LP Foundation: alcohol again! And drug treatment centers.

And finally the movement became a political party. But that was much later. It was still the 1940s, and the Pentecostal movement's image of itself included adversity as a leading element.

Those who were scorned and hated joined forces and grew strong.

Because they joined forces in unity, against the enemy, meaning the adversity, it was even more important to expel the doubters and those who were skeptical. Congregational chastisement! At the height of the Franklin dispute Lewi had written a book entitled *Christian Congregational Chastisement*. The last four chapters had revealing titles: "Congregational Chastisement, But Not Expulsion"; "Expulsion"; "Expulsion Is Intended to Break the Member Who Has Sinned"; "Reasons for Expulsion."

As Kant and Lewi both would have said: It is the calling of every individual to think for himself. But the dissidents shall be spit out of the mouth of the congregation, and for this, specific rules must exist.

3.

Efraim himself, as a dissident, was expelled from the Pentecostal movement.

We are told very little about this. In the *Lebenslauf* there is a prelude to the final battle that includes an unnamed wife.

This is the first time that Efraim recounts an incident involving his wife. There is a conflict between them. Up to this point she has been strangely absent, she is mentioned only in passing, with kind words: "a marriage in marvelous grace and the love of Christ."

Never anything personal.

Efraim had come home and when he stepped through the door, his wife went into another room so as not to show him that she had been crying.

But he realized that something had happened.

"What is it?" he asked. "Are you crying? What is it?"

She then reacted with great emotion, which was surprising because she had a calm and quiet nature and was a devoted Pentecostal.

"What is it?!! I'm the one who should be asking that question! The brothers have been calling, full of alarm! What have you been doing? Efraim, what have you done!!!"

"Done?" he said, claiming not to understand a word of what she said, or any reason for her incomprehensible outburst.

"As if you didn't know! You have betrayed Brother Pethrus, and the brothers have had a serious talk with me and urgently asked me to try to sway you! So you won't have to be expelled as . . ."

She was now sobbing so hard that she couldn't go on.

He simply asked: "As? As what?"

"As a dissident!!! What if we're expelled, like Franklin? And his wife! What if we're expelled? How shameful! They say that you've voiced criticism to the deacons and cast aspersions and are taking Lidman's side, Lidman's side! And that you blame Lewi for the finances. Why are you getting involved!!! And that you said that Ottosson . . . what haven't you said?"

"Calm down," he said. "I've just been feeling uneasy."

"Uneasy! And what if Lidman has the Pomeranian disease, like they're saying, and has to be put in the hospital!"

"What's that?" he said with the utmost self-control. "The Pomeranian disease?"

"That he's insane! Actually insane!"

"So that's how they're planning to resolve things," he said, but didn't explain it to his wife.

Only after a few hours did she stop crying. He assured her that he loved Brother Pethrus, but that a conflict was brewing. It might be unavoidable, and it probably would develop.

If the Lord tarried.

No further explanations.

The incident is connected to what was to come.

In the *Härold* Sven had written an article about the political aspects of the Pentecostal movement, and that's when the conflict began brewing. Sven claimed that the Pentecostal movement repudiated party politics.

Lewi, on the other hand, was in favor of them.

At this time Lewi seemed to have changed sides regarding the issue of politics. Previously he was certainly of the opinion that it was the duty of the Pentecostal movement to become involved socially. But that didn't mean party politics. "A true, warmhearted Christian does not get involved in politics," he said in 1937. "Christianity is something infinitely higher than politics, and the true Christian must invest all his forces in spiritual work. Can history present any examples of someone who was, in my opinion, a warmhearted Christian and at the same time political? I don't know, but it doesn't seem likely."

Later he would consider these remarks foolish. Undoubtedly the most foolish thing he had ever said.

Lewi had changed. It was the same thing with the dispute about the daily newspaper *Dagen*. "Lidman thought it was a matter of going out to the gutters and the streets." Lewi countered that the Lord had commanded them to do just that. It was there, on the streets and in the gutters, that the people were to be found.

And now it was a question of party politics.

The Pentecostal movement was now being pulled in many directions. Especially by the Social Democrats. The brotherhoods were pulling particularly hard; Lewi had many friends there. But the Liberal Party was also a possibility. At one point he happened to be negotiating with party leader C. G. Ekman—"that was before his somersault," meaning his political fall due to taking bribes. Lewi had indicated that the Pentecostal movement, on certain conditions, might collaborate with the party. Preferably with an agreement.

"What would this agreement include?" asked Ekman.

"Every Liberal Party parliament member," replied Lewi, "who pledges to vote for a ban on Sunday entertainments can count on Pentecostal votes in the thousands."

"What would a ban on entertainments mean?" asked Ekman.

"It means a ban on theater performances and movies on Sundays, and of course a ban on dancing, but also . . ."

Ekman then, nearly losing all control, stood up and said that he had no wish for such a ban. He said that Pastor Pethrus might as well turn to his God and pray for a miracle, then maybe this ban on entertainments might be introduced in modern-day Sweden. But if so, a political miracle would be required. And he was absolutely convinced that the Liberal Party would not want to participate. Furthermore, it was his opinion that it would be better if Herr Pethrus formed his own party. Then he wouldn't need to enter into agreements of this nature. And he wished Herr Pethrus the best of luck.

Lewi stood up and, with a little smile, said:

"Thank you. I'll remember that you wished me well. It might be necessary to follow your excellent advice."

"I'm afraid in that case," Ekman then said, "it will be quite a small party."

"There will always be some party that is quite small," Lewi replied. "We'll see which one it will be."

Sven Lidman wrote an editorial in the *Härold*.

Everyone knew what Lewi was after. It was a political showdown in the fight against sin. And the instrument, the vehicle, the booster rocket would be a political party. Which one, no one knew; he would keep searching. But not the Liberal Party. And the Social Democrats were reluctant because the electorate liked soccer on Sundays. Later Lewi looked to the Conservatives, and even once had lunch with Tage

Erlander. In the old days Lewi had imprudently declared that he "always voted with the Social Democrats," which he later corrected to "the left"—whatever that meant, since he in any case regarded communism to be the Leviathan. The term "left" was vague. Gradually he had also been struck by an almost passionate hatred for the Liberal Party, which he regarded as a vipers' nest of cultural radicalism ("a Pentecostal can vote for any party except the Liberal Party"). But perhaps he included the Farmers' Party in the left. Who knows, who knows?

But it was all in vain.

Lewi's hundred thousand Pentecostal votes did not seem tempting, or it could be that his demands were too dangerous. The agreement was not sufficiently enticing: Campaigns against dance floors! A ban against movies! A ban against sports on Sunday! Was this really the modern and dynamic Sweden? Who could win control of the government with such election slogans? But that was where he started: by searching for a political party as a booster rocket in the battle against sin on Sundays.

He analyzed the political field and got started. He didn't wish to be decapitated and dismembered and put on the wheel in silence, like Struensee, his much too culturally radical Moravian predecessor. He wished to enter the political game, in the name of Jesus, and in the battle against sin.

He wanted Sweden to get out of sin, as if Sweden were an alcoholic.

But on September 21, 1944, Lidman wrote an article in the *Härold*.

And for the first time, it was a negative one. It was against Brother Lewi.

"But surely it can't be true that an individual was ever saved just so that clever electioneers can fill that person's pockets with election literature and ballots and newspapers or so that speakers can hound him toward voting locations and ballot boxes. The Pentecostal movement has been a true apostolic revival beyond, above, and outside of everything called politics and culture. May Jesus ceaselessly keep us in this position so that we, when we fulfill our voting obligations at the ballot box, never exchange our spiritual faith for a faith in any political program. Election speeches and election sermons, election promises and election disputes disappear and are forgotten as quickly as all the thousands of ballots are swept together and beyond and outside all the thousands of voting locations all over our country when the election itself is over. Yet God's solid foundation is permanent and has a seal with these words: The Lord recognizes His own, and whoever invokes the Lord's name will turn away from injustice."

It was a declaration of war. Sven knew it. So did Lewi. And Efraim.

A week later Lewi decided that Lidman's articles should be sent to him to read, before publication. Perhaps for proofreading.

Perhaps for inspection, and to put a stop to them.

That was also a declaration of war. And Sven, who had been yearning for a major battle for such a long time, and whose family history included so many soldiers, and who had dreamed of death on the battlefield and about war like a torrential rain, seemed ready to take up the fight.

He asked to have a talk with Efraim. He knew that Efraim was Lewi's man, but he also knew a different Efraim.

They took a walk through the woods.

A period had arrived in the history of the Pentecostal movement when certain conversations had to be carried out in the woods, or in places where they would not be observed.

Something had changed.

Efraim reported on the directive which stated that from now on all of Lidman's articles would be inspected by Lewi before going to press. But Sven already knew about that. That was why he had called.

"Censorship, in other words. And he knows I can't accept that. He wants me to quit in protest."

"I can't give you any advice," said Efraim. "I was born a simple, poor working-class boy, and you've lived your life among books and newspapers. But my view is that a person should never quit in protest. It'll be forgotten in a week. You should threaten to stay. That will scare them."

Sven was very quiet and pensive. But then it came.

Everything in Sven and Lewi's relationship had become so personal, he said. It had become so personal, and touched their families. There was a rumor that Sven had allowed his children to dance at home. It had been done in all modesty. But it was counter to the fight against the abomination of dance floors. And he couldn't explain how it had gotten out. The dancing in the Lidman home had become an evil story in Pentecostal circles.

And then there was the matter of infant baptism.

He recounted the conflict between Lewi and Ulla, Sven's daughter. She gave birth to a child and then had the child baptized. She had allowed infant baptism. Lewi was outraged. It was against their ideology, and Sven was a prominent figure, after all. If the prominent figures didn't keep to the ideology and beliefs and guiding principles, then who would? But Ulla's husband was a minister in the state church.

And now there was animosity between the families, although Lydia was still friendly.

"Stay," Efraim finally repeated.

"But it all depends," Sven added thoughtfully. "If a person doesn't stay, it all depends on how he leaves."

"Are you longing to leave?" asked Efraim.

"Sometimes."

"Yes, you can always write books and live your life. And you'll be applauded by our enemies."

"Should I keep quiet, then?" Sven asked calmly. "Keep quiet and watch the empire grow and die its own inner death?"

That was the occasion when Sven used the phrase "inner death." He didn't explain what he meant, but Efraim remembered the expression. And later, when he read Sven's descriptions of his youth, and the story about Margot, he understood more.

"Yes, I think so," said Efraim. "I think you should stay, because in spite of everything the movement needs you. You know what I think about your political views. And you know that I love and admire Lewi. And I don't love or admire you, Sven. Not in the same way. I'm just telling you how things are. But without you, Lewi would be only half. And there's something about you that we need. So you should stay."

"You're asking a lot," Sven said. "But if I leave, it won't be by the back door. It will be by the grand staircase."

"I wouldn't expect anything else of you," replied Efraim.

Why did Efraim agree to the walk in the woods? Within the movement people had already labeled Efraim as a dissident.

Although they didn't use that term.

Efraim later noted that whenever he sat down on one of the chairs reserved for congregation elders and deacons up front on the platform, and if he arrived early and was the first to sit down, no one would sit next to him.

This was something he noted. At first he refused to see it. Later he saw it.

4.

It was a stormy board meeting at Filadelfia.

Lidman was indignant. He stated that if Pethrus refused to approve an article, he would go to the board. If he found no support there, he would go to the elders. If the brothers did not approve his views, he would ask the congregation for a vote of confidence. If there too he was voted down, he would leave the *Härold*.

"Go ahead," said Lewi. "That seems to be the appropriate procedure, which God has earmarked for you."

But the threat hung in the air. War was declared. After the meeting Sven said:

"Just imagine, Pethrus, if the newspapers reported that I had suddenly died after a stormy meeting of the board in the Filadelfia corporation."

Lewi gave him an ice-cold glare and replied:

"I'm sure you wouldn't die that easily."

And Lidman, suddenly smiling and as charming as he could be, especially when the chill was the strongest, then laughed and said in a friendly tone:

"Oh, it's too bad you have such a great mortgage on my heart that I can never help feeling fond of you!"

But Lewi now seemed to be immune to his charm. He merely said:

"You must have taken out a loan on that mortgage by now."

In this new atmosphere, these were the proper metaphors. Love, mortgage, loan.

Yet the *Härold* was now, to a certain extent, blocked from any attacks against Lewi. Lidman would have to choose other means if he wanted to attack.

It would have to be through his preaching.

* * *

When my mother, whose name was Maja, passed away I spent several weeks at the old folks' home in Bureå, cleaning up. Mail had piled up from the past month. In the mail there was an amazingly thick stack of money orders that she had not been able to send. They were voluntary contributions to various groups, from "Bibles in the East" to the "Israeli Mission."

Normally she would have sent them in. All the old ladies at the home did that. They had their secure pensions. I looked at the stack and then tore them all up. I don't know why I was so mad. I wasn't mad at her.

It was silly for me to be so mad. I assume those contributions were symbolic of the normal and almost daily sacrifices made by her and others of deep faith. They were also, in a way, the explanation for the enormous success of the Pentecostal movement, what some called "the Pentecostal movement's money machine."

It was the women in the sea of old ladies.

The problem arose because this successful movement was theocratic, after all, and not democratic. The two systems did not mesh. And all those increasingly influential gentlemen up on the platform behind Lewi were most likely not directly chosen by God. And thus exempt from an obligation to keep accounts.

A quiet, imploring, whining, and finally piercing shriek could be heard.

Lidman was now standing on the grand staircase, at the very top, preparing for his exodus.

And now he started talking.

The amazed and bewildered sisters and brothers at Rörstrandsgatan received ever more startling lectures that seemed to be about their beloved movement, hinting that everything was not as it ought to be. *"Alas, how easily, how quickly dust falls upon even the most vigorous spiritual movement! How easily it becomes petrified and its arteries harden into an autocratic bureaucracy when the bread of life becomes a livelihood. The movement was propelled by free men and killed by bureaucrats. Their wages became an end in itself, their ideals an advertising poster, and their philosophy of life a gramophone record. 'In 1898 founded Church Company,' I once read in a biographical reference work about someone in one of our neighboring countries. A famous Social Democrat recently told me: 'When I was young we fought over who would carry the union's banner at the May Day demonstration. Now they pay five kronor to anyone who will take the trouble!'"*

And that far the brothers and sisters, not yet alarmed, could follow. No one had yet been singled out, no one! And the part about the dust on the movement was the way Lidman usually spoke: images! images! and metaphors! But then the insinuations began pouring down harder. *"There are many poor unhappy people who never come to believe in Jesus, but instead come to believe in the preacher who preaches about Him."* Yes, that too was true, but what did it mean? What did it mean? Was there any truth in the steady rumors about a great, profound conflict between Lewi and Sven? *"Each time a revivalist wave gushes forth there are always people who think they can cash in and make good profits from the whole thing."* Certainly, certainly, but where was Lidman heading? These constant references to the Bible, but with a subtext which, as was becoming more and more evident, pointed in the same direction. *"But Peter and John said no, this is not a business enterprise, this is a revival from God!"* And that odd story about Simon the Sorcerer, who was actually just an economist and not part of the revival, yet he had taken a place up on the platform among the leading brothers. On the platform! There they sat! The congregation's elders and deacons and the leading brothers, who were now so intensely involved in the growing financial empire of the Pentecostal movement. *"And then Brother Simon might be allowed to stand up there on the platform and conjure with prayers and pious phrases. For he could only CONJURE with everything. He had, after all, no SPIRITUAL part in what was at issue here. And so it was easy to turn it all into conjuring tricks."* And then how would things turn out with this property manager, because he wasn't a textile manufacturer like Ottosson who would soon weave his inscrutable textile manufacturing business together with Filadelfia and take possession of *Dagen*. What was Lidman getting at? *"The representative of gold, who will start to run his business in God's holy room—and open a real estate firm dealing in temple properties,"* and then even clearer: *"a real spiritual revival is not run from outside or from above the way a political party or an amusement park is run. In a spiritual revival the truths of faith are not used as discussion topics or as reassurance, the way promises are thrown around in an election to entice sympathizers or knock out competitors. Speakers are not called artistes, making use of new diversions and a variety of programs to perk up those who are lazy, satiated, asleep, or indifferent. A spiritual revival comes from within, and its true instruments and leaders are the thousands of unknown people who pray at*

prayer meetings and in prayer corners, who genuinely hunger for sanctity, jus-
tice, purity, and the Holy Spirit. "

And then those puzzling, or rather increasingly clear, images.
About the explorer in Africa who meets a native tribe and is especially impressed by the chieftain. So simple, handsome, and proud in
his simple royal robes! He tells a friend about it. Then his friend goes
to that country ten years later. Upon arriving he meets a clown–like
figure: It's the same king! But now he's wearing a tall hat, an old tail-
coat without a vest, and a pair of women's patent-leather, high-button
boots that he had been forced to cut up to make room for his toes. The
handsome king is wearing the insignia of European culture! however
misunderstood. And then the inference: But who was Sven talking
about? It couldn't be Lewi, could it? It couldn't be the transformation
of the original revivalist leader he was talking about, could it? Lord,
let that not be the case! But perhaps? What does Lidman mean? And
then he goes on, implacably: *"You must understand that precisely the same*
thing could happen to our revival. Persuasive and smart religious agents might
thrust upon us, nice innocent Pentecostals, suits and clothes that have nothing
at all to do with our true being or with the spirit that carries and animates our
revival. "

And then the characteristic conclusion, repeated three times, two
phrases juxtaposed with two other phrases:

Lack of love—power struggle
Brotherly love—hunger for truth

Sven was in the process of recounting a story.

It was not yet clear. It still existed in the subtext of Christ's love.
But he stubbornly kept on telling it, and soon it would become clear
and rise up to the surface. Efraim was now sure of that.

And soon everyone would know and understand.

5.

Was it Brother By-ends who was sitting on the platform behind Lewi,
next to Mr. Money-love?

In the *Lebenslauf* there is suddenly a bitter tone.

But, Efraim writes, he loved Brother Pethrus. He truly did. He
wanted people to believe him on this point. In fact, the cancerous

tumors he saw were not the fault of Brother Pethrus. They couldn't be. Yet he saw the way the businessmen, the brothers By-ends, were crowding around Lewi. The congregation looked the same as it always had, the lonely and despairing and those whom no one saw, but were now seen by Christ, those who hid in his wounds and in hope, and who made offerings and prayed.

But the sharks! Those bloodthirsty! entrepreneurs surrounding the Pentecostal business! Those leading colleagues around Lewi who were growing in number, all of them affluent, and directed more toward Mammon than toward Christ! Increasingly, gleefully focused on the money machine of the Pentecostal movement, increasingly ingratiating toward the leader, less and less spiritually alive.

The first holy men at Uppsalagatan 11 came to mind.

Where were they now? And even earlier: Where were the fallers? Where were those who went out to the stables to find peace to pray, those who went into the forest and knelt down next to rocks and pine trees? Where were they?

Oh yes, they were still there. But this seine-fishing . . . In the past they pulled in souls. Now they were pulling in the banknotes of the souls.

The revivalist meetings proceeded in such a fashion that the preacher sought to provoke a consciousness of sin in his listeners.

There were songs and prayers and songs and prayers and talking and shouting and silence. But when the actual meeting was over, then the so-called post-meeting began. This was the so-called seine-fishing. They pulled the fish, meaning the souls, to land. And first the preacher and seine fisherman asked the people if they were saved, and then they began shouting, often loudly, and it wasn't the same as with the fallers, but in some ways it was similar. They often shouted no. No! And then it was a matter of persuading the sinners that the hour was at hand. And then they walked among the pews and, if it had been especially powerful, then the people felt the misery of sin. Then it had been very powerful.

It was right now that mattered. Tomorrow might be too late. Jesus was coming. Those who were not yet saved would be lost. For all eternity. And that would be terrible. They would go to hell and to the eternal cries of distress and torment. And eternity is very long. Sometimes the preacher would tell the terrible story about the mountain in the sea, ten kilometers long and ten kilometers wide and ten kilometers tall, and made of the hardest rock. And every thousand years a bird comes and rubs its beak against the mountain. And when the entire mountain is worn down, then only one second of eternity will have passed.

That's how long the torment would last; it was like being lowered into boiling oil, or like going to the dentist—just imagine! And after death there is no time for salvation. You are lost forever. The moment for salvation is now. And then the cries of distress might rise out of the mouths of those who were saved, and then the moment of salvation might come.

But there was nothing strange about this. It was the way things had always been. The sermon was powerful, but sin took a fierce grip on the sinner, as if you were going down into a sinkhole. And the quagmire was sucking you down. It required a powerful sermon. Efraim had seen and heard a good deal, and in its way it was all necessary. But since they had started the daily newspaper *Dagen*, there had been such a need for extra contributions for the paper. A million kronor after another to cover the losses. But since Ottosson owned the Godvil corporation, which owned *Dagen*, and at the same time he owned textile factories, they never knew for sure where the offerings were going.

They had to rely on the brothers.

But Efraim was growing more and more gloomy. He obviously asked himself where the money was going. And of course he knew. To the mission. And the fight for salvation.

And yet. Efraim had his own political views. And for him that's when the grumbling began. Because it was still quite strange that these poor Pentecostals, who were basically working-class sisters and brothers, should take up collections for this newspaper that was fighting against the labor movement party. There was no better way for him to express it.

And at these post-meetings the preachers had increasingly become activists for *Dagen*. It was odd. At first the agents spoke a great deal about sin and torments and the mountain in the sea and eternity. But later they drew the down-and-out and despairing wretches into the prayer room and saved them and then hauled out a paper which the poor sinner had to sign that committed him to give 200 kronor to *Dagen*. It had become almost systematic. And then there were offerings, and extra offerings, and special offerings, and whatever else they might be called.

They had different names, but they were all offerings.

And sometimes the brothers would travel around the country and seek out the members who were the most affluent. Sometimes they would look up obituaries, and then the widow might be so grief-stricken that she would purchase extra insurance, in the form of an offering. In a sense the deceased would make an offering so as not to stay in the boiling oil of Gehenna.

Efraim knew that these kinds of things went on.

But sometimes it was necessary to question what was said because it sounded like pure slander. It was said that those who collected money were given a commission, even though this was always denied vigorously. And for his part, Efraim was glad that it was denied, because this idea of a commission was a stock phrase that was spreading, but it might also be coming from what Pethrus called the direction of cultural radicalism and be pure slander. And Efraim was glad to have this clear confirmation that it was not true.

Because Lewi never actually lied. He might withhold the truth. And often he didn't know the truth. But he never lied.

Lewi never lied.

Yet the worst thing of all was the politicization.

In 1944 Efraim became infuriated. That's when the reversal occurred. That's when he joined the Brotherhood movement, which was the Swedish Social Democratic organization of Christians and Believers. Efraim was, of course, a Pentecostal. But should the funds of poor people, intended for the mission and revival of the spiritually mute, now be used against the labor movement? He could see what the leadership was thinking.

The blackcoats around Lewi were like a wall.

It was clear what they were like. And a Nazi cell had even existed during the war. This was something he knew. How the sharks had gathered around Lewi! Whom he loved! Yet Lewi was still talking about campaigns against the movement, and prohibitions! and persecution! and there were plenty of examples! such as when they weren't allowed to put up the revival tent at Ladugård field! because of the others who took walks around there! You had to understand Lewi!

But the sharks! those bourgeois men! And yet.

How could Lewi, whom Efraim no longer fully understood, how

could Lewi allow them to acquire such power? And silently watch as the supplicants' coins went to the political battle. No, Efraim joined the Brotherhood movement.

It was a form of protest. It was 1944.

That was the year in which Lewi wrote that "it would be irresponsible, not to mention criminal, if we failed to do what we could to get those who represent our views placed in the legislative bodies of the nation."

They started with Brother Per Jacobsson, an elder, in the general election. He made use of congregation funds, Efraim writes, "in a completely reckless fashion." He used congregation offices, and membership records, which were otherwise secret, as well as staff and money.

The handwriting in the *Lebenslauf* is now indignant.

The *Lebenslauf* depicts an event at the beginning of 1944, but Efraim writes his account much later.

It's true. He knows the results. He anticipates long-term goals that may not have existed in 1944. Although they did come to pass. The Pentecostal movement was going to enter politics. This meant thinking in the long term. Or else there would be religious persecution of the movement.

Lewi was thinking in the long term.

First they would try to place their candidates on the list of some party. Then they would start a daily newspaper, *Dagen*, which would pursue political issues and prepare the electorate. Next they would start a radio station to break the state monopoly. Then create a political cooperative organization for the political ambitions of the free churches, called KSA, which in Swedish stood for Christian Community Responsibility. Next create a party, which would be named the Christian Democratic Party.

But it was in 1944 that the reversal occurred.

6.

Lewi had a dream of purity.

In this sense he was an organic part of the Swedish modernism of the twentieth century, even though it might be difficult to see this. He sat in his functionalist castle on Rörstrandsgatan and was part of this modernism, this dream of purity which manifested itself in various ways within architecture and art and film and literature, and he was practically the only one who spoke of the purity of the mind and morals.

It didn't fit in with the overall picture, not in any obvious way. The cultural radicals hated him. He was no Georg Brandes, no Poul Henningsen, absolutely not Elise Ottesen-Jensen. He was the other side of the modernistic coin, ostensibly the foremost enemy of modernism, and yet part of it.

Without Lewi's dream of purity it was impossible to understand modernism in its Swedish form. The question was whether it was possible to understand the twentieth century in Sweden without including Lewi's moralistic modernism, which was the battle against sin and for purity. If modernism was seeking liberation from history, dreaming of the pure and unsullied, Lewi was dreaming of this same purity, but liberated from what was modern. What was modern was the sullied agrarian society, contaminated by jazz, theater, and dance. What was modern was sports, car trips, dancing, sexuality, popular music, and the city! the city! It was machines and greased pistons that led the mind to fornication, it was everything that covered up the memory of Hunneberg and the forest below the precipice where he as a child had contemplated the world. Lewi's modernism was perfect purity, the chaste mind in the chaste body of a modern building, and yet somehow placed in a chaste, unsullied nature.

Enlightenment placed in the Swedish primordial forest.

Was there something that had frightened him? Perhaps himself? Or the women in the congregation, with their tremendous emotionalism, the reminder of the vipers' nest of passion beneath the functionalistically pure and unsullied covering?

Or was it Chicago? Maybe what was modern also included those six months in Chicago, the booze and the whores in the Promised Land, that time when he fled from the City and out into the Country to heal his feeling of being broken down.

Maybe Chicago was what was modern. And he had been seized by terror and anger. Now he took up the fight against what was modern, as part of modernism's dream of purity.

* * *

He now had a forum, a newspaper, *Dagen*.

Right up until his death, Lewi made use of this forum. He wrote between thirty and fifty editorials every year. No Swedish religious leader has ever, to the same extent, devoted his life to the political debate. He became a journalist, like his admired mentor Tingsten, or like his admired opponent Moberg, whose books he hated and fought, but whose journalistic efforts he much admired during the battle over corrupt legal practices.

Corruption! That was the word.

The list on that topic seems endless. His calling was to conquer consciences. That was the new empire-building. Before his journey to the Forest of Despair, Lewi had wanted to build a revivalist empire that was physical: meeting houses, congregations, missionary work; in the end a world congregation of 250 million faithful Pentecostals.

Now his dreams of an empire were different. He took up the fight for purity. That was where Lidman failed to understand him. Lidman was an anarchist and not a builder of associations. Lidman was a dreamer who was not afraid of the vipers' nest beneath the purity of modernism. Lidman talked as if they were still at Uppsalagatan 11. Lidman talked as if history had not moved on. Lidman was still in the prologue of the Pentecostal movement's great story; he was still tarrying! still tarrying! but he had not seen evil or sin or what was modern. Sven Lidman, who had been the greatest evangelist of sin! who told such terrible stories! who enchanted so many with confessions of his own wretchedness! his accounts of sin! Sven, who now failed to understand that they had to carry the fight against sin further using political means. The Devil wasn't going to be allowed to have a monopoly on the best melodies, as Lewi had once said, paraphrasing William Booth, and that's why the Pentecostal movement had to become a singing movement. Now the Devil wasn't going to have a monopoly on the political instruments.

Sven and Lewi had traded roles.

How can a mind be explained? The same is true of a mind as of love. They're both impossible to explain. But where would we be if we didn't try?

7.

The last time I visited Christiansfeld and God's acre it was a clear and mild January day. No snow, and the center aisle through God's acre was muddy.

I stood at Efraim's gravestone for a while, thinking about how his mind had not changed very much during his lifetime. He had stood firm, and watched everything else change. It's also possible to do that. To stand firm. And then I suddenly looked at the stone next to his; it had a German inscription. The birthplace was Halle.

There was a kind of logic to this. Halle, in the early eighteenth century, that remarkable university that was the center of the Enlightenment and radical pietism at the same time. Halle, where Struensee's father was a theologian, and where the Moravians and men of the Enlightenment were crowded together.

Sometimes crowded into one individual.

Yes, there was a kind of logic to it. Efraim was resting next to a messenger from Europe's strangely ambivalent, vague, and fantastic spiritual midpoint: that point existed everywhere in the obscure mind of Europe toward the end of the eighteenth century. The Rationalists and magnetists, the men of the Enlightenment and the occultists, and the Free Masons! the visionaries! revolutionaries! They seemed to merge with each other and stimulate and combat one another, to die off and flourish, ultimately on Azusa Street and at Uppsalagatan 11, and in the functional palace on Rörstrandsgatan.

Yet turning toward each other with obscure, terrible points of contact.

Efraim from the realm of fallers. And this unknown person from Halle. Perhaps they spoke to each other down there. And attempted to figure out what was not crystal clear. Nothing in the European mind was crystal clear. No doubt that was what made it so formidably alive.

Lewi began a campaign for the conquest of morality.

In some sense his point of departure was that of the solipsist. If you close your eyes, the world ceases to exist; if you open your eyes again, it's there. If you shut your eyes to sin, it doesn't exist. Sin would be closed off. Sin would be starved. Most of what he wrote about sin had this as a subtext. It didn't mesh very well with Lewi's other side. For example, he might carry on a campaign in the newspaper to collect funds for pianos to be given to juvenile prisons ("for the youths who have landed on the dark side of life. Their heavy lot is often caused by the unhappy circumstances of their homes and environment. It is a statistical fact that most of them come from homes that have been torn apart and destroyed by divorce or other unfortunate circumstances"). It's not known how he thought these pianos would be used, but the children of alcoholics in the tattered proletariat, those who came from morally broken homes (and shouldn't it be the parents who were punished? he thought, and not the children?)—the children who were homeless criminals, in other words, and that was how he often viewed criminals—perhaps they would pay attention to the distant and then ever-approaching melodies that were the songs of the Pentecostal movement.

To the promises, to "The Promises"! as if to the tones of the heavenly harps, and thereby achieve grace.

He had once dreamed of writing the great proletarian novel; now it was with particular interest that he wrote about the degradation of artists. The battle against obscene literature! Which he defined broadly. In general, it included everything that was not edifying literature— although he himself read everything, almost manically, everything! The battle against obscene literature became a focal point. Together with the battle against theater, film, and dance, particularly dance instruction in the schools, or rather the threat that this might be instituted.

His fight against Vilhelm Moberg's novel *The Emigrants* was carried out with vigor and fury. Lewi had personal reasons for this, after all. The portrait that Moberg presented of the emigrants did not mesh with the one his mother had once given him when she wept over those fine letters from America. This book, *The Emigrants*, "and its disgusting contents"! In article after article Lewi laments this "dreadful example of how deep our Swedish nation has sunk in terms of morals, when authors can write and sell something so base and vulgar. But Moberg is not alone in taking the ideas for his books from the cesspools of society. A large part of the substance of modern literature is taken from the same source. Moberg is not solely responsible for his manner of writing. The society that demands and tolerates such literature is equally responsible, to the highest degree."

Moral decay had to be countered with prohibitions, but he sees dangers everywhere. From his beloved America come reports that even the revivalist movement has begun using theater performances and movies in its work.

Where was it all heading?

Every week new headlines and it seems as if, in the battle for the restoration of the Christian nuclear family, he was now carrying on a war against all enticements, except for the merging with Christ's love. The Christian should close his eyes. Shut things out. Lewi's articles became in a way an impressive and enduring catalogue of political topics. Youth in need. Juvenile criminality. Dance floor abomination! Christianity's vulnerable situation on the radio! The Pentecostal movement had been allotted only five stations in twenty-five years! The dictatorship of monopoly! The terror of cultural radicalism!

The list was a long one. Moral decay! The sanctity of marriage! Homosexuality! The tabloid press! Church and state! Israel! He applauds the creation of the state of Israel, because the prophets in the Bible clearly asserted that Israel should be restored to Palestine as a first condition for the Jews to acknowledge the Messiah, who, in Lewi's opinion, was Jesus Christ. And so on.

Occasionally old topics crop up, such as the question of a church association. Or new ones, much later: Bishop Helander! Or the profanation of the Lucia celebration!

And perhaps Lewi imagined this as the battle at Mal-Ola's grotto: the way in which he single-handedly was carrying out the fight against the upward-climbing cultural radicals, armed only with a wooden cudgel; the way he shoved them down into the abyss, one by one, using his cudgel. Lewi all alone, in the service of God.

8.

Lewi had built an enormous cathedral on Rörstrandsgatan. Now he had found a media cathedral, and he wrote with joy and desire, and with a fury that even Sven found both astonishing and frightening.

Lewi had his particular points of departure, and he was no friend of compromise. But Efraim noted that Lewi, "whom he loved"—once again he repeats this like a mantra—that Lewi, in his fight against moral decay and dissolution and the tabloid press and degenerate art (no, that wasn't the term he used, but what's the difference?) had attracted friends that he actually might not have cared for.

"A number of brown lice became attached to the flypaper," as

Efraim writes in the *Lebenslauf.* And that was a problem, although an almost invisible one.

But there was another problem for Efraim personally. It was the fact that he couldn't remain silent. He couldn't express things as subtly as Sven Lidman, he didn't couch his criticism in metaphors as Lidman did, he was not a speaker as Lidman was. But he had started to raise his voice at the elders' meetings, and among the deacons. And finally he realized that there was a reason why sometimes, and more and more often, he found himself sitting alone on the platform.

Lewi had asked Efraim to come over for a private, spiritual talk.

It was at Rörstrandsgatan. Lewi had sounded depressed on the phone, and when they met, Efraim suddenly noticed that Lewi had aged.

He was pale and seemed to have lost weight.

It was hard to know why he suddenly looked so fragile, but that was often the case with Lewi. If you sat directly across from him, he appeared tired. He was a good listener and smiled often, his little, childishly warm smile—that keeps recurring: "his childishly warm smile." In photographs he never seems childish or warm but instead solid and unflinching, with his little mustache and now thinning hair; he gives an impression of wholeness that is the epitome of the restrained, strong, and efficient bureaucrat. Yet in private he seemed good-natured and considerate, and almost childishly gentle.

Now he looked worried and pale. He was sixty-three years old, after all. He had a hard time getting to the point.

Finally he looked Efraim in the eye and said:

"Efraim. My friend. There's one thing I have to know. I want to know whose side you're on. On the side of God and the Pentecostal movement, or on the side of the dissidents? And by all means tell me what it is that you hold against me. You have to tell me the truth."

"You know what the truth is," replied Efraim. "I've merely requested that everything should be accounted for, openly and democratically. And not just recited from the pulpit. Who could understand without actually looking at the figures? That's all. There's no oversight. That's not how things should be done with an annual report. Where are the offerings going?"

"You don't trust me," said Lewi.

"I don't trust them," replied Efraim. "All those elders who have no understanding of finances and yet run the business. All the ass-lickers. This is an ass-licking dictatorship, and you're in the middle, but you refuse to do anything about it."

"I don't care for your tone of voice," said Lewi.

"I don't care for what I see."

That was how the conversation started. Lewi became furious. He said that he understood. It was Efraim's friends within the Brotherhood movement who wanted to break away. Efraim and C. G. Hjelm were in cahoots with Erlander. That was well known. It was a matter of politicization. And they were using poor Lidman as an instrument. Lidman, who was simply the way he was.

The tone grew increasingly rancorous.

"Pethrus Lewi Johansson," said Efraim, "let me tell you something. I have always believed in you. I have loved you. And I have been afraid of you. That's all true. But those days are over. I'm going to tell you point blank: I don't give a damn about your admonishments."

"So it's war?"

"A pawn can't declare war against a king. You're the king, Lewi. I'm nothing. You're going to end up kicking me out, and no one will even notice. But it's a different story with Lidman. And you know that."

"I'm not afraid," said Lewi.

"Oh yes, my beloved Brother Pethrus. You *are* afraid. It's the only thing in life that you're afraid of. You're going to end up destroying him, that's what I believe. But then you'll be cutting off part of yourself. And part of the revival."

They sat in silence for a long time. At last Efraim said:

"And that, my oldest friend, is something that frightens you, and you know it, and that's why you don't say anything."

There is another version of this conversation. In that version it was concluded out in the hallway, with a fierce exchange of words, and it's at the end of this exchange that Efraim grabs hold of Lewi Pethrus's lapels and shouts:

"I don't give a damn about you! I don't give a damn about you!"

And Lewi, who is much shorter than Efraim, says:

"Are you planning on hitting me?"

But Efraim wasn't planning on hitting him. And the brothers intervened. It would take some time before Efraim was expelled. It was not as he thought: that the pawns would be sacrificed first and after that would come the more important men. No, they were saving Efraim for later. It was as if the Pentecostal movement had brushed off the dust from its lapels and straightened its tie and wanted nothing to do with administering a Christian box on the ears. In fact, it was as if everything had returned to normal, although nothing was normal, nothing, and Efraim the pawn was not expelled until two years later.

And then everything was done according to the rules. It's still possible to read paragraph sixteen, in which the congregation unanimously resolves to dismiss Brother Efraim, with the support of Titus 3:10-11, which reads: *"As for a man who is factious, after admonishing him once or twice, have nothing more to do with him, knowing that such a person is perverted and sinful; he is self-condemned."*

But that was later. There isn't much about this later event in the *Lebenslauf*, which is strange, since it was the great catastrophe of Efraim's life. In the *Lebenslauf* there's no more than a note about the paragraph, and a summary of the brief speech that Efraim gave in his defense before the group of brothers who were elders.

He writes that this is what he said in his own defense:

"My sins are as follows: I know too much. I have requested financial oversight in the movement, meaning democracy. On the other hand, I have not slept with women, as many other brothers have done. I'm not divorced, I'm a faithful husband, and I'm not married to a divorced woman. I have no broken engagements in my past. Nor does my wife. My wife wears the proper clothing of a Pentecostal, with her hair properly pinned up, and she does not wear jewelry. I have not been found guilty of bookkeeping crimes or the illegal handling of client funds. On the other hand, I have served the Pentecostal movement since 1911. I am one of the first brothers, who all served the congregation in poverty and joy. I have not, like certain brothers, studied sin in Paris nightclubs. I have never tasted liquor. Never smoked. But I know too much. I now await the judgment of the congregation."

And after such a speech in his defense, there was only one possible outcome. But that was later. First came the final battle. And after that the conquered foot soldiers could be mowed down.

9.

It would become the story most heavily covered and observed in the press, and the most scandalous dispute in the spiritual history of Sweden. But I don't know . . . in the end there seemed to be only sadness.

I can't think of any other word for it. Sadness. It was the story of a popular movement that triumphed and did not break apart, surviving even this conflict. But it was mostly sadness that they all felt, and mostly sadness that I too feel. I don't know why.

It might have something to do with the congregation, with the believers, the devotees, those without hope who had found a way to love. It might have something to do with the love of those four thousand people who sat there in Filadelfia and anxiously hoped that the rumors would turn out to be false, that what was being said about Brother Sven and Brother Lewi was not true. And they would again be able to fall to their knees in harmony and then walk home through the streets of Stockholm, saying to each other that it had been a blessed evening.

And everything would be as it was before. When it was all so magnificent. Especially like the summers back home. Wasn't that, in reality, what Efraim wanted? Back when they used to gather in large groups, and people would come from other towns? Even if they had to walk for ten or twenty kilometers. And they would go out to the woods in small groups. Prayer groups. They would go out to the woods and pray. They knelt down next to rocks and stumps and prayed to God the Almighty. And the whole forest was filled with the murmur of prayers, and the Spirit fell upon them.

But somehow this had been lost, that was how Efraim saw it. Not for those who sat down there and listened. They had the same needs. But for those up on the platform. That was what Lidman had said.

And as far as Lidman was concerned, Efraim didn't care for him. He loved Lewi and actually detested Lidman. But as far as Lidman was concerned, perhaps he was right.

That was the awful part. That was what caused the sadness.

The last great sermon that Lidman gave before the conflict exploded had to do with the swine spirit.

That's what he called the commercialization of the Pentecostal

movement. The expression became famous. Efraim would never forget
that evening, perhaps because it was then that everything became obvious. There was no turning back, and he suddenly knew that he detested Lidman, and that Lidman was right.

And he finally realized that he loved Lewi. That was the most difficult thing of all.

They were all sitting on the platform: Sven, Lewi, and Efraim, who
was still an elder in the congregation. A few more years would pass
before his own expulsion would occur. They sat there and gazed out
over the crowd of several thousand, and then Lidman began his long
sermon about the movement and the swine.

> *"My dear friends,"* he began, *"this morning I was reading Mark, chapter
> five, you understand. You know it well, it's about how Jesus drove the unclean
> spirit out of a man in the city of Gadara. And the unclean spirits in this poor
> man were drawn away into a herd of two thousand swine, and the swine
> rushed into the sea and were drowned.*
>
> *"But then, you see, the whole city went out to meet Jesus, and when they
> caught sight of Him, they shouted that He should leave their neighborhood.*
>
> *"How odd, don't you think? What was it that happened, my friends? A
> madman was cured, wasn't he?"*

Lidman was asking a question. And he would answer it. They knew
that. But things weren't right, not the way they were before. There was
no mumbling of *"Yes, Lord Jesus, thank you, sweet Jesus, yes, Lord Jesus,"*
words that could swell and die away, like the waves of the sea, words
that were especially present when there was a sense that this was a
blessed evening, when the certainty about the Power and the
Benediction was practically overwhelming. No, right now there was a
tension in the air. Something was on the way, a story, but maybe not
one that would provide peace and warmth. No, a different kind of
story, no doubt a great one, but not soothing or happy. Perhaps a great
story was on the way that dealt with something terrifying. Oh, there
was such a feeling of anguish. What was it all about? Why was Lidman
tarrying? What would he come up with? Would it be about all of
them?

About the fact that they had been deceived?

About the fact that they had forgotten something when they built
this fantastic cathedral, or this fantastic Sweden? That something had

been lost? It felt as if a silent anguish were spreading. There was no redemptive bliss that was now going to be confirmed!!! Lidman was not going to confirm anything!!! He wanted to threaten them! Reproach! Correct!! Tell them that something had been lost. And the whole time Efraim sat there behind Lewi, off to the side, and he looked at Lewi and thought: What is he thinking? Is he afraid, or full of hate? Hatred was not allowed! What was Lewi thinking? This builder of the empire of faith, this peddler from Västergötland, this kind and decent man whom Efraim had known almost his entire life. And suddenly Efraim felt a fear that was somehow emanating from Lewi.

As if he had completely identified with Lewi, and was already preparing a shared statement in his behalf, shared! Because the two of them were one! Even though he had almost struck this man, his brother. But faced with this attack! Was it an attack? And then Lidman went on, relentlessly, relentlessly.

> "Because, you see, and this I can tell you with confidence, because it's the truth: Jesus saves, but the swine interests were opposed. You see, the fact is that the great, famous key industry of the city of Gadara was harmed by the actions of Jesus. It was the swine industry. And the loss of two thousand drowned swine carried more weight than the fact that a madman was cured and healed and saved and freed from his terrible suffering. The economy was more important.
>
> "That's obvious. Or is it?
>
> "Recently the newspapers have been using such nice compound terms. We read about the 'steel interests' in the United States, and the 'mining interests'—the 'shipyard interests—the 'wool interests.' And by this they simply mean the capitalist power that is behind an industry, and these interests exist behind the hundreds of thousands and millions of employees.
>
> "The steel interests. The mining interests. The shipyard interests.
>
> "And in the city of Gadara there was something called the 'swine interests.' Yes, you see, it's no wonder that the city of Gadara, with its councilmen and industry leaders and all manner of social bigwigs in the lead, should dash out and shout at Jesus: 'Go away—get out of here—you terrible creature, go as far away from here as possible!
>
> "My beloved friends, there's a great deal of talk these days about revival. But it's going to come about in the same terrible way as the revival that came to Gadara. And then it will come into conflict with the swine interests and the steel interests and the mining interests and the oil interests. Because when Jesus

comes, He will plunge His terrifying spiritual sword right into the heart of the
societal and human economic centers of interest. And that is a terribly painful
story. We understand so well these councilmen and men of industry who rush
out, saying: 'Dear Lord, go away! You've harmed our swine interests—the
trembling life-blood of our society: our swine interests!'

"Because our world today is more than ever intertwined, entangled,
ensnared, in the enormous network of economic interests. And our weakness is
that the swine interests can so easily gain a foothold among Christians. The
swine interests have not only been given free rein, but they have even, in certain respects, become essential. And then the swine interests shout at Jesus:
'Get out of here!'

"The swine interests could come up here on the platform, you see; there's
nothing to stop them. The sheep could sit in the congregation and be sheared,
while the swine interests sit up on the platform, leading the prayers, and shearing the sheep and cutting out coupons. Things go fine for a while. But when
the swine have sat on the platform for too long, leading the prayers, the sheep
start to get tired of being sheared. There's no wool left. And the revival grows
cold, as the saying goes."

It was very quiet.

Lewi stepped forward and thanked Brother Lidman for his blessed
words. Everyone kept their eyes fixed on Lewi, everyone. He was actually the one who had been singled out as the swine on the platform.
He was the one who was responsible, but he had merely expressed his
thanks. And then there were songs, though not "The Promises." And
prayers. And Lewi, as usual, asked those who had felt the mighty power
of the Spirit to come forward and speak with the congregation's pastors afterwards. A few came, but not many, not like they usually did,
but a few stood murmuring up in front below the platform, which
now all of a sudden seemed sullied. And as usual they received some
murmured prayer guidelines, and as before a hand was placed on their
heads.

But it was ice-cold in Filadelfia, and there was dead silence among
the thousands. Heaven and earth had not burned; the heights and the
mountains were iced over.

And everyone knew.

*   *   *

Afterwards Efraim ran into Lewi in the hallway to the prayer room.

Lewi seemed calm but very tired, as if it was only with the greatest exertion that he could remain on his feet. He stopped and asked Efraim:

"So what did you think?"

Efraim didn't say anything about what he had felt, or that a tremendous sadness had come over him. Or that he loved Lewi, that he so dearly wished he could have formulated a speech in his defense, and in defense of all those who were sitting down there in the congregation. Or that Lewi had the same view as Sven, that he too was a wild ass, but that the role of the wild ass was not his only role; he was also the driver. And that Jesus could not ride into Jerusalem on an unruly wild ass. Somebody had to be the tamer. And that Lewi was his friend, in fact the only one he had ever had in his whole life. But Efraim merely said, and this too was something he meant:

"It was all very true."

Lewi gave him a long look, and in a low voice replied:

"And then the cock crowed for the third time."

And then he left.

CHAPTER 23

The Traveling Companion

1.

HE WAS NOW SURROUNDED BY ICEBERGS. HIS ENEMIES WERE LIKE
the tips of icebergs, invisible, but the chill could be felt in the water.

And it was getting closer.

In his dreams his mother came to him, and her voice sounded
worried.

And she asked him: *Little Lewi, you're not getting arrogant, are you?*
You know that arrogance is the worst of all sins. You mustn't put on airs.

And he replied: I know my weakness, Mother.

What is your weakness, little Lewi?

He answered: My weakness is my greatest strength. Then she wanted him to explain. I know my weaknesses, he replied, and only the person who knows his weaknesses and surrenders to the knowledge that he
possesses them, and arranges his life so as to combat these weaknesses,
and establishes the Pentecostal movement's organization and growth so
that these weaknesses will not become a burden, only such a person can
be a good leader. I know my weaknesses, and that is my greatest strength.

But what in fact are your weaknesses, little Lewi? she asked.

It's a tendency toward arrogance, which I'm always fighting, he
replied. Arrogance and despair, and for me these two are connected.

Why despair? she asked.

I know that I'm just a little peddler from Västergötland, and I don't
have the learning that someone like Lidman has, and I haven't gone to
the schools where you can learn about the financial prerequisites for
running a large enterprise, which is what I'm actually running, dear
Mother, and with success, with success!

Lewi!!! his mother then admonished him in his dreams, shouting so loudly that he almost woke up. *I can hear in your voice that you're now starting to put on airs! Humility!*

And then he continued his confession. No, I don't have the great talents possessed by those preachers who are truly instilled with the Spirit, those who can bewitch the masses, like Lidman, and I actually shouldn't be the leader of such a large business. And when anyone contradicts me, I often fall into a rage, and I can never be a great poet like Birger Sjöberg, who got mixed up in boozing, and I know how easy it would be for me to end up in sin, and that's why I fight against this weakness. I know it's not the temptation itself that's the greatest sin, but giving in to it! Being weak and giving in! And that's why I'm constantly fighting against my weaknesses and my temptations. These are the weaknesses that I know so well.

That was how he answered her in his dreams.

But then his mother interrupted him and said: *But your talent! Little Lewi, your talent! Don't just dwell on your weaknesses but think about your talent. How should you use your talent?* And she suddenly seemed very gentle. *Lewi, I've seen your wanderings. Little Lewi, I've followed your journey without you knowing it, because heaven is set up so that each person has someone following him from up above.*

Are you an angel now? he asked.

She replied: *Little Lewi, do you think I would boast by calling myself an angel? Don't you know me?*

All right, Mother, he said, but then what are you?

I'm a traveling companion, she replied.

What is a traveling companion, Mother? he asked.

I'm here as a traveling companion, she said. *I'm here, and you know that I'm waiting for you. I am your solace and protector and your only benefactor.*

How can you be my only benefactor? he asked.

And she replied: *Little Lewi, in order to have strength in the long journey of life, a person must have a benefactor, someone who travels along, who accompanies him.*

Oh, Mother, are you the one I'm traveling with? he asked.

Yes, she replied, *haven't you realized that? A traveling companion is the one who has given you your talent—and taught you everything—and the one who accompanies you. I accompany you in times of distress, when I support you, and in the Forest of Despair. And I admonish you when success strikes you. I'm your traveling companion.*

Are you truly my traveling companion? he asked. I thought others were my traveling companion, but now I understand.

Yes, she said, *you know that I'm your traveling companion, always. Haven't you realized that? I'm your traveling companion, little Lewi!*

Yes, he whispered, and you taught me everything, everything, and I will try to use your talent! Because it's yours, yours alone. You have given me everything, everything. Everything that I think and believe I have received from you, do you know that?

Yes, I know that, and I'm your traveling companion! she went on. *That's why you keep going, and will continue to keep going! And now the conflict is coming, but I'm your traveling companion. You've known that all along, even though you weren't aware of it. I'm the one who is your traveling companion, and that's what I have always been, little Lewi. You surround yourself with so many people, but I'm your traveling companion, your traveling companion. And I always have been and always will be, in the eternity of eternity, for all time, for all time.*

When he woke up, the dream slowly sank away, like an image fading, though two words remained. Those words were: traveling companion.

And he knew this meant Kristina.

2.

A brief note in the *Lebenslauf* about the sadness.

Efraim was standing outside the entrance on Rörstrandsgatan, waiting for someone—he doesn't record who it was—when Lydia came out the door.

She was alone.

Efraim took a step toward her and began to speak.

"Lydia, allow me to say how . . ."

She stopped and looked at him. Suddenly she seemed on the verge of tears, but she shook her head vigorously and then swiftly moved past him, walking along the sidewalk toward St. Eriksplan without looking back.

Efraim had always liked her, and admired her. And this was painful.

The only remark he writes is: "People have often asked me what was the reason for Lidman's rebellion. It was obvious that he wasn't happy. But why now, when he had felt so happy before? The answer, when I study the documents in the case, is that Lidman was rebelling against something, and he may even have been right about also finding it within the Pentecostal movement."

Quite an odd conclusion. The incomprehensible part is in the last line, that he "may even" have found it "also" within the Pentecostal movement.

Where else? That's not apparent from the "documents."

But Efraim seems to do everything for his love of the movement, and for Lewi. That's why Lydia's silence was so painful.

It should be kept in mind that they were trying to describe something that was intangible; they had only language to assist them, and that's why they often despaired.

They were all trying to describe the most difficult of all things: the religious experience. And they had only their own words to turn to. No one actually knows what Lewi or Sven saw in the farthest hazy seas of stars—that which could not be sketched on paper, not on sandwich paper or any other kind of paper. And it was not like the clear constellations; it was something that was found only beyond the comprehensible, the rational, and what could be sketched. Some people feel small before the farthest constellations; others feel bigger. Some people shrink before the inconceivable; others experience excitement, magnification, almost ecstasy.

Sven once wrote that he could feel a thoroughly sexual excitement when he preached. Maybe he was one of those who felt bigger when facing what was least comprehensible. Others became smaller, and rather humble. Did not put on airs, as Kristina or my mother would have expressed it. Did not boast. And perhaps for Lidman the excitement diminished over the years. No one knows. Outwardly he retained his faith, whole and without compromise, until his death. What this meant, beyond his confessions, is not something that anyone knows.

Descriptions of the incomprehensible can become mute over time. And then the revival grows cold, as Sven expressed it, although he meant something else.

The language of the Pentecostal movement in terms of the miracles of faith was always impenetrable. The enormity of what was supposed to be described never came through properly in words. The

words were somehow too grand and were repeated too often.
Everything was enormous, and they assured one another; they were
convinced, unwavering, and assured, and in the end they fell mute. The
enormous gratitude for the enormous grace of God and Jesus, and the
enormous joy He allowed to flow through humankind, it was much
too enormous. They were constantly confirming the glorious.
Everything was glorious, and they were convinced, in some ways
before it even began, like an advance pledge, almost a command.
Occasionally it was reminiscent of a communist party congress that I
witnessed in the old German Democratic Republic. They were constantly "confirming" the "absolute resolve" or "definite certitude" that
they would "triumph." They confirmed and confirmed, and in the end
there was that little question: But how?

What was the substance? What did the words mean?

What possibilities did the religious language offer? Which words
should be used to describe what was so enormous? Other than silence,
one to one, before God. Was it even possible to describe the religious
experience of God? Or was it simply like a cat that goes to sleep and
dies next to your cheek? It could not be said in a more complicated
or simpler fashion, but surely that's not how it might be described?
Not a cat?

What was the enormity that was constantly confirmed by the men
up there on the old-man platform? Enormous in what way? The little
human being thirsting for grace—the one who sat down there among
the pews, down in the sea of old ladies, as they used to say, as opposed
to the old-man platform where the decision-making brothers sat—
that person began to ask: But how? And if my own mother were somehow to be found down there in the sea, like the drop that she was, even
though she was never a Pentecostal, wouldn't she too have asked,
imploring and perhaps despairing: But how?

Enormous grace, but how? Did she ever receive an answer?

Sven tried to answer this question, more tenaciously than most.

But perhaps the ecstasy was beginning to weaken, and the images
to fade. Enormous grace, enormous assurance, firm resolve about the
happiness in Christ, but how? And perhaps that stubborn "but how?
but how? but how?" became painful little trumpet blasts through the
rhetoric of salvation.

He talked about the swine interests, and he was right about this "also" existing within the Pentecostal movement, as Efraim oddly enough had expressed it. But the fact that he grew weary and then suddenly better and truer in his furious attack on the movement and the friend he had loved and served for decades, this too might have had something to do with the dearth of words for describing the religious experience. Hypocrisy was a mute word, after all, although impressive and therefore applauded, in contrast to the dearth of words.

Heaven and earth had once blazed for Sven, even though it was Lewi who had composed the song. But it was no longer burning in the Pentecostal movement. No one knew better than Lewi how important it was for it to burn, but it was Sven who formulated this insight.

It was also logical, since they were parts of the same body.

Salvation's dearth of words: what a terrible phrase. And what were they supposed to do about it?

Sven repeated to Brita what he had said to Efraim:

"There are so many outcasts hanging around in the cellars of the Pentecostal movement. But I have no intention of hanging around there. I intend to exit via the grand staircase. And Lewi knows that."

"What are we going to do?" she asked.

Then he looked at her with a little smile and said:

"That was nice of you to say 'we.' But you know that what I've done is unforgivable. I have questioned Lewi's power. And the telephone lines are buzzing all over the country. They've started saying that Lidman is crazy."

"But you've always been like that," she said. "How amusing that they've finally opened their eyes."

And he liked what she said so much that he laughed for a long time, and then murmured anxiously:

"The grand staircase. The grand staircase. But there has to be some pretext."

3.

And so he left the Pentecostal movement, and he did, in fact, exit via the grand staircase.

Afterwards none of the parties involved could actually remember what the pretext was that triggered the attack, and it didn't really matter. But open conflict was inevitable. An error was the cause of it all, a routine memorandum on January 8, 1948, stating that Lidman was going to retire from the *Härold* when he reached the age of sixty-five. A notice in the great auditor's report about Swedish spirituality, which was corrected by the board on the following day. But by then it was too late.

Lidman understood that they wanted to get rid of him. "They" meant the group surrounding Lewi. But an equally strong group surrounded Sven.

Error or not, it was like the shot fired in Sarajevo, as he expressed it.

It legitimized the grand staircase.

On January 23 he was ready.

Before the elders and the board of the Filadelfia congregation he read a statement in which he submitted his resignation as editor of the *Evangelii Härold*. This was obviously not of great importance. The *Härold* no longer played a decisive role in influencing public opinion; it was *Dagen* that was now important. But Lidman didn't want to write for *Dagen*: it had too much of the gutter about it. And his involvement at the *Härold* had declined. Editorially his contributions were insignificant, actually nonexistent.

But the motivation for his resignation! The motivation!

Before the dead-silent group of elders, he began with the pension threat. It became slightly technical, but everyone knew that something else was coming. And it did. "For years, both around the country and here in Stockholm, there has been talk of a 'tension' between Brother Pethrus and myself. This is absolutely true." Then he praised their years of harmony. "I collaborated in full concord, harmony, and confidence for almost twenty years with Brother Pethrus, until the time came when he, dazed by success, thought he was called to appear in the United States as the apostle of the Swedish Pentecostal movement on a worldwide level. At the same time he was also impressed and influenced by Hitler's *Mein Kampf*, which he regarded as the best presentation of how a real leader should be and act."

And then it came.

It was as if *Mein Kampf* was the signal, and the symbol of the rancor of the attack. What he now sketches is the picture of a "grotesque religious tragedy."

"After the winter peace in 1940, Pastor Pethrus's fear of a Russian attack on Sweden rose to monomaniacal proportions"—and this was the explanation for why he "fled" in 1941. But after his return, "I know that the years following this disastrous year were marked by a series of the most irresponsible and profane decisions and measures, insults, persecutions, and attacks on dissident Pentecostals and dear brothers and sisters in faith. Confused and contradictory measures, often driven by an uncontrolled desire for power and dominance, which finally culminated in the fateful episode with the newspaper *Dagen* and the destructive consequences it prompted, both within the preacher circles of the Pentecostal movement and with regard to the external position and reputation of the revival and our congregation." And he is grateful that when the newspaper was started he had already expressed his reservations. "The revival that casts itself into the daily yapping on the street runs the risk of landing in the gutter."

He then moves on to the financial leadership of Filadelfia, since the spiritual work during these years "became commercialized and industrialized." Here he mentions Lewi's flight to the United States ("at a cost of 13,500 kronor"), the fact that Lewi was allowed to buy back his property in Bredden even though there were other buyers, the fact that Kaggeholm Castle had been purchased and for that purpose funds were borrowed from the Rescue Mission accounts, the fact that the *Härold's* printing presses had been transferred to *Dagen*, and that a loan had been granted to an American Pentecostal publisher.

He closes with a metaphor. And it's as if the circle is now complete. What was once a metaphor for the power of the Spirit and the strength of salvation for Lewi at the beginning of the century—the metaphor of the mine horses in Wales that were well-treated by their saved tormentors, who became almost unrecognizable—was now replaced by a different account from the coal mines.

"It's said that in the old days the English coal miners would take along a caged canary down to their workplaces in the mines. Quite often poisonous gases would build up, and a man would suddenly fall over, dead or deathly ill, because he hadn't noticed that he was inhaling the odorless poisoned air.

"But the little bird would notice faster than the big strong man what was happening in the atmosphere around him. If the bird suddenly stopped singing or dropped to the bottom of the cage, the worker would know that something was happening that might endanger his life, and he would leave the place as quickly as possible.

"Maybe I'm a little songbird like this, who can sense that the atmosphere around him is gradually being poisoned, and now he is fleeing for his life—and to save his soul."

This last metaphor, in his farewell sermon to the leading brothers of Filadelfia, was beautiful, even though some noted that the mine's little bird was condemned to die as the workers fled, while Lidman, on the other hand, was fleeing and leaving behind the brothers and sisters in the poisoned atmosphere. The fable didn't quite hold up, but it was still true. Lidman did in fact view himself as the sensitive little bird, the one with the utmost sensibility.

In terms of the points at issue—from the use of the *Härold's* printing presses for *Dagen*, to the matter of the Bredden property, to the other financial insinuations—the future would no doubt show that there was very little substance behind them. Lidman had rightfully pointed out the movement's much too expansive commercialization, but his examples were meager, and that wasn't so strange: Sven had never been much of an economist.

His objective was a character assassination of the Pentecostal movement, with Lewi as an example of financial avarice. The aim may have been good, or even bad, but the target was poorly chosen. It was not Lewi personally who was an example of financial corruption. A few months before his death, Lewi stated, "I would regard it as shameful if I should die a rich man. I think it would be a disgrace to my position." And in this regard he succeeded. When his estate was settled, it showed a balance of 3,200 kronor.

But what turned out to be effective was the accusation about *Mein Kampf*, though it was impossible to verify, and it would prove to be a tenacious charge. Lewi also imprudently fanned the coals several times, rather awkwardly. It was always the battle against obscene literature that made him put his foot in his mouth—the last time on a TV show when, with remarkable political and media naïveté, he stated that surely there was nothing wrong with the Nazis' fight against obscene literature.

But it was the metaphor of the canaries in the poisoned mines that remained. And the image of Lewi as dictator.

The accusations crumbled, but the force of violence in the attack remained, like an ominously lingering echo, until in the end it was the only thing that many people would remember about the story of Lewi and Sven.

On January 28, 1948, Sven published the entire accusatory document in *Aftonbladet*.

He had exited via the grand staircase. No doubt he envisioned the staircase at Stora Tuna, or perhaps other grand staircases he had seen and walked down—perhaps the one to the Thiel palace in Djurgården. The palace also had a staircase. Whether to climb up or down it all depended on the story.

Now there was only one thing left. Slowly and with dignity, to leave the last palace from which Sven would depart.

He had decided it would be a soldier's departure.

What were they to do?

In haste, on the very next day after the article appeared in *Aftonbladet*, they gathered in Rörstrand Castle, which stood right next to the temple and is still there today, in the room with the beautiful ceiling decoration from the seventeenth century, with the blue and red gleaming stove, and the portrait of a young Lewi on the wall—a painted portrait, as opposed to the photographs of the elders in which Sven still held a distinguished central position.

It was the last elders' meeting in which Efraim participated. It's true that another year would pass before he was expelled, but this was his last meeting. In the *Lebenslauf* he gives a brief description of the meeting. The atmosphere was "tuned to a minor key." They agreed that Lidman had to be expelled, but they disagreed on how to do it. Lewi was gray-faced and hardly said a word. Several of the brothers discussed the risk of a schism occurring, with the Lidman phalanx taking the rest of the country along with it.

The Lidman phalanx was strong. Half the movement was bewitched by Lidman.

It was unclear how many would stand by Lewi. Special attention had to be given to the Örebro Mission. Lewi merely said yes, yes. After an hour he finally took the floor.

"It's obvious that I feel sad," he said. "I'm going to have to refute him on these charges. The idea that I kept *Mein Kampf* as a substitute Bible is pure nonsense. And the notion that the movement is not democratic. Also pure nonsense. Isn't it?"

He looked around. And a fierce murmur of agreement erupted. Efraim said nothing. The movement was theocratic, not democratic; he knew that, yet he said nothing.

"But this claim," Lewi went on, "that there is a general feeling of mistrust toward me. Tell me, my dear friends, is this true?"

And now fierce protests broke out.

The meeting lasted three hours. Afterwards Efraim went out to the kitchen, and by chance Lewi came in, all alone. At first he didn't see Efraim and so he was unprepared. Efraim noted that he was crying. When he became aware of Efraim, he quickly pulled himself together.

"You didn't say much today, Brother Efraim," said Lewi. "But then, you don't give a damn about me now, as you expressed it the last time we met."

"No," said Efraim. "I didn't mean it."

Lewi then poured a cup of coffee from the pot. It was cold, but Efraim knew that Lewi liked to drink cold coffee with a lot of sugar cubes, and he handed Lewi the sugar bowl.

Lewi took four lumps, with a little smile.

"Do you remember, Efraim, the pot we used to make coffee in on Uppsalagatan?" he said. "With the jute bags? Do you remember how that coffee tasted?"

"Awful," said Efraim. "It was quite frankly awful. Weak and awful."

"Yes," said Lewi, "those were glorious times."

Efraim merely nodded because he was unable to say a word. He writes that he couldn't reply because he suddenly felt so upset that all words deserted him, and his tongue refused to obey.

"There were so few of us," Lewi went on, "and we were so poor, and the coffee was so weak. And it was all so wonderful. But it's when the movement grows that problems arise."

"Yes, but why?" asked Efraim.

"I've met so many good Christians, Brother Efraim," said Lewi. "That has always been a great experience for me. Pure and simple. But isn't it true, Efraim, that deceit, hypocrisy, and duplicity, that infernal duplicity—I don't think it's ever encountered as much as in religious circles. Those brothers, called Mr. By-ends. You know, like in Bunyan."

"Are you thinking of Lidman?" Efraim asked, but then Lewi seemed indignant and protested.

"No, not at all. I'm not thinking of Lidman. He's just the way he is. No, I'm thinking of other people."

"And what did you ever do about it, Lewi?"

But Lewi had no answer.

"I'm thinking of speaking my mind at the congregation meeting on Monday," Efraim then said. "No matter what you say about how things used to be."

"Don't do it," said Lewi. "I'm telling you: don't do it."

"I'm going to. No matter what happens. Even if the worst happens, I'm planning to say what I think."

Lewi simply looked at him in silence, took a gulp of cold coffee, set the cup down, and then, almost pensively, said:

"Well, Efraim, my oldest and best friend, then we're going to have to say goodbye to each other because of this Lidman. But the worst part is . . . Do you know what the worst part is?"

"No," said Efraim. "What's the worst part?"

"The worst part is that I'm going to miss him terribly."

4.

By six o'clock the Filadelfia temple was already packed for the congregation meeting on February 2, 1948.

Everyone knew that it would be crowded and had arrived early. Those who came right on time had to settle for seats in the hall seating five hundred, where the doors stood open to the big hall. This was the decisive moment.

In a certain sense it was amazing: over four thousand brothers and sisters on a Monday evening. Lidman arrived at five minutes to seven. The long front row on the platform was empty; it consisted of sixty chairs that were reserved for the congregation elders. Lidman sat down in the middle, right behind the pulpit with the name JESUS shining on the front.

It was not phosphorescent.

At precisely seven o'clock the congregation elders and deacons came in and sat down. No one sat next to Lidman. During the fifteen minutes before the brothers came in and joined Lidman, without actually joining him, a sort of battle of songs had taken place.

A faction in the hall had taken up Lewi's song "The Promises," and more and more had chimed in. *Heaven and earth may burn /Heights and mountains vanish /But whoever believes will find / That the promises are forever;* but after the first verse, originating in the gallery, another faction took up Lidman's song "O Bliss, O Mystery," which begins *O bliss, O mystery, O Christ's crown of thorns, which more than worldly wisdom knows and every sin absolves.* The songs became intermingled. At first "The Promises" seemed to die out, but then the congregation interpreted "O Bliss" as a direct attack, as taking a stand against "The Promises."

The nature of the factional battle and taking of sides grew clearer: the "O Bliss" faction was in the minority, and people once again took up "The Promises," while "O Bliss" could be heard only faintly, and, as most people later would testify, it came mostly from a group in the middle gallery and possibly from the orchestra seats on the left, though "The Promises" was also strong there. It could be said that "The Promises," after the first few minutes of uncertainty when the songs had collided the hardest, had clearly taken over the entire orchestra section, though possibly with the exception of the back section on the left, as well as parts of the middle gallery.

In this manner many were able to confirm that "O Bliss" was defeated, almost crushed, by "The Promises."

Yet when Lidman entered, complete silence fell.

They began with routine messages, and then Lewi stood up. He took the eight steps to the pulpit with the word JESUS on it, which stood at the exact midpoint where the acoustical analyses from Paris had once said it should stand, before it was moved diagonally to the left where the acoustics were worse, but that was later, after Lewi was called home and gone and the temple was remodeled and the acoustics were ruined. He stepped up and began to speak.

He was completely calm and focused, and every single word was heard.

He spoke without a script, as usual, and suddenly everyone realized that this, surprisingly enough, was going to be Lewi's night. He spoke calmly, almost extemporaneously, and told them of the animosity that had been awakened toward the Pentecostal movement during the past few weeks all over the country.

People were even spitting in the collection boxes. *The pranksters have awoken,* he said, and now his voice grew more forceful. *Like an army of bats and vampires they have thrown themselves at us. People have called me a rat, people have called me a goat; that's what Lidman called me. People have said that I stole money from the poor. This is a sad meeting,* he said. *It's like a funeral. I loved Lidman, and I still do. It's tremendously painful for me to stand here and talk about him in this way. But if there were so much as a pinhead of sin in my life, I would have left this work long ago. They have looked for sins in my life, but found none,* and later he would eat these words too—Lewi who had not even a pinhead of sin! The pure one! The man cast in one piece! It was too much! And he tried to defend himself by saying that of course he had sinned, but this was not what he was accused of, but that was later, in the long-lasting, distressing repercussions of the great conflict.

Lidman has compared the Pentecostal movement to an industry, he went on, *but the movement has to be funded, and it's growing, and the mission requires money, the hundreds of missionaries, and Lidman himself wanted to be the head of the Filadelfia publishing company.* At that, Lidman stood up and shouted protests, but after a brief pause Lewi continued, refusing to be interrupted. In the middle gallery a few people, not many, ten at most, had started in on "O Bliss, O Mystery," but fell silent after a few, not many, perhaps fifteen, sang the *Leitmotif* to "The Promises," meaning the last verse, and this time too "The Promises" defeated, almost crushed "O Bliss, O Mystery." But after a few minutes of shouting and singing, silence once again set in, and Lewi could go on.

He did not have all of them in his hand—not the "O Bliss" faction—yet even those unruly ones loved him. He seemed so calm and sad. There was something about that small, familiar figure that they recognized, also in themselves.

Oh, if only he might triumph.

He concluded by saying that the debate had nothing to do with retirement. He himself was going to retire the following year, and at that time he promised to withdraw (he kept this promise, though with a slight delay of fifteen years). No, it was a matter of the attacks in the press. And that meant it had to be put to a vote of confidence.

Then Lewi left the pulpit. Afterwards everyone agreed that his demeanor had worked in his favor. Calm, sad, and clear. And a man from the Pethrus phalanx had stepped forward to support him, but loud voices could be heard shouting "Lidman! Lidman! We want to hear Lidman!" The Pethrus supporter then hesitated, stopping halfway there. "O Bliss" started up again, this time with many voices.

The "O Bliss" faction also seemed to have supporters in the orchestra section on the right, in the back—not many, but they hadn't been heard earlier.

And then Lidman walked up the steps to the pulpit with JESUS on the front.

Lewi and Sven passed each other, though without a glance.

And then it was dead quiet.

Perhaps it was the fact that Sven was not holding a Bible in his hand that made him uncertain. How many times had he stood at that pulpit with a Bible in his hand, quoting from it and swinging it like the staff of Moses, and using it for support. Now he had only a piece of paper. This man who never used to follow a script. And suddenly he seemed uncertain, even frightened.

"I have just left a home filled with flowers," he began, and it was not a good start because someone down there in the orchestra section on the right began to laugh! They knew where those flowers came from! From the heathens! From those who gloated at the misfortunes of others! The cultural radicals! The defamers from *Expressen*! The insulters from *Dagens Nyheter*! And what good were those flowers?

Funeral flowers! Filthy flowers!

Lidman looked up in surprise and for a moment lost his train of thought.

But then he went on.

He was reading from the paper, but he stumbled again and again. He said that he had no intention that evening of acting out some religious drama or of carrying out some quasi-religious cat-and-mouse game, because he was looking for the truth, and he had lost all confidence in the spiritual and financial leaders and leadership of this congregation (which prompted strong shouts of protest). And after that bad start, it didn't get any better.

He could feel the animosity in the congregation. He was not the Lidman they had learned to know. He did not speak freely, but instead read from his piece of paper. At the most important moment of his life, the gift of preaching had deserted Sven.

He left the pulpit amid silence. Brother Allen Törnberg then quickly stepped up to the pulpit and explained that he too had come from a home filled with flowers (this brought merry laughter), but in his opinion they could leave the flowers and the flowery words back there. He gave a forceful speech in behalf of the Pentecostal movement's chief and urged a vote of confidence for Pethrus.

But the matter was not at all clear. The congregation seemed restive, as if the last speaker had forced something that should not have been forced. "O Bliss" started up in the back rows of the orchestra section on the right, and this support was unexpected; the orchestra section on the right had previously been one hundred percent for "The Promises." Now a spontaneous support for "O Bliss" seemed to be growing. "O Bliss" spread to the orchestra section on the left, where "O Bliss" had previously had a strong foothold.

Suddenly a commotion occurred.

It started in the front row of pews in the orchestra section where some of the most well-known members of the congregation were sitting. Not all of them were seated on the platform; that was the strange thing about that strange evening. Efraim stood up and took a step toward the pulpit, but several of the leading brothers nearby grabbed hold of him and tried to pull him back. But since Efraim was a big man and not easy to restrain, the commotion grew more heated. He dragged himself several steps toward JESUS, with two of the leading elders hanging onto his arms. Then the Lidman faction in the orchestra section on the left noticed what was happening, and with loud voices began shouting "O Bliss, O Mystery," and several yelled: "Brother Efraim! Brother Efraim wants to speak!"

The brothers holding his arms then released their grip, and he stumbled forward and fell right in front of the JESUS on the pulpit, but he put out his hands and quickly got to his feet, as "O Bliss, O Mystery" faded away in the confusion and excitement. A few cries of "Justice!" and "God's grace and compassion!" and in any case scores of shouts invoking God could be heard. And in this manner Efraim managed to reach the pulpit with JESUS on the front.

His speech has been preserved in the *Lebenslauf*. It's quite long.

He began with a criticism of Lidman for going to the press "because it's a terrible thing to abandon the congregation to the howling hyenas and roaring wolves in the world." For that, Lidman should be reprimanded. But the damage had been done, and that's why the facts of the matter had to be seriously considered. "The charges that Lidman has brought are all the more dangerous because they refer to suspect transactions or tampering with collection funds." But, he added, "It's odd that it has to come to a catastrophe before the congregation's members find out anything about their own congregation, for which they have sacrificed and prayed. Much too great a burden has been placed on the shoulders of Brother Pethrus. But a board member must have spiritual qualifications as well as general competence, not just the merits of compliance and a good nature, as is now the case."

He spoke for a long time, and again and again called for oversight. The movement lacked democracy.

Again and again during his speech he was interrupted by applause from the congregation. But finally Brother Törnberg stood up from the row of elders and furiously shouted: "Are we going to stand for this in God's congregation? Applause has no place here!" But Efraim went on, refusing to be stopped. And when he came to the matter of the loan to the American publisher, the accountant Ernst Petterson stood up in the orchestra section on the left—this was in the middle of the "O Bliss" faction—and in a loud voice shouted: "Shame on you, Pethrus, shame on you! That's the only thing I can say!" And this later became a famous remark.

Loud booing was heard, and "The Promises" was started up, without success.

Efraim continued as soon as things calmed down.

Finally, Efraim talked about the democracy of the congregation. And everyone down there in what the elders—who were all men—jokingly used to call the sea of old ladies, listened in dead silence. Efraim spoke in favor of transparency, clarity, the right to choose the congregation elders, the right to choose representatives who possessed integrity and were not compliant and good-natured. Then he put down his script and spoke directly to the people down there in the sea of faithful, suddenly gripped by something that he perceived as a holy wrath.

Yes, it must have been a holy wrath. He threw out his hand toward the row of congregation elders, who were deathly pale and resolute, and shouted:

"Here before you, here sits a group of old ladies!!!"

And that was when the miracle occurred.

Lewi stood up and went over to Efraim, and the laughter and booing stopped, and everyone was utterly still. What was Lewi going to do? But Lewi, quietly and kindly, just put his arm around Efraim's shoulders, turned to the congregation with a little smile, and said:

"Brothers and sisters, don't we all feel that at a time like this, it's men like Brother Efraim that we need?"

And then the cheering broke loose.

One year later Efraim was expelled from the Filadelfia congregation with the by-then familiar justification from Paul's letter to Titus, chapter 3, verses 10-11.

As for a man who is factious, after admonishing him once or twice, have nothing more to do with him, knowing that such a person is perverted and sinful; he is self-condemned.

On the day the judgment came, he felt great bitterness and recalled the moment when Lewi had embraced him. And he thought that it had been the greatest cleverness on Lewi's part. Great cleverness, perhaps too great. Almost cunning. The fact that Lewi had seized the opportunity on the spur of the moment and turned the congregation to win their support.

It had not been honest.

But the years passed, and his bitterness faded. And again he remembered what he had actually felt back then. Lewi had come toward him, as if toward a friend. And they *had* been friends, after all, during that long journey. Lewi put his arm around him and uttered those words of acknowledgment. Suddenly everything felt the way it had in the past. They were together, in the battle. And after those words Efraim couldn't say a thing; he was overwhelmed by such joy and gratitude before God that afterwards he would call that moment the greatest in his life.

And finally, in the autumn of his life when he wrote about this in the last pages of his *Lebenslauf*, what remained of all the emotions was the joy.

He had found a purpose. He had been chosen by God to unite this divided, confused, and bewildered congregation. Hadn't Jesus Christ once chosen Judas to betray him? And wasn't Judas struck by eternal shame? But was it Judas's fault?

No, the Lord had chosen Judas as His instrument. And surely there was also some purpose in the fact that God had chosen him to unite the Pentecostal movement, during those brief moments of bewilderment. And God had given Lewi the inspiration to make use of Efraim.

Efraim had been used.

He would always remember the way they left the pulpit, together, with Lewi's arm still around Efraim's shoulders. And they had left very quietly and lovingly, and the congregation started singing "The Promises," and later the congregation would unanimously decide to appoint an investigative commission, which much later concluded that no misdeeds had been committed. And who would be surprised at that, considering the composition of the commission? The Pentecostal movement had survived its worst crisis. And Efraim was the pivot and the instrument, God's instrument, and the movement would live on, perhaps chastened and wiser, as he hoped, but it would live on.

He used to think that was it, that was how it happened, that was the whole story—even though it was not the whole story. But if he ever in his life, in truth, had wanted to use the word "blessed" or "miraculous," it would be to describe that brief moment. The feeling of what it was like as he went down to the other faithful, with Lewi's arm around his shoulders, having been used by God—that feeling was true. It would stay with him, like the promises, for as long as he lived. And finally, from the anguish of division they were united in song, so blessedly resounding, as if in their love they all wanted to embrace the two brothers: Lewi who was the chief, and Efraim who at the movement's most difficult moment had become God's instrument, and who now in unity and love went down to those who loved him. And now they sang in unison and the song united all the beloved, the song with the strong, swaying rhythm, the one that carried them all, and elevated them and made them understand how everything fit together:

Heaven and earth may burn,
Heights and mountains vanish,
But whoever believes will find
That the promises are forever.

An hour after the meeting ended, Lewi and Sven met at the general manager's office.

There wasn't much to say. But Sven, at any rate, asked:

"I assume you're thinking of expelling me, because I have no intention of retracting what I said."

"I assume so," replied Lewi in a low voice. "I suppose that's how it will have to be."

"Yes," said Sven.

They stood and looked at each other, almost shyly, since there wasn't much to add, and then Lewi said:

"And what are you thinking of working on now?"

Sven replied in the same friendly tone of voice:

"Well, I suppose I'll write. I'm an author, after all. So I guess I'll sit down and see if anything comes."

Lewi merely nodded.

"What about you?"

"Well, I thought I'd come to the office early tomorrow, around eight o'clock, as usual. The brothers in Skövde are having problems. The same old drudgery."

"Yes," replied Sven.

"Things have been piling up lately," Lewi added.

And then they nodded to each other in silence and each went his own way. And that was how Lewi and Sven finally parted: one of them waiting to see if anything would come, and it did; the other to the same old drudgery, and that too would come.

It would be possible to write an article about the conflict at God's acre, choosing the victor and the loser.

But sadness was shared by both those who may have been the victors and those who were the losers. Why did it have to be that way?

Or was it necessary?

There were no judges, no sentence was handed down, other than a sentence of sadness. Or the sentence from the one Lewi called his traveling companion, and that's what she was. Her name was Kristina, a traveling companion on his journey, and in sadness, and for all time, for all time.

Epilogue

WHAT WAS LEFT?

In the end Lewi seemed to return to where he had started. In an interview several months before his death, during the summer of 1974, he was asked what he valued most of everything he had done. And suddenly he was back where he started, with the social involvement. "I think that without hesitation I can say that it's my work among the children in need. The people in distress that I helped get back on their feet—that's the greatest of all." And, on the same occasion, he almost sounded like Sven during the great conflict. "One of the biggest dangers for the Pentecostal movement is its success and growth. There is a great danger for the leadership of a movement to become cocky as the movement grows, and they become aware of their strength. All the wondrous material that exists in terms of devotion, loyalty, love, and the spirit of self-sacrifice can be made into a platform for the exercise of power. I see that as one of the great dangers in all movements."

Perhaps it was the quiet admonishments of his traveling companion that, in the end, remained. And also her words about the talents, which were put in our charge.

But Lewi and Sven would meet one more time.

The Lidman conflict was the Pentecostal movement's most difficult time, and it was as if the movement withdrew to nurse its sorrow, to lick its wounds. Maybe they had also learned something. Outwardly the movement that continued was not fundamentally damaged; if you looked only at the outside, its success seemed to go on. The membership numbers may not have increased in Sweden, but internationally the Pentecostal movement continued to grow, and by the turn of the century in 2000, there were 250 million members around the world. In Brazil alone—the country that was so beloved and cherished by Lewi, and where, back in 1930, he had turned over the entire organization to the "locals"—the Pentecostal movement had 30 million adherents. Not everything was due to Lewi, but much of it was. It was the Västergötland piece of board from Västra Tunhem which, with its particular mixture of burning belief and pragmatic gift for organization, had in just the right way calmed the sloshing of the ecstatic barrel.

And that was what distinguished the movement from all the other radical pietistic revival movements. That was what made the Pentecostal movement grow and, in spite of everything, survive.

He might not have succeeded without Sven's efforts as the evangelical renewer during the critical 1920s. Lewi knew that, and this too caused pain and sorrow. He never got over it even though he, and the movement, tried for many years to suppress Lidman's name.

They were not even allowed to sing "O Bliss, O Mystery." No doubt it hurt too much.

Lewi would live to be ninety years old, unceasingly active to the very end. Yet over the years his mind seemed to soften, becoming more tolerant and forgiving in areas in which he had always been unforgiving in his old-fashioned battle against sin, or his fashionable battle for purity. He became increasingly quick to gentleness, and to tears. He began to be a gentle listener and a much beloved myth. He had always listened, but now it was with a growing understanding for those unhappy people who were not cast in one piece. He wept often, as if the years had made his skin thinner, and he understood more and more.

He was still, within the Pentecostal movement, the absolute authority on questions of sin, but he frequently gave surprising answers. "People have made God more religious than He is," he might say. Or, to a pastor who as late as the 1960s sought guidance regarding the proper appearance of faithful sisters, regarding the matter of hats and hairstyles. Then Lewi "with the deepest indignation" replied: "Keep in mind, Brother, that there may often be something sickly hidden inside those who constantly and fiercely concern themselves with such matters."

Perhaps he realized, in the end, how true that was.

With his talent for being farsighted and for seeing things close up, and his matter-of-fact pragmatism, he could have been a brilliant politician; but that's not what he became. He was able to leave the sin catalogue behind; there were more important concerns. He had dealt with so many issues, and the list had grown: there were conference centers and new missionary fields and international activities and IBRA's eighty radio stations in fifty-four languages and newspapers and the LP foundation for drug and alcohol abusers, and finally a political party as well which, like the Pentecostal movement, started out very small but later became very successful. Yet during his last years Lewi lamented the fact that it had shifted to the right: it should have been a Christian center party.

It's true that opinions varied widely about Lewi. He continued to be controversial. Yet he was possibly, as Efraim writes in one place, the greatest spiritual leader that Sweden ever had, and the greatest we will ever have. The twentieth century was his time, but the spirituality, or lack of spirituality, would change, along with the world, the way we think, and progress. And the new century probably has no place for spiritual empire builders, which is what Lewi was, in spite of everything.

He held his last policy speech—occasionally it was possible to use such political terms for Lewi—during Nyhems Week, three months before he died.

He had had several heart attacks, and he now seemed weak and frail, but he still wanted to speak, although everyone was concerned. No one knew whether he would have the strength to stand at the pulpit for very long. Even he wasn't sure that he could.

During the hours before his speech, he was very frightened, and he knelt in his room for a long time, praying for strength. But it went well. He kept a tight grip on the pulpit, and the brothers who were anxiously watching him from behind, ready to catch him if he fell, did not have to intervene. At first his voice was frail and trembling, from age and nervousness, but as he spoke his voice grew stronger. And he had a message for them, one last message.

He wanted to admonish them, and tell them that a human being meets God one on one.

"We are living in the age of the great religious campaigns," he said. "But this is not the biblical revival method. God saves people, one by one. It is in the private encounter between the individual and God that grace is to be found. God is interested in the individual human being." And this brilliant organizer of mass meetings seemed, in the end, to have returned to the Christ-centrism of Zinzendorf and his own youth. In the end it was the single individual's meeting with the Savior that mattered. Everything else was unimportant, or inconsequential, or merely organization.

And then he stumbled down from the pulpit.

One by one. Before God.

He died on September 4, 1974. During his last days he was often unconscious.

Now and then he would wake up. Then he might suddenly start talking about listening to Sven-Bertil Taube on the radio, and how well he sang. They were such nice songs. Were they by Evert or Theodorakis?

Then he would sink farther away. During the last hours before he passed away, he woke up and said: "It cannot be explained." Those were his last words; they were recorded, as the last words of great men are always recorded.

What did it mean? No one knows.

But last words are meant to be used. And then we have to take responsibility for them ourselves.

Lidman also passed away surrounded by his loved ones; he too was gentler and perhaps also, in the end, wiser. That was on February 14, 1960. His last words were also recorded. He muttered a single word, four times: "Fiasco. Fiasco. Fiasco. Fiasco."

We can interpret and make use of the last words of others in whatever way we like. We are the ones who decide and who have to continue to live with them.

When my mother died, in 1992, she had been unconscious after a series of small cerebral hemorrhages, only waking up now and then, but apparently unable to speak. I sat by her bed and fed her a chocolate cream. It was starting to melt, and I brushed my hand over my pants and cautiously wiped my fingers. Suddenly she said in a surprisingly clear and firm voice, though her eyes were still closed and her face was turned toward the ceiling:

"Don't wipe your hands on your pants!"

After that she never spoke again. Those were her last words. I've grown quite fond of them and have tried to live up to them, if that's at all possible. I think that Lewi, in any case, would have also been fond of them.

Lewi, Sven, and my mother, whose name was Maria although she was called Maja, lived to approximately the same age, and all three of them experienced the twentieth century within the revival. Each of them in his own way, and in very different levels of society, was a great twentieth-century personality. I have tried to interpret my mother's last words, to figure out how I should live by them, and have done my best to understand them. No doubt a person has to interpret and do his best. But sometimes I think about those three: Lewi, Sven, and Maja, and their last words, as if together they contained a solution to a mystery or were a sort of combined code message from the twentieth century and the revival, about what it was like to live, and how difficult and despairing, but rather pleasant it was too, and about what we ought to do.

It cannot be explained.

Fiasco.

Don't wipe your hands on your pants.

Lewi and Sven would meet one more time.

On an early summer day in 1954 someone called Lewi and said that Lidman wished to meet with him. The contact person said that Lidman was sincere. He had thought about everything and felt regrets; he said that the reason for his attack was that "the love had died out in his heart." No one could explain what this actually meant, but a meeting was arranged.

It was at Lewi's house in Bredden. Both Lewi and Sven were nervous before the meeting. They met on the stairs and shook hands and looked each other in the eye, and then suddenly, without either of them being able to explain it, everything was the same as it had been in the past. They ate dinner together with Brita and Lydia and "relived old memories," and laughed.

And it was incomprehensible, or by the grace of God.

Lewi was seventy years old. Sven was seventy-two.

After dinner Lewi suggested that the two of them take a stroll along the ridge. They walked for a long time. It was a very beautiful evening in early summer, and they talked about old times and then, suddenly, Lewi stopped, took Sven's arm, and said:

"Listen, didn't we have a splendid time during the years we worked together?"

Then Sven clasped his hands, raised them up to his face, and said in a voice so full of sorrow and despair that tears came to Lewi's eyes:

"And we tore it all apart!"

"But it can be repaired," Lewi replied.

But Sven merely gave him a long look, with tears in his eyes, and then took Lewi's arm, turned around, and they walked home along the ridge. It was too late. It was too late.

That was the last time. After that they never saw each other again.

It's Lewi himself who describes this incident in one of his last books before he died.

He says that he learned to love Sven Lidman as one of the best friends of his life, and he never stopped loving him. The loss of Sven was a loss that could never be replaced. "We were as different as two people can be, but we complemented each other."

Perhaps the love was mutual.

Many summers have passed since their last walk together, the inscriptions in God's acre have grown less distinct, and Efraim rests there in his exile. Perhaps, in a final protest after being expelled from the congregation he loved so much, he had chosen the great ecumenical congregation in the European spiritual house, where he, in his final diaspora, could speak to the others. Also to the woman who was humble, but who did her best. I can almost imagine the conversations beneath the rectangular stone slabs that form the floor and roof of the extraordinary European twentieth century, of revival and reason, radical pietism and enlightenment, despair and ecstasy, hope and confusion.

But I think Efraim would be happy if he had seen Lewi and Sven meet that last time. He would have said that it was a good thing.

No one saw Lewi and Sven on their last walk, which was their last meeting, but if Efraim had seen it I think he would have felt . . . well, peace. That tall, gaunt man and the thin, short one, arm in arm, quite a funny pair, actually, not comical but slightly funny, a couple of funny human beings. And when they disappeared beneath the trees on the ridge, they would have reminded Efraim of the time when Sven and Lewi met for the very first time, in Kölingared.

Back then they had taken each other by the arm—wasn't it in 1921?—and walked along a path that led through a field of grain. The tall man was wearing a frock coat and vest, the short man had on a serge suit. And they had taken the path through the field, down into the valley, and it looked as if they were slowly descending through God's acre, not the kind in which Efraim was now resting, but a living acre that was growing, and from which God was awaiting His magnificent harvest, and they had wandered away and very slowly disappeared into the valley, arm in arm, until they were finally swallowed up by God's acre, inseparably united.

And in truth: they had been so happy.

I am writing this in the spring. I would like to go to Christiansfeld one more time.

It was there it began, and it was there I received the last, posthumous message from Efraim. I still don't know why he wanted to rest there. Perhaps it was because in the end there was no other affiliation than God's. And it existed only in God's acre, where the words finally become invisible.

Then the smallest and most independent congregation arises, the one that is not an association: Alone with God. One by one.

Efraim Markström's gravestone will also end up being erased and illegible, like the others. In a few hundred years only the stone slab will remain, with no inscription. Undoubtedly there is a rational explanation for it, as there is for most things. The horizontal stones, lying there so meekly, may suffer the most exposure from the wind and weather. Perhaps that was the intent.

By then the oldest inscriptions that are still visible in the slanting morning sunlight will also be gone. In a sense this is the Traveling Companion's admonition to Lewi, but it's carved on the gravestone of an old Danish woman. She was eighty-nine years old when she was buried in God's acre. "She was humble, but she did her best." Very simple, very beautiful, a thumb verse about the talent bestowed.

Copenhagen–Stockholm, 1993–2001